C8 000 000 328361

KU-535-646

BIRMINGHAM LIBRARY SERVICES

DISCARD

SPECIAL MESSAGE TO READERS

This book is published under the auspices of

THE ULVERSCROFT FOUNDATION

(registered charity No. 264873 UK)

Established in 1972 to provide funds for research, diagnosis and treatment of eye diseases. Examples of contributions made are: —

A Children's Assessment Unit at Moorfield's Hospital, London.

•

Twin operating theatres at the Western Ophthalmic Hospital, London.

•

A Chair of Ophthalmology at the Royal Australian College of Ophthalmologists.

•

The Ulverscroft Children's Eye Unit at the Great Ormond Street Hospital For Sick Children, London.

You can help further the work of the Foundation by making a donation or leaving a legacy. Every contribution, no matter how small, is received with gratitude. Please write for details to:

**THE ULVERSCROFT FOUNDATION,
The Green, Bradgate Road, Anstey,
Leicester LE7 7FU, England.
Telephone: (0116) 236 4325**

**In Australia write to:
THE ULVERSCROFT FOUNDATION,
c/o The Royal Australian and New Zealand
College of Ophthalmologists,
94-98 Chalmers Street, Surry Hills,
N.S.W. 2010, Australia**

THE NATURE OF MONSTERS

It is 1718 and, in a parish near Newcastle, Eliza Tally, a girl of sixteen, embarks on a love affair that will prove her undoing. When her lover casts her off, she is forced to travel to London. There she takes up a position in the house of an apothecary, Grayson Black, whom she trusts to salvage what remains of her reputation. Black, however, has a quite different plan in mind. Shunned for years by the men of science, the apothecary is convinced that he is finally about to achieve the fame and success he thinks he deserves. And it is Eliza he is determined to exploit to realise his long-held ambitions, with consequences that are terrifying for all who inhabit the apothecary's house.

CLARE CLARK

THE NATURE OF MONSTERS

Complete and Unabridged

CHARNWOOD
Leicester

First published in Great Britain in 2007 by
Viking
the Penguin Group, London

First Charnwood Edition
published 2007
by arrangement with
the Penguin Group, London

The moral right of the author has been asserted

Copyright © 2007 by Clare Clark
All rights reserved

British Library CIP Data

Clark, Clare
    The nature of monsters.—Large print ed.—
Charnwood library series
    1. Teenage girls—England—History—18th century
—Fiction 2. Pharmacists—England—London—History
—18th century—Fiction 3. Human experimentation
in medicine—Fiction 4. London (England)—Social
conditions—18th century—Fiction 5. Historical
fiction 6. Large type books
I. Title
823.9′2 [F]

ISBN 978-1-84617-877-1

BIRMINGHAM LIBRARY SERVICES
LP 2/|
09/07
H

Published by
F. A. Thorpe (Publishing)
Anstey, Leicestershire

Set by Words & Graphics Ltd.
Anstey, Leicestershire
Printed and bound in Great Britain by
T. J. International Ltd., Padstow, Cornwall

This book is printed on acid-free paper

For Charlie. Just Charlie.

Prologue

September 1666

Everyone was agreed that the fire would burn itself out before it reached Swan-street. In Tower-street they had embarked upon the blowing-up of houses for a fire-break. She had felt the shocks of the explosions in the soles of her feet as she bent over her mending, but, although the glass rattled in the windows, she had not been alarmed. On the contrary, her mood had been one of tranquillity, even contentment. The pains that had dogged her throughout her seventh month had eased. When the child kicked, she had stroked the dome of her belly with the palms of her hands, moving them in reassuring circles, her lips shaping lullabies so old and familiar that they felt as much a part of her as her own breath. That night she slept deeply, without dreams. Even when the night-lanthorn thundered upon the door of the shop, shouting that the fire was coming, that those who remained abed would surely burn alive, she remained untroubled. Quietly, she eased herself to her feet and settled her shawl about her shoulders. For all that it had been a hot, dry summer it would do the infant no good if she were to take a chill.

The bird must have sought refuge in the chimney. Its high-pitched cry caught in the

1

mortar, setting the irons shrilling in echo before it plunged into the empty grate, its wings brilliant with fire, setting wild shadows thrashing against the wall. Bright scraps of flame spiralled upwards as the bird lashed and twisted, its bead eyes lacquered with terror. Beside the grate the stuff spilled from her sewing basket, spangled with sparks. Languidly, as though wearied by the very notion of combustion, a pale scrap of muslin smouldered. When at last it caught it did so with a burst of flame and a sucked-in gasp of surprise. The blaze took quickly. From beneath the stink of burning feathers came the distinct smell of roasting meat.

Then she was down the stairs, outside, running, the skirts of her nightgown bundled in her arms. The streets were filled with people, twisting, screaming, pushing. Above them the fire was a vast arch, grimed with oily black smoke. The wind bayed and twisted amongst the flames like a pack of dogs, goading the blaze, urging it onwards. Suddenly she turned. Mr Black. It had not occurred to her to think of her husband. Sparks gusted upwards, swarming like maddened bees around her face. In their frames panes of glass shrivelled to yellow parchment. Someone screamed, falling against her with such force she was almost knocked to the ground. Hardly thinking where she ran, she stumbled away, fighting against the current of people spilling downhill towards the silver sanctuary of the river. Above her, birds wheeled and shrieked, twisting arcs of flame. The dust and smoke burned her eyes and throat. It hurt to breathe.

On the great thoroughfare of Cheap-side the kennel ran scarlet with molten lead, the liquefied roof of the mighty church of St Paul's. The noise was deafening, her cries drowned out by the crowds and the screams of horses and the crack and rumble of falling houses and the howl of the wind as it spurred the flames forward. Behind her the wooden beams of a church tower ruptured with a terrible crack. Time ceased as she turned, her hands before her face. A column of fire, as high as the mast of a ship, swayed above her. The flames billowed out behind it like a sail. There was a rolling roar of thunder, like a pause, before it groaned and fell in an explosion of red-gold and black, throwing thousands of brilliant fire-feathers into the air.

The fit of terror that possessed her then palsied her limbs and shrivelled the thoughts in her head to ash. She could do nothing, think nothing. The breath smouldered in her lungs. In her belly, the child thrashed madly but though its elbows were sharp against her flesh, it could not rouse her. All sense and impulse banished, she stood as though bewitched, her eyes empty of expression, her face, fire-flushed, tipped upwards towards the flames. Had it not been for the butcher's wife who grasped her arm with one rough red hand and dragged her bodily to the quay, she would doubtless have stayed there and burned.

Years later, on one of the few occasions when he had permitted himself to speak of her, his father had told him that afterwards, when it was all over, she had confessed that she had thought

3

herself dreaming, so detached was she from the physical mechanism of her body and the peril of her predicament. In the extremity of her fear she had ceased to occupy herself but had gazed down upon her own petrified body, observing with something akin to detachment the calamity that must certainly ensue and waiting, knowingly waiting, to discover precisely the nature of the agonies that awaited her.

She had waited, but she had not prayed. For she had known then, as surely as she had known that she must perish in this searing scarlet Hell, that God was not her Father in Heaven but a pillar of fire, vengeful and quite without mercy.

1

1718

Afterwards, when I knew that I had not loved him at all, the shock was all in my stomach, like the feeling when you miscount going upstairs in the dark and climb a step that is not there. It was not my heart that was upset but rather my balance. I had not yet learned that it was possible to desire a man so and not love him a little.

Oh, I longed for him. When he was not there the hours passed so slowly that it seemed that the sun had fallen asleep in the sky. I would wait at the window for whole days for the first glimpse of him. Every time a figure rounded the corner out of the trees my heart leaped, my skin feverish with hope even as my eyes determined it to be someone to whom he bore not the slightest resemblance. Even Slack the butcher, a man of no more than five feet in height and several times that around the middle, whose arms were so pitifully short they could barely insert the tips of his fingers into the pockets of his coat. I turned my face away hurriedly then, my cheeks hot, caught between shame and laughter. How that beer-soaked dumpling would have licked his lips to imagine the tumbling in my belly at the sight of him, the hot rush of longing between my thighs that made my fingers curl into my palms and set the nape of my neck prickling with

5

delicious anticipation.

In the dusty half-light of the upper room, breathless against the wall, I lifted my skirts then and pressed my hand against the slick muskiness within. The lips parted instantly, the swollen mouth sucking greedily at my fingers, gripping them with muscular ardour. When at last I lifted my hand to my mouth and licked it, remembering the arching fervour of his tongue, the perfect private taste of myself on his hot red mouth, I had to bite down hard upon my knuckles to prevent myself from crying out with the unbearable force of it.

Oh yes, I was alive with desire for him, every inch of me crawling with it. A whiff of the orange water he favoured, the touch of his silk handkerchief against my cheek, the remembrance of the golden fringe of his eyelashes or the delicate whorl of his ear, any of these and less could dry my mouth and melt the flesh between my legs to liquid honey. When he was with me my sharp tongue softened to butter. I, who had always mocked the other girls for their foolish passions, could hardly breathe. The weaknesses in his face, the girlish pinkness of his damp lips, the irresolute cast of his chin, did nothing to cool my ardour. On the contrary, their vulnerability inflamed me. Whenever I was near him, I thought only of touching him, possessing him. There was something about the untarnished lustre of his skin that drew my fingertips towards him, determining their movements as the earth commands the sun. I had to clasp them in my lap to hold them steady.

The longing intoxicated me so I could barely look at him. We sat together in front of the empty fireplace, I in the bentwood chair, he upon a footstool at my feet. My mother's knitting needles clicked away the hour, although she kept her face turned resolutely towards the wall. For myself I watched his hands, which were narrow with long delicate fingers and nails like pink shells. They dangled impatiently between his legs, twisting themselves into complicated knots.

It never occurred to me to offer him my hand to hold. Slowly, as though I wished only to make myself more comfortable, I adjusted my skirt, exposing the white flesh of my calves. His hands twitched and jumped. I lifted my petticoats a little higher then. The fingers of his right hand stretched outwards, hesitating for only a moment. I could feel the heat of them although he did not touch me. My legs trembled. And then his fingertips reached out and caressed the tender cleft behind my knee.

The ungovernable swell of desire that surged in my belly knocked the breath from my lungs and I gasped, despite myself. Silently, he brought his other hand up to cover my mouth. I kissed it, licked it, bit it. He groaned softly. Beneath my skirts his right hand moved deftly over my skin so that the fine hairs upon my thighs burst into tiny flowers of flame. I slid down towards him, my legs parted, and closed my eyes, inhaling the leather smell of his hand on my face. Every nerve in my body strained towards his touch as inexorably, miraculously, his hand moved upwards.

Unhooked by longing, my body arched towards him. When at last he reached in to touch me, there was nothing else left, nothing in the world but his fingers and the delirious incoherent frenzy of pure sensation they sent spiralling through me, as though I were an instrument vibrating with the exquisite hymns of the angels. Did that make him an angel? My toes clenched in my boots and my belly held itself aloft in a moment of stillness as the flame quivered, perfectly bright. I held my breath. In the explosion I lost sight of myself. I was a million brilliant fragments, the darkness of my belly alive with stars. When at last I opened my eyes to look at him, my lashes shone with tears. He raised a finger to his lips and smiled.

Oh, that smile! When he smiled, his mouth curved higher on one side than the other, dimpling his right cheek. That dimple spoke to me more eloquently than his eyes, for all their untroubled blueness. And it was surely one hundred times more fluent than his speech, which was halting at the best of times and rutted with hiccupping and frequently incomprehensible exclamations. Even now, when so much time has passed and I must squint to recognize the girl in the bentwood chair, the recollection of that tiny indentation can unsettle me. Back in those days, it was as if, within its perfect crease, there was concealed a secret of unimaginable wonder that might be known only to me. For like everyone who falls for the first time under the spell of corporeal desire, I believed myself a pioneer, the discoverer of something never before identified, something perfectly extraordinary. I was god-like, omnipotent, an alchemist who had taken vulgar flesh and somehow, magically, rendered it gold.

Had you asked me then, I would have said I loved him. How else to explain how desperately, ferociously alive he made me feel? It was only afterwards, when the lust had cooled, that I saw that I was in love not with him at all but rather with myself, with what I became when he touched me. I had never thought myself handsome. My lips were too full, my nose insufficiently imperious, my eyes with their heavy brows set too wide apart. I was denied the porcelain complexion I secretly longed for. My face seemed always to have a sleepy, bruised look about it, as if I had just awoken. But when he touched me I was beautiful. It was only afterwards, as he offered his compliments to my mother and prepared to return home, that I became a girl once more, commonplace, cumbersome, rooted by my clumsy boots to the cold stone floor.

He patronized my mother from the beginning, his address to her exaggeratedly courteous, a pastiche of itself. As for her, she bridled at every unctuous insincerity, her habitually suspicious face as eager as a girl's.

'I am but your humble servant, madam. There could be no greater privilege than to oblige you,' he would say, bowing deeply before throwing himself into the bentwood chair and allowing my mother to loosen his boots. He did not trouble to look at her as he spoke. His tongue was already

9

moistening his lips as he smiled his lazy smile at me, his eyes stroking my neck and the slope of my breasts.

I'm ashamed to say that at those moments I cared not a jot for her humiliation. He could have called my mother a whore or the Queen of Sheba, it would have been all the same to me. The pleasantries were a necessary chore to be endured but my heart beat so loudly in my ears I hardly heard them. I thought only of the tug of my breath inside my chest, the shimmering anticipation between my thighs. As long as he touched me, as long as he smiled at me and caressed me, his fingers drawing a quivering music from my tightly strung nerves, my mother's dignity was not a matter of the least concern. As long as that tiny indentation in the corner of his mouth whispered its secrets to my heart and to my privities, he might have unsheathed his sword and sliced off my mother's head and I would have found reason to hold her responsible for his offence.

If I allowed my desire for him to obscure his failings, then so too did my mother, though her desires swelled not between her thighs but in the dark recesses of her purse. They were at least as powerful as my own and they sent her into shivers of breathless anticipation. Once, just once, I mocked him for his creaking courtliness. Well, I was peeved. He always refused my mother's offers of food, declaring himself quite without appetite while gazing at me with a greed he did not trouble to disguise. On this occasion, however, he smiled at her — at her! — and set about the plate of victuals she put before him with gusto and extravagant praise.

'The finest mutton you have ever eaten?' I echoed scornfully. 'Do you think us such knuckle-headed rustics that we would swallow such claptrap? Still, I suppose we should be grateful to have anything to swallow at all. A handful of empty compliments — shall we make a dinner of them, Mother, now the meat is gone?'

He said nothing, only raised a languid eyebrow and continued to eat, his chin greasy with meat. But my mother shot me a look of such brutal force that it might have brought an eagle down from the sky.

Afterwards, when he was gone, she struck me about the head and told me angrily that it was time I learned to hold my tongue. Was it beyond me to learn a little humility? The boy was the son of the wealthy Newcastle merchant, Josiah Campling, whose own father had made a notable fortune in the shipping of coal to the port of London and who himself had expanded the family business to include the more lucrative trade in Negro slaves. This was not his first-born, it was true, but there was enough money to ensure that he would be settled well. The family lived in a fine new house, some five miles from our village. It was close by there that I had met him for the first time, when he had dismounted from his horse to watch the bringing-in of the first harvest. The day had grown hot and, when we stopped to take our midday meal beneath the shade of the oak trees, the dust from the threshed corn hung like a gauzy shawl against the blue sky. Laughing, he had called out that he was parched and surely we could find it in our hearts to spare him something by way of refreshment. When one of the girls offered him a drink of apple cider he took it, his eyes fixed upon me as his lips caressed the neck of the earthenware bottle. Determined not to blush, I held his gaze. When at last he lowered the bottle he smiled. I knew then that I was lost. That evening, as dusk silted the hedgerows, he walked with me along the white lane and kissed me. Around us cow parsley floated on the deepening darkness like soap bubbles, exhaling its thick, licentious scent. He did not tell me his name. He did not need to. I knew who he was. We all did. We knew about the collection of Chinese porcelain that the maids were expected to dust daily. We knew their livery, their carriage, that they owned a lake stocked with exotic golden fish. We knew that all of the children would be expected to make propitious marriages.

As for us, my mother was but the village midwife, respected and respectable still then, her hand clasped by the curate after the Sunday service and a few words exchanged as to the weather, but as foreign to the Camplings as a tiger to a fly. My father had been curate himself until he died and my mother had always struggled to manage the expenses of a family on his meagre stipend. She had been helped in this by the unwitting cooperation of my seven brothers and sisters who, perhaps more sympathetic to her difficulties than I, had none of them

12

chosen to burden her for long. I alone among her children had persisted in life beyond my fifth birthday. I remember my father as an anxious face beneath the shadow of a round-brimmed hat and a voice that clung to the cold stone of the church like cobwebs. He was no sermonizer. Rather, he spoke of God with wary circumspection, as an exhausted manservant might speak of his capricious master. More than anything he feared enthusiasm and religious fervour, reserving particular abhorrence for the onion-munching papist peasants of France. When he died, succumbing to a pleurisy when I was perhaps seven years old, and my mother told me that God had taken him up into Heaven, I felt a little sorry for him. Despite my mother's insistence that Heaven was a paradise of eternal joy, I could not shift the picture I had of my father, his face creased into its usual expression of weary fortitude as he coaxed flames from the Heavenly fires and sponged the angels' starched wings ready for them to put on in the morning.

After that it was only my mother and me. Ma Tally, as she was commonly known, was more than just a midwife. Renowned for the efficacy of her medicines, she was consulted frequently when conventional physic had failed to bring the patient to health. She mixed her recipes from waters, herbs and roots that she gathered herself, mindful of the very best time and place to collect each one, and knowing instinctively, without recourse to scales and measures, the precise amount of each ingredient required for each of her numerous draughts and ointments. So effective were many of them that she might, if she had been a man, become rich upon the profits of them.

As it was, however, she, like all midwives of her sex, was prevented by law from charging for her services and was forced to rely upon presents from her patrons, a precarious business since their generosity was inclined to run in inverse proportion to the fullness of their pockets. From time to time there had been money enough to allow me to attend the village school. I learned my alphabet and the rudiments of reading. By the time I was grown I had mastered the words in all of the school's small library of chapbooks and my handwriting was adequate, if not elegant. But there had never been anything to spare for a dowry. In her more cheerful moods my mother gave me to believe it did not matter. My face, she observed consideringly, might not be handsome in a conventional manner but it had a wantonness about it that might serve me well, if I used it carefully. Fine-looking girls, she asserted, might be divided into two categories: those that men liked to display in glass cabinets like figurines and those that they preferred to handle. I, my mother assured me, was one of the latter type. A man might do a great deal against his better judgement on the promise of a face like mine.

I believed her less because I thought her right than because I had little or no interest in the matter. I had thought nothing of marriage before I met him. What dreams I had were all of Newcastle, a magnificent town many miles from the petty limits of our small parish. I was perhaps sixteen, a woman who should perhaps already have been pushed out to make her own way in the world had my mother been ready to relinquish me. Headstrong and opinionated, I was none the less young for my years and had yet to learn the shaded skills of subtlety or prudence. I occupied the present moment entirely; my mood was jubilant, or it was desolate, and there was little of anything in between. It was easy for a girl of that nature to pin such extremes of feeling upon the simplest of precepts, and I did. With him I was joyfully, entirely alive; without him the days dragged, as bleak and dreary as winter fields. The simplicity of it entranced me.

It occurred to neither of us to speak of the future. He declared me enchanting, delightful, delicious, and I only placed my finger upon his lips, wishing them silent, only warm and insistent against mine. He brought me gifts of clothes but it was my mother who clapped her hands with astonished glee when she saw them, a scarlet cloth petticoat with a broad silver galloon lace to it and a black scarf lined with blue velvet. She hung them in the press and her brown face creased like an old apple. As for the sonnet he penned in my name, which I hastened to burn before I might find some clumsiness in it to offend me, she insisted upon folding it in a clean rag and placing it in the tin box on the dresser.

'We shall have him,' she murmured to herself, the words ripe with triumph. 'Oh, my girl, we shall have him, all right.'

It was a gamble for her, I understand that now, and I do not blame her for it. She knew that the risks were considerable, and that the price of failure was high. But she knew too that time was running out, for her as well as for me. They had already begun, you see, the whispers and the nudges that were to be her undoing. It was not unusual, when a woman grew old and sour and there were fears she might become a burden on the parish. My mother sought no charity but the gravel in her urine made her snappish and disagreeable. Even her own carefully pounded preparations did little to ease her discomfort.

It should have surprised neither of us that fingers began to be pointed in the direction of our cottage. Already some of the village children had been strangely affected with unknown distempers. One, the son of the baker with whom my mother had exchanged angry curses, had vomited pins; another was frightened almost to death by nightly apparitions of cats which all of a sudden would vanish away.

It made no difference that the second was a child my mother barely knew and with whom she had no quarrel. There were rumours that she kept a lead casket beneath her bed in which she concealed the caul and afterbirth of infants she had delivered so that she might use them to revenge herself against those who crossed her. Osborn the grocer claimed that the balance of the scales in his shop was sent awry whenever she set foot in the store. It was not long before several of the village women who could afford the extra expense contrived to send for the man-midwife when it came to their lying-in. When one of the infants refused to suckle it did not take long for the gossips to agree that it was Ma Tally who, in a fit of jealous temper, had stolen away its appetite.

Not everyone shunned her. Her remedy for dropsy, made to a secret recipe that claimed seventeen ingredients including elder, betony and foxglove, remained sought after. But there was a wariness now, a faint sharp whiff of fear and suspicion that rose up off our neighbours like the smell of unwashed skin from a child sewn too long into its winter clothing. My mother dismissed such foolishness, declaring that words were only words and could not harm her, but she was too shrewd not to be afraid. And so it was that she narrowed her eyes and set about securing her future, hers and mine together. An opportunity like the Campling boy came along once in a lifetime and then only if you were very lucky. She had no intention of losing him.

The second harvest was brought in, despite heavy rains. His lips grew hungrier, his hands more insistent, and I strained towards him, crushing myself into his embrace. Beneath the canopy of her shoulders, my mother's knitting needles clicked faster, louder, the whistling of her breath almost a hum. Then, one blowy afternoon, he cleared his throat and suggested she find something with which to occupy herself in the other room. My mother turned, her expression unnaturally bland, her knitting needles held aloft.

'But what of my daughter's virtue?' she asked placidly. 'Of course, sir, there is another way.'

The ceremony took place less than a week later. He did as he was bid but made no attempt to conceal his amusement. My mother fixed him with a beady gaze as she spoke the necessary words. As a midwife she had baptized many infants too weak to cling to life until the parson might be brought. Over the years she had perfected a tone of affecting piety that might have put many a loose-toothed Sunday sermonizer to shame. My mother's cousin, who acted as landlady at a half-respectable inn on the turnpike a few miles north of our village, had been persuaded to leave the business for a day or two and sat as witness in the window seat, her wattles shaking appreciatively as she pressed her handkerchief against her mouth. I wore my scarlet petticoat and a bodice that my mother had cut down and retrimmed so that it might show the pale swell of my breasts to best advantage. Even as my mother laid the broom upon the floor and we jumped backwards over it, our fingers woven together, my palms were damp and I could think only of his mouth upon my nipple, his hand between my thighs. Afterwards we drank the French champagne he had brought. As the wine took hold of me, trailing its golden fingers over my skin, I desired him so acutely I could barely stand. My mother begged him to say a few words but he shook his head, declaring her charming country ritual obser-vance enough. Instead, he bent to kiss me. His eyes were blurry with lust and I saw myself reflected in them as I melted against him. Then, bowing to the two old women, he took my arm and, guiding me to the adjoining room, the bedchamber I shared with my mother, he closed the door.

I had once overheard an aunt mutter to my mother that it was worth enduring the indignity of marriage only so that one might enjoy the privileges of widowhood. When I recalled those words, as I tore off my petticoats, I pitied her. She had never had a husband for whom she ached with unrestrained longing. She did not know what it meant to take a husband into her arms, so that she might close her eyes and lose herself, time and again, in the perfect sphere of her own private ecstasy.

My memories of that afternoon are sharp-edged, bright and deceptive as the shards of a broken looking-glass. I remember it grew dark and he lit a rushlight which he set upon the floor, casting strange shadows upon the draper-ies that hung around the bed. I remember the salty reek of the burning fat, saved from the skimmings of the bacon pot, and the sweet scent of the bed linen which I myself had laundered and starched and set to stand in the pine chest with bunches of drying lavender. Most of all I remember the dismal twist in my belly as I saw him naked for the first time. As girls we had liked to hide by the river on summer evenings so that we might spy upon the farmer's boys as they stripped to swim. Their bodies had been hard and wiry, the round muscles moving like unripe fruit beneath the sunburnt skin of their arms. The apricot sunlight had dappled their brown shoulders and tangled itself in the dark triangles between their legs.

He by contrast was pale as milk, his flesh as pliable as a child's. The hair upon his groin was blond and sparse, and from it his yard rose thick and pink as a stalk of rhubarb. I closed my eyes hurriedly, pulling him beneath the covers, straining for the explosive rush of lust in my belly in which I had come to place my faith. The flesh of his buttocks was yielding and slightly sticky, like bread dough. I caressed them warily. I had never touched his skin before. Now he barely touched me. He was greedy and rough and it was quickly over. Soon afterwards he returned home, where business associates of his father's were expected for supper.

We were married.

The night-lanthorn calls eleven of the clock, I
should to bed. My hand aches & my stomach
too (the calomel has not eased it & my turds
were hard as gravel) but not my heart, not
tonight, despite the lateness of the hour. My
discourse sits before me virtually complete, the
title page so creamy bright in the glow of the
candle it seems that the light comes from
within the pages themselves.

UPON THE MOTHER'S IMAGINATION:
A TREATISE BY GRAYSON BLACK.

How it thrills me to think of it in the hands
of fellow men of science, its meticulously
chosen words pondered, deliberated & — let it
please God — praised. If modesty permits me,
I must confess to believing the analysis of the
physiological effects of imagination masterly. Of
course the raised temperature of a woman's
blood when in a violent passion must heat the
fluid parts of the body. & of course, when
those passions duly weaken, the salts contained
within those fluids must be deposited within
the body, precisely as salt marks the interior of
a cooling cooking pot. Where else could they
then collect but in the unshed blood of the
menses? It is inevitable, then, that, when the
menstrual blood is ingested by the child for
nourishment, the salts impress themselves upon
the as yet unhardened muscle & bone of the
foetus. And so the child bears the imprint of

the mother's passions as sealing wax receives the imprint of a stamp.

There is a beauty in the simplicity of it that touches me even as I write. Does the thesis not share the characteristics of the greatest scientific discoveries: so lucid, so plain, that it seems impossible, once it is set down, that it was not always known?

Of course I cannot deny that there remain imperfections, though hardly of my making. My fieldwork in the parish has yielded little but frustration. The difficulties lie in the women themselves who, despite my repeated imprecations, seem unable to remember the particulars of their activities from one moment to the next & are as careless of their hours as flies. For all that I tell myself that I must be patient, that the nature of such women can never be altered, I confess I grow discouraged. It was with some considerable envy that I watched on Friday last the anatomization of a live dog at the College of Surgeons, while I seem unable to compel my women so much as to open their mouths. Surely the exchange of one for another, appreciated by so very many, would be regretted by none!

2

It was an abundant autumn. But as the fruits swelled and sweetened upon the hedgerows, our encounters grew brusquer and more tart. The uneasy distaste I felt for his white fleshiness had not so much diminished my appetites as honed them, ground them to a sharper point. I set about their gratification resolutely and without any pretence at affection. I no longer kissed him, indeed I barely touched him, but, far from displeasing him, my coolness served only to provoke his desire. He gripped my arms, trapping them painfully above my head as he thrust deep inside me, biting at my neck, goading me to cry out. When I wrapped my feet around his buttocks, spurring him with my heels, forcing him deeper, harder, his face twisted with an ardour that was close to hatred. Fierce though they were, our lusts were quickly sated. We grew adept at securing our own private pleasure. The heat could be relied upon to explode through my belly, although it cooled more rapidly on each occasion. But though I longed for him to be gone, I sulked as he dressed, heavy with a resentment I could neither alter nor understand. When I called him husband, maliciously, insistently, knowing that it agitated him, he laughed without smiling and the lump in his throat bobbed.

He laughed in the same manner when my

mother requested an interview with his family. His father was a man of sanguine humour, he told her, with the red face and popping eyes characteristic of those with an abundance of blood. Even in the most favourable of circumstances, the old man was given to outbursts of strong temper, and the circumstances at the present time were far from favourable. A ship in which the merchant had had a substantial interest had recently been lost, attacked by Portuguese privateers before it had the chance to exchange its cargo of silver for Negro slaves. Given the profits that its investors had sought to realize from the venture, it had not been considered economic to insure either the ship or its consignment. This unwelcome intelligence had been communicated in a letter delivered to the breakfast table, and the old man's roar had echoed so violently through the house that the Chinese vases had chimed together like bells.

Since then the slightest provocation was likely to produce in the merchant an attack of splenetic fury that had the veins upon his forehead standing out in purple ropes. The household tiptoed around him, fearful he would find his dish of coffee too hot or his coat inadequately brushed. One of his sisters had waited more than a week before she dared approach him for a new gown, and then his howl of outrage had been enough to bring the last of the rose petals tumbling from the bushes beyond the window. It was hardly a judicious time for a son, even a son as well loved as he, to present to him as a prospect a girl with no family nor fortune of any kind to recommend her.

* * *

It was my mother who saw the signs first. Unused to illness, I had thought myself struck down by a cold which filled my head with fog and left my limbs heavy and disobliging. I longed to sleep. When he lay heavily upon me, biting at my breasts, I cried out in real pain. My distress inflamed him. He bit harder, burying his nails in the soft flesh of my arms, forcing himself with painful abruptness between my legs. I said nothing as he dressed but hunched my back against him and closed my eyes, sunk in soreness and despondency. I did not answer him when he bid me good night. Although I had a powerful need to urinate I could barely summon the strength to drag myself from the bed. When at last I squatted on the pot, the quilt wrapped clumsily around my shoulders, I had to drop my head between my knees, so certain was I that I should faint.

My mother discovered me in that position some minutes later. She considered me for a moment, her head on one side, her mouth puckered. Then she left the room. I heard the clank of the kettle over the fire. When she returned she carried a cup of steaming liquid which she held out to me.

'Drink this, Eliza,' she instructed. 'It will revive you.'

I took the cup. The liquid was dark green with

25

the harsh aroma of sage. The queasiness roiled in my stomach and I swayed, slopping the hot tea over my fingers.

'Hold it still, you clumsy baggage! You will spill it.' Snatching the cup from me, my mother held it to my lips and ordered me to drink. 'This will help with the sickness. It will also stay the child.' Her face softened and she stroked my arm a little, as though it was a cat. 'You have done well, my dear. This will bring this boy out like a blister.'

★   ★   ★

It shocked him, you could tell, although he turned the twist in his knees into a swagger as he steadied himself against the back of the bentwood chair.

'A child? But — '

The astonishment in his voice was undeniable. I felt the coarse rub of irritation against my chest. What did he expect to have sired, a calf? My mother gripped my hand painfully, warning me to remain silent. I bit my tongue but I stared at him beadily, daring him to show discomposure. He himself kept his gaze on the floor: His cheeks were the bluish white of skim milk. For a moment I thought he would swoon and the sharp tang of dislike flooded my mouth, souring my saliva.

'I — but — I never — '

'You never what, exactly?' I demanded, aiming at haughtiness, but my voice came out reedy and strained. He looked at me for a moment, blinking rapidly, his lips trembling, his hand

26

groping at his waist for the hilt of his sword. It was a moment before he understood that he did not wear it, that it sprawled instead upon the floor where he had discarded it shortly after his arrival. His fingers flexed as he regarded it. Then, stiff-backed, he turned to my mother and jutted out his chin.

'Given your daughter's proclivities, how can I be sure that the child is mine?' he drawled.

My mother clenched my hand so hard it was a miracle that the bones did not break.

'How do you dare speak so before your own wife?' she hissed. 'I had thought you a gentleman, sir. You have shamed my daughter enough by your refusal to acknowledge your vows to her before your family. Would you tarnish her virtue further by doubting her fidelity?'

The boy raised one eyebrow. I noticed then how like glass marbles his eyes were, protruding a little too far from their sockets. I had a sudden powerful urge to shake him with all my strength until they fell from his head and rolled upon the floor. The thought of his plump fingers palpating my flesh, insinuating themselves between my legs — the gooseflesh rose upon my chest and neck, twisting the skin away from its bones. Despite the warmth of the day I shivered.

'My wife?' he echoed mockingly. 'My wife? I fear you are mistaken, madam. I have no wife. I have taken no vows. None, that is, that might be regarded as such by any civilized person. Or by the law.'

'What — ?'

27

'Quiet,' Ma Tally barked at me, jerking my hand. She glared at the boy, her eyes hooked into his face. 'If anyone is mistaken here, sir, it is your good self. You see, I was there. I officiated at the ceremony. There was also a witness, if you care to recall.'

'You claim that superstitious rustic gibberish to be a binding contract of marriage?' he sneered. 'Jumping over a broom? Really! I hate to disappoint you, madam, but there is not a magistrate in the land that would consider me legally wed. Jumping over a broom, I ask you!'

A spike of bile rose at the back of my throat. Dizzily I tugged at my hand, certain I would vomit, but my mother only tightened her grip. The tip of her nose sharpened to a white point.

'Ah, but that is where you are wrong, sir,' she said smoothly. 'You see, my husband was a curate before he died, so I know a bit of something about these things. Maybe a magistrate might have his niggles with what we done in the legal way, but not the Church, not for a minute. The Church considers you married before God, good as though you made your promises in St Bede's itself. You ask Reverend Salt if you doubt me. He'll tell you just the same. Cottage or cathedral, it don't matter to the Archbishop, he don't see a jot of difference. You're married, you are, no question about it. The two of you's bound together for life now, for better or worse. Married, fair and square.'

The boy opened his mouth to object but Ma Tally knew when to press her advantage. On and on she went, until I was so chill and giddy that I heard only the roaring in my own ears.

The boy blinked and bit his lip. His thrust chin began to quiver. Then, at last, to my shame and disgust, he burst into noisy sobs. It was hard to distinguish his words but the sense was unmistakable. He had made a mistake. It had been only a bit of amusement. He had never intended matters to run so out of control. I was a harlot, a sixpenny whore who was out for her own gratification. He had given me presents, had he not? He had honoured his obligations, had behaved like a gentleman. It was I who had lured him on, encouraged him, tricked him. This child, well, he doubted it even existed. He had always made it perfectly clear that there was not the slightest possibility of marriage. His father would never in a thousand years entertain the prospect of a union with a girl of my kind. He would see both of us dead first. And if he so much as attempted to defy his father's wishes, the old man would not hesitate to cut him off without a penny. He would be thrown out into the streets, forbidden to see his mother and sisters. He would lose everything.

As for me, I could think of nothing but my own nausea. I saw the expression upon my mother's face, I understood its meaning, but I gave only the scantiest consideration to the scandal that would certainly follow, to my own ruin. I could think only of the sickness, the sickness and the disgust, coiling and curdling in my stomach. I could hardly bring myself to look at him, at his weak, sticky face and his streaming nose which he wiped on the back of his cuff like a child. If he had tried to touch me I think I would have struck him. He had addressed not a single word to me since the interview had begun.

I clenched my eyes tight shut, willing him gone. Inside me the child twisted like a worm, its marble eyes peering into my private darkness, its hooked claws clutching and squeezing at my stomach as piece by tiny piece it devoured me. I would have torn into my own abdomen and ripped it out with my fingernails, there and then, I would have flung its tiny bloody corpse in his face, I would have stood over him as he gagged and kicked my boot into the soft parts of his stomach, if I had only had the strength. But it was too late. The worm had no intention of relinquishing its grip. It would see me dead first. Already it had sucked the animal spirits from me like the juice from a plum so that I was shrivelled to nothing, nothing but a stone wrapped in dried-up skin.

I wanted to die. My mother on the other hand was aflame with righteous fury. She danced about the room as though the floor beneath her feet was a grate of hot coals. The boy watched with growing horror as she took his letter from the tin on the dresser, gathered together her wrap, her cloak, her pattens, and thrust his coat and hat into his arms. He would not tolerate it, he stammered desperately, blowing his nose with attempted authority and almost dropping his hat. He would brook no interference in his affairs. No, indeed not. It would behove Ma Tally to remember her position. He demanded she respect his wishes. Of course his father would never condescend to see her, he spluttered. She was a fool if she thought he would permit her to place so much as a toe across his threshold.

My mother said nothing. Instead, she smoothed her hair in front of our scrap of glass and placed her bonnet upon her head, pulling its strings together with a smart tug. Then, picking up his discarded sword, she spun around to face him so abruptly that its jewelled hilt grazed against his nose. His voice wobbled as he snatched it from her. If she was to be granted an interview, what then? His father was a malevolent, rancorous old man. Surely she could not be such a fool as to expect a sympathetic hearing. The merchant would have mother and daughter thrown in the pillory for lewdness and insolence, horse-whipped at the cart's tail. He would not rest until they were drummed out of the parish in disgrace. Was Ma Tally so comfortably settled that she could afford to be stripped of her right to parish relief in her dotage? Or did she truly believe that the village would move to defend her against the old man's wrath? If she did, she was even more soft in the head than she appeared. For he knew without doubt that they would be only too happy to be rid of her. Did she not know that there were many out there who had already declared her a witch?

Ma Tally fixed him then with a look that might have shattered stone. His mouth opened and closed but no words came. Afterwards I wondered if this speechlessness was a curse she set upon him but I think it unlikely. My mother was a wise bird and would have known it quite unnecessary. He was cursed enough already without her efforts, cursed with vanity and stupidity and the simple-minded greed that comes with a lifetime of having the idlest of your fancies indulged.

'I shall be back in due time,' she barked at me over the sag of his shoulder as she pushed him out into the darkening afternoon. 'When things are settled.'

I said nothing but stared miserably at the floor. She slammed the door. The faint tang of orange water quivered in the air, wistful as dust in a slice of sunlight. I breathed it in. Everything was still. Then the blackness rushed back in.

Seizing a bowl from the kitchen table, I vomited.

★ ★ ★

My mother did not return that night. I did not think to worry about where she might be. I seemed barely capable of thought at all. I lay alone upon our bed, without troubling to undress. I did not weep. My heart was leaden, the hundreds of words I had failed to speak heaped heavily upon my chest, but my skin prickled and twitched and my fingers were taut with restlessness. To quiet them I wrung the rough blanket between my hands until my palms ached. The rawness comforted me.

When I woke a bright rent of light slit the bed-hangings. I blinked, my eyes still bleary with slumber, and raised myself on to one elbow. I wore a nightgown I had owned as a little girl, white cotton trimmed with lace, presented to my mother at the christening of one of her charges by a grateful godparent. Although the gown had long since been worn into rags I felt no surprise to be wearing it. The fabric was soft as a kiss and I shivered, my belly flushed with sleep-warm desire.

I pushed back the curtains. The room was filled with light. He was not there. I felt a sharp tug of apprehension, even as I chided myself for expecting him. He never came before dinner. Instead, my mother stood at the window, her back to me, pouring water into the cracked yellow bowl. She wore a muslin cap I did not recognize, its lappets loose over her ears. I called out to her. She turned around. The cap was edged with a frill of such startling whiteness I had to shade my eyes. When I looked again I saw that it was not my mother at all. Instead, it was his golden curls that writhed beneath the cap, coiling sinuously around his shadowed face. His face and at the same time not his but something far more brutish, sharp-featured with the textured coarseness of thick dark fur. I saw the gleam of teeth as he lifted the ewer high above his head and poured its contents upon the floor. Not water, now, but blood, a terrible unstoppable stream of blood, lumpy with large black fibrous clumps that fell in splatters upon the flagged floor.

I struggled to sit up, my heart pounding, the scream caught in my throat like a fishbone. It was still dark. My bodice squeezed my chest

33

until I could hardly breathe. I reached round to pull loose the lacing, my hand shaking. The skin between my shoulder blades was slippery with sweat. Gobbets of blood flashed and slithered in the shadowed folds of the bed drapes. I ground my fists into my own eyes until the redness blurred. But I knew what I had seen. I could not pretend to misunderstand it. I had made a covenant with the Devil, and the Devil, who must always betray those that deal with him, had staked his claim upon me. I might escape him for as long as I lived upon this Earth but he had come to tell me, without equivocation, that my soul belonged to him. I had sinned against God and against goodness and no number of petitions for forgiveness could restore me to grace. I was damned and I would burn for eternity in the sulphurous flames of Hell.

I write these words calmly now, my quill quite steady. I am older now and have seen too much of the world to be so sure of either the truthfulness of dreams or the Old Testament apoplexies of a pitiless and vengeful God. It is harder, surely, to forgive yourself for your own follies and failures than it must be for Him, who has so many cases to consider. But then I was young and ignorant and awash with emotions so violent I might, I think, be forgiven for imagining them real. I considered myself worldly, after all. I had more education than many of my acquaintance and could read tolerably well and even write a little. I had a wide knowledge of the plants and herbs to be found in our district. And I had known a man, had felt in my stomach and the soles of my feet the violent thrill of ecstasy. It is not then surprising, perhaps, that I believed my instincts were to be trusted.

What armour did I have then against fear? Only the sooty flame of a rushlight, which I huddled over until a hard white dawn set about scouring the darkness from the hem of the sky, forcing its bleached fingers through the last of the leaves beyond my window.

What an evening! Indeed I hardly care that, despite my express instruction, that damned drab of a girl has once again failed to light my fire. Who cares that this room is colder than a tomb! Tonight I can even overlook the full inch of dust upon the chimneypiece, although she shall surely find me in less indulgent temper on the morrow. Not only is she the idlest creature on God's Earth but she flaunts herself before the fat apprentice like a two-penny whore. But enough, enough. After an evening of such eminence, even the vexations of that foolish strumpet shall not tarnish my high spirits.

The Royal Society, how the words thrill upon my pen. The President of the Society himself, the distinguished Mr Sloane, was present & all the most prominent men of science, gathered together in a room hardly larger than a parlour. What was more, Mr Johanssen, at whose invitation I attended, introduced me to several illustrious Fellows, among them Mr Halley, the astronomist, who described to me a case, personally witnessed, of an animal resembling a whelp delivered by the anus of a male greyhound. He promised to send me his account of it, or at least to have the Secretary at the Society do so as it is already published in the Transactions. In my turn I told him of the Dog-headed race of savages known as the Tartars whose physiognomy results from the godless practice of fornication more canino. He was most interested and encouraged me to send to him the latest draft of my thesis. Imagine if he were to endorse it, Mr Halley himself, & propose it for presentation at the Society! I should like to see Simpson's face then, and the faces of all those stationers who would reduce the art of science to nought but shock & sensation. The thought of it is intoxicating.

As for the debate itself it was only through the exercise of strenuous self-discipline that I obeyed Mr Johanssen's stricture that guests must remain silent during the proceedings. For, to my delight, the thrust of that night's discussions turned upon that matter essential to my work: if indeed the body is, as Descartes would have it, mechanical in its structure & workings, with all God-created beings obeying the immutable rules of mathematics, who or what drives the machine?

The debate that followed was most vigorous. There were those who asserted animation as a matter for God alone, & others who argued for a nerve-juice issued from the brain which moved the heart, but it was the eminent Mr Tabor who in my view put forward the most powerful argument. His doctrine, recently published, contrives an ingenious blend of a soul & an external & divine principle that guides motion, an arrangement that combines gravitation, subtle matter & the intervention of the Almighty to direct the heart to throw blood to the ends of the arteries & thereby drive circulation.

When he was finished speaking there was violent applause for some ten seconds before the debate broke out once more with redoubled force. I was amongst those who rose to their feet & cannot describe to you the powerful feelings it roused in my breast to stand as an equal amongst these men & imagine myself the subject of such applause. I fear I paid little heed to the remaining experiments of the evening, so giddy was I with all that had already taken place & the certainty that one day I shall stand before them & they shall stamp & huzzah & I shall know that the work I was placed upon this Earth to do has indeed been satisfactorily done.

I only wish I could say the same for that good-for-nothing harlot of a maid. I have swallowed a purge but fear it comes too late. My stomach tortures me & the cold sets my teeth to chattering so violently I fear I shall take a chill. How dare she make me ill with her carelessness, when she has been told so many times of the delicacy of my constitution and of the grave demands placed upon me by the rigours of my work. When I rebuke her she pouts those lips & smirks & thrusts her hips at me in her harlot way but I shall not be put off so. I have half a mind to go to her now, while she sleeps, so that I might acquaint her with the full extent of my displeasure. Let her see how she likes it, to stand before me on such a night in nought but her thin nightgown. A whipping & a night in the coal cellar would surely serve to improve her memory & subdue her unruly spirit.

3

Naturally I blamed my mother. She was all that
was left. Besides, it is easiest to strike out at
those who make no effort to defend themselves.
Their very passivity drives one to greater fury, to
more violent assault. Our Lord Jesus understood
this. Consider His instruction that, struck by our
enemies, we should turn the other cheek. Only a
fool would mistake this for the meek acceptance
of injustice. On the contrary, turning the other
cheek is a considered act of aggression. It is
distressingly, brilliantly cruel. For if, despite the
frenzy of your beatings, your victim refuses to
express his pain, what then must become of your
own, bloating and blackening inside you? It must
tear open the very crown of your skull.

When at last Ma Tally returned, a little after
dinner-time the next day, her skirt was ruffled
with dust and she looked weary, her face
collapsed somehow, as though the bones that
buttressed it had rotted and crumbled beneath
the wrinkled skin. She did not greet me. Without
taking off her cloak she sank into the chair by the
empty fireplace and closed her eyes. In the
endless hours of the night I had thought myself
quite without hope. But some faint desperate
flickers of optimism must have persisted in me
for it was only when I saw my mother's face and
the leaden way in which she dragged her feet
across the floor that those last feeble glimmers

were snuffed out. My heart clenched like a fist and my nose prickled but I did not cry.

Instead, I was flooded with a bitter venomous anger. I wanted to hurl my stool at her, to bite her, kick her, smash my fist into her nose. I wanted to shake her by her shoulders until the few teeth she had left were jolted from her gums. Everything in her posture incited me to violence. But I did not move. I peered grimly at her from under my cap, my head resolutely lowered, and I said nothing. Even as the tide of rage swelled inside me, a part of me congratulated myself on my control. Let her be the first to break the silence. Demands for news would serve only to dignify her condition and implicate me in her failure. I had no intention of doing either. It was she, after all, who had contrived this devilish venture, she who had put up my virtue for a wager. My reputation had been all my fortune. Now, with a single throw of the dice, it was gone. My life was over. I would hate my mother for ever.

Ma Tally sighed, sinking lower in the chair. Her chin sagged on to her chest. I clenched my teeth together. Let her say it. Let her say: *I have failed you. I have ruined us both.*

'Sage tea,' she whispered, without opening her eyes. 'Brew me some sage tea, girl. I have had a long walk and no breakfast.'

I dragged myself over to the grate, pushing the black kettle over the flames with such force that the iron bracket struck the chimney. Ma Tally flinched but she said nothing. We watched in silence as the water grew hot and the stump of a

40

spout let out a feathery shriek of steam.

'So?' The word belched from me before I could swallow it.

'So,' echoed my mother, staring at the gnarled roots of her hands in her lap.

I laughed then, a choke in the back of my throat, as I sloshed boiling water into the teapot, scalding my fingers.

'Don't bother to tell me,' I spat, shaking my hand furiously. 'I have no interest in the pitiful future you have brokered me. Why should I concern myself with such foolishness, now that I am ruined?'

My mother did not reply. Her face was impassive as she watched me clatter a single cup from the shelf. The tea was weak and fragments of dried sage leaf floated on its surface. I slopped the cup at her feet and turned away to the fire. My face burned and unshed tears clumped behind my nose. I would not give her the satisfaction of seeing me cry. Slowly, as though the movement pained her, she reached down to pick up her cup. I heard her suck at the hot liquid. Her slurping disgusted me.

'You go to London on the stage, Market Day next,' she said quietly.

I wheeled round.

'That's right, child,' she said, her face bent over her cup. 'London. There's a position for you there. With an apothecary. A respectable man.'

'But — '

'They'll know what needs doing. All the necessary expenses have been agreed and a little extra to ease your passage. We settled on a year, longer if they like you. That way there'll be no arousing suspicion. Three pound a year and a new gown too, which isn't bad, considering.'

Ma Tally raised her head to look at me. Her smile was lopsided and her little eyes were unusually bright. I put it down to the mention of money. She was a greedy little magpie, my mother, and never happier than when presented with something shiny. Abruptly I felt the dizziness return. I grasped the chimney breast to steady myself and rested my forehead against the cool stone.

'And how much did he pay you, Mother?' I whispered, 'That you would sell me?'

Ma Tally pretended not to hear me.

'As for that boy, he is sent to Newcastle this morning.' She scowled at the floor. 'He's to sail immediately for the colonies. We will pray God his ship may sink and the fishes make a fine dinner of him.'

Shakily I drew myself up to glare at her.

'I shan't have you speak that way of my husband,' I said, but my lips were white and stiff and formed the words only with difficulty.

'There is no husband, not any more. In London you will be a widow, your husband lost at sea. It's best. There you'll be free to begin again. Your pay will do for a portion. They say London husbands don't come cheap.'

Her voice wavered then and she buried her face in her cup.

'He would've had you sent by the waggon, the tight-fisted scoundrel, but I wasn't having none of it,' she mumbled into her tea. 'I will not be bullied by such a dog, for all his rich man's bluster.'

'I am a married woman,' I said more desperately. 'My husband lives, whatever you say. You can't sell me like a Negro.'

Ma Tally slammed her cup down.

'Don't tell me what I can and cannot do, girl. You will go to London and forget what's been and you will be thankful for your good fortune. There's not many gets a second chance.'

*   *   *

And so it was that I found myself cast off, abandoned not only by my erstwhile husband but by my own mother too. She might have helped me herself, if she had wished to. She had long since been sought out by women of the parish who found themselves inconvenienced and had secured something of a reputation for her belly-ache teas. But she refused. She even had the effrontery to chide me for my foolishness. For all that the situation had not come out in the way that we had wished it, there was profit to be made from it and profit I would, if it was the last thing she made me do. She protested that she had no wish to be parted from me but that there was nothing to be gained by keeping me where I was, and much to be lost. In London I might find myself a better future, better perhaps even than the one I had already glimpsed.

For a while I was stupid enough to muse upon her words, to imagine that she might care for me

43

as a mother should, that she did indeed have my best interests at heart. For a few days we were gentler with each other. She made me savoury broths to ease my nausea and rubbed my shoulders to loosen them. She bound a hare's-foot to a thong of leather so that I might wear it about my neck for good luck. For my part I accepted her kindnesses with something close to gratitude. I no longer blamed her quite so completely for my misfortunes. I remembered the passion with which she had defended me and I felt a warm twist of affection for it. It occurred to me that I might even miss her a little when it came time for me to go. At night, when I found her hand upon my shoulder as she slept, I did not throw it off.

And then I found them. I hadn't been searching, not specifically. Or not for that. When I lifted the loose flagstone and felt to the back of the damp press I had no intention of taking anything that was not mine. I was simply curious and I was running out of time. My life was to take a new course in an unknown city. Most people never came back. If I was never to see the cottage again I wanted to be sure I took its secrets with me. I knew my mother's business. Women came to the cottage with child; they left alone. I felt a thrill of awful anticipation as I fumbled in the loose brickwork in the chimney. My fingers touched something stiff and slightly greasy above the ledge where we set the bacon to smoke. It was a package, wrapped in a piece of oilcloth. It occurred to me then that I could

44

leave it, dust my hands off on my apron and put it out of my mind.

Except that I couldn't. My hand trembled as I reached it down and unwrapped it. And there they were. Rolled up like a slab of meat, like a corpse in a winding sheet, four shiny golden guineas. *Profit we would.* How she must have cackled to herself as she watched me softening towards her. How she must have longed me gone, so that she could lay them out in a row upon the bed and trace the shiny implacable shape of them with the tip of one avaricious finger. A victory, then, in the end. Her only child's future traded to soften her own.

For my remaining nights at the cottage I slept wrapped in a blanket on the floor and woke with my limbs stiff and cold. I refused to answer her, to acknowledge her. I could barely stand so much as to look at her. The creak of her leather stays or the trace of her old-woman smell was enough to send me into a blind black fury.

When the time came for me to leave the cottage, and the waggoner hoisted my box into the cart that would take me to the staging inn, I looked directly ahead, my eyes fixed upon the flat white sky. My mother hesitated as though she intended to speak. Then she turned and went back into the cottage, closing the door quietly behind her. Sharply I urged the waggoner to hurry. He shrugged indolently, scratching his balls and hawking with slow deliberation into the ditch before finally hauling his bulk up beside me. He nudged me then and I frowned. Laughing, he slapped the reins against the horse's withers and with a jolt we moved off.

I had sewn the guineas into the lining of my padded petticoat, along with my hare's-foot for good luck. I liked to imagine the soft paw patting each one in turn like children, keeping them steady. All the same, the coins dragged at the fabric so that my skirts caught against the splintery wooden bench of the waggon. If I moved suddenly I could feel them shifting, their muffled edges bumping the side of the cart. Inside the oilcloth I had left four round flat stones. It had taken me a full afternoon to find four of precisely the right shape and thickness, and I had polished each one upon an old rag to bring it to something close to a shine before replacing the bundle in its hiding place in the chimney. I felt a sour shiver of satisfaction in my bowels when I pictured how her face would fall when she discovered the treasure gone, her greedy smile shrivelling faster than a slug sprinkled with salt.

I smiled grimly to myself to think of it, perhaps I even laughed, for the waggoner gave me a sly sideways glance and shifted his thigh so that it touched against mine. Disdainfully I moved away, turning my shoulders from him, but the smile still twitched grimly at my lips. I was determined never to see Ma Tally again but I wished her to remember, long after she had stamped out the last embers of my existence, that I was the kind of person who was not to be trifled with.

To Mr Grayson Black,
Apothecary at the sign of the Unicorn
in Swan-lane

Grayson, my dear fellow,

I beg you to accept my apologies for my tardiness in responding to you with regard to your manuscript. Business has proved uncommon brisk these past months & there has been little time for the mountain of manuscripts that await my attention.

I have now had the opportunity to consider yours, perhaps the weightiest of the lot, & I am obliged to confess that I can see no market for it at present. While the subject is of considerable interest to many of my customers, those volumes that have proved themselves most in demand are principally illustrated compendia of examples of the many strange creatures born of woman around the globe. I have had particular success with Swammerdam's *Uteri mulieris fabrica* — among his many fascinating examples, I would cite in particular the tale of the pregnant woman who took care to wash herself after being greatly frightened by a Negro so that the ill effects of her imagination might be reversed, only to discover her child born black in those places she was unable to reach.

Where then are the similarly intriguing cases

in your account? An idiot girl & a child born
with uncommonly large moles as a result of her
mother's affection for currants hardly satisfy. I
would add here that Swammerdam's book contains many fine illustrations, while your volume
is more notable for the very considerable
number of pages you commend to scientific
discourse of a frequently opaque nature. I fear
my customers have not the inclination to read
so great a quantity of words — nor I the ink
for them neither!

I regret that I cannot help you further. As an
old acquaintance I would only enquire whether
you had considered finding a patron, perhaps a
physician or other educated man of science, to
assist you in the promotion of your efforts? You
might find both the standing & the counsel of
such a man of considerable value.

Please extend my warmest regards to Mrs
Black. I enclose the page you requested &
remain, sir, your loyal friend & servant,

SEPTIMUS GAULE

2nd day of July 1718

Extract of a letter, written from Paris, containing an Account of a Monstrous Birth & Published in the PHILOSOPHICAL TRANSACTIONS OF THE ROYAL SOCIETY in the year of our Lord Sixteen hundred & Sixty Six

In the House of M. Bourdelots was showed a Monster in the form of an Ape, having all over its Shoulders, almost to his Middle, a Mass of Flesh, that came from the hinder Part of its Head, & hung down in the form of a little Cloak. The Report is, that the Woman that brought it forth had seen on Stage an Ape so clothed: the most remarkable Thing was, that the said Mass of Flesh was divided in four Parts, correspondent to the Coat the Ape did carry. The Woman, upon Inquiry, was found to have gone five Months with Child, before she had met with the Accident of that unhappy Sight. Many Questions were on this Occasion agitated: viz. about the Power of Imagination & whether this Creature was endowed with a human Soul; & if not what became of the Soul of the Embryo, that was five months old.

4

I had never travelled in a coach before and my
first experience of it was uncomfortable enough
for me to wish never to have to do so again.

It rained incessantly for the nine days it took
us to drive to London, sheets of molten cloud
that thundered against the roof of the carriage
and turned the road to swamp. The horses made
slow progress. On more than one occasion we
lost the road altogether and had to traverse some
miles out of our way to rejoin it. Frequently we
were required to stop so that the wheels might be
dug out from the mud. The coach moaned and
buckled as though every rut and puddle in the
path were an agony to it. I had thought myself
fortunate to have secured a seat facing forward
for the length of the journey but our trunks,
tumbled any which way in an iron basket
suspended on bars upon the rear of the coach,
struck against the wall behind my head with a
barrage of such ferocious blows that I was
certain they must burst clean through it.

The ceaseless bangings were not the only
inconvenience to the passengers inside. The
weather required us to keep the tin windows
raised so that the rain might not come pouring
in. In the closed space the air quickly became
stale and brackish with the powerful smell of
bodies and wet wool. The only illumination came
from a pattern of holes punched in the metal and

a thin tear of light where the plate of the window did not quite fit in its frame. The draught from this gap spread a veil of tiny droplets across our laps, but it conceded only the most grudging suggestion of daylight. The darkness was intensified by the dull black leather that covered the interior of the coach, studded with grimy broad-headed nails which were, I supposed, intended by way of ornament and instead gave it a faintly menacing atmosphere. It would not have been possible, had I cared to, for me to make out any more than the vaguest features of my fellow passengers.

I did not care to. In the inn, as we took breakfast prior to departure, I noticed one woman, a buxom madam with a yellowed cap and a scarlet complexion, who picked at her teeth with her fork and clucked disapprovingly at everything her husband had cause to say. The chariot's occupants were mostly men in their middle years travelling alone and, when it came time for us to take up our seats, I took care to position myself beside her. She enquired my name that first morning but, finding me to be uncongenial company, promptly forgot it and occupied herself instead with the joint pleasures of a bag of sugary pastries and incessant admonition.

Her husband, a man even wider than she, seemed to take offence at neither the crumbs nor the criticisms. Indeed, on the few occasions that a remark of his passed uncensured, he took care to repeat it so that she might have a second opportunity to find something about it that

51

displeased her. Otherwise the conversation proceeded as it always must among men, with long silences punctuated with grunts and curses or, more frequently, gusts of flatulence and immoderate laughter. I curled myself into my corner and wished only to be left unmolested. At night, when we disembarked to take supper and lodgings in yet another roadside inn, I declined to accompany the others into the parlour.

Instead I took myself directly to bed, requesting my meal be brought to my room on a tray, although I seldom ate it. The worm inside me was fattening itself, tightening its grip on my guts and sickening me even as the worms of my childhood had sickened me. My appetite failed. I had a dry cough and a poor colour and my eyes were hollow and bruised with dark shadows. Even the treacly black rage that had sustained me in the first miles of the journey had begun to ebb away, leaving only a sooty scum that smeared the inside of my chest and tasted bitter on my tongue. I felt empty, bereft, my dress hanging from my thin shoulders like a child's poorly altered. I refused to think of my mother but, when in the long dreary hours my head fell forwards in a chilled half-sleep, it was the image of the door of our cottage quietly closing that jerked me back into consciousness. In the seat opposite to mine a man sucked incessantly on a long clay pipe. The smoke caught in my throat and stung my eyes until they watered.

The jolting movement and stuffy interior of the coach compounded my already uncertain stomach and rendered me weak with nausea.

Each morning, when I was roused at dawn to take my place once more in the carriage, I vomited so violently that I was sure I must turn myself inside out. But, for all the miseries of the journey, I longed for it never to end. I had met only one person who had been as far as London in all my life, a baker's apprentice, who, his face pale with flour, swore an oath that he would never return. He had remained there only a month and, in that month, he claimed, he had been daily taunted, admonished, jostled, pissed upon, and frequently stripped of his money. There had been not an inch of space to think, not even a sip of clear, clean air to breathe. The clamour of the streets had been insufferable, the choking fogs that pervaded them foul with disease, the famous river no more than a stinking brown ditch of rotting shit. London itself was a vast and fiendish carnival, an endless Hell stinking of tainted meat and swarming with footpads, swindlers and whores. A place of the damned, he had muttered grimly. There was no kindness to be found there, no trace of sympathy for one's fellow man. One might wander for ever as one street twisted into another, on and on, pressed on all sides by the rush of people until one fell, exhausted, to the ground. And when you did, no one would think to stretch out a hand to help you. You would be trampled instead beneath the heedless feet and irritated curses of a thousand strangers.

London. The very name had the whiff of brimstone about it. A city the size of twenty Newcastles? It was unimaginable, horrible. As the days passed, and the miles grudgingly gave themselves up beneath our wheels, the airless lightless clamour of the coach in which I endured from hour to hour took on the awful tension of a purgatory from which, however much I prostrated myself and begged forgiveness for my sins, there might be no deliverance. My fate was already decided. All too soon I would be cast out into London's fiery and pitiless abyss.

There would be nobody there who would wish to deliver me. I harboured no false hopes of sympathy from the apothecary and his family. It was plain that they would despise me and mistreat me cruelly because, quite aside from the satisfaction it affords a man of means to abuse a servant, it would, as associates of the merchant, surely profit them to do so. I could hardly expect kindness from a master who, paid to unyoke me from my troubles, knew the full extent of my shame. My sins would not be forgiven. God Himself would smile with fatherly approval upon the resourcefulness of his chastisements and buttress his thrashing arm. But he would rid me of the worm, thank God. He would give me something that would flush it out as a clyster purges a stubborn turd from the bowel and, like a turd, it would be tipped away, buried in one of the stinking cesspits that city houses grew upon. It cheered me a little to think upon it, the white worm in the rank darkness of a foul cellar, sucking desperately, hopelessly for air as it drowned, abandoned in a filthy mess of shit.

★ ★ ★

Early on the eighth day I was startled to be roused from a thin doze by the brisk shouts of ostlers. The coach had come to a stop and I saw when I opened my eyes that I was its only remaining occupant. The stillness of the carriage was startling. It was no longer raining. The door stood open, and the air had the green river taste of freshly washed skies. Tentatively I allowed my limbs to relax.

'We are arrived at Hampstead Hill.'

I looked up to see the fat woman's husband standing in the doorway of the chariot. He had a kind face, brick-red, with deep grooves into which a smile might be conveniently slotted.

'You are indisposed, I know, but the waters here are well known for their medicinal properties. Perhaps you might feel a little stronger if you sampled some.'

He proffered his hand but I shook my head. Fatigue knotted my limbs and made my neck ache. The fat man opened his mouth to say something. I closed my eyes. There was a pause.

'Sleep well, my dear,' he murmured.

His heels clattered on the cobblestones as he walked away. I squeezed my eyes shut, leaning back against the musty-smelling seat, but the noises of the morning pressed in upon me. The horses' harnesses rattled against the struts of the carriage as the animals were unhitched. Metal buckets clanked against stone. Voices called out orders. A dog barked. Several clocks competed to chime the hour. Nearby someone was striking a hammer against wood. There was a warm reek of fresh horse manure. I opened my eyes.

55

Beyond the open door there was a courtyard and, beyond that, its thatched roof frayed with watery sunshine, a long low inn. I was thirsty and I realized that I needed urgently to piss. Slowly I swung out one leg, groping with my foot for the step. My legs were weak with hunger. Holding tightly to the iron rail so that I should not fall, I climbed down.

And there it was. I shall never forget it. The clamour of the yard, which until that moment had clanged and echoed inside my skull, seemed to cease, so that even the twitters of the birds fell silent in the face of it. There was no building, no wall to break up the prospect, only a slope that curved away, its scrubby turf scabbed with churned mud. Beyond the hill it stretched away into forever, a glittering carpet of low black-tinted mist pierced by the sharpened points of innumerable spires and unrolled like a gift at my feet. London. And, in its centre, triumphantly, rose up a mighty orbed mass, a dome of unimaginable majesty, its silvered patina shadowed with midnight's inky blue. For all its immensity, it seemed to float above the city, borne up upon a solemn wreath of cloud. As I stared, a thin shaft of sunlight broke through the mottled sky above it, striking the lantern at its crown and turning its apex to liquid gold. My heart constricted but something deeper inside me stirred. It was faint but unmistakable, the warm quiver that ran through my belly. I clenched my fists then, for safety, but I could not take my eyes from the city. It glistened in the pale light like a promise. Even as I watched it seemed to grow, as all around it and beyond it smoke curled endlessly and proprietorially upwards from a thousand chimneys to join with the clouds and claim ownership of the heavens themselves. The noise too, the noise rose up from it like the shimmer of heat from sand, a hollow roar like the echo of a vast and distant ocean, eternal and unceasing. It seemed to me that the force of it moved the spires like the sea-swell of a tide, sucking at the pebbles beneath my feet, pulling me onwards.

I did not go in but stood at the swell of the hill until the coachman summoned his passengers for the final stage of the journey. As I climbed into the carriage, one of my fellow passengers enquired what it was that amused me. It was only then that I realized I was smiling.

At last I am well enough once again to take up my pen. My indisposition was severe but never, I think now, grave, a chill which took hold first in my chest before moving to my abdomen where it lingered, keeping me to my bed these full twelve days. But today I am much recovered in strength, owing to a new tincture of my own devising, that mixes two grains of opium with five of rhubarb pounded with a little camphor & taken in a tumbler of Canary wine, bloodwarm. It has proved uncommonly effective in relieving the pain. It is some years since I felt so powerful an energy surge within me. Tonight the candle shall give out before I do.

It is an unseasonally mild evening in London & I sit before the window, careless of the draught through the casement, with a bottle of Portugal wine at my elbow. Of course such pleasure does require that I am obliged to gaze upon the monstrous dome of our new cathedral. It is truly a grotesque creation, the vainglorious grandiosity of its design trumpeting a Popish enthusiasm that is an affront to any sober Anglican. Can the burghers of this city have already forgotten that it was those heretics who set the fire that destroyed the great Cathedral upon whose hallowed ground this vile boil now swells? Resurgam, indeed! It is nothing but a pustulous wen on the face of the city, a monument to corruption & to superstition &, of course, to Mr Wren himself who charges a scandalous 4 shillings for entry to the place &, it is said, squats like Moloch in the nave on Saturdays, receiving guests as though it were his own parlour. It matters not to him that it was our taxes that paid for its erection, nor that the place is not yet even complete & painters continue to swarm over the inside of his dome like spiders on their ropes. On the contrary I am sure he demands a considerable share of the admissions. The man's vanity is outlandish. I do not doubt he would erect an altar there in his own honour if he could only manage it.

How my quill flies across the page! The wine I have taken would seem to have an intoxicating effect quite at odds with the quantities I have consumed. The letter from Samuel Marlowe rests beneath my elbow and sends a thrill of anticipation directly into the pit of my arm. Surely, it is surely a sign, the answer to my prayers. The prospect of uninterrupted study is matchless and, from what Marlowe writes, the subject ideal, shaped of precisely the manner of crude clay most suggestible to stimulation. Oh, praise be to the Lord God who, in His wisdom, has chosen me, His faithful servant, & has placed the flaming torch of Truth in my hand so that I may light the way. May His glorious will be done!

5

There was a warning shout and the coach came to a sudden stop.

'The New Road already?'

Yawning, the man opposite me reached up to lower the window and peered out. Pallid sunshine powdered his short wig. I glimpsed a jostle of smoking chimneys and the hazy orange of an open fire, before I was overcome by a powerful stink of pig shit and rotting refuse and something harsh and chemical like burning hair. I swallowed and pressed my hand over my mouth as the man brought his head sharply back into the coach, struggling to raise the window as he did so. But even as he wrenched at the strap a blackened hand pressed down upon it and a grey face loomed at the window. Male or female, it was impossible to know. Its hair was long and straggled and coated with a thick white dust. Its yellow eyeballs rolled like egg yolks in their deep sockets. The hand clawed at the air and the mouth opened. Its two remaining teeth, set together in its lower jaw, were skewed and mossy as old gravestones. Beside me, the fat woman gave a little shriek.

'Come, kind sir, a little something — '

There was a shout from the coachman, the sharp crack of a whip, the jingle of harnesses. Then, with a sudden jerk, the carriage leaped forwards, almost throwing me from my seat.

'What the Devil — ?' demanded the fat woman's husband, leaning forward to settle his buttocks more categorically across the bench. His wife swallowed and hurriedly pressed a pastry into her mouth. Her upper lip was bristly with sugar.

'Thieves?' one of the gentlemen enquired anxiously.

'Damned beggars,' said the one at the window. 'Bed themselves down in the ash-heaps out here full winter through. Acquaintance of mine owns a brickfield out here. Isn't a damned thing he can do about it. It's the kilns, of course. Warmth draws 'em out like lice.'

Relieved to have escaped a robbery, the men fell to a pleasurable complaining. I did not listen. So this was it. We would soon be there. Our progress had slowed to a crawl. There were other coaches alongside us. I could hear the lascivious suck of mud upon their wheels, the shouts of the coachmen as they traded curses. Horses whinnied and danced. Herds of cattle on their way to market blocked the road, bellowing their reluctance. The foul stench grew stronger. Several of the gentlemen held handkerchiefs to their mouths. At last, I begged the gentleman opposite me to lower the window so that we might all breathe some fresher air, but he only snorted. It was the air out there I should be worried about, he retorted. Where did I think the stink was coming from, anyway? Besides, the ditches along this road were several feet deep and so full of malodorous filth that, with the windows open, we would be knee-deep in rancid

61

mud before we'd gone a half-mile.

'First time to London, then,' he said. He was a thin man with hunched shoulders and bony legs that folded beneath him like a grasshopper's.

I nodded curtly, not wishing to prolong the exchange.

'Come up to snare yourself a city husband, I don't doubt.' He leaned forward to peer into my face. 'Quite a comely little baggage, aren't you?'

I replied stiffly that I was recently married and was to take up a position with the family of a relative while my husband attended some necessary business in the Indies. The rest of the carriage had been occupied in their own conversations. Now, to my displeasure, they turned their attention to me.

'Man must be a knucklehead,' said his neighbour, a milk pudding of a man with protruding teeth who showered the carriage's occupants with spittle as he spoke. 'Sending a lonesome wife to London, of all places? The bastard'll be sprouting a cuckold's horns afore his ship's so much as hoist anchor.'

'It is you, sir, who is the knucklehead if you think — '

The grasshopper leered.

'My, a spirited little vixen, isn't she?' he observed, with no little spite.

'Anger becomes her,' drawled the milk pudding. 'Brings a pretty colour to those pale cheeks. Say, if it is a position you seek, why not come and work for me? I can think of at least one hundred positions I might be able to offer you, and each one more gratifying than the last.'

I blushed angrily as the other men laughed.

'The greatest gratification you could give me, sir,' I replied with as much dignity as I could muster, 'would be to drop down dead.'

The fat woman's husband chuckled approvingly and leaned across his wife to pat my leg. She slapped his hand hard, sending up a cloud of sugar.

'The girl should be welcome in our house, should she not, madam?' he said equably to his wife as he inspected the damage to the back of his hand. Before she might empty her mouth to speak, he turned back to the other gentlemen, his round belly shaking with laughter.

'My wife could not countenance a handsome girl about the place. Last maid she hired was blind in one eye and so much disfigured with the smallpox, 'twas a wonder I did not mistake her for a strawberry and eat her with cream. Mrs Tomlin is a green-eyed harridan when it comes to servants, is that not so, my dear?'

His wife shook her jowls crossly, choking on her pastry.

'It's a wise woman who doesn't trust her husband,' the milk pudding declared.

'And a weak-minded fool of a husband who permits his household to be ruled by a shrewish wife,' sneered the grasshopper.

The fat woman's husband smiled without rancour.

'I assure you, sir, that my wife is as obedient and dutiful as any man might wish and is invariably in agreement with me. It is simply,' he

63

added, with a twinkle in his eye, 'that I am not always cognizant of my views upon certain matters until she informs me of them.'

There was a burst of laughter among the assembled company. The atmosphere was suddenly convivial, the passengers expansive with one another now that the journey was almost over.

I alone remained silent. We had descended Hampstead Hill some time earlier. With every uncomfortable turn of the wheels my spirits rose and fell, and with each jolt of the carriage I felt the breath suck and shiver in my chest and the grip of the worm in my belly tighten and relax, as though in the first pains of labour. We were in it now, the cloudland I had seen from on high, and every moment brought me closer to its centre, to the place where the dome ascended skywards and the door stood open upon my grim sentence of servitude.

A satisfactory day.

My stomach is easier, though there is an alarming bruise beneath the surface of the skin close by the right hip bone. I have taken comfrey to disperse the congealed blood & applied a poultice of the same to draw the obstruction outward. It is imperative that my blood & juices be kept in a due state of thinness & fluidity, whereby they may be able to make those rounds & circulations through those animal fibres with the least resistance that may be, or I shall grow stale & sluggish. To that end I bleed myself weekly & continue to swallow three grains of opium each day, for not only does the poppy relieve pain in the severest degree but it harmonizes the whole constitution, so that each part may act in just proportion to the other. Truly I have never worked so quickly nor with such clarity.

Everything is arranged. A matter of days, only days, and then at last — at last I shall set about the essential elements of my proof.

It occurs to me, suddenly, that I understand precisely how, in utero, it is decided whether an infant be violently deranged or, as in this case, inertly idiotic. I must commit it to paper before it is lost and yet it is so plain to me I cannot believe I have not seen it before. Surely, this is decided by <u>the nature of the maternal passions,</u> so that violent madness results from those passions which manifest themselves violently through bulging eyes, distended veins, redness of face, hard pulse such as <u>anger</u> or <u>excessive sexual appetites.</u> Idiocy by contrast must be the result of those strong emotions evidenced by paleness of features, dead faints, coldness of extremities, irregular pulse such as <u>excessive fright.</u>

It is quite plain, plain & undeniable. Not for the first time, I find myself elated & yet calm, quite without doubt. The opium works like a whetstone on the blade of my intellect, sharpening it until it slices through ambiguity & ignorance like an anatomist's knife, revealing all its secrets.

I shall have Mrs Black bring the idiot to me forthwith so that I may examine her further. Surely her injury is mended now, for it was hardly a violent blow & her childish bones are too waxy easily to break. She must learn to endure. With my powers of perception exalted so, I can afford to waste not a single moment.

6

And so it was one dishwater afternoon in January in the year of our Lord 1719 that I set my foot for the first time upon London's tainted and abundant soil. The coach set us down at an inn in Holborn. I hardly knew where to look, so astonishing was the clamour and the bustle of travellers and coaches and horses, but from what I could make out each one of the inn's seven coach houses might have provided ample accommodations for the most discerning of country squires.

As for the inn itself, with its fine columned porch and its rows of grand windows, each fashioned from a single great sheet of glass, I could not imagine that the King himself could live in a palace more magnificent. I stared around me, my mouth hanging open, unable to take it all in, until a coachman drove his horses so tightly alongside me that I could feel the heat rising from their flanks and might have felt the tang of the whip across my cheek if I had not stepped backwards into a puddle. Moments later a man in a tight black coat instructed me to close my mouth and move on before he stopped the hole himself with the bung he kept handy between his legs. By the time I had thought up an appropriately scornful reply he was gone. Everyone arriving in London, it appeared, was intent upon business so urgent that the loss of even a minute would have the direst of consequences.

It was barely past dinner-time and already the afternoon was grey as dusk. From inside the long lower windows of the inn there came the supple glow of clustered candles, the red blush of a fire. Heavy with exhaustion, I felt the clutch of hiccups at my chest and gripped my left thumb in my right hand as tightly as I could; I could not risk ill fortune on such a day. For a moment I thought to secrete myself inside the snug golden belly of the Eagle and Child for as long as I could contrive it, perhaps for ever, but before I could take one step towards the door a messenger boy ran up to me. Asking if I was come in on the Newcastle stage, he informed me that the apothecary had sent him so as he might bring me back to his house without misadventure. I was not to trouble myself about my box. Instructions had been left for it to be sent on with a porter later that afternoon. We could leave immediately.

The boy's face was stained purple around the mouth and his hands were dirty, but his eyes were bright and he looked well fed enough. Remembering the warnings of the baker's boy, I drew myself up and demanded how I was to know that he was indeed sent by my employer. I had no intention, I declared, of allowing myself to be gulled out of my possessions by a common thief. This little speech had sounded impressive as I composed it in my head but, for all my bluster, I made a poor job of delivering it. Fatigue caused my voice to tremble. To my great vexation I realized I was not far from tears. The boy shrugged and rubbed the back of his hand against his nose, leaving a bubbled trail in the dirt.

'It was Mrs Black had me come. Said you was like to get yourself lost or somefink, not having been to London before. Said you'd be glad of someone to show you the way. Gived me sixpence and all.' He scuffed a toe in the mud, then looked up with a sudden grin. His teeth were startlingly strong and white. 'Said you might give me somefink too, if I minded me manners and let you take the wall.'

The unexpected kindness of Mrs Black was too much for me. The tears spilled over and rolled down my cheeks. I yawned widely and rubbed my fists against my eyes, so that the boy might not see them and pity me.

'But it don't matter,' the boy said anxiously, reaching out a hand towards me. I glared. Changing his mind, he plunged it instead into his pocket and shrugged. 'I was only sayin'. You don' 'ave to fret yerself 'bout the extra, not if you ain't got it.'

If this was a trick then it was a very superior one. I had neither the spirit nor the inclination to resist further. I shrugged and followed him.

Outside the street was paved in stone and so broad across a farmer's hay waggon might have turned itself quite around in a single manoeuvre had it not been for the impenetrable press of traffic. As it was, I had never seen so many vehicles gathered together in one place, chaises and chairs and carts and coaches and waggons,

69

crowded together three deep, each blocking the next, their wheels rattling in their sockets and their drivers engaged in a ceaseless exchange of shouts and curses. Frequently an irate passenger would thrust his head out of his conveyance and yell his own abuse, fist aloft. Above this clamour, horses stamped their hooves, pedestrians called to one another, street vendors cried their wares, and bells sounded out the hour from what must have been one hundred church steeples. At the corner of one street a street organ creaked out its tune, a moth-eaten monkey in a plush skullcap crouched atop it, while only a few feet further on a fiddler sawed out an Irish jig, accompanied by a tiny ragged girl with a tambourine. A trumpeter commanded the crowd to see a calf with six legs and a topknot. A tinker banged a frying pan with a tin spoon, singing out his business and calling for kettles and skillets to mend. The fishman's bawled chant collided with the oyster lad's and clattered against the ditty of the pudding man: *two for a groat, and four for sixpence!* The cry of the milkmaid pierced them all, her long shriek like the wail of a dying cat. A man in an ancient tricorn hat carried a cage of birds slung around his neck, each one frenziedly chirruping and flapping its wings against the flimsy metal bars. Parsons, lawyers, porters, excisemen, water-carriers, milk-girls and pedlars of all kinds elbowed their way through the throng, their heads lowered in the headlong rush. Doors banged, taverns and coffee-houses belching raucous groups of men out into the street. And, without pause, children wove like flying needles in and out of the crowd, their shrieks streaming behind them. They leaped across the kennel, a stinking slurry of refuse of every imaginable kind which in places was close on three feet across, ignoring the stones that had been set into it by way of a crossing, and dodged between wheels taller than they, which creaked ominously over them as they disappeared. Their heels threw up sprays of mud, splattering the beggars who squatted, grimy with dust and soot, among the heaped-up rubbish in the shelter of doorways and, plucking at the hems of passers-by, implored them to spare a few pence.

It was like an enormous, extravagant puppet show. I watched agape, aching to lift the joiner's sawdusty hat for a better look at his seamed face, to finger the flashing silver buttons upon a dandy's coat, to feel the coarse texture of an old man's campaign wig. I wanted to raise my own voice and add it to the clamour, so that I might become part of it. I would have been content just to linger and stare about me but even that was impossible. I was carried along by the relentless tide of people. I could not stop. Besides, I dared not lose sight of the boy, who slipped ahead of me with the sinuous assurance of an eel.

Determined to arrive at the apothecary's house with my dress unsoiled, I refused to give up the wall, though it bore the grimy trail of a thousand skirts at hip height smeared along its length. I surrendered my privilege only when a sooty chimney-sweep with elbows like a pair of folded umbrellas walked directly up to me and, refusing to budge, stood with his arms akimbo, rolling his creamy white eyes in his blackened face, until I was forced to step out into the road where directly a nut-seller rammed his wheelbarrow hard against my shins and several chairmen cursed at me to clear out of their way. Alarmed, I pressed myself back against the wall but, as I passed the entrance to a narrow courtyard, two mangy curs unleashed themselves at each other, twisting themselves into a growling eight-legged blur of teeth and drool. I screamed, stumbling away, my heart pounding against my ribs and my head filled with a kind of blind roaring. The boy turned impatiently, gesturing at me to follow. I clenched my fists, struggling to regain my composure. Once, as a girl, I had been badly bitten by a dog and I retained a powerful fear of them. Reflexively I reached up to touch my scar, a ragged purple seam where the nape of my neck met my shoulder. I called for the boy to slow down, to walk with me, but he was too far ahead to hear me above the racket. Biting my lip, I hastened to catch him, my legs shaky and treacherous.

I was almost abreast of him when, ahead of us, a gentleman with red-heeled shoes and a sword two feet long was jostled by a greasy porter pushing a barrow of boxes. Wheeling around with a yell of outrage, the gentleman threw the startled porter head-first into the gutter. Immediately a mob clotted around the pair, laughing and jeering and urging them to a fight. Meat-faced men and urchins pushed roughly around me, angling for a better view. The stale smell of beer and old sweat mixed with the mouse-nest reek of breath and bodies and greasy clothing. A boot came down heavily on one of my feet. Yelping, I tried to squeeze between the men as they crowded forward, but they pressed together like roof slates, one overlapping another, allowing no opening. Their rough coats grazed my cheeks. Behind me there was the dull inhaled thwack of a nose crumpling beneath a fist. The men cheered but, for all their outward high spirits, there was something ugly about their faces now, something gaunt and greedy. There was another punch, a piglet's shrill squeal. A roar went up from the crowd. The men jostled harder. For a moment I lost my footing and feared I would fall. Scrabbling upright, I pushed again, turning myself sideways to slip out. The bodies pushed back. Someone cursed. I felt the castellated knuckles of a clenched fist against my ribs. Another hand plucked at my cloak. Out of the corner of my eye I saw the flash of a drawn blade. I felt the scream swelling in my chest.

'Come on.'

The voice was low and clear, like a voice from a dream. Someone seized my hand. Against my chilled skin the fingers were warm and insistent. Comforting. Furiously I tried to pull my hand away.

'Get your hands off me, you thieving good-for-nothing!'

The hand tightened its grip, wrenching at my arm. The men shoved against me so that my ears twisted painfully against the scrape of their

73

sleeves. I tugged frantically. Then, abruptly, I was free. Behind me the crowd, tiring of spectatorship, set quickly upon one another in a barrage of blows and curses. Blood splattered shiny red across the dull grey stones of the kennel. The messenger boy glanced up at me as he dropped my hand.

'Come on,' he said again, and pointed across the road. I followed him through the perilous press of vehicles, my hands shaking, my face hot with fear and anger. The fear I dismissed as no more than the panicky apprehensions common to those weakened by tiredness and hunger. Had the contemptible maggot in my belly not insisted upon draining me of my habitual strength and vigour, I would doubtless have found myself less susceptible to foolish fancies. The anger, however, I clung to gratefully. I fumed at the boy as he turned in to a narrow lane, gesturing at me to remain close to him. It was too late for such niceties now, I muttered angrily to myself. Surely he could not expect a gratuity from me after such a thorough-going display of carelessness. It was true that I had never really been in danger. But all the same, I told myself firmly, if I had been alone I would have more quickly understood the possible risks of the situation and taken steps to avoid it. I was not worldly, exactly, having been denied the rich man's pleasure of travel, but, as the daughter of a cunning woman, I had met many of the diverse and devious characters who populated that world and lent it its flavour. My mother had taught me to listen to what people did not say, to winkle out the meanings that concealed themselves inside the hard shells of words. In the village I had been known to be sharp-witted and sharp-tongued. Only once had I allowed my passions to rule my instincts and I had paid a very great price for my folly. I had no intention of making such a mistake again. There would not be many in London who would contrive to get the better of me.

There was considerable comfort to be derived from these assurances. As I walked, I repeated them to myself several times until my heart ceased its frantic knockings. When at last we stopped in front of a door, and I realized that we were finally arrived, I spat once upon the ground, for luck, and dismissed the messenger boy with only a casual sneer as a gratuity.

He did not leave, however, but lingered beside me as I rang the bell. It jangled within the shop and fell silent. No one came. There was a small latched flap in the door through which customers might be examined before being admitted, but it remained closed. Feeling my heart quickening once again, I stepped to the window and peered through. The inside of the shop was not lit but, behind the glass, the ledge was crowded with dark-coloured glass bottles and jars. Between them I could make out a large volume placed upon a low stand, set open. Beside it was a tray of coloured stones strung upon strips of leather and a yellowed skull. Beyond the ledge I could make out the outline of a counter set with more, larger bottles and, behind it, an open doorway, leading into another room. I leaned closer to the glass so that I might have a better view. I made out the shape of something long and ridged suspended from the ceiling before my breath misted the glass. I rubbed it with my sleeve and looked again. Beside me someone cleared their throat.

'Mrs Campling?'

Startled, I stepped backwards, glancing over my shoulder. My foot sank into a puddle of mud but there was no one behind me.

'Mrs Campling?' the voice said again. 'I am Mrs Black.'

A woman stood in the doorway of the shop, her arms crossed, a woman made entirely of precisely ruled lines. Her face was long and stern, its planes sharpened by iron-grey hair pulled tightly back from the crown. Above the two angles of her cheekbones, her eyes were curt incisions, while her nose was a narrow triangle, pinched to a white tip. Her plain white cap was so crisply starched it might have been folded from paper while, beneath the jutting lines of her collarbones, the rigid bodice of her plain dark dress made another precise triangle of her chest, permitting no softness or curvature of flesh. It was impossible to imagine her sighing with pleasure when her stays were finally loosened at the end of the day. It was impossible to imagine her sighing with pleasure at all. A man would cut himself one hundred times before he so much as got his buttons unfastened.

Mrs Black considered me, her fingerbones drumming upon her sleeves. I looked anxiously over my shoulder. Apart from the messenger boy who still waited, shifting from foot to foot, we were quite alone. The bunch of iron keys at her waist clanked a little as she drummed. Beside them, on a separate loop, a birch switch dangled, its leather handle worn to the shape of a hand.

'You are Mrs Campling, are you not?'

Still I hesitated. Perhaps it was a trick. If I answered in the affirmative, would punishment follow? After all, it was his family who had arranged my position. They had dispatched me to this place not as the wife of their son, never that. The Campling name must not, under any circumstances, be besmirched. I was no more than soiled sheets to them, a musty ill-used bundle which must be bleached clean of ignoble stains. The expenses of the laundry had been met. That, as far as they were concerned, would be the end of it.

And yet the apothecary's wife addressed me with his name. Eliza Campling. The anticipation of it caused the saliva to leap in my mouth. I swallowed, tasting excitement and disgust. Often I had imagined myself taking his name, owning it — what girl in my position would not have? — but it had always been like a new dress that belonged to someone else, something to be admired, stroked a little perhaps, but never taken out of its paper, never put on, for fear of spoiling it. Now I thrust my arms roughly into its sleeves, wrenching it over my shoulders. Who cared if it ripped? I would wear it with as much destructive pride as I could muster. I would eat in it, sleep in it and, when at last I was rid of the vile worm, I would bleed in triumphant scarlet across it. If there was to be punishment, let it come. It would have been worth it. For a bright fleeting moment, I would have taken what was rightfully mine.

'Yes,' I said firmly. 'I am Mrs Campling.'

That first evening, when Mrs Black saw the bare finger on my left hand, she gave me a brass ring to wear and chided me for being careless with my own. There was not the faintest trace of archness in her voice. Indeed, in all the time I knew her Mrs Black never once betrayed, by the slightest gesture, any knowledge of my true circumstances. To her I was always someone's wife, always Eliza Campling.

And I was fool enough to be glad of it.

She is here.

I can hear her lumbering feet as they thunder up the stairs, her strangling Northern inflections as she does battle with the rudiments of the English language. I shiver a little as I imagine the effects of this great metropolis upon her undeveloped sensibilities. I know of no stranger not bewildered & disturbed by the glare & clamour of it, be they perfectly familiar with European cities of some considerable size. How powerful a provocation, therefore, must it prove to a rustic sprung only days ago from a mire of mud? Indeed, I have instructed Mrs Black to warn her repeatedly of the city's dangers, for a dread of unseen horrors beyond her immediate environs must surely stimulate a heightened state of imagination which shall serve the work to its considerable advantage.

So too with myself. Though the particulars of the situation contrive to blur the line between the domestic sphere and the precision of the laboratory, it is imperative that I maintain a rigorous distance between subject and examiner. I shall neither acknowledge her outside this room nor address her upon any matter not pertaining directly to the study in question. There must be no easing of formality, no moderation of the strict & objective rules of science. This is not simply a matter

79

of correct procedure, although the objectivity of my observations shall gain from such rigour, but a part of the work itself, for fear & unease are as vital as the subject's intrinsic susceptibility to the success of the enterprise. My work with the parish women has shown me clearly that the low faculty of imagination that so dominates women is brought most effectively to the fore by the cultivation of such fear. It weakens the solids & fibres of the body, already so much feebler than those of the male, so that they are at their most receptive to impression.

On no account may she be permitted to grow comfortable.

7

Mrs Black took me first to the kitchen, a dark, low-ceilinged room tucked beneath the street. A small fire burned in the wide grate and, by the window, a linnet bounced on its perch in a wire cage. I could smell meat roasting with rosemary and the shitty reek of the cesspit in the cellar beneath. A muddle of boots and hooves and wheels hustled through the upper panes of the grimy window. The rain had once more begun to fall and the kitchen was thick with shadow. In the half-darkness a girl busied herself kneading dough, her face bent low over the table. Flour danced in a dust around her, blurring her outlines, while around her ankles a yellow cat made a sinuous figure of eight, its tail hempy as a length of rope.

'Mary!'

At the sound of her mistress's voice the girl startled backwards, bumping into a ladder-backed chair which fell with a crash against the stone flags and sending the yellow cat streaking away into a corner. The girl giggled and then tried to swallow her laughter, covering her mouth with a floury hand. Mrs Black sucked in her breath but said nothing. Instead she set the chair once again on its feet and, taking a taper to the range, lit the stick of candles on the kitchen table. The girl did not attempt to assist her. Instead she blinked in the light, tracing a large circle on the floor with one foot. Her large head hung a little to one side as though its weight was too much for her. She wore no cap and her amber hair was caught at the nape of her neck with a scrap of ribbon. It was not a modish colour but it glowed like polished copper in the candlelight and for a moment I almost envied it. Then I saw that there was a bald patch the size of a man's palm on the right side of her scalp. Its lower rim was crusted with a dark black scab.

'Mary,' Mrs Black said more harshly. 'This is Mrs Campling. She is to stay with us a while, remember?'

With an effort Mary lifted her head. I saw immediately that she was an idiot. Although her face lacked none of the individual features requisite to its construction, it had all the same an unfinished air about it, a slackness as though the clay that fashioned it had been too wet. The mouth hung open, and so too did the eyes, pink and lashless as a rabbit's. Naked and oddly vulnerable, they bulged from their flattened sockets, their swift sliding movements giving the unsettling impression that they were able to look in two directions at once. Their gaze slid over my shoulder and across the top of my head before, together, they came to settle upon the smudge of flour that whitened the bridge of her indistinct nose. Her cheeks were an inflamed red in her pale face. Meanwhile her fingers busied them-selves in her mouth, her large wet tongue probing at the lumps of uncooked dough caught in her bitten fingernails. She mumbled some-thing inaudible. Bubbles of saliva gathered at the corners of her mouth.

'Fetch Mrs Campling some water,' Mrs Black instructed. 'She will be thirsty after her long journey.'

Slowly Mary dragged her hand from her mouth. Her upper lip was cleft from the base of her nose so that it fell in two loose flaps over her protruding front teeth, exposing a slice of wet white-pink gum. Blinking her rabbit eyes, she smiled in my approximate direction, a slack, lopsided grin. Her chin was crusted with a paste of spittle and flour. Several of her bottom teeth were missing. I shook my head firmly.

'Thanks all the same but I don't think — '

Mary rolled her head around, her bulky tongue struggling to form a word. Then, with painstaking slowness, she took down a wooden dipper from a nail on the wall and a cup from the narrow dresser and carefully scooped a dipperful of water from a bucket by the range. When I took the cup from her its belly was scummy with dough. She waited expectantly, her loose eyes slithering around me and over me and through me until I could stand it no longer. I took a hurried sip and set the cup upon the table. The water was unpleasantly warm and had a brackish taste. I forced myself to swallow it. Mary clapped her hands together and smiled so widely that her tongue fell from between her lips and her rabbit eyes disappeared into two curved slits. Her delight was obvious.

It was also repulsive. Quickly I looked away. What could possibly have possessed Mrs Black to hire such a freak I had no idea. The girl's mother must have had a hare run across her path when she was with child, or maybe even eaten hare meat. It was well known in my village that, if no action was taken to reverse such damage, the child would be born marked by the animal. My mother had favoured tearing the dress of the mother which, if done directly, was known to neutralize the hare's abominable influence. Clearly the mother of this mooncalf had been something of a half-wit herself.

'You will do your utmost to speak clearly,' Mrs Black informed me crisply. 'Or you will struggle to be understood. I fear we have a rather more gracious way of speaking in London than you are used to in the provinces.'

Outraged, I opened my mouth to protest. Me, harder to understand than this rattle-head who could barely squeeze out a grunt without falling over with the effort? Mrs Black pinched her face together and studied me, her eyes somehow angry and impervious at the same time. Very gently her fingertips plucked at the switch that hung at her belt.

I closed my mouth.

'As to the arrangements here,' she continued, 'you are to sleep with Mary in the garret. I'm sure you will be comfortable. Come, let me acquaint you with the house. Then you may rest before supper.'

So there was to be punishment after all, I muttered to myself as we made our way up the dark wooden staircase. I was to be forced to sleep with an addle-headed idiot of a maid who could barely utter a syllable and who would doubtless piss in the mattress and dribble into my hair. I thought of my mother, her curled body compact as a walnut in the bed beside me, and my heart squeezed. Once again those vexing tears, whose foolishnesses I had been obliged to check all day, threatened to fall. I rubbed my nose with the back of my hand, biting down hard on my tongue. There was no future in such nonsense. My mother had betrayed me. I would shed no tears for her.

Instead I forced my attention towards the particulars of my new home as Mrs Black briskly pointed out its arrangement. It was considerably larger than I had expected. The ground floor was mostly taken up with the shop and the laboratory, the first looking out over the street, the latter over a small patch of yard to the back of the house. I would be required to assist when necessary in the shop, Mrs Black informed me, but the laboratory was kept locked. I would be permitted to enter it only with her authority and then I was to touch none of the apothecary's scientific equipment. Any breakages would be deducted directly from my wages. Behind the shop was also a narrow dining room where the apothecary and his wife took their meals.

On the first floor Mrs Black pointed towards the private chambers of herself and her husband. Both doors were firmly closed. On the second floor, she paused. As on the floor below, there were two doors, set at right angles to each other. Again both were closed. The one on the left, Mrs Black informed me, led to the room occupied by the apothecary's apprentice, a Mr Pettigrew. The other was the door to the apothecary's study. As she spoke, she placed herself firmly between it and me, as though to block my path.

'You are never to lay so much as a finger upon the handle of this door, do you understand me? The apothecary will countenance no intrusion.' She spoke severely, as though to a wicked child. I felt a flush of resentment warm my neck. 'Mr Black is engaged upon a work of extreme importance. He will not endure his papers to be disturbed. Even Mary is bid never to enter. If there is cleaning to be done then I will undertake it myself. If he calls for victuals you will knock to announce yourself and leave the plate outside the door. You will not tread heavily in your chamber nor make any other noises that might upset him. You will remove your shoes as you go up and down the stairs. It is your duty and responsibility while remaining in his house to guarantee the apothecary the privacy and silence that his work necessitates. If he finds even the least cause for complaint you may expect no leniency in his treatment of you. Do I make myself clear?'

She glared at me. I shrugged. The pretence seemed ridiculous to me, ridiculous and futile. The apothecary might wish to keep the more unsavoury particulars of his business a secret from the prying eyes of the Justice, but it seemed a little far-fetched to attempt to deny the existence of such services to those who sought to profit from them. After all, for what other reason had I been dispatched here?

'Answer me, girl,' she barked, skewering me with her gaze.

So much for Mrs Campling, then.

'Yes, madam,' I muttered sulkily, staring at the floor. If she considered the time for courtesies concluded, then so did I. As I followed her up the splintery wooden stairs to the garret I let my feet strike the boards with as much force as I could muster.

Ahead of me Mrs Black bent to open the low door and stepped back so that I might enter. I set one foot across the threshold and gasped, my ill temper quite forgotten. The room contained a large bed, furnished with a heap of rugs and a flock mattress and hung with heavy dust-coloured drapes, and, in the corner, a rickety three-legged stool propped up under the eaves and bearing a chamberstick and a small leather book. But it was only later that I noticed them at all. If the room had boasted no more than a pile of greasy rags to sleep on I would still have been unable to prevent myself from crying out with the sheer wonder of it. For the enchantment of that room was not contained within its four sloping walls but framed by the plain peeling border of its single window.

In a moment I was across the room and throwing open the casement. The houses on the west side of the lane were rather less tall than their neighbours opposite them, and the roof of the house across the street sloped down towards me, so close that, had I looked, I might have seen the brown streaks in the white splatters of bird dung, the soft mouse-grey balls of lichen that nestled among its slates. But I did not look. I did not see the shop signs beneath me as they shifted and creaked on their rusting brackets, distorting the noise from the street below. I vaguely heard Mrs Black calling out to someone on the stairs but I did not turn. I could not tear my eyes away.

For there, above my head, rising with glorious disregard from a low jumble of roofs and smoking chimneys, was the dome I had seen from Hampstead, only now it soared before me, its vaulting magnificence held aloft by a vast coronet of pillars. The columned lantern at its summit reached upwards into the smoke-bruised sky like Jack's beanstalk in the chapbooks at the village school. A golden balcony encircled it and, at its top, triumphantly, it held aloft a vast golden orb and cross, burnished bronze in the twilight. There was nothing of supplication in its appeal to Heaven, nothing of the humility before God so beloved of the Bible. On the contrary, it rose from the mud as a magnificent testament to the boundless ambitions of men, realized in all their inexorable glory. It was flanked by two great towers, like a pair of footmen in splendid livery. One bore the most enormous clock I had ever seen.

I could hardly bear to blink my eyes and lose the sight of it, even for a moment. As I stared the bells pealed out the quarter hour, rattling the slates of the roof about my ears. In all my life I had never dreamed that such a thing might exist. Beside it I felt tiny, as irksome and inconsequential as a louse, but at the same time it filled me with a rush of excitement. My heart quickened.

And, for all that I urged myself to fear what was to become of me in the apothecary's house, as I stared at the dome, I felt once again the faint stirrings of anticipation in my chest. In the shadow of this magnificence, I felt somehow safe, cheerful even. Who cared about the idiot maid, about the trials I was about to endure? I was not so much a fool to be careless of the pain ahead. I had heard the terrible moans of the women who sought out my mother's belly-ache tea. Afterwards I had washed the blood from the twisted linen. I knew that the next few days would be fearsome and dangerous, but, when the time came to purge me of the vile worm, I would take my chances in this room. I would drink whatever they gave me and rejoice. If I could but gaze through this window as my body racked and cramped then I might tolerate the pain. All the perils and injustices of the world would be powerless to harm me while a structure of such majesty stood sentinel against my slice of the London sky.

NOTES FOR OBSERVATIONS UPON A CONGENITAL IDIOT

1. *PHYSICAL EVIDENCE that solid fibres of body significantly <u>weakened</u> by effects of the mother's imagination: slack assemblage of limbs & muscle; cleft lip & palate; very large head [circumference about twenty four inches & a quarter]; small eyes with weakened eyesight; very large tongue of a full five inches in length; unusually small ears (no more than two inches in length); flattish nose prone to blockage; sparse hair; urine thick & with sweetish taste [deficiency of salts? though tears appear to contain customary amount]*

2. *CALLOUS ORGANS OF SENSATION: slow to thought & insensible/dull to small pains [pinching/pin/candle flame applied to skin of arm]; stronger stimulus [physical blows/knife/hot coal] → surprise & confusion —* BUT NOT ROUSED TO ANGER

3. *MEAGRE POWERS OF REASONING matched by EXCESSIVE EMOTION: deficient grasp of logic e.g. patterns, basic mathematics; little stimulation required to produce foolish laughter/abundant tears; unreasonable terror of darkness; superfluous response to sudden noise — screaming, dropping of held items [weakness of solid fibres?]*

4. *GODLESSNESS: poor grasp of rudiments*

of faith; refusal to repeat [recall?] simple prayers/oft-repeated verses; lack of conscience; moved by self-interest over virtue [NOTE: ** _Is an idiot in possession of a soul?_**]

↓

LOOSENING OF NERVE STRINGS LIKE STRINGS UPON A VIOLIN: RESPONSES SLOW, SENSATION DULL, REASONING SLACK & CARELESS

8

Those first nights at Swan-street I lay awake, my fist closed around the hare's-foot beneath my pillow, certain I should never sleep again. At home the nights were silent, disturbed only by the straining of tree branches in the wind or the distant muffled bark of a fox. But in London the noise of the city never ceased. The darkness was alive with yells and shouts and whistles, shrill with anger or drunkenness or desperation, I could not tell which, and with the rattling of coaches and the groaning of shop signs and the impatient tolling of bells quarrelling amongst themselves. When at last I contrived through sheer exhaustion to sink into an uneasy drowse, I was roused every hour with the fearful din of the watchman thundering at every door, bawling out the hour and the threat of rain. By dawn, when the shutters of the shops clattered open and the waggons laboured up the lane on their way to the market at Smithfield, churning up the chill grey air with their great wheels and drowning out the birds with the lowing of bullocks and the neighing of horses and the foolish gurgling frenzy of forlorn flocks of sheep, the day was once more begun.

Beside me the idiot girl stirred in her sleep. Tugging the rugs roughly over my shoulder, I rolled as far away from her as I could manage. The sickness was worst when I lay down, the night-blackened room lurching and rolling beneath me. Something bit at the back of my right knee. I cursed softly, humping myself upwards so that I might scratch it better.

The sudden movement cramped my belly and I dug my fingernails into my flesh, pressing downwards and squeezing as though I could tear the contemptible worm clean from my flesh. I saw it clearly, its blind eyes blank as it ground into my belly, stabbing its claws yet deeper into my flesh. Each day it grew stronger, more implacable, and yet, since my arrival, nothing had been said, nothing done. At first I thought the tea we drank in the mornings bitter and assumed it to be a preparation of sabine or some other such herb that might dispose of my troubles, but Mary drank it too, chipping extra sugar from the loaf to stir into it when Mrs Black left the kitchen. When I carefully enquired about it, Mrs Black informed me that I was privileged enough to be drinking tea made from leaves brought all the way from India, which was steeped first for the apothecary and then a second time for our breakfasts. This tea was so precious it was kept not in the pantry with the other provisions but in a locked canister in the dining room to which only Mrs Black had the key.

'It is something the apothecary wishes to do for Mary,' Mrs Black said with an expression that was neither frown nor smile but a curious mixture of both. 'He claims she has a fondness for it, although how he can tell — ' She cleared her throat. 'Doubtless you will develop one too.

93

I've found that girls who marry above themselves are not slow to acquire expensive tastes.'

And so I drank the bitter, purposeless tea and I waited. Although it had never sat comfortably with me, I attempted to learn patience. I told myself that it was a matter of waiting for the right time. There was the alignment of the moon to consider, I knew, and doubtless there were others who had waited longer. Neither would it be prudent if I fell ill immediately upon my arrival in London. It would favour us all not in the least if the neighbours were roused to suspicion. Besides, and surely most decisively, I had been hired by my mistress as a servant, on full and proper pay. Our agreement ensured that I would remain in her household for a full year, regardless of what else it was that went on beneath her roof. She made it clear from the outset that she meant to make as good a maid of me as she could manage.

The routine of my new life was rigid and unchanging. On every day except Sunday I rose with Mary when the watchman called six o'clock. When we were dressed and the bed straightened, Mrs Black would unlock the door to our chamber. When she was persuaded that both we and the room were in satisfactory order she would take our pulses and demand view of the contents of our chamber pots before she permitted us downstairs. She studied the turds as though they were tea leaves, swirling them round in the pots with her eyes narrowed in concentration. On several occasions in my first weeks she had me deposit my pot, still full, outside the door of the apothecary's study so that he might subject it to a further examination. She would not have a girl of hers taken ill, she told me sternly. It did not look well, not in an apothecary's house. To that end she also insisted upon sniffing about me like a dog, peering into my eyes and ears, and ordering me to open my mouth so that she might count my teeth. On one occasion she even took measurements of my brow and the circumference of my skull, tapping my forehead hard with her pencil when I fidgeted.

When these formalities were completed, and their conclusions noted in the big book Mrs Black kept for this express purpose, I assisted Mary in the daily duties of the house while Mrs Black went to the market for the day's provisions. I pitied the unfortunate tradesmen forced to bargain with her. She knew nothing of compromise or concession. Certainly she took no account of the fact that the very air of London was suffused with a sticky soot that blackened everything on which it lit, so that it required unceasing vigilance to maintain the appearance of cleanliness. Even a plate, untouched for a week, would, when finally lifted from the shelf, instantly begrime a clean apron and stain the tips of your fingers to bruises. If the mistress discovered such a thing the punishment was swift and severe.

The work was hard, monotonous and wearisome, and each night I fell into bed barely able to stand for fatigue. But, for all that, to begin with at least, even the most commonplace of the tasks assigned to me were brightened by the gleam of novelty. I had never before seen a house with so many possessions in it and I liked to touch them. It gave me a quiver of greedy pleasure to beat the dining-room carpet and see its riot of colours revive, to rub a cloth over the abundance of varnished wood and pewter and glazed Fulhamware and discover the rich gloss that lurked beneath their veil of grease and soot. Every time I passed the looking-glass in the dining room the perfect precision of my reflection made me start. I could not bear for that reflection to be smudged or smeared. I polished that glass until it shone like a white winter sun on its dark wall.

The only duty I refused to have anything to do with was the emptying of the chamber pots and close-stools. I left those to Mary. She never objected, although I resolved to misunderstand her if she ever tried. We were under instruction to empty them in the vault beneath the house once their contents had been examined and recorded, but, if Mrs Black was not yet returned from shopping, Mary would giggle at me, her eyes leaping in her skull like marionettes, and, slopping the pots with gleeful abandon, would throw the contents out of the window. We would both wait for the splash, hoping for a cry of outrage from a passer-by. On the occasions that it came I laughed too but slyly, snorting in my throat, for if I showed my amusement too openly Mary would tug like a delighted child upon my sleeve and bring her great slack face up to mine until our noses almost touched. Her chin was chapped raw with saliva and her breath was foul. I preferred to keep her at a distance.

When the first round of chores was completed and a meal prepared for the apothecary and his wife, we were permitted to take a breakfast of bread, cheese and small beer in the kitchen. Mary chewed loudly, with her mouth open. Above us we could hear the occasional jangle of the shop bell and the clunk of a customer's footsteps across the floor. On the rare occasions when the shop was busy, I was required to assist with fetching and carrying and with the wrapping of packages.

I liked the shop. It did not have the dark, sealed-up airlessness of the rest of the house. Although the door was kept closed, even on warm days, the thick round panes of glass in the windows caught sunlight like syrup in the bottom of a bottle, showing the auburn tints in the wooden floor. I liked the flap in the door that allowed you to consider a customer before permitting them in. I liked the shop's smell, the harvest scents of dried flowers and herbs dancing over the sharp reek of vinegar and the exotic resin of the Oriental medicines. I liked the stretch of polished counter in which you could see the pale gleam of your eyes, the wide shallow drawers with brass handles shaped like shells, the walls lined with shelves and crowded with bottles and jars: the blue and white ones on the lower sills fat and ponderous as aldermen, the amber stoppered flasks like petrified drops of medicine, the green glass jars that glowed emerald when struck by the early-morning sun. I liked the chatter of the customers, the tilt and clunk of the brass scales as Mrs Black weighed out tea and tobacco. I even liked the strange prehistoric creature called an alligator that hung from the ceiling, his hide cracked, his teeth brown and dull as wood chips in his parted jaws.

The only thing that discomfited me was the skull upon the table. It had a habit of grinning, as if taking comfort from the knowledge that, although its own decease had been grisly enough, yours would be much worse. I refused to look at it, examining instead the living faces of the customers for marks of the great capital. But to my disappointment, apart from their accents, which required them to speak in a penetrating but frequently incomprehensible shout, I could see little difference between them and the villagers I had grown up with. I had hoped for much more.

I comforted myself that I saw hardly enough of them to judge. I was never permitted to go out, except to the stand-pipe and to church on Sundays. To begin with I had no strong objection to these arrangements. The stand-pipe was located close enough at the top of the lane and I liked the short walk for there were diversions enough to lighten the weight of the buckets. When I wished to see more of the city I crept up to our attic and gazed out of the window. The sight of the dome, flanked by its two magnificent towers, never failed to lift my spirits. It presided over the smoke and the filth and the chaos of the city like a King, careless of its power. It never looked down. All might fall into the mud around it and still it would continue to stare away towards the smudged brown hills of Surrey, enormous and immutable. It was impossible to believe that it had been built by the men who scuttled in its shadows. I preferred to imagine it, complete and perfect, pushing its way up from a city beneath this one, a city of unimagined magnificence and splendour, where men as tall as houses strode the jewelled streets arrayed in coats of gold. I liked to imagine the moment that its golden cross had shattered the crust of London's tainted earth, the dome rising inexorably and scattering the tiny citizens of the metropolis and their matchwood houses with glorious disregard. On cloudy days, it seemed the dome was rising still.

On my first Sunday at Swan-street I accompanied Mrs Black to church. She warned me to stay close to her, for the city, she claimed with a warning frown, was quick to devour the unwary, but I lingered all the same, agreeably confused by the noise and the jostle of the streets. In London, at least, God appeared to make an exception to his Sabbath strictures. As for the church, it was grander by far than any I had ever before encountered, almost a Cathedral, with an aisle twice the width of my father's and pillars fatter than a mayor. The parson was a nervous man with a curd-cheese complexion and a permanent frog in his throat which afforded the unexpected amusement of words that sometimes escaped him in a shrill squeak and at other times failed to emerge altogether, causing him to blush scarlet as a girl. When I grew tired of such pleasures I diverted myself by studying the congregation. There was one woman in particular who caught my attention, since she had the habit of mouthing to herself in silent echo every word that the parson uttered. When a word slipped away from him she craned forwards, her mouth open, as though she hoped to catch it like a communion wafer on her tongue. Such amusements turned out to be poor compensation, however, for the hour or more I was required to spend with Mrs Black afterwards as she read aloud from the Bible. Occasionally she asked me to repeat verses after her, so that she might correct my pronunciation. Mary, lucky sow, was allowed the day off, which she took in bed. That night the bed was hot and tumbled and coarse with crumbs. I cursed her violently for her carelessness but in truth the night was bitter and I was grateful for the fusty warmth of it.

There was no shopkeeping on a Sunday. The house was even darker then, with the shutters locked and shades made of cambric pulled down over the shelves of bottles and jars. I thought such pi-jaw hardly necessary. For most of my first week, the shop might just as well have been closed. Customers came only infrequently and there were days at a time when the shop bell did not sound at all. On those days, if the mistress was out, the apothecary's apprentice, whose name was Edgar Pettigrew, would come down to the kitchen and warm himself in front of the range.

Edgar was a flabby youth with plump hands

and a pale complexion that put me in mind of a softly set junket. His buttocks and thighs were soft as dough in his tight breeches and his uncut hair hung in sausage curls around his ears. Even his voice was plump, fatty with cheese and self-satisfaction. He had a habit, at meals, of leaning over my shoulder and helping himself to the tastiest morsel on my plate. When I slapped his hand away he only laughed, closing his fat fist around whatever he had chosen and pressing it hurriedly into his mouth. In the laboratory, a narrow, dreary room with shelves on all four walls and a deal table in the centre crowded with books, flasks and ferocious-looking metal contraptions, all of the glass cups and flasks were smudged with his fingerprints.

'You impudent sluttikin,' he goaded, the words greased with butter. 'I have a mind to take you over my knee and paddle your bare arse for your insolence.'

'Try it and I'll hack off whatever it is you keep in your codpiece,' I retorted hotly, brandishing my knife.

Mary squawked unhappily, banging her fists upon the table. Edgar's presence always unsettled her.

'Such sauciness,' he murmured. With an insinuating finger he lifted a stray curl of hair from the back of my neck. I twisted my head away. Unmoved, he slid his round bottom on to the edge of the table and took another fragment of buttered biscuit from my plate. He chewed slowly, like a cow, his eyes fixed upon my chest. In the past month my figure had swollen extravagantly and now my bosom rose in a white bow above the brim of my stays.

Edgar licked his lips.

'So the master does not object to his idle apprentice keeping his customers waiting?' I demanded, scraping my chair back and turning away towards the sink.

Edgar shrugged.

'What customers? I have better things to do than freeze myself half to death waiting for business that will never come. Why, doubtless you can think of a few yourself, Eliza, my brazen little puss. You must have offered entertainment enough for some wagtailed dog to find yourself as you do.'

Before I could answer, he grabbed my waist and, spinning me around, pressed his tongue into my ear. I wriggled ferociously but he held me tight. Mary whimpered.

'Besides,' he whispered, his lips wet against my ear. 'Mr Black is gone out. Seeking 'the company of fellow scientists', self-deluding fool, as if there are any in London that would so much as pass the time of day with a worthless quack like him. Still, he is gone, and what he does not see will not grieve him. It seems a pity to waste that vulgar mouth of yours on words, when we might persuade it into action.'

'I'd fuck a dog before I'd let you lay a finger on me,' I hissed, trying to free myself. 'You let go this instant or, I swear it, you'll get a pair of black eyes for your trouble. I am a married woman.'

He released me then and smiled, his cheeks

plumping into two pillows.

'Oh, yes,' he purred. 'A married woman. Of course.'

Displaying a remarkable nimbleness for a man of his size, he skipped around me, lowering his mouth to my bosom and biting me hard. As I yelped in pain and rage, Mary gave another whimper and covered her face with her hands.

'Edgar?'

Edgar did not trouble to answer the mistress's summons. Instead he rolled his eyes at me, stretching up his arms in an exaggerated yawn. He lowered them only as Mrs Black opened the kitchen door.

'Madam,' he drawled, executing an unctuous bow. There was a smudge of coal dust on one of his stockings. 'What is your pleasure?'

'Edgar,' she said again and, to my astonishment, her mouth turned up a little at its edges. Upon the sharp points of her cheekbones two faint blushes of pink had bloomed. 'If you will. I require your assistance.'

'You flatter me,' Edgar replied. 'I am of course entirely at your disposal.'

'Of course.'

Mrs Black's fingers fluttered at her sides. She appeared a little out of breath. The blade of her Adam's apple sliced up and down her throat, several times in quick succession, as if it would cut the flesh in two. Edgar bowed again, gesturing at her to ascend the stairs ahead of him. Then, over Edgar's shoulder, she observed me. On my breast the bitten skin reddened. Hastily I placed a hand over the mark.

'What do you think you are looking at, missy?' she snapped, her face folding into its habitual crisp lines. 'And cover yourself up, if you please. This is a respectable house, not a bagnio. I will not tolerate any girl of mine disporting herself like a sixpenny strumpet. Any more of that and you shall find yourself in the cellar.'

She swept up the stairs. Edgar bared his teeth at me in a silent growl, raising his fat hands like claws. Then, smirking, he followed her. Furiously I hurled my plate into the sink. Mary, who until then had kept her face hidden, rose and came over to me. Very carefully she reached out to touch the bruise on my breast with one finger. The nail was bitten so low that the tip of her finger looked fat and swollen but her touch was cool, light as a moth. Impatiently I pushed her hand away. Mary said nothing but blinked at me, her mouth slack.

'What?' I demanded angrily. 'Cat got your tongue?'

Above our heads the bell of the shop jangled. There was work to be done. But, as I slammed out of the kitchen, my heart was heavy. I banged my mop against the dark boards of the hall, sloshing too much water from the bucket. I knew Mrs Black would rebuke me for squandering it but I did not care. If I was to be friendless in London I might at least grant myself the dignity of believing that it was a matter of my own personal choosing.

★ ★ ★

Every long dark day of that first week, I told myself firmly that neither the waiting nor the disagreeable nature of my fellows were matters of the slightest consequence to me. I declared myself careless of the strangeness of the new house and the strictness of my mistress. I was not in London to please myself, after all, but for a purpose, and I determined to see that purpose resolved. I had only to execute my duties and avoid punishment and, when the time came, to pray for a safe deliverance. A year would soon be over. Then this page of my life would be torn from the record and a fresh one begun. I would be at liberty to do what I wished, to go where I pleased, to take another position, perhaps, or even to return home. I tried not to think of my mother's face as she closed the door of the cottage. I was no longer her concern nor she mine, treacherous, double-dealing, foul-smelling crone that she was. I missed my mother not one jot.

No, there was nothing at Swan-street that unsettled me. What did it concern me that I never once laid eyes upon my master? After all, this was not a country cottage, with everyone heaped one on top of the other like puppies. It was doubtless quite usual in a London household with many rooms that a maid might go weeks at a time without encountering her master. It was not as if he was not spoken of frequently. On the contrary, his requirements and desires were discussed and worried over, his health and comfort a source of unceasing concern.

Nor was his authority in doubt. Mary was afraid of him, thrusting the tray into my hands when it was time to take his dinner up to him, pushing me out of the kitchen with her head turned away and her eyes squeezed shut. I rolled my eyes at her but all the same my knees trembled a little as I bent to place the tray before the closed door. When later I returned, the smeared dishes gleamed in the half-light, their contents gone, the folded napkin twisted and marked with wine and gravy. Each day I washed his dirty plates, brushed his coat and wig, rinsed out his worn white stockings. Sometimes in the mornings there were signs that he had walked about the house while we slept. I smelled the burnt sweetness of his tobacco when I shook out the rug in the parlour, gathered up the curls of orange peel discarded in the grate, rubbed with a cloth at the pale grey mark on the wall above his chair where he liked to lean his head. Often, as I lay in bed, I heard him pacing the room beneath me, his feet drawing figures of eight on the varnished boards, round and round, his voice a taut black thread pulling the darkness into folds. Then I held on to my hare's-foot a little tighter and rebuked myself for being absurd.

And still I did not see him. I grew uneasy, peering around doorways and jumping at shadows. For it was not quite true that there was no mystery at all about my master. On my very first day at Swan-street, before my box had so much as been brought to the door, Mrs Black had commanded me that I was never under any circumstances to look directly at the apothecary,

106

nor was I to express any surprise or dismay at his appearance. If I chanced to encounter him on the stairs, I was to keep my eyes to the floor. If I disobeyed her in this I might expect harsh and certain punishment. She provided no other explanation except to pull Mary's sleeve from her shoulder and show to me a line of dark purple bruises that blotched her pale skin.

I never dared ask why. It was almost as though I feared the taste of the question in my mouth. My master was as present and yet as invisible in the house in Swan-street as God himself was in church except that, as Mrs Black and the frog-voiced parson liked to instruct me, God was the one true Light. My master on the other hand seemed to me to be composed of darkness, of shadows and locked doors and windowless stairwells and the sour black smoke of extinguished candles. In the gloom of the house his absence was unyielding. It clung to the murky corners of every closed-up room, as sticky and persistent as cobwebs.

It was to be a full eleven days before I saw my master for the first time. I was sweeping the stairs when the door opened and he entered the house. The landing was dark and he did not see me. When he paused in the hall to peer at his reflection in the mirror, his shoulders and the crown of his hat caught the dusty sunlight from the high slice of window behind his head. At first glance he appeared almost comically ordinary. He was of unexceptional height and build. His hat was round, of the kind favoured by country curates. He wore a black frock-coat with a stiff skirt grown slick and greenish with age, and old-fashioned square-toed shoes with buckles. The silver was tarnished, the leather cracked. The cuffs of his shirt were marked with ink. The overall impression was commonplace, drab even. Despite myself, I felt a stab of disappointment.

Then he turned to face me. I squinted so that I might see him better. My knees buckled. He moved towards me. Steadying myself against the wall, I forced myself to keep my gaze fixed upon his approaching shoes, to observe the smear of mud upon one leg of his breeches, how his pale stockings had a shapeless grey patch across the front of his ankle as though he had put them on upside down. The wooden heels of the shoes struck hollowly against the wooden floor. A far-off part of me noted that one of the boards was loose and would need nailing. He was at the bottom of the stairs now. Screams bubbled in my lungs, my ribs pulled so tight together I could barely breathe.

In all my imaginings I had never dreamed that my master would have no face at all.

I closed my eyes, my fingernails digging into the palms of my hand, but I could not shift the image, the round hat and beneath it the moving patch of dark shadow, the blank of blackness with holes for eyes that loomed between two fogged slabs of wig. Where there should have been nose, cheeks, mouth there was nothing but darkness, swirling darkness that shifted and moved, devouring the light, draining its warmth. The wall behind my shoulders was cold as a corpse. What would one touch if one reached out to such a face? Would it strip the flesh from your fingers, shrivel the bones to ash? I whimpered, the darkness of my closed lids spangled with silver dust. Beyond the roaring in my ears all the commonplace daytime noises had ceased, as though the house was holding its breath.

At the bottom of the stairs the shoes paused. I heard the knock of the wooden letter box, the hiss of something being dropped on to the cherrywood table, the leathery creak of a fart, each noise sharp as a spoon against a glass so that the silence vibrated with its echo. Then he began to climb. I pressed myself flatter against the wall, clutching my broom against my chest with both hands, wishing myself invisible. Usually I would have done anything I could to avoid the ill luck that must surely come from passing another person on the stairs. I only wanted him past me, gone, disappeared once more behind the safety of a locked door. He drew closer, so close I could smell ink, the lingering reek of tobacco and spilled wine, the stale powder of his wig. I squeezed my eyes shut, concentrating all my attention on willing him gone.

Suddenly I felt the press of his fingers around my jaw. My stomach fell away.

'Good,' he murmured. 'It is time. We shall begin tomorrow.'

His grip tightened. Hot tears swelled behind my eyelids. Then, abruptly, he released me. My head jerked forward.

'Mary! Have your mistress come to me directly. And sponge my hat. Those rooks are become a plaguey nuisance.'

Then he was gone, his shoes clattering up the stairs to the next floor. I heard the scrape of the key in the lock, the slam of the door. Then silence. As it settled softly about me, my legs began to shake. I slid down the wall, huddled into my dark corner, pulling the gloom about me like a quilt, letting the tears slide unheeded down my cheeks.

My master was no apothecary. He was a fiend, a demon, the faceless agent of the Devil himself.

What kind of Hell was it that I had come to?

In her belly it floats, conceived in perfection by the father but as yet imprecise in form, its limbs soft as wax. A male child perhaps but, born of woman, powerless against the violent passions roused by the ardent nature of the female imagination & the failure of the weak & suggestible female body to resist the effects of such passions.

Suspended in milky darkness, it grows dimly aware of the raised temperature of the liquid in which it floats, the irregular palpitations of the muscular heart located directly above it, the strong paroxysmal movements of the organs of respiration & the convulsions of the fibres & the nerve-strings of the body as breath comes faster & more wildly. Already it senses that the more rapid respiration during a seizure of imagination is driving the heated blood more violently than is usual through the woman's body, hurling it to her extremities so that the womb pitches in her belly like a boat on a stormy sea.

The storm abates. The blood steadies & cools. The foetus settles, resuming its curled slumber, soothed once more by the unshed blood of the menses which provides its nourishment. It cannot taste the difference in its composition nor turn away its mouth, for the blood enters its body without its compliance, by means of the navel string. It cannot know that the high temperature of blood has heated the fluid parts of the body & that, even now, as

111

these parts cool, the contents of those fluids are deposited in the woman's body, as salt marks the interior of a cooling cooking pot, & collect in the same pool of menstrual blood that provides its sustenance.

& so it is begun. The salts in the blood impress themselves upon the waxiness of the foetus, before muscle & bone might have the opportunity to harden. It can only endure, as the force of her passions pressed into its tiny form the embodiment of its vilest extremities.

I stare into the glass & the opium sharpens my eyes so that I see every detail of my damaged cheek with perfect clarity, every tiny flake & hair & hole in the skin as though I examine it beneath a microscope. It seems to spread as I look, each scarlet scale of skin its own betrayal, repository of another's sins, the weakness & imprudence of woman imprinted without mercy upon the innocent flesh of a child, the truth not a balm but an agitator, its message simple & incontrovertible: the absolute impossibility of forgiveness.

9

I cannot say precisely how long I remained there, crouched on the landing. Certainly it grew dark, the light draining from the glass pane above the door until it closed over, shut tight. The clamour of the lane leaked into the house as though strained through muslin, pure drips of sound without sense or substance. Nothing felt real, not even the cold plaster of the wall against my back or the coarse bristles of the brush that grazed my shins. My hands made pale shapes upon its splintery handle, ghosts that drifted free of my arms in the twilight. Around me the house contracted, distilling into night, pooling every-where into eye sockets and gashes of mouths and the brimstone whiff of demon breath. I did not dare to move, although I thought longingly of the hare's-foot concealed beneath my mattress. Instead I observed the worsening cramps in my legs distantly, without curiosity. Inside my belly the worm stretched and squirmed. For a brief, bright moment, like the spark of a tinderbox, I was lit with a kind of desperate comradeship.

It is time. We shall begin tomorrow.

The spark went out. I pressed my knuckles against my belly, pushing them together. Something moved within it, a faint twist of resistance. I pushed harder. Suddenly, below me, the shop door opened, discharging voices and a puddle of yellow light. The ordinariness of it was

113

startling, shocking. Shadows leaped against the walls of the stairs as someone carried a candle into the hall. Light crept up the stairs, catching the peaks of my knees, the lappets of my cap. I longed to crawl into it and away from it at the same time.

'You are mistaken, madam. He is come home already. His hat is — well, that's a pretty sight, I must say.'

Edgar stood at the bottom of the stairs, the candle held aloft. Narrowing his eyes, he tilted his head to get a better view. Awkwardly I pressed my legs together and tried to stand, but my cramped muscles refused to oblige me and I stumbled, jabbing myself painfully in the chest with the handle of my broom. Edgar's mouth twitched. When Mrs Black called something to him from within the shop he shook his head at me, running his tongue lazily over his lips.

'I imagine you shall require that shiftless chit of a maid to work it over, madam,' he called back without taking his eyes from me. 'It would appear that birds have made something of a cesspit of the brim. Do you wish me to fetch her for you?'

Mrs Black must have concurred, for Edgar gestured at me and then at the hat that lay upon the cherrywood table.

'Eliza!' he feigned, his hands cupped round his mouth. 'Eliza, where are you?' And then in a low hiss, 'It may be customary for a maidservant to sleep upon the floor in whatever godforsaken corner it is you come from but I should warn you that in civilized society it is considerably frowned upon. I would advise you to get down here before I am obliged to inform your mistress of your insufferable idleness.'

Scowling, I limped down the stairs, my broom bumping behind me. A slice of light came from beneath the shop door. I could hear my mistress conversing with a customer and, from downstairs, the clattering of pots as Mary prepared the supper. An ordinary evening. I refused to look behind Edgar where the tall clock threw a looming shadow and the glass pane above the door was black and bottomless as a well.

'I was not sleeping,' I muttered, and my voice tasted sour on my tongue. 'I — I was — '

'What?' Edgar reached out and pinched my cheek. I twisted my face away, my eyes on the ground. 'Indisposed? And why would that be, I wonder?'

Before I could answer the door to the shop opened and Mrs Black leaned out, vexation whetting her sharp features. Edgar's hand vanished into his pocket.

'Edgar, those pills, if you please. Mr Butterfield is waiting.'

'Madam.'

'As for you, girl, what are you doing lurking about? Get to the kitchen, and quick about it. There's supper to be got and a thousand other things besides. And take the master's hat with you. If it is left any longer that stain shall mark.'

The hat squatted on the table, dark, malignant, a wide white streak across its crown. In the laboratory a drawer slammed and Edgar cursed loudly. Mrs Black watched me, her arms

115

crossed, her fingers drumming upon her forearms. Summoning all my courage, I snatched up the hat. As I lifted it from the table, something soft and dark fell out from the crown, a swathe of congealed shadow that clung to the felt brim. I gasped and almost dropped it. Impatiently my mistress seized the hat from me and peered at it.

'Damned birds. Use soap. And wash the veil separately. It is perfectly filthy. Ah, Edgar, at last. Mr Butterfield, I am so sorry to have kept you.'

Placing both hands lightly on the small of Edgar's back, she pushed him before her into the shop, closing the door behind her. As for me, I barely noticed the immodesty of the gesture. Instead I stumbled down the stone steps to the kitchen as though my legs were made of wood. Mary blinked at me as I entered. She held a wooden spoon in her fist and her face was flushed pink with exertion.

'Help Mar'?' she asked tentatively, waving her spoon so that splashes of gravy hissed against the hot metal of the range.

I did not answer. Instead I half-threw the hat upon the kitchen table. It was then that I saw it properly for the first time. The hat had a veil. The dark gauzy fabric was perhaps a foot or more in length and attached to the crown with a series of small black hooks so that it fell over the brim to the shoulders, protecting the face in the manner favoured by bee-keepers. The hem of the veil was blurred grey with dust. Streaked across the crown of the hat, and clotted in the brim, was a thick trail of bird shit. I bent over, my

116

shoulders seized with a fit of shaking.

Mary's hand was soft and warm upon my shoulder.

'Ill?' she whispered.

I shook my head impatiently, stepping away, but still I could not stop the shaking.

'Laugh?' Mary persisted, following me. 'Is joke?'

'For the love of peace — !'

I wheeled round and thrust the fouled hat in her face. Mary stumbled backwards, her hands flapping and her mouth working with alarm. I glared at her. She blinked back. I sucked in a long ragged breath. Then, dropping the hat on to the floor at her feet, I smoothed my skirts and walked slowly around her and over to the sink.

★　★　★

After supper Mrs Black informed me that the master wished to see me the following morning, directly after breakfast. When in my confusion I choked and had to press my hands over my mouth, she gave me a narrow look and warned me that she would tolerate no impudence. If my master informed her that I had been anything but entirely obliging, she would not hesitate to use the birch.

That night I lay awake in the darkness. My head ached with exhaustion but I could not sleep. At last, when the night-lanthorn called midnight, I rolled over and dug Mary in the ribs. She muttered, sucking on her tongue as though it were a sweetmeat. The sound of it disgusted

117

me. I poked her again, more harshly this time. She groaned.

'Mary,' I hissed. 'Mary, wake up!'

'Wha — ?' she mumbled, humping herself over on to her side.

I pulled her hair. She yelped in surprise. I could see the whites of her eyes as she squinted at me in the darkness, the gleam of her irregular teeth.

'Have you ever seen it? The master's face?'

'Mn.'

'So? What is it?'

'Red. Fire,' Mary mumbled, humping her back from me. 'Sleep.'

'Burned?' I shuddered, imagining livid flesh melted into waxy folds.

'No burn. Red.' The words were muffled, slurred with sleep. 'Stain. Fire stain.'

I turned on my back, gazing up into the darkness. Fire stain. Could a commonplace red stain upon his face be the extent of the master's terrible secret? The pettiness of it soothed and agitated me at the same time. Beside me the idiot burrowed deeper into the bed, flatulent snores snagging in her throat. The sound filled me with a murderous irritation. Was idiocy contagious? What nature of fool was I to trust the word of a tom noddy, who could hardly tell a fart from a farthing? Kicking off the covers, I rose and went to the window, pressing my face against the cool glass. Beyond the casement the mighty dome held sway against a moon-metalled sky, indifferent to the dark jumble of roofs that cringed before it, reaching up their chimney pots like arms in supplication. There had been a farmer's boy in our village who'd had a crimson stain across his brow and down one side of his face. The marked skin was raised and rough, its surface studded all over with little yellow pimples. His ear on that side was always scarlet, as though mortified to be appended to so unsightly a blemish. We had tormented him and called him names but my mother had always been kind to him.

'It's hardly the poor child's fault,' she had sighed, shaking her head. 'That mother of his, she's been a greedy lass her whole life. Longing for strawberries in February? She must have known it would mark the boy.'

A responsible mother, she told me firmly, controlled her appetites or, if she could not, made sure to satisfy them. Otherwise they grew so powerful that they took her over, burning themselves into the flesh of her unborn child. Was that how it had been for my master? On my first day at Swan-street my mistress had warned me against profligacy, insisting candles and coal be used only when strictly necessary. I had a sudden picture of a woman, large with child and wrapped about with a shawl, her lips blue with cold, crouched shivering before the empty brick hearth in the kitchen as the ice glazed the low window and she dreamed of a fire so high that it stung her cheeks and caused the infant in her womb to thrash with the heat of it. I shivered, all at once aware of my cold feet, the gooseflesh on my arms, but still I lingered at the window, staring out into the darkness towards the invisible smudge of the hills. In nearby streets and houses lights still burned despite the lateness of the hour but there was no comfort in it. Rather, it seemed to me that across the city, the thousands and thousands of voracious mouths sucked in what remained of warmth and light, exhaling in return a darkness blacker than any night so that, with each vast polluted sigh, another lantern died in a curl of sooty smoke. As for the first pale shell tints of dawn, they would be drained from the sky before they could pink the lowest of the red rooftops. It would be night for ever.

The cold had penetrated my bones so that my teeth chattered. Chafing my skin with my hands, I climbed back into bed. Mary murmured and rolled against me, her slack body warm as a muffin. I did not push her away. I did not permit myself to think of her protruding eyes, the way her tongue lolled wetly in her mouth. Instead I tucked my cold feet into the snug bend of her knees.

In the darkness she could have been anyone.

I am so beside myself with outrage that I can hardly hold my quill. I remind myself that a man of science must always remain dispassionate but there are surely circumstances in which such an expectation is neither reasonable nor desirable. The body of a man may operate by mechanic principles but he is not a machine.

The evening began well enough. I dined with Wright at the chop-house & was comforted by his opinion of Gaule, the odious bookseller. It was Wright who reminded me, after all, that even the distinguished Mr Harvey was compelled, long after his proof of the circulation of the blood, to continue to teach to his students the Galenic principles which his discoveries had emphatically disproved. Despite the company he keeps, Wright is a fine & decent gentleman.

It was at the Folley that we encountered the insufferable Simpson. To my annoyance Wright greeted him heartily & called for more wine, which Simpson & his companion fell upon like locusts. Sodden with liquor, the dog then began an account of a paper he had recently read into the science of physiognomy, & in particular the ways in which the particulars of anatomy reveal the hidden heart of a man.

New experiments made in Germany, he informed us, had proved beyond doubt that it was no longer appropriate to assign the defects of babies to the passions of the mother, since women lacked the authority to make anything distinctive of their own without male agency.

Instead the source of such deficiencies could be traced directly to the <u>intrinsic corruptions of the child</u>. A hump, therefore, reflected not the exposure of the pregnant mother to a crippled man but rather the affected child's inability to bear responsibility, while a hare lip revealed the loose mouth of one who might not be trusted & two Siamese twins, conjoined at the waist & sharing only a single vagina, had been shown to harbour depraved & deplorable sexual desires. As for facial staining — and here he fixed me with his reptilian eye — it was attributable to vile thoughts, thoughts that would cause a respectable man to blush.

Perhaps I should be grateful that Wright intervened to prevent injury but I cannot say that I regret drawing my sword. Open discussion between men of education is one thing; the peddling of pernicious & perfidious untruths quite another. Oh, how mankind corrupts itself & takes as its innocent victims those upon whom suffering has been visited to excess already. The very thought of it hastens my pulse & sets my quill to shaking against the page. Will those of us who have all our lives been forced to endure the burden of another's wickedness be once again the innocent repository of man's hatred?

Simpson is a rogue & a villain & I wish him every ill fortune.

10

Dawn came all the same, bound by a low rope of cloud. As soon as the first tasks of the day were complete and breakfast eaten, my mistress sought me out and required me to go directly to my master's room.

'But my duties — ?' I stammered.

'They shall keep,' Mrs Black said crisply. 'Now, upstairs with you. It does not do to keep the master waiting.'

Slowly I mounted the stairs. The day had grown sunny and the glass pane above the front door was a clear pale blue. It was too bright a morning for ghosts or demons. There was nothing to be afraid of. I would glance at his face, I told myself, just so that I knew, and I would be done with it. In the meantime, there were more important matters to consider: whether he would have me drink something or if it would be a plaister, how severe the pains would be and how quickly they would come upon me. You might die, I told myself fiercely as I raised my hand to knock upon the closed door. What do you care for your master's face when you might die?

There was the scrape of a key in the lock and the door swung open. My master was a black shape against the sunlight that filled the room. I blinked, dazzled, and allowed myself to be directed towards an upright chair that stood close to the table, encircled on all sides by towers of papers and pamphlets and cloth-bound books bristled with markers. This room looked out over the lane, affording a view only of the house opposite and, above its gabled roof, the cloudless blue of the sky. You could not see the dome from here. The low sun slanted through the chimney pots and drew patterns on the grimy window panes. When I blinked, the undersides of my eyelids were marked with golden discs.

The apothecary did not greet me. Nor did he invite me to sit. He said nothing at all. Instead, he pressed his hands together as if praying, his fingertips against his lips, as, very slowly, he walked around me, his eyes moving meticulously over every inch of me as though I was a horse he thought to purchase. Careful of my mistress's orders, I kept my eyes fixed upon the sky.

In front of me he stooped, considering the slope of my belly beneath the folds of my skirt. Hurriedly, queasily, I glanced at his face, clasping my hands together to stop them from trembling. That I had half-expected it did nothing to ease the shock of it. His disfigurement was so — so ordinary. The stain was sizeable, it was true, extending from his temple down into the folds of his neck-cloth, but, although unsightly, it was hardly grotesque. Had he not attempted to disguise it with wig powder, which clumped in the coarse grain of the damaged skin like mould, it would have looked less disagreeable still. As it was, the powder gave the purple mark an unhealthy, greyish tinge that was reminiscent of decomposing meat.

124

'Move your hands.'

Hastily I glanced away, unlacing my fingers so that my arms fell to my sides. The apothecary gazed at my abdomen, his lips pressed together as though resisting the urge to smile. I sucked the wall of my belly in, compressing the worm, daring it to protest. It made no movement. Soon it would be gone. As my master reached out and took my left wrist, pressing his first two fingers against its underside, a spike of elation pierced my throat. It left my mouth dry, metalled with fear.

I swallowed.

'Shall it soon be done with?' I asked, keeping my voice light.

My master frowned then but he did not answer. Instead, he bid me hold my tongue while he completed his examination. For the next few minutes I stared out of the window while he palpated my flesh and peered into my ears and mouth. Even when his face was only inches from mine I kept my eyes averted from it.

For his part my master said not a word but only jotted notes on a scrap of paper. He lifted my eyelids, pulling them out by the lashes so that he might study the hidden parts of the white. He had me state the habitual pattern of my monthlies, the approximate age I had been when they had begun. He pressed the point of a pin against my finger until a bead of blood appeared, examining the blood closely before licking my finger to consider the taste of it. The pin did not hurt, although when he pinched me I yelped.

When at last his investigations were complete

he bid me sit in a chair turned away from his so that it faced the wall. For perhaps an hour or more, then, he required me to join with him in what I could only describe as idle chatter. He had me write out my letters and read a little from one of his books, a purposeless humiliation which caused me to flush hot with indignation, but otherwise he displayed more the sensibilities of a lady at the tea table than a man of learning. I might even have found such a conversation pleasant, or at the least preferable to the usual round of my household duties, had it not been for the apothecary's rapid and disquieting shifts of humour so that he was one moment amiable, even avuncular, and the next, as grim and unyielding as a gaoler. On one occasion he even struck the table with a whip, marking the varnish and startling me so exceedingly that I cried out in surprise. It unnerved me greatly, for without sight of his face I had no way of predicting his fiercer gusts of rage. Nor did I have the least notion of what it was in my answers that provoked him so.

As the hour passed, I grew more tentative in my responses. At last the apothecary fell silent. His chair creaked. I could hear the faint whistle of his breathing, the rustle of papers being gathered together, the oyster slap of a man sucking at his teeth. I stared at the wall, my hands clasped in my lap, awaiting his prescription, my belly tumbled with eagerness and apprehension. He sighed, a long exhalation, and drummed his fingers upon the desk.

'I shall require you to come to me every other

day at this time, with the exception of Sundays. Go now. Doubtless you have much to attend to.'

I frowned, shaking my head at the wall.

'But, sir. I had thought — that is, I had hoped — I — I don't understand, sir.'

My master did not reply immediately. There was a rustle, the chink of glass. A moment later I heard the scratch of his pen upon the paper.

'I do not imagine you do,' he said at last. 'I do not mean to take dinner today. Have Mary bring me tea.'

I twisted around, catching sight of the top of his head as he bent over his work before I recalled myself and hurriedly turned away. He had not seen me but, all the same, I felt agitated, alarmed in equal measure by my master's indifference and my own recklessness.

'Is there not — I mean, surely sir, if I could only — ?'

'Tea,' he repeated coldly, placing the page to one side and beginning another.

I was dismissed.

EC — interview I

Confinement advanced some four or five months, with noticeable swelling to the lower belly and some enlargement of the breasts. Born in the village of W — in the county of Northumberland of English parents. Father deceased [pleurisy]

General health of subject robust:
- eats and drinks heartily — detail of daily diet attached
- faeces firm with good colour/odour; no sign of worms
- urine straw-coloured/copious, free from sediment/clouding; no discernible taste
- blood watery but sharp with fine colour — no clotting or phlegm
- spittle clear and well-digested — no knotting or toughness visible
- breath odour strong but sour/noxious, indicating healthful lungs
- teeth almost complete — rear gums slightly swollen
- eyes clear, with unnaturally white surround

Character and Physiognomy:
- short of stature, standing no more than 5 feet & 3 inches
- strong physique with pronounced breasts & rear, advertising crude sexuality

- *thick dark hair with large dark eyes & choleric complexion of Latin breed*
- *skull tapered with indentation above right ear & low brow, indicating limited intelligence*
- *reads & writes to elementary standard [unusual — effects on imagination?]*
- *but, despite education, credulous & of superstitious nature ['a broom left bristles down has all the strength run out of it']*

→ *early impressions indicate subject likely to display strongly* choleric *temperament, fortified by the rough instincts of the rustic: quick-witted, bold, furious, hasty, quarrelsome, fraudulent, persuasive,* exceeding stout-hearted

↓

CONCEALED TERRORS?
NB. coarse & resistant:
persistent reinforcement critical

11

It came as little surprise that Edgar had lost no time in seizing upon my disquiet. The prentice's brain might be all in his breeches but he had a nose for weakness that might have put a terrier to shame. He was quick to acquaint me with the master's particular fondness for young girls. Indeed, despite the old man's churchgoing and Sunday closing and all his other pretences at virtue, he was, in Edgar's assessment, little more than a salacious old rogue, much addicted to the comforts a pretty young maidservant might confer. Edgar himself had several times made use of an expedient crack in the door to observe the old lecher with his britches around his knees and his bare breech jerking up and down like a fish on a line. It was said that the previous girl, an impudent chit if ever there was one but with curves to make a grown man weep, had refused his advances, and what had happened to her, on the streets without good character? Edgar regarded me consideringly before finally declaring me less fetching than my predecessor but possessed of a homely kind of allure which the master would doubtless find satisfactory. A girl of my type would surely seize her chances where she might find them. Edgar sighed contently as he bit into a muffin. He was certain it would not be long before it was my plump white thighs that he would have the pleasure of observing through that convenient imperfection in the grain.

Although I knew better than to swallow Edgar's assertions whole, his predictions left me uneasy. He told the truth about the hole in the door for I saw it for myself. And if the master did mean for me to give him comfort, he would hardly have been the first. How many girls in my situation were required to endure in silence the burden of their master's attention or lose their position without reference? Even without Edgar's vigorous stirring of the pot, a sensible girl would have always to be wary.

★ ★ ★

Two weeks passed, then three. Days were brief twilit breaks in the relentless sooty darkness of winter. Even on the rare clear days the pallid sun seemed barely to manage to crawl across the rim of the tight-packed roofs before it sank exhausted from sight. Even at midday, we were required to burn tallow candles so that we might see our way about. The shadows were slick and salty with the stink of melted grease.

Nothing more was said of my situation, nothing done. I grew anxious and then fretful. I knew that it was crucial to act with all possible haste and, try as I might, I could not fathom the purpose of the apothecary's examinations nor the benefit of further delay. Each day, as I performed my duties, as I responded to his purposeless questions, trying to draw from the blank plaster of the wall some clue as to the answer that would best please him, the worm swelled and strengthened in my belly. Thinking on it caused my palms to sweat and pimples to break out in a band around my brow. Had I not been sent to the apothecary's house for one purpose, and one purpose alone? Had the apothecary not been chosen specifically, hand-picked, his instruction to remove and to exterminate any evidence of impropriety or boyish bad judgement? There was no one in the world who wished the vile worm alive, least of all here in the house at Swan-street.

All the same, as the weeks passed, I found myself unable to shake the terrible and persistent dread that my condition had somehow been over-looked or forgotten. I began to suffer headaches, bellyaches, rough rashes that bloomed beneath my arms and around my neck. My master noted them all, making precise sketches of the inflammations that crusted my skin, but he said nothing. Any attempts I made at questions were met with silence or, more frequently, a strike of his rule across my palm. It was not long before I stopped asking. I took instead to complaining whenever my mistress was nearby, praying that accounts of the nagging pains in my reins, the cramps in my belly, the vomiting, might provoke her to acknowledge me, to assist me. They did not. Mrs Black only smiled her thin smile and advised a tonic of industriousness and forbear-ance. It was a woman's duty, she informed me, to suffer such discomforts patiently. I dug my fingernails into my palms and felt the not-knowing stiffening my arms and twisting my face into lines. When she harried me into the parlour to black the grate, the bray of the hawker crying cabbages and Savoys in the lane grated upon me so insufferably it was all I could do not to run into the street and shove the largest of his vegetables down his detestable throat.

It was the next Sunday, as she intoned the words of the Psalms, her hands clamped around the heavy book on her lap, that I came to a startling and fearful conclusion. Mrs Black wished me to suffer. She might not be able to prevent what was to happen but she could delay it, she could make quite certain that I was properly punished for my transgression. My hasty departure to London had saved me from the shame and the whipping I would surely have been forced to endure if my village neighbours had discovered my condition, but she had no intention of sparing me. On the contrary, she intended me to suffer, to pay for my sins.

The more I contemplated this possibility, the more certain it became. I tried not to listen but it was impossible not to heed the frequent references to wickedness in her carefully chosen passages. My mistress was a godly woman, her very flesh desiccated with piety. It was as difficult to imagine her ripe with child as it was to expect juicy fruit to spring from curls of dried-up orange peel. And yet Edgar had informed me that she herself had borne five children, not one of which had survived infancy and whose names were never permitted to be spoken in the house. Before Mary had come to Swan-street her name had been Henrietta. On her very first day, however, Mrs Black had informed her that such a name was unacceptable for a servant and that from henceforth she would be known as Mary. Henrietta had been her second child, her only daughter. Edgar could not recall the cause of her passing, though he was reasonably certain that at least one of the infants had succumbed to the influenza.

Mrs Black cleared her throat, glaring at me and tapping her finger on the page.

'Attention! *Let death seize upon them, and let them go down quick into Hell: for wickedness is in their dwellings and among them.*'

For the first time since arriving in London I missed my mother. I missed the cottage with its stone chill and the low branches that tapped against the windows. I had a longing for the familiar must of our bed so profound that it made me dizzy. That night I had a fearsome headache. I longed to creep up to the laboratory for the master's willow oil but I did not dare. Instead I snapped at Mary as we laboured over the linen and kicked out at the cat who yowled and retreated beneath the dresser, his yellow eyes bright with reproach. Even when the work was finally done I could settle to nothing but picked at the splinters on the underside of the kitchen table, taking a kind of savage comfort in the needles of pain as they jabbed the raw wrinkled skin beneath my fingernails.

The next morning was not one of my master's mornings and I dragged myself through my chores. It was a little before the midday meal when Mrs Black beckoned me into the dining room. The room was cold, the fire not yet lit, and

I shivered as she closed the door behind us, folding her hands together and bowing her head a little. I breathed shallowly, my belly churning with impatience.

'I wished to inform you that, from henceforth, there shall be no further Bible classes on a Sunday,' she said. 'Nor shall you be expected to attend church.'

She looked up at me abruptly, her face twisted with anger as though she granted such exemptions only under extreme duress. It was clear she meant to say more.

'As you wish, madam,' I said, willing her on.

'That is not all. I wish you to tend to the carpet in here. You are to dampen the saved tea leaves from our breakfast and brush them over its length to restore the pile. Then I would have you paint out the worn spots with ink. Mary must be kept out of the room while you perform these duties. Last time she attempted to eat the mess of tea from the floor.' She nodded at me and, pressing her lips together, reached for the door handle.

I gaped at her, appalled. 'But what about — surely — '

Mrs Black's mouth tightened.

'You understand the task, do you not? Well then, lose no more time.'

'I thought — I just thought — isn't there something you — we — should I not be given something? For the . . . ' I floundered, gesturing helplessly towards my belly. Mrs Black frowned but I could not stop now. I was perilously close to tears. 'I beg you, madam. I mean, the weeks are passing and I — '

'Ah. Of course.' Mrs Black inclined her head and I was certain her features softened a little. 'I understand. And you are quite right to bring my attention to it. We have left things long enough. I shall speak with Mr Black today.'

★ ★ ★

All that day I toiled in a state of delicious fear and anticipation. Each time I passed the laboratory I could not resist the temptation to glance in but there was only Edgar there. Just before supper I went again, peering through the crack into the cramped room with its strange contraptions. Edgar was seated before the table, a book open before him. All about him upon the long counter lay dirty phials, bottles and retorts, heaped together with unscrewed jars and lidless boxes. I recognized none of the contents. As I turned to go, Edgar looked up.

'Spying on me now, are you?' he called after me. 'I must warn you, I have little patience with Peeping Toms.'

I thought of Edgar peering through the door into his master's room but I said nothing. I had no wish to make an enemy of him tonight. Instead I leaned against the door frame and shrugged.

'My mistress said she meant to give me something: I thought perhaps it might be ready.'

Edgar smiled, picking his teeth with a scalpel.

'Well, I may be able to assist you there,' he said winking lasciviouly. 'Provided you were to offer me some manner of favour in return, of course.'

My desperation for the medicine overcame my natural distaste.

'You will always have my friendship, Edgar,' I managed to say.

'Friendship!' he mocked. 'A harlot's friendship! Well, well. Doubtless you would have me converse with a sirloin of beef before I carve it?'

Before I could reply the bell rang for supper. I ate little. Though Mrs Black made much of the beef she permitted us, the meat was dry and tough and caught in my throat. It was only much later, when we were putting out the fire, that my mistress came to me. She held out a cup of Lambeth delft from which a curl of steam uncoiled in a kind of promise. My hand shook as I took it from her and lowered my head over the cup, inhaling the tea's flowery scent. It smelled strangely sweet for something so injurious.

'An infusion of honey and nutmeg with a little syrup of motherwort,' Mrs Black said. 'It will provoke the urine and settle the womb.'

I shrugged away her fictions, swallowing the hot liquid so quickly it blistered the inside of my mouth. I licked my gums afterwards, seeking out a bitter flavour, but I found none. My mother had pounded fern with the pink-flowering hyssop which some country folk called gladiola, which she sent me to gather in early summer on the boggy ground near the river. She claimed the tincture helped ease the inflammations of the dropsy and the gout but I knew that most of the women to whom she gave it were swollen with a quite different condition.

What Mrs Black's prescription might be I could not guess. The liquid mixed with the fear in my belly until I almost retched, tasting soured honey in the back of my throat. When I asked Mrs Black, my voice trembling a little, if I might depend upon her coming to me when I called, she snorted a little through her nose and bid me cease my nonsense. I did not doubt that she would derive some considerable satisfaction from finding me drowned in my own blood.

Taking a bundle of rags that I had been meant to char for tinder, I took to my bed. Mary came as usual and as usual fell instantly asleep. For several hours I lay still, listening to her breathing, waiting for the cramps to come. I could sense them massing at the edges of my belly, dark and silent, gathering their strength. Biding their time. In the lane two dogs bellowed and howled, locked in ferocious battle. Their baying scraped down my spine, sharp with teeth, splattering across my skin like hot saliva. I buried my face beneath the pillow but the snarls crept into the spaces between the feathers and twisted themselves into my hair. They mixed with the churnings in my belly, with the silent moaning of the worm as the liquid blistered and burned and tore its tiny fists away from my flesh. The fear in my mouth tasted strong and gristly, like tainted meat.

Perhaps I fell asleep. When I woke it was almost dawn. There had been no blood, no cramps, no pain. Between the brackets of my hips the swell of my belly rose matter-of-factly, resolutely.

In the hall Mrs Black frowned as I seized her hands. Coldly she detached my fingers.

'You look tired, child.'

'But nothing happened!' I said frantically. 'Nothing at all.'

'I myself was kept awake by the fearful racket of a dog fight,' Mrs Black observed calmly, as though she had not heard me. 'Edgar tells me you are frightened of dogs, is that right? I have to confess last night I was somewhat unsettled myself.'

Another time I might have taken pleasure in the idea of Mrs Black being unsettled. Now I cared only for myself.

'Bugger the dogs!' I wailed. 'Do you not hear me? Nothing happened!'

Mrs Black glared at me. For a moment I thought she would strike me for cursing. I tried to stand straighter, to return her gaze without flinching. Then, abruptly, she pressed her lips together and let out a sharp puff of breath.

'What on earth did you expect?' she snapped, turning away. 'Your stools indicate that your bowel is moving adequately. It would hardly do to purge you at such a time. Now, I suggest you rest. You would not want to overtire yourself in your condition.'

And that was the end of it. Nothing more was said.

Jewkes came today. He was in sickeningly high spirits, having come directly from the Cathedral which he claimed magnificent. He had climbed to the gallery in the dome & had had his man carve his & his companion's initials upon the stone. 'For Posterity', he said, as though his graffito was as great a gift to history as the works of Harvey & Sydenham together. I can only despair of such a patron. He insisted upon raising objections to my method, most of them dull & all of them unscientific. No man questions the virtue of anatomizing felons, who have been hung from the neck for their crimes against their fellow men. Why then can he not see that the subject has, through her actions, placed herself beyond the bounds of civilized society? At least this way she may atone in some way for the sin she has committed. If the man is so damned keen on Posterity, why can he not permit me to make my mark upon it unencumbered, & in his name? Truly, he is a Philistine.

Still, he pays & his visits calm Mrs Black whose thoughts are all for the tedium of pounds & shillings. Would that they calmed me too. For all that he cannot rob from me the pleasure I continue to derive from my work here vexation with the man takes its toll upon my health. My stomach, though not painful, is unsettled, my digestion erratic & plagued with wind. The tincture does not soothe me as it

140

once did but rather inflames my blood, striking in my breast a strange agitated feeling, so that my legs jump & twitch. My skin itches ferociously, upon the surface & deep within itself, as though ants crawl in my veins. Sleep is no comfort. I dream of dark shadows, bright with eyes & teeth, & wake exhausted.

But I must not succumb. All will be well. I must think always, only, of the work. Complexity & confusion rendered simple, perfectly clear. No tricks, no manipulations. Just the living proof. Nullius in Verba. The mysteries of Creation laid bare, in their magnificent simplicity.

Jewkes informed me today that the dome of that Cathedral is not a single dome but rather three, one set inside the other like eggshells. The dome that may be seen from the inside is quite a different structure from the lead casing that encloses it, & there is another of brick, or wood, I do not recollect which, that forces the two together. Jewkes of course thought it brilliant, his builder's brain quite unfit to grasp the iniquitous cheat of it.

Wren is a charlatan. He may deceive the citizens of London but only a man of his arrogance could presume to deceive God.

12

I meant to escape. I dreamed of it, planned it, staring out of the window at the dome that was not afraid of anything. All I had to do was to go as far as the stand-pipe and keep on walking. I had the four guineas I had taken from my mother. I could find lodgings somewhere else in London, find someone willing to expel the worm. It was the part after that I could not imagine. Four guineas was a fine fortune until it was spent. I knew not a soul in London. I thought of the thieves that lurked in the dark courtyards along the Strand, the villains and the swindlers, the pimps and the drunks and the whores and the half-wild dogs. I thought of the fights that broke out like boils, the thundering carriages and rearing horses, the trampling crowds, the dark doorways of Cheap-side where the broken-down beggars clutched at your skirts, half-naked and famished for the want of bread, and I thought — tomorrow. Tomorrow, if still nothing is done tomorrow, then I shall go.

The day I overheard the conversation was one such day. It must have been mid-morning because the dome's clock had just struck ten times. My breakfast finished, I had heaved a bucket of water upstairs so that I might mop the parlour. Distressed as always by the onset of her monthlies, Mary had wept when I asked her to assist me, complaining of pains in her stomach, and I was in a poor temper. In the hallway I clattered the bucket down, slopping water. The door through to the shop stood open and I could see Mrs Black outlined in the street door, the alligator hanging down above her head so that, from where I stood, it resembled a vast and jaunty hat. She was conversing with someone, I could not see whom, and I stopped to listen. It was the unusual timbre of her voice that caught my attention. There was something almost confiding about it.

'Oh yes, indeed,' I heard her murmur. 'The girl's husband is a relative of my husband's, a very good family, of course. But he has interests in the Indies that require him there, and now there are fears of smallpox in the parish. Naturally we offered to have her stay with us for the duration of her confinement. It is a great relief to his mother. After all, here we may attend properly to her needs.'

'You are a good woman,' I heard a woman reply. She moved a little so that she might more easily peer into the shop and I saw that it was the wife of the chandler, Mr Dormer, whose shop faced ours. She was a whey-faced woman with a weakness for fancy lace which she wore in a soapy lather around her neck, and a powerful interest in her neighbours' affairs. It was said she possessed an archbishop's instinct for a sinner.

My mistress shifted a little, obscuring her view.

'It is no more than my duty,' Mrs Black corrected smoothly. 'Ah, Mr Nicholls, good day to you. I have your prescription already prepared. Mrs Dormer, will you excuse me? I

143

should not wish to keep a customer waiting.'

Stepping back, she ushered Mr Nicholls into the shop. I caught a glimpse of Mrs Dormer on tiptoes, squinting and stretching for a better view, before Mrs Black closed the door. As for me, I barely had the presence of mind to hide myself. My head swam. Mrs Dormer knew. But how? Though I was a sturdy girl I was naturally narrow at the waist. My breasts were swollen but as yet my belly protruded only a little way and I was still able to wear my usual stays, albeit more loosely laced than usual. Even a friend of long acquaintance might not yet be quite certain. Surely Mrs Black would never have confided such information of her own accord. Such an indiscretion might prove ruinous, particularly for the wife of an apothecary. It would take only a neighbour with a grudge, perhaps someone whose expensive preparations had failed to cure them, or who owed the Blacks money. A woman of my mistress's disposition would hardly make so elementary a mistake. It wasn't even as though she was fond of conversation. Most of the time her lips were cramped so tightly together the sharp lines around them might have been stitches, sewing them shut. And yet had I not just heard her speaking of it openly, without a trace of shame?

I leaned dizzily against the wall, my legs unsteady. My hands were perfectly cold as I placed them flat against my belly. The worm's features pressed outwards from their blank clay, making of the lump a nose, ears, two hands. A child. Until this moment I had never thought it a child.

★ ★ ★

That night Mrs Black brought Mary a tincture to soothe her stomach.

'White Archangel,' she said, and set a cup before me too. 'It is to be hoped it may improve your temper somewhat. Come on now, drink.'

She crossed her arms, waiting. I hesitated. Then, quickly, hardly caring what it was, I snatched up the cup, drained it and handed it back to her. My mouth burned. Mrs Black raised an eyebrow and said nothing, turning instead to Mary who gazed into her tea, her eyes crossed in concentration. The steam made sparkles in her sparse eyebrows. By the time she was finished, my nerve strings were stretched so tightly that my toes clenched in my boots.

That night I could not sleep. Questions writhed in my skull, frenzied and senseless, packed so densely it was impossible to know where one ended and another began. Beside me Mary snored, her mouth slack. More than once I kicked her but she slept so deeply that she did not even turn over. But though I twisted and thrashed, I could not get comfortable. The rugs wound themselves about my legs, tethering me to wakefulness. Beneath me the apothecary traced his perpetual circles, the low murmur of his voice licking up through the floor like the suck and rush of a tireless sea, and beyond the window the dome gleamed, closed tight. I turned away from the casement, squeezing my eyes shut, but still the questions pressed in, closing my nostrils, filling my mouth with their metalled tang. I buried my face in my hands, my fingers plaited into my hair as though I might tug the answers from my scalp.

All of a sudden there was a noise on the staircase, running feet, hardly human, and something of iron like a chain clanking against wood. I hardly had time to be alarmed before the door to the garret banged open. Light blazed on the narrow landing, so brilliant that for a moment I was certain the house was on fire. Immediately I started out of bed, my eyes dazzled, shaking frantically at Mary's shoulder. She grunted but she did not wake. I struck her with my fist.

'Wake up, you gowking — '

The words died on my lips. For, at that moment, with a most awful roar, a monster from the depths of Hell hurled its full weight into the room, its chest held out before it like a shield, its front legs aloft. Its teeth mauled the darkness, great streams of slaver looping from its jaws. Its eyes were bright with murderous rage. It roared again, the length of its fiendish body resonating with the noise. It was so close I could smell its foul breath, sulphurous with sin. My ears were full of a deafening clamour but I could not move. I stared instead at the creature's collar, a dark circlet set with iron studs and an iron chain that shook and banged. I could feel the warm

146

seep of piss down the inside of my thigh. My bowels melted.

It had come for me. It was not the house that burned. It was the fires of Hell itself that licked up the stairs, crimson flames bloody with vengeance. The envoy of the Devil had come to claim me, to drag my wicked soul back down into Hell's perpetual inferno. Frantically I tried to think of something, a prayer, a curse, anything to keep the monster at bay, but my mind was blank, empty with shock.

Help me. Oh, sweet Jesus.

The words were meagre and weak as cobwebs. It was too late now to plead for mercy. The deal was already struck. The thin stuff of my nightdress clung to my shaking body, soaked with sweat and excrement. The ghastly beast strained ever closer towards me, its tongue Satan-red, the sinews standing out from its neck in hang-man's ropes, its teeth bared in a ghastly voracious grimace.

I could do nothing. I could only wait for the suffocating bulk of its body pressing down on mine, for the meaty stink of its fur, the scream of its claws burying themselves in my neck as its teeth tore into the flesh of my stomach. The beast roared again and hurled itself forward. I screamed, falling backwards and striking my head against the corner of the bed. For a moment the room was streaked with colour, scattered all over with a fine silver dust.

Then it went black.

UPON THE MATERNAL IMAGINATION
Notes for Section ix, revision xvii

The female imagination is a temptation sent by God, to test a woman's virtue & determine her fitness for the Kingdom of Heaven, just as a man must do battle with the grossness of his carnal appetites

A chaste & virtuous woman may be certain that her imagination, be it ever so strong, may find, in the purity of her soul, a mighty shield, an unassailable fortress that may protect the soft & blameless flesh of her unborn infant

But in the bosom of the sinful the soul is <u>weak,</u> a rusting armour, a crumbling buttress, defenceless against the dark forces of the imagination which must then vanquish the citadel of the womb, just as the gout seizes an old man's foot

The imagination imprints itself only upon those women who are sinful, godless, corrupt, but the woman senses it not & suffers not. She feels no pain. It is the child who must wear always the bitter stain of her sin, the child whom the world judges as monstrous

THE BASE WOMAN FEELS NO PAIN

13

When I woke it was morning, cold grey light pressing flat the awkward angles of the room and illuminating the sounds of the new day: the clatter of horses and carriages, the heavy rumble of shop barrows, the calls of the criers. It was late. I tried to raise my head from the pillow but it was heavy and stupid, stuffed with sleep. My eyes and mouth were gritty and dry. With an effort I turned my head. Beside me Mary lay sprawled on her back, her mouth open, her twisted bolster blotched with spittle stains. I felt a choppiness in my guts, like a premonition. Why had the mistress not roused us? Then, humping the mess of rugs over my head, I closed my eyes and sought to burrow back into sleep. One of my hands was prickled with numbness, as though I had laid upon it all night, and I flexed my fingers sleepily. Mary would wake me when it was time. For an addle-head she was vexingly punctilious.

'Colly Molly Puff! Colly Molly Puff!'

Again the uneasy twist in my guts. Reluctantly I pushed the blankets away from my face and, with an effort, struggled to sit up. Colly Molly, the pastry man, did not pass this way until after nine o'clock. My breath made smoke as I shook at Mary's shoulder. She grunted in her sleep, sucking upon her tongue, but she did not wake. On its nail my stomacher hung empty, slack without the shape of me, but still I could not

149

summon urgency, only a chill and queasy dread. Ice glazed the inside of the casement window. It was bitterly cold.

There was the brisk tap of footsteps upon the stairs, the rap of the mistress's knuckles upon the door as the key scraped in the lock.

'We are all slept late today. Up now and quick about it,' Mrs Black instructed crisply, but there was no harshness in her voice. Hurriedly I stumbled out of bed, gasping at the shock of the cold floor against my stockinged feet, but she did not open the door. Instead her soles tap-tapped away down the stairs. I shivered and, thrusting my arms into my dress, shouted at Mary to shift her idle backside out of bed. She half-raised her head, her eyes slitted against the light, and let it fall.

'Go 'way,' she muttered, already almost asleep again.

I yanked hard at the laces of my bodice, pulling the waist as tight as I could bear. It steadied me somehow. Twisting my hair into my cap, I stepped into my boots and, with a great sweep of my arm, pulled the rugs from Mary's prone body. She cried out, her face contorting with befuddled indignation.

'Didn't you hear the mistress?' I muttered. 'Get up. Don't think I shall do your work for you.'

Chafing my arms with my cold hands, I stamped across the room. A mess of bells rang out the hour. In the rippling silence that followed a dog barked fiercely. I stopped, the fear rising in my throat like vomit. I swallowed hard, shaking

150

my clogged head to clear it. The cracked basin with the blue stripe contained an inch of icy water. Steeling myself, I thrust my hands into it and splashed some on my face.

The chill of it ached against my temples. I pressed my fingers into my eyes, waiting for the pain to disperse, and abruptly the dusty red-black of my closed eyes gaped in a ghastly roar, framed by glittering silver teeth. I managed only a shudder of remembered terror before the bitter nausea spiked my throat. Hauling the chamber pot from beneath the bed, I was violently sick.

Groggily Mary raised her head, her hands tugging at her wild hair, but I did not look at her. I had to get out of the garret. Snatching up my shawl, I stumbled towards the door. I refused to notice the fresh white marks scored in the floorboards by the door but stepped over them, my fists clenched for balance. In the kitchen everything would be ordinary, dull. The cups would be lined up in their usual places on the dresser. I would listen as I always did to the giddy peeps of the linnet as it hopped upon its perch, and know before I saw it the rapt greed on the face of the yellow cat as it pretended not to watch. Mary would come down and smile at me in her squinting, lopsided way and wipe her nose against the back of her hand and another dreary day could begin.

The dog barked again, his snarls stretched into an undulating howl. I fled downstairs.

The apothecary was in his study. I could hear his footsteps on the floorboards as he paced to and fro. But before I had set my foot upon the landing he opened his door, craning his head out. His face was uncovered. He wore neither cap nor wig and his shaved head was hazy with grey stubble. I could not endure any of his questions. I tried to slip past him but he caught me by the sleeve. His grip was tight. In his other hand he held a glass bottle, quite empty. His lips were dry and cracked and coated with something white as though he had been sucking on a stick of chalk. The white gathered in thick scabs in the corners of his mouth, making the stain on his cheek look redder than ever, and behind his spectacles his eyes were huge black holes ringed with a thread of pale blue.

'Good morning,' he said, and the tip of his tongue flickered over his lips. 'You slept well?'

Too late I realized that I looked him directly in the face. I twisted my gaze away, gripping the handrail. The lateness of the hour suggested surely that he meant the question sardonically but there was something fervent in his tone that belied mockery. Although I had looked directly into his eyes, I had no idea what it was he wanted of me.

'Thank you, sir,' I replied carefully, trying to steady the tremble in my voice. 'Though I think I am not quite well.'

The apothecary took a step closer to me. He smelled of stale wine and liquorice and something charred and foreign like burnt caramel. I closed my eyes, willing him to let me go.

'Feverish. I shall see you directly I have taken

breakfast. Or perhaps — yes. Before supper, I think. When the sun has set.'

My legs fell heavily against the treads of the stairs as I stumbled downstairs. The kitchen was empty, although the kettle whistled to itself on the range. I took a rag and lifted it from the heat, pouring the water into the waiting teapot. Then I took cups from the dresser and set them upon the table, along with a loaf which I put to warm among the ashes of the fire. The cheese was flecked with weevils, so I cut out the black spots before placing it on a plate. I still felt nauseous but the routine nature of the tasks calmed me a little. As for the dread, I swallowed it down with all my strength and would not look at it. Gradually my hands ceased their shaking. When I sat I concentrated on the feet of the people hurrying through the high slice of window and tried to imagine the missing parts of their bodies. I had often amused myself this way, but on this particular morning I set about the task with uncharacteristic resolve. When Mrs Black rapped my shoulder with her knuckles I jumped as though I had been burned.

'I am most displeased with you,' she admonished me. 'You disturbed the entire household with your hollerings last night. You are fortunate the apothecary is in merciful humour this morning. He sleeps ill at the best of times without a thoughtless chit of a girl bellowing the house down.'

I stared at her helplessly.

'Don't look at me that way, my girl. You should be falling over yourself to thank me. After all it was I who was roused, I who was obliged to change you when you had soiled your night-gown.'

I rubbed my face.

'My nightgown — ?' I managed. My mouth was dry.

'Ranting on and on like a Tom o' Bedlam when frankly it would have behoved you to show some gratitude,' Mrs Black continued. 'Next time I shall surely leave you to rot in your own filth.'

'I — thank you.'

'Indeed. It is clear something has inflamed you. I have asked Edgar to make you something up to cool your liver. But let me say this. Your lurid inventions have no place in this house.'

'Inventions!' The tears started in my eyes. 'But — '

Mrs Black held up her hand for silence. Her face was grim.

'If you are to remain under my roof, you shall endure the sufferings that God sees fit to send you with considerably more courage than you have displayed thus far. I shall not tolerate hysteric distempers in my house, Mrs Campling.'

She pressed her fingers hard into my neck, feeling for my pulse.

'I shall see your pot when you have opened your bowel,' she ordered. 'Now eat and be quick about it. And where is the other girl? You are already lamentably behind with your work.'

The day passed with agonizing slowness. I stumbled through my duties hardly noticing the movements of my hands. When at last the idiot

154

troubled to drag her idle bones downstairs she chattered on in her unintelligible way but I heard not a word of it. My head was already frantic with its own manner of gibberish, all distressed flappings and squawks that bounced off my skull and skittered out of reach in the darkness. Despite the chill I sweated into my stays. Again and again the dog's jaws gaped in the soft bruised space between my eyes and I had to squeeze them shut, my fingertips pressed into the sockets, until the shifting yellow patterns behind my eyelids forced the image away. In their place were scratches, long pale scratches, dug with claws into the soft timber of a floorboard. Not inventions. Not inventions at all.

It had grown dark when the apothecary's bell sounded, the moon no more than a curved gash in the black sky. The bells in the apothecary's house were used so seldom that we never troubled to oil them and this one scraped tentatively, as though it cleared its throat. Mary bounced up and down on the balls of her feet, tugging at her apron and pointing. The bell rang again.

'For pity's sake, enough!' I snarled. 'Must you ring that damned thing off the wall?'

The anger was solid, consoling. Snatching up a tallow light, I stamped up the dark stairs with enough force to make kindling of them. When I reached the master's door I did not tap it with the knuckle of my index finger as I had been taught. I beat upon it with my fist.

'Come.'

My master sat at the heavy oak table, a quill

155

held aloft in one hand. In the centre of the table stood two great heaps of papers, one secured by a coffee cup, another by the sugar bowl, and beside them a tarnished girandole bearing five dripping candles. The flames dipped as I entered, shifting the shadows so that the furniture itself seemed to move about the room. He had put on his wig, the old-fashioned one with the horns, and a suit of rusty black. He reached for the girandole, bringing it closer so that it illumined his face. Quickly I looked away.

'So,' he said.

Even with my eyes averted, his restiveness was striking. He moved like a draught around his papers, lifting corners and letting them drop. Even when he sat, his legs twitched beneath the table, his toes dancing a precise and dogged jig, around and around, while his fingers drummed on the arm of his chair and his wig flicked about his shoulders like a horse's tail. Even the stuff of his plain black clothes seemed constantly to shift, like a nest of stinging ants arranged in the shape of a man. Crumbs swarmed about his feet.

'What is it you want?' I demanded.

I waited for him to reprimand my insolence but, although his fingers flexed dangerously, the apothecary said nothing. Instead he gesticulated at my usual chair with his quill, sending an arc of black ink spots across the floor. His hat hung from the chair's back, its veil almost touching the floor. I sat stiffly on the edge of the seat, as far from it as I could manage.

'Hmm. My wife tells me you suffered a nightmare last night.' The apothecary unglued his tongue from the roof of his mouth but still the words came out stuck together. He took a sip from a glass at his elbow. 'You may begin by relating to me all you can recollect of the apparition.'

Immediately my anger deserted me, leaving nothing but the cold roil of sickness in my stomach. Around me the shadows seemed to darken and shift. My lips were numb and dry, making words impossible. Pleadingly I shook my head.

'From the beginning, if you please. You shall describe first the particulars of the dream itself. I will then have a number of questions I wish you to answer. I would press you to speak clearly and pause when I tell you. I shall wish to make notes.'

He reached out to dip the quill into the inkwell, his hand shaking so violently that he was required to steady the wrist with the other hand. I stared down at my lap, my head still moving from side to side. In the silence a log shifted in the fire, sending a fan of sparks up the chimney.

'Dammit, girl, speak! I shall not tolerate defiance!'

His eyes were red with agitation, the stain on his face dark as a bruise, as he hurled the quill on to the table. Hot tears swelled in my eyes.

'Come, come now, my dear, so distressed?' the apothecary said with sing-song gentleness, the rage so rapidly extinguished it seemed certain I had imagined it. With quiet deliberation he picked up his quill and, turning away from me, studied the nib before taking a knife from his pocket and carefully sharpening it. I could see his reflection in the window pane, the way his mouth smiled. The purple stain was a dark hole through which I could make out the flaking white paintwork of the chandler's window opposite. I sniffed, wiping my nose on my sleeve.

The apothecary took a slow deep breath.

'You are quite undone, are you not? Shall I have Mary bring us chocolate?'

Mary kept her eyes on the floor as she rattled the tray on to a side table and scuttled from the room. I had only ever tasted chocolate before on those occasions when I was the first to the master's empty cup and could run my finger around its bottom to rescue the last gritty dregs. Now the warm creamy liquid coated my tongue with its silky sweetness. I rested the rim of my cup against my chin and inhaled, allowing the fragrant steam to soothe the queasiness in my belly.

'I would encourage you to begin,' the apothecary said smoothly to the window as I took another slow sip. 'I shall need to know everything. And I shall not permit you to leave this room until I am satisfied.'

He smiled again and his fingers drummed impatiently against the arm of his chair. I swallowed and pressed my teeth into my lips so that the pain might restore me a little and lend me the composure to begin. In my hand the cup rattled in its saucer.

'You would not wish me to impel you to speak, would you?'

Although the smile still curved his lips all trace

158

of it had vanished from his voice.

'I — I — '

'Yes?' The quill stabbed.

'I — I don't understand.' The words rushed from my mouth. I hardly knew I was thinking them until they crowded into the space between us. 'It is — I don't understand, sir. Why you wish to know.'

I gazed at him helplessly, braced for the wooden rule to slice the air. Instead the apothecary stared out of the window, his chin resting upon his hand.

'Why I wish to know,' he said at last.

'Yes, sir,' I whispered.

The apothecary blinked rapidly, several times. Then, laying down his quill, he turned his chair around so that he faced me. I quickly looked away. Pushing aside a pile of papers, my master leaned across the table and motioned to me to give him my hand. I hesitated. Then, keeping my eyes averted, I did as he asked.

'Look at me,' he commanded.

'But — '

'I said, look at me.'

Slowly I raised my eyes.

'Yes, that's right, look. Look hard.'

He was breathing hard, as though he had been running. I looked. Unpowdered, his stained cheek was the muted purple of blackberry juice, its surface pocked and coarse. It faded out gradually on the upward slope of his nose, like a wine stain on a tablecloth, but, across his brow where the mark was raised and puffy, it came to an abrupt stop which contrasted starkly with the

159

yellowing wax of his high forehead. Observing the direction of my gaze, he traced the raised border with the tips of his fingers, inviting me to study it. In its dull purple frame, the white of his right eye was a livid red, its black centre no more than a pinprick. I shifted unhappily, my gaze sliding away.

'Well? What is it you see?'

'I — '

'You are disgusted. Doubtless you think me grotesque, a fresh-faced young girl like you.'

'No, sir, no — that is, I — '

'Well?'

'It is not so very bad,' I whispered.

The apothecary expelled a strange, strangled snort of laughter. His brow sparkled with perspiration.

'Not so very bad. Is that so? Let me tell you something. All my life people have looked upon my face and seen only this, this mark upon my skin. To them I am not a good husband or a loyal friend nor even a fine and original mind. To them I am only this, this patch of ruined flesh! A disfigurement, made man!'

He seized his wooden rule and brought it down hard upon the table. I bowed my head, squeezing my hands in my lap, stiffening myself against the blow. I could not imagine how this must end.

'All my life I have suffered fearsome dreams.' Once again, he spoke softly, cupping his stained cheek tenderly in his hand. I had to strain to hear him. My back ached, my stomach too. I wrapped my arms around it, willing the interview to be over. 'Apparitions that stalk the darkness and cause me to wake with sweat upon my skin and a scream in my mouth. You seem surprised. Perhaps you thought a man of science impervious to, or even dismissive of, such imagined horrors. But you are wrong, quite wrong. I have embarked upon a study of such things. Yes, indeed. A study for no less than the Royal Society itself. And I require your assistance. Even a humble maidservant may bear witness. A man of science cares more for truth than for distinctions of birth. Come, let us begin. We have already wasted enough time.'

His cajolery had a hysteric edge, the desperate conviction of a prophet or a madman. The candles guttered. The wooden rule twitched in his hand, pleasuring itself against the edge of the table, as very carefully I lifted my chocolate cup to my lips. The liquid had grown cold and a sticky skin adhered to my lips. My throat pulled into a knot as I picked it off with my fingernails. In my lap the cup rattled in its saucer. I knew then that this would never end, that, unless I told him what it was he wanted to hear, I would remain here in this room for ever.

'If you wish it, sir.'

'Excellent.'

The master's face clenched, his eyes blinking frantically. Then, clearing his throat as he pulled a pile of papers towards him, he set about his questions. What was the nature of the dream? Had I believed myself asleep or awake? How had it affected my pulse, my bowel? Had I sweated with fear or had I been rendered cold? Had I feared death? Had I suffered cramps, bleeding? How had I felt upon waking?

At first my answers were brief, each hesitant phrase requiring a great effort of will, but, to my surprise, as the interview progressed, my tongue grew looser and more willing. The words came in sudden unexpected surges that scoured the inside of my chest. It felt good to be rid of them.

To my considerable relief it seemed that the responses I gave were the right ones. My master's head nodded in convulsive little jerks as he wrote and wrote, his mouth working furiously as he numbered each fresh page. Sometimes he even sighed and closed his eyes, smiling tenderly as though he too had suffered just as I had. When he grew tired, he raised a hand to silence me, putting down his pen and making patterns with his fingers to ease the cramps. It was easier when he bid me turn my chair so that I no longer faced him. The wall made for an easier confessor. When I admitted that I had been sure that the beast was the agent of the Devil, sent to claim me for Hell, I surprised even myself. Behind me my master drew in his breath sharply. I clenched my fists in my lap, horrified by my recklessness, but, to my astonishment, he said nothing. He only wrote faster, pressing so hard with his quill that he tore right through the paper.

Then, suddenly, he dismissed me. He did not trouble to raise his head from his paper as I left the room, so engrossed was he in the act of scribbling. I rose unsteadily from my chair. I had no idea how long I had been there.

'My studies show that the most alarming dreams have a propensity to recur,' he mused. 'I hope for your sake that you do not suffer the same miseries tonight.'

I flinched.

'I fear that the more afraid of our dreams we are, the more they haunt us. And you, I think, are very afraid. Go now.'

'Sir.' It was barely more than a whisper but all the same a strange compulsion drove me on. 'Sir, about the — about my condition — '

The apothecary looked up.

'What do you think you are staring at?' he barked, suddenly enraged.

I shook my head helplessly.

'Nothing, sir.'

'I should damned well hope not, if you do not wish a night in the cellar. Brash little strumpets, the lot of you. Now get out, before I thrash you!'

He snatched up the wooden rule. Whimpering, I staggered to the door, wrenching it open. On the dark landing I leaned against the wall, my heart thumping. The taste of chocolate soured in my mouth. Suddenly a light loomed up the stairs.

'Been helping the apothecary with his studies, have we?'

Edgar stood before me, a rushlight flickering in his hand. A smirk tugged at his lips.

'I don't see what business it is of yours,' I retorted, but Edgar knew a winged bird when he saw one.

'Make sure you lace your stomacher back up before the mistress sees you,' he drawled,

163

fumbling a key into the lock of his door. 'I wouldn't like to think what would become of you if she was to discover any of your smutty little goings-on.'

'You shut your scurvy mouth before I shut it for you,' I spat. 'What kind of a trollop do you take me for?'

'Ah, let me think,' Edgar shot back. 'The kind of trollop who needs to come to an apothecary's house to be relieved of her troubles?'

He blew me a contemptuous kiss and shut the door behind him. The landing went dark but the echo of his laughter clung to the chilly air, acrid as smoke.

Mr Johanssen,
Apothecary at the sign of the Golden Hind at
Cornhill

Dear Mr Johanssen,

I received your letter by this morning's post.

I would like to think, sir, that we are both
men of science, distrustful of long words &
fancy metaphors. I know you would desire me
therefore to express my opinions to you with
the utmost candour.

Like you I hold the institution of the Royal
Society in the highest esteem. Unlike you, I
have not been cowed by the disrespect in which
apothecaries have always (& frequently without
justification) been held by physicians & their
kind. Unlike you, I do not consider my intellect
deficient because I have not purchased myself a
degree in France & have not a tame bishop
who might be persuaded (for a price) to confer
upon me the distinction of Doctor of Medicine.
It would behove you to remember that there
remains a difference between one skilled in the
art of physick & one skilled in the art of promoting himself as a physician.

As for your criticisms of my treatise, I take
issue with almost every one of your remarks. I
stand upon the brink of a great discovery, the
proof of which I hold in my hands, _in my
hands_. How dare you then to direct me that
'when & if you discern anything of note, it

165

would be appropriate to submit your observations to the Society without the encumbrance of attempted analysis or interpretation', as though I were no more than a common witness? Are you so blinded by the reputation of your fellows that you do not see what it is they do, extracting from men such as myself the work of a lifetime so that they might claim it for their own? I may be a simple scholar, sir, but I for one am not a fool.

Mr Johanssen, I have been frank & I intend to be franker still. I would not presume to question the agency by which you contrived your election to the Society. I would, however, regard it as no less than my duty to counsel you that there is a considerable danger, when a man enjoys a measure of success, either through his own merits or the patronage of others, that he will become vain & self-regarding. Far from reaching a hand to others so that they too may ascend to greater heights, he kicks the ladder away so that he might protect his position & defend against those who would challenge his position.

A man's conscience may over time, & for greater ease & comfort, grow deaf & blind. But let me say this. Remember that the Lord God, into whose hands we must all surrender ourselves at the Day of Judgement, looks ill upon such men, for all that they are Fellows of this society or that, or held in esteem by the powerful few to whom they take care to ingratiate themselves.

It is imprudent in this short life to make

enemies on Earth. It is surely calamitous to make them in Heaven.

I am, sir, & c

GRAYSON BLACK

14

Mindful of my master's warning, I endeavoured not to be afraid, but I found only that fear feeds upon itself, raising an edifice of apprehension from which I could not escape. The first night I drank the infusion that Mrs Black gave me to help me sleep but still the ghastly apparition came, so real to me I could smell the stink of meat upon its breath. After that I did not drink, though I pretended to. Instead, I fought sleep with all my strength, terrified of the horrors that lurked within its dark walls. And every night, when at last it overtook me, these horrors returned, not the same every night but altered in their form so that I was never able even to seek that shred of comfort that may come from a nightmare's dreadful familiarity. I woke to the sound of my own screams and, on the third night, to the shrill scrape of Mary's cries as well. Mrs Black was roused and came to the garret, her face creased with sleep and her grey hair plaited in a rough rope that hung stiffly from her unadorned nightcap. When she had struck me enough she informed me that tonight would be the last night she would tolerate my disturbances. From henceforth, I was to sleep in the kitchen.

The following morning Mary wept as I gathered my few things and placed them in my box for removal to the kitchen. She clung to me with her chapped hands, shaking her head.

'Doan', doan',' she pleaded, her clumsy tongue flapping in her mouth like a fish. 'Doan' go. Pliss. Pliss Lize. Stay Mar' — '

She buried her face against my shoulder, smearing me with snot and tears. I stared down at the top of her head. The sight of the bald hairless patch made the tears spring in my eyes. I felt a powerful urge to strike her. Instead I pushed her roughly away. When I took up my box its sharp edge barked her shin.

'See how you've unsettled the child,' Mrs Black reproved me when she came down to the kitchen later.

'You will take no more beef for the remainder of the month. Its melancholic vapours have quite corrupted you.' Mary herself refused to look at me. Her cheeks were marbled with scarlet, the back of her hands pinched and shiny with dried snot.

At night, when the small fire had died, the kitchen was fearful dark. From the window of the garret it was possible to stretch one's neck and see not only the dome but the glow of Cheap-side, ablaze with light through the small hours of the night. Even in the lesser thoroughfares the laws of the City required the residents, on those nights of the month when the moon was slight, to display lamps until midnight in the winter so that the circles of light came close to touching one another. But in the kitchen one lay beneath the level of the street and, besides, ours was too insignificant a lane to be bound by such an obligation. At night, when the

169

few faint lights in the windows across the way had been extinguished, the kitchen was as black as a tomb. Somewhere beyond the window the dome traversed the sky like a lead ship, impervious to my subterranean misery. It would not remember me.

My first night alone there was windy, thick with rain. Outside the shop signs creaked and groaned and a cascade of water poured from a spout in the wall, splattering the kitchen window with mud. The water bubbled and dripped where the frame had rotted. From time to time unseen feet hastened past the window, rattling the glass. I had overheard the chandler's wife tell of the thieves who had stolen from an open window a pair of new and valuable curtains from their pole. These days the picklocks were so bold, Mrs Dormer had sighed, that they might enter a man's house in broad daylight and carry out every last stick of furniture before you could say 'Stop, thief!' One might know such brigands, she added firmly, by their white stockings. At night it was too dark to make out white stockings.

I shivered, pulling the thin blanket around me. Beneath my palliasse the stone floor exhaled a damp chill, its crumbling mortar lush with the stink of the cesspit in the cellar beneath. I missed the haphazard slopes of the garret roof, the yeasty smell of our bed, its affable sag. I missed Mary's bulk beside me, her warmth, even the exasperating sticky sound of her champing on her tongue. In the kitchen the noises of the street came so close. I could hear the suck of muddy boots tramping past the window. They slowed, stopped. A lantern glowed lemon against the low slice of window, transforming the raindrops on the glass into one thousand brilliant splinters. My heart squeezed.

'Past eleven o'clock and a rainy night,' the night-lanthorn wheezed, and he stamped his feet in the mud before taking up his lantern and moving on. A buttery smear of light greased the window frame and was gone.

Sleep came suddenly, unexpectedly. That night the beast came at me through the window, forcing its hideous head through the narrow opening. The following night it leaped out from the doorway; on the next from the narrow recess we used as a pantry. Each time it was lit with a brilliant dazzle of fire that stamped my eyelids like a seal. Each time the fear closed its hands around my throat and pressed out the hairs from my skin until my body burned with it. Every morning, when I had drunk my tea, Mrs Black had me hold out my hands for the birch. When I wept, she sucked in her cheeks so hard that the bones above them threatened to pierce the skin. One morning she had me march out into the lane so that I might show her the prints of this beast I insisted upon. There were none, only churned mud and a single bootprint, freshly made. I did not know whether to be comforted or terrified out of my wits.

I sickened. My head shrilled with exhaustion. There was an unceasing pain in my reins so that I had to grip my back tightly with my hands whenever I bent over. My eyes were red and sore, my eyelids lined with sand. A necklace of boils encircled my neck. My teeth ached in their gums. I ate little, unwilling to subject them to the rigours of the gristly mutton Mrs Black insisted I took in place of beef. My lack of appetite angered the apothecary's wife who snatched up my plate when I pushed it away, poking with her finger at the food I had left there. She gave me meat to build my strength, she told me sharply. The apothecary would be angered if I did not eat. It would look badly if one of his household sickened. People would talk.

I hardly heard her. Words rattled in my head like dice in a cup and were as quickly dispatched. I performed my never-ending duties in a grey haze of misery and fatigue. I stopped thinking about the worm. I did not have the strength to care what became of me. I feared I might be going mad. At other times I despaired that I was not.

On the sixth day I bled. When I felt the first slippery wetness between my thighs I hardly knew what had happened. It was only when I raised my skirts and saw the rusty stains on the flesh of my thighs, the smear on my cambric petticoat, that I understood. The pains followed quickly, bringing with them a wild exhilaration. At last, at last, it was to be over. The waiting was over. Triumphantly I dragged myself up towards the garret. The pains were stronger now. I clung to the handrail of the stairs as another spasm clamped my belly, pressing around from my back like a metal band, twisting and tightening as if it would tear me in two. I gave myself over to the agony, moaning aloud, urging it forward, biting down hard on my bottom lip so that I might bear it better. I had nothing to fear from the pain. Each cramp brought me closer to my release, my salvation. I arched my back, the sweat greasing my face, tasting blood in my mouth. I no longer attempted to move. By the time Mrs Black found me squatting on the stairs, my arms wrapped around my belly, I was already exhausted. As the paroxysm retreated, leaving me gasping for breath, I looked up at her and laughed, a racking, breathless sound that caused her to stare at me in undisguised alarm.

Taking both my arms, she pulled me to my feet. Her touch was not unkind. Her starched voice wrinkled at the edges as she bade Mary bring me wine and a warming-pan. Once she had me in the bed she placed a pillow behind my back and charged me to sit as upright as I could manage. Through my half-closed eyes I could see the curve of the dome, its outline categorical against the smudged grey sky. The pain came in great cramping swoops, as though the Devil pulled my stays. In the breaths in between I stared upon the dome's burnished cross and ball. When the pain came again I could see the shape of the cross behind my clenched eyelids, red as blood. I could feel my strength failing, exhilaration leaking away.

I knew I would die.

The light faded from the sky, twists of cloud scattered like potato peelings across the darkening blue. The apothecary came to the door of the garret and conversed in urgent whispers with my mistress. The golden cross mellowed to bronze

173

and then to a dark velvety plum. By nightfall the cramps had eased a little, the respite between them longer. Mrs Black bound a hot plaister about my belly. She would not let me sleep, although fatigue weighted my eyelids and fogged my head. Instead, she gave me warmed wine with herbs and rubbed my shoulders with a strong-smelling oil. She took no supper, although she had Mary prepare some for her master, but remained with me, watching me closely. By the time the night-watchman called twelve o'clock I had ceased to bleed. Mrs Black had Mary take away the worst of the soiled linen for laundry. Then she blew out the candle and bid me goodnight. She took the pillow with her.

I laid myself down carefully, inhaling the stale bed frowst of sweat and blood. It hurt to move. Beyond the window, the half-moon lolled upon its back, wan and listless on a narrow bolster of cloud, but the sky was brisk with stars. When at last Mary came to bed the mattress shifted, jolting my aching belly. I whimpered. Mary gave a strange animal grunt and humped her back against me. Her breathing was thick, lumpy as porridge, and she sucked at her tongue as though she meant to swallow it. Twisted in with the familiar twinge of vexation was something else, something that tugged at my throat so that I swallowed.

For several minutes I lay there, listening to her. I did not kick out at her legs as I usually did or poke a sharp finger in her back, muttering at her to be silent. Instead, very slowly, my hand reached out and laid itself lightly upon her back.

I could feel the soft bumps of her spine beneath their wrapper of flesh. Mary stiffened. Abruptly I pulled away my hand and turned over. The pale moon gleaming through the casement etched a dusty cross of shadow on the floor. Mary sighed. Rolling over, she burrowed against me, her sticky child's hand reaching for mine. I hesitated but I did not push her away. Champing busily, she plaited her fingers through mine as her warm body shaped itself against my flank. She was hot as a bed jar beneath her nightgown and hardly awake. When I was certain she slept, I pressed her hand to my cheek, feeling the soft curve of her knuckles against my temple. Her fingers smelled of salt and cinnamon.

Then I slept too. This time there were no dreams.

Too close, too close. My heart is still racing for I thought it lost, I thought we had lost it. See how my hand trembles. The fear is still upon me, the stink of blood in my nostrils though I stayed away, unable to trust myself to wait. <u>All care must be taken to still the foetus;</u> bed rest for several days mandatory, clarified juice of plantain three times a day to stay the bleeding

I have taken a little tincture & feel myself calmer, my heart slower, propelling my blood less violently to my extremities. Clearer too & caught suddenly by the evident desire of the subject to be rid of child
IS THAT A POSITIVE CONTRIBUTOR TOWARD SUCCESS OF IMPRESSION?? I had not considered before the <u>effects of maternal ill will</u> upon the foetus but now it occurs to me that surely the mother's abhorrence for the foetus <u>must</u> alter the impression of imagination

Consider the excessive incidence of monstrosity amongst the poor & <u>in particular in those depraved alliances unsanctioned by matrimony.</u> Of course such women suffer an increased exposure to ugliness & deformity & thus a higher risk of imprinting; also their imagination is untempered by the civilizing effects either of pious faith or of reason & scholarship & therefore wilder & more savage in its effects

BUT THIS IS NOT THE SUM OF IT

For is it not undeniable that amongst the low ranks of women many, perhaps most, pregnancies are <u>unwanted/unwelcome</u>, because such women lack the gentler maternal virtues & the means with which to support their offspring, & therefore the fear & passion that elicit impression may be roused not only by external factors but by the <u>fact of pregnancy itself</u> RESULTING IN a violent antipathy to unborn child; aggressive nature of ill will exaggerated by ignorance & coarse instincts

→ additional heat generated causing pronounced fermentation & consequently <u>increased salt deposits</u> that settle over the solid parts of the body of the unborn foetus & contaminate them with their image

↓

ADVANCE SUBJECT'S ANTIPATHY
TOWARD FOETUS
WHEREVER POSSIBLE

15

The worm survived.

After the bleeding I suffered a fever that persisted for nearly a week, confining me to my bed, and which, inflamed by the bitter weather that gripped the city in the latter days of March, weakened me severely. When the writhings of the worm roused me at night I thought of the cramps like iron rings around a barrel, the dark patch where my blood still stained the landing, and I was filled with a bleak terror that squeezed the piss from my bladder in hot brackish trickles. One thought preoccupied me to the exclusion of all others. Dead or alive, the vile creature would be required to come out. I did not think I had the strength to withstand either.

It was more than two weeks before I was able to resume my duties and even then I grew quickly fatigued, exhaustion fogging my head and dulling any appetite but the craving for sleep. But, in spite of me, my waist thickened, my belly arching into a dome. The waiting was a scream buried in my lungs. I coughed and coughed until my throat was sore but I could not shift the weight of it. As the days lengthened, the worm grew angles that jabbed my agitated bladder and pressed the curves of my belly into corners. At night it pounded upon my spine. My stays no longer laced. Even though Mrs Black pronounced me much recovered, it was no longer considered appropriate that I assist in the shop. On the few occasions that the master received visitors I was instructed to remain out of sight. I heard voices behind closed doors, caught the vague unfamiliar flavours of strangers on the stale dark air of the landings, but, beyond the occupants of Swan-street, I saw no one. When I caught sight of myself in the hall mirror, for all my bulk beneath my loose gown, I had the pallid, insubstantial cast of a ghost. I had the strange sense that if I were ever to venture out into the lane, I might find myself quite invisible.

* * *

As for the master, the tread of his feet paced through my nights. According to Edgar he walked and wrote incessantly, covering sheet after sheet of paper with his close writing which he kept in a locked wooden cabinet in his study. Every page was printed at the top with the motto of the Society of Apothecaries, *opiferque per orbem dicor*, which he had Edgar write out in readiness on to countless fresh sheets each day before breakfast. Edgar grumbled that while his dreams had once given him considerable consolation, they were now reduced to those four mean words, chasing one another like dogs around the circle of his skull. I wondered uneasily if the apothecary had intended it so and meant to include Edgar's dreams as well as my own in his study of the subject.

'What do they mean, those words?' I asked

Edgar once, when I needed to hear the sound of my own voice.

'Your ignorance never ceases to astonish me,' he declared. 'Damn this wretched pen, must it smudge every line?' He glared at the paper and crumpled it into a ball which he tossed towards the fire. It bounced off the chimney breast, skittering across the flagstones. I picked it up and smoothed it out. 'Since you ask, it translates loosely as 'I am called throughout the bringer of aid'. Something of an irony, when you consider it. What aid could our esteemed Turk of a master possibly claim to bring anyone? If there is a soul in this house who deserves such a title, surely it is I. I am up and down to that study with 'aid' so frequently it is a miracle that the soles of my shoes are not worn clean through. And burn that paper, for the love of peace, before the mistress delivers another of her lectures about household thrift.'

Edgar exaggerated, but it was true that Mr Black had come to rely heavily upon an infusion of opium to ease his discomforts. He suffered from agonizing stomach cramps and, when the pains seized him, he would swallow a preparation of his own devising, a mixture of opium, rhubarb and camphor taken in a tumbler of Canary wine. The effect upon him was at the same time remarkable and deeply disquieting. In the midst of an attack the apothecary might be bent double with the pain, unable to walk or even to speak. But when he had swallowed his laudanum his eyes shone like two black pearls, bright with dark fire, and his breath came in shallow, excitable

180

gasps, his whole frame seized with a fevered energy that danced in his fingers and caused the muscles in his face to jerk and leap.

One morning as I scrubbed the floor in the hall, the master came up behind me. He wore his hat with the veil so that I could not see his face, but from his awkward gait I surmised it was one of his bad days. I shuffled back against the wall, afraid to rouse his displeasure, and kept my eyes upon the bubbled puddle of water before me. I prayed he did not step in it and soil his shoes. He stopped above me, stooping down so that the burnt caramel odour of him filled my nostrils. His fingers were bruised black with ink.

'Soon,' he murmured, so quietly I almost did not hear him. 'Soon.'

He swept towards the door, flinging it open.

'Such a sky!' he marvelled. 'Surely all the pearls of the Indies do not gleam with so rare a luminescence.'

I hardly heard him. *Soon.* The word clung to me like a cobweb. *Soon.*

That night the worm writhed and thrashed. I was roused frequently by the overwhelming urge to piss. The dome rose above me as I squatted, a cold moon of lead. *Soon.* An unsatisfactory dribble trickled into the pot. Suddenly, without warning, the worm butted my chest with its head. I gasped, the breath knocked from my lungs, and it was as though an obstruction had been shaken from my gullet. I swallowed, blinking, and stared up at the dome, pulling my nightgown over my knees.

Soon. What had become of me? I felt as

181

though I was waking from a long and fevered sleep. *Soon.* I had waited so long, with such blind conviction, that my condition was already far advanced. My belly was round, my breasts heavy. The worm was fat and growing fatter and soon, very soon, it would come out. It would be real, solid, ruin made flesh. And I had no possible idea of what would become of it, what would become of me. I had been in the apothecary's house for weeks and weeks and weeks and in all that time I had done nothing. I had allowed myself to be given over to the household, had waited meekly for them to do with me as they chose. These people, whom I hardly knew, held in their hands my life, my good character, all of my future. I had done nothing.

My brain worked hectically. I might never have been shown the particulars of such matters, not formally, but I was my mother's daughter. It was as yet only May, too early for hyssop or yellow bugle or most other of the flowering remedies notorious as helpmeets to women in difficulties. But not too early for gladwin. Gladwin might be found at all times of the year where there were ponds and rivers. My mother had pounded the roots and rolled them into pessaries which she had given to women in the earliest stages of pregnancy. I had only the haziest recollection of the ingredients and their quantities but I could not think of that, not now. Nor could I think of my mother's face, the familiar walnut creases of her face as she frowned at her mortar. There could be no distraction. *Soon.* It could not be too late. It simply could not.

It was a simple matter to find myself in the hallway when Mr Black came down after breakfast. I made sure to hand him his veiled hat, his silver-topped stick. He nodded, settling the veil around his shoulders.

'Forgive me, sir, for my boldness,' I ventured. 'It is only that I — it is early in the year, I know. Too early for many things. But even now, there are many roots and barks I might fetch you that might be worth something. Mrs Black always says the old woman's charges are extortionate. So I thought I might go for you instead, if you wished it. I used to collect for my mother and I know what to look for.'

The apothecary said nothing but only tapped my belly with the top of his stick. I shifted. His face was invisible behind the black shadow of his veil.

'I — I should like to be more useful to you, sir. After all you have done.'

There was another long pause.

'How fearful you must be,' he murmured. 'How very fearful indeed.'

I was left staring after him, the saliva cooling in my open mouth.

Several days passed. Then, one morning as I polished the hall mirror, I overheard the master and mistress in heated discussion in the parlour. I paused outside the door and listened.

'Are you gone mad? Of course I must have the books! How else may I work?'

'But so many? Might it not be possible to curb your expenditure a little? Our creditors grow so

183

impatient, sir. There are mutterings of Newgate and worse.'

'Madam, I stand at the threshold of greatness and you threaten me with a debtors' gaol? I will not be goaded so, do you hear me? Was Mr Sydenham assailed with petty concerns such as yours? Was Hippocrates? If you wish to make economies, send the girl herbarizing. Her mother was a cunning woman, was she not? Then she knows the primary herbs. Next time, I would have you demonstrate similar resourcefulness before you come complaining to me about your difficulties.'

The following afternoon, while Mary polished the pewter, Mrs Black handed me a pottle. I was to go north, to Islington Spa, a village famed for its waters some two or three miles away. I was to gather what I could. The soles of my feet tingled. It was not yet too late. I nodded eagerly at Mrs Black but she was not finished. I was on no account to go alone, she informed me. Edgar would be my guide.

Edgar smiled. My heart sank.

'Be home by nightfall, I beg you,' my mistress added softly to Edgar as we prepared to leave. 'It is a favoured road for footpads.'

It was a gloomy day but mild, the air syrupy with certain rain. Even the dull light made me blink. I stood on the step, breathing in, tasting smoke and soot and animal dung. It had been more than a month since I felt the sky against my skin. Outside the closed crate of the house I felt dispersed somehow, vague as cloud.

As soon as I stepped into the lane, however,

my feet grew heavy, my borrowed pattens soled with sticky mud. Edgar walked briskly ahead, his hands thrust into his pockets. At the north end of the lane, where it tipped its contents into Cheap-side, he paused so that I might catch him up. Like a river in flood, the great thoroughfare roared and coursed between its banks of bright-windowed shops. Edgar had to shout to be heard over the din.

'Follow this road as far as the Cathedral. And in case you wondered, you little savage, a cathedral is a church, only bigger. The road north from there will take you directly to Islington.'

I frowned, bewildered and still a little out of breath.

'But Mrs Black — '

'Dear Mrs Black. I should not wish to have to turn her against you.' He squeezed my arm, digging his nails into the flesh. 'You will meet me at the church of Mary-le-Bow when the watchman shouts eight of the clock. Ask someone if you do not know it. It would be most imprudent to be late.'

He thrust his face close to mine. He smelled of sweat and Stilton cheese. All around us people pushed and shoved, or stopped and shouted, creating rapids and swirling pools in the traffic, while sedan chairs tilted among them like boats. Then, abruptly, with one last pinch, he released me. I caught a glimpse of the crown of his hat before he was swept away by the current.

I stared after him uncertainly. The people eddied around me, each man as contained within his own importance as a sausage in its skin. Almost immediately, a ragged chicken-seller swung around, almost knocking me off my feet with his baskets of moulting fowl suspended from a pole over his shoulder. Stiffening my legs and thrusting my basket before me like a shield, I pushed myself out into the stream. A clothes trader shoved ahead of me, a bent old man wearing his own hair and over it three hats, one on top of the other. His velveteen coat was worn through at the elbows and was fashionably short, not by design but because its hem was quite rotted away. He stumbled and almost fell. I had to step smartly around him so that he might not take me with him.

Snatching up my skirts, I lowered my head and began to walk, pushing roughly through the crowds, my eyes fixed upon the muddy tips of my boots. I had walked without stopping for perhaps a mile before the road began to rise steeply and I was forced to pause to catch my breath. Only then did I permit myself to look back. Behind me the dome floated gracefully away from the choppy mud of roofs and chimneys, untouched by the petty concerns that measured out the lives of men. I held my basket tightly against my stomach as I looked. Then I closed my eyes and spoke the words aloud.

'Forgive me, Lord. For what I am about to do, forgive me.'

★ ★ ★

I was fortunate. Although the spring had been unseasonably wet, in the low woodland beyond the city's ashy boundaries I quickly discovered many familiar and useful remedies; dragonwort, butterbur, black alder bark for purging the spleen and liver, late primroses, even dandelion, which ignorant folk call Piss-a-Beds. And root of gladwin.

I waited for Edgar outside the church, my feet set carefully upon unconsecrated earth, but all the same I felt the eyes of the godly boring into me through the closed oak door. He was late. It was already dark as we walked silently home, the moon muffled by cloud, but the light that poured from the shops was extravagant, excessive. The liquid white light of lamps overflowed their glass globes while forests of candles flamed in sticks and sconces. It danced in glass windows and spilled lavishly out on to the thoroughfare until even the dung in the kennels glistened silver. Faces loomed towards us, white masks, inked with shadow, their expressions comical or grotesque. Where the light stopped at the end of our lane, the darkness was complete, as though no individual scrap of light would dare to venture there alone. There was never darkness so absolute in the country.

Safe in the fire-lit kitchen, I wrapped the gladwin in a clean cloth and buried it beneath the other linens in the dresser drawer. I might have brought some for the apothecary if I had not been afraid to draw attention to it. It had such a strong odour that where I came from folk called it Stinking Iris. Not my mother. She

187

refused to set a curse against a plant with so many diverse and powerful properties. The roots and leaves, powdered and added to wine, eased the pains of the belly. A decoction of the roots purged corrupt phlegm and choler. Or you might boil the roots with wine and roll the resulting paste into short fat fingers which you wrapped in muslin. I was almost certain that that was all that was required. If you thrust them in as far as they would go, the pains would follow.

Perhaps I mixed the preparation wrongly. Perhaps there were additional ingredients of which I was ignorant. I think perhaps it was simply too late, the worm grown too resilient. Certainly there were cramps. There was bleeding too, a little. But, despite the storms, the worm clung to the wall of my belly, as a sailor clings to the wreckage of his ship, and waited for the gales to blow themselves out.

For some days after that the worm was quiet, its movements subdued. I had more gladwin. I might have tried again. But I did not. I could not explain it, even to myself. I only knew myself defeated. The optimism that had prickled my feet as they hurried towards Islington was gone, replaced by a grim acceptance. The worm was stronger than I, the dark forces that fortified it too inexorable. At night I pressed my fingers into my stomach, willing it to move, to strain towards my touch. When it did I was not tender. I clenched my fists and pushed my knuckles into the angles of it, filled with rage and dread at the tenacity of the creature. But on those nights it did not come to me I felt lost.

June blew in like a sneeze, hurling hard rain at
the windows. Though the nights were short there
was no sign of approaching summer. Instead,
patches of greyish light seeped into the house,
furred with sooty dust. Often the master was
absent during the day, returning late to work for
the greater part of the night. He brought with
him cold air and the tobacco smell of
coffee-houses so that the house no longer felt so
sealed up. As a result he saw me less often than
before and always late in the evening. Once he
had examined me, his hands fluttering in their
particular way over my belly like moths too
skittish to settle, he had me sit facing the wall as
he always had. But now the questions came
rarely. Instead he talked almost to himself.

At night, when I removed my petticoats, the
skin stretched over the egg of my belly, taut and
insistent, and the navel poked forward, inquisi-
tive as a nose. The size of it was startling. There
was nothing of me about it, nothing of
conventional human shape. It protruded from
me like a wen, a sickness my body was
determined to expel. Except that it did not. One
afternoon, Mrs Black had me bring the baby
linens down from the cedarwood chest in her
chamber so that they might be laundered. I
turned away then but she recalled me sharply,
bidding me to pay attention. When she shook out
a gown, its soapy lace yellowed with age, her
brow twisted and her eyes seemed to slide back
into her head. Slowly she put it to her face and

inhaled. It was hardly bigger than a handkerchief. I could not bear to look at it. Instead I tugged the remainder of the linen roughly from the chest, careless of the frail stuff. Then, from beneath a pile of musty napkins, I unfolded a large white stretch of cloth. A winding-sheet. I bundled it up, thrusting it back into the chest, but the stuff caught upon my skirt, tangling itself around my legs. The omen was unmistakable. Crying out, I fell to my knees, the sheet wrapped all about me.

Mrs Black glared, her lips peeled back from her teeth.

'Cease that bleating, for pity's sake,' she spat disgustedly. 'Repentance shall avail you nothing now.'

★ ★ ★

At first the stories were no more than noise to fill the nights. As the bells quarrelled over the quarter hours, counting the hours off till my confinement, the words wove themselves into ropes that bound me to my past, to myself, so that I could not drift away. As the time of my confinement drew ever closer, the house at Swan-street closed in on me until I could hardly breathe.

The present was impossible, the future unimaginable. Only the past was safe, its pleasures certain, its privations softened by time and wistfulness. It did not matter that I had only the idiot for an audience. It was myself I sought to divert, to console. I fixed my eyes upon the hole in the garret ceiling where the lathes poked through like fingers and I talked. I talked of the village where I had grown up, the cottage, the school, the people. I unearthed old affections I had quite forgotten, Dilly the butcher's daughter who wove me necklaces of grass and daisies, the rough blacksmith with his missing finger who let me watch him as he twisted scarlet metal, the soldier with the strange accent who had stayed for the harvest and who had tasted of cider when he kissed me. But the man I spoke of most was my husband, away at sea.

At first he was thin, insubstantial, but little by little my words nourished him until I might have reached out and held his hand against my cheek. His eyes were the glossy brown of horse chestnuts and, when he smiled, his mouth curved more in one corner than the other, dimpling his right cheek. His family had not wanted us wed, desiring him to find a wife with a good portion. But he had refused to heed them, proclaiming me rich not in coin but in beauty and good humour. Indeed, if I were to accept him, he declared, he would consider himself the most fortunate man alive for he loved me with all his heart. That part was Mary's favourite and she had me repeat it many times.

Of course his family had relented. From that day until his father's business required him to sail to the Indies, I confessed dreamily, we had not been parted. I touched the ring Mrs Black had given me, turning it round and round on my finger before lifting it to my lips, and I pictured him standing alone at the prow of a great ship, his shoulders thrown back and his legs braced against the swell of the sea.

Mary sighed, tugging at my nightgown.

'Nay?' she asked. 'Wha' nay?'

The picture blurred and I frowned. I had quite forgotten her.

'Lize, plea. Wha' he nay?' Mary asked again.

I hesitated, although I understood her perfectly.

'Daniel,' I said at last, and through the darkness he smiled at me, etching a dimple in his right cheek, and tipped his hat.

It is nearly time. Perhaps a week now, surely not more than two. This will be it, I am certain of it. My heart jumps in my chest, so frantic with keen blood that I am certain it must burst. Infusions of dittany cannot calm it. On the contrary, my body is become like the plant itself, so that the faintest spark of an idea ignites a flash that illumines my whole self. And, like dittany too, there seems no end to its combustibility. The fire comes again and again, each time intensifying the light.

I shall not permit Jewkes here, for all his insistence, & have instead dispatched an invitation to Mr Halley & await his reply. He shall come, I know it, for we are Englishmen both & cannot fail to recognize our duty as instruments of God's holy will. Was it not an Englishman who first understood that the plain white light that illumines us contains within itself all the colours of the universe? There were those who claimed we could know no more, that God would allow us no more of the blessed secrets of His creation. And yet, here I stand, humble and a little afraid, ready to hold aloft the lantern of my understanding so that the world's dark corners might be bathed in light. How wrong, how very wrong they are proved!

The pain eases, and the opium flows through me, cool as water, its effects quite restored now that I have increased the dosage by three grains. Lemery was quite wrong to assert that the gummy resin of opium emulsifies & retards the spirits in the brain. On the contrary, it scours the channels of my mind so that the dust & rubble of human weakness & delusion is swept away & I see only Truth, plain & purposeful, which suffers no cheat of words, no obfuscation but seeks only the simplest of expression — the <u>creature itself</u>, ignorance and godlessness made flesh, the living embodiment of darkness against which might be discerned the purity of the light.

The scent of my coffee lingers in the air, holding within the structure of its aroma all the odours of the Orient. I breathe in and the tiny hairs inside my nose tremble with perfect pleasure. I have never seen such colours. The fire burns with unmatched ardour, the red-gold of its centre trembling with a liquid brilliance. It imprints itself upon my skull, pouring its molten light into its darkest recesses, so that I understand everything. A bird hops upon the window ledge. Each one of its feathers is a perfect symphony of colour and grain and its eyes are fathomless. I could gaze at it for all Eternity. It raises its wings and I feel the tears start in my eyes for I know I look upon the flawless beauty of an angel.

I am overcome.

16

Mrs Black came quickly when I screamed.

Immediately she had Mary set a fire in the dusty grate. Unused for many years, the chimney was blocked and the fire smoked, sending bitter clouds into the room. Mrs Black opened the window and had Mary fetch the rags we had prepared for the purpose while she instructed me to lie back with my knees raised. The contractions came fast, compressing my ribs. The sweat greased my hair. I cried out that I could not lie, that the pain was bearable only when I sat up, that if I lay down the agony would surely kill me, but Mrs Black paid me no heed. She rubbed her hand with duck fat and, pushing me back against the pillows with a sharp shove, she forced my knees apart and thrust her hand up between my legs. I screamed again. Then the cramps seized at me, so that the scream died upon my lips. I could barely breathe. The tears rolled unchecked down my cheeks. The pain was intolerable. I would surely die. I clutched my hare's-foot against my cheek. The fur stuck to my skin in dark lashes.

'Hush,' she scolded, but she spoke gently. 'I wish only to feel how the child lies.'

I gasped as her fingers probed me. When, with a sharpening of her cheekbones, she hooked her fingers and wrenched, I screamed. The room swam before me, its walls dissolving into a

195

silvered dust of tiny stars.

'The neck of the womb must be stretched to allow for the baby's passage,' she said briskly. 'How else do you suppose it may be born?'

The pain that followed was more terrible than I could have imagined. For all that my mother had been a midwife, I had no experience of childbirth. In my village, confinements had taken place behind locked doors, closed shutters, guarded by the taut and secretive faces of the gossips who attended the labouring mother. Birth to me was whispers, anxious faces, glimpses of dark, hot rooms before I was bundled outside. Even after a successful delivery, the gossips stood sentinel at the door, warding off anyone who might attempt to enter for as long as it could be contrived. An infant was a week old or more, and its mother considerably recovered, before their vigil might be abandoned and the family permitted to enter.

Part of me was thankful I had not known what to expect or I might have died of the dread of it. The room was stifling. Mary was kept busy with the tasks Mrs Black assigned to her, hanging a thick rug over our window so that sunrise might not disturb the darkness of the room, bringing a caudle of warmed wine sweetened with sugar for me to sip when I was able, fetching water and rags and other necessaries, but between her duties she crouched next to me, stroking the sweat-sticky hair from my forehead and murmuring sing-song strings of words beneath her breath which I took for prayers. When the pain receded a little I prayed with her, begging God for mercy and deliverance. Mrs Black bade me sharply to be silent then but I whispered the words anyway, far beyond the reach of her admonitions. I would do anything, I implored Him, I would submit to the cruellest of terms, if He might only deliver me from my terrible agony and let me live.

By the time the creature was finally expelled from me I was so weak I could no longer raise my head to drink. Mary tried to pour a little cordial into my dry lips but she was clumsy and most of it dribbled down my chin. Mrs Black alone was brisk. She sliced through the cord that bound me to it and, snatching up the bloodied mess, took it to the window, holding the curtain back with the spike of one shoulder. I heard her draw in her breath sharply, mutter something under her breath. Then, letting the curtain fall again, she snapped angrily at Mary to go directly to the apothecary and tell him that the child was delivered, although she feared there was little cause for hope. It would of course be brought to him directly so that he might examine it himself.

Mary kissed my hand and placed it carefully back on the blanket. I did not have the strength to protest. I closed my eyes. The pain trembled expectantly between my legs, waiting for me to move. The bed beneath me was slick with blood. In a corner of the room Mrs Black busied herself with a basin of water. There was a dull splash and then a thin high shriek like the call of a bird. Mrs Black crooned, singing softly under her breath. For all the pain a kind of tingling peace spread through me. I closed my eyes as sleep pulled insistently at me, dragging me down, dark and blissful as drowning. I let myself be taken —

The slap on the cheek sent spasms of pain through my damaged body. I cried out.

'Do not sleep, you foolish girl,' chided Mrs Black. In one arm she cradled a tightly swaddled bundle. 'Mary will fetch you a compress to ease the pain but you must remain awake. Do you hear me?'

I nodded and at once my eyelids began again to droop.

'What did I just tell you?' Mrs Black scolded, shaking my shoulder. 'Would you die now, when we have come so far?'

As though she was two different people contained within a single skin, she laid the bundle with great tenderness upon the bed and, turning away, stamped furiously over to the corner of the room. Her impatience made her clumsy. When the basin of water smashed to the floor she cursed and bawled for Mary. No one came. Cursing again, this time more violently, she slammed out of the room.

With the fire banked high the room was hot as an oven and my eyelids too heavy to fight. I sank backwards, surrendering to sleep. Then something whimpered. The noise caught in the fissures of my ripped flesh, sending quivers of pain through my belly and between my legs. I clenched my fists, refusing it, pressing my eyes closed. The whimper came again, louder this time, plucking at me. It would not stop.

With considerable effort, I raised my head. The creature had rolled on the sagging mattress so that it lay almost beside me. It stared up at me. I stared back. Its squashed face was purple and wrinkled but its eyes were the dark vast blue of a midnight sky and it blinked them slowly, sagely, as though it already understood everything that there was to know in the world. Its hands flailed at its sides, each tiny finger curled like the frond of a new fern. Its nails were soft and long and needed paring. When it opened its mouth I caught a glimpse of a petal-pink tongue. Then it squeezed its eyes tightly shut and, with a great gulping breath that seemed to suck every last gasp of air from the stuffy room, it began to scream.

The scream tightened the strings of my nerves until they sang. I no longer thought of sleep or of the pain that turned the saliva in my mouth sour and thick. Instead, I reached over and placed my hand on the bundle. It was warm, almost hot, as though all the vigour it would have need of in a lifetime already thrummed in its tiny body. My palm tingled.

Very slowly my hand slid upwards, following the fragile rise of its chest, the slope of its shoulder. It paused then, the root of the thumb resting almost imperceptibly against the line of its delicate jaw. Then one finger, more courageous than the rest, reached out and touched its face. The skin was thin and silky, expensive-feeling. The eyebrows were perfect twin curves of surprise, soft and fragile as shadows. My fingertip traced their shapes before moving downwards, memorizing the tilt of the miniature nose, the downward curve of the open pink mouth, finding the folded corners of its lips.

Something about the mouth made my heart squeeze. The upper lip formed a perfect bow, as though outlined with ink, tipped by a tiny bead of flesh. In that moment I separated from the pain of my torn and bloody body. All I could feel, all I could be, was in the tip of my index finger, where the rough skin of that bead gently grazed against my skin. I touched it only for a moment. Against my uncurled palm the infant scream was hot and insistent, vastly bigger than the body from which it came. Then, abruptly, greedily, the mouth seized upon my finger and closed around it. Immediately the screaming stopped. I could feel the soft rasp of the petal tongue against the blister where I had burned myself upon the kettle. The toothless gums clamped around the fingertip, pressing down into the flesh as though they feared to let it go. Every part of the creature seemed given over to the effort of it. The face creased with concentration, its eyes squeezing tighter shut with every pull of its mouth. Even on the top of the creature's downy head, a circle of flesh the size of a penny pulsed in and out in time with the sucking. I stared at it and my heart thundered in my throat, so that I too was caught in the precise metre of my baby's mouth.

Around me, the room faded and withdrew. There was no pain, no smoke, none of the childhood stinks of blood and shit. There was only finger, mouth, pulse. Everything was contained within them. We were complete.

All of a sudden the door swung open. Mrs

Black stood on the threshold, a fresh basin of water in her arms. When she saw me she slammed the basin down upon the stool and snatched the infant into her arms. Immediately it began to bawl.

'Mary!' she commanded. 'Here now!'

I gazed at my curled finger, bereft on the blanket, the saliva drying to nothing around the nail. The pulse in my throat jumped hopelessly, its rhythm quite lost. The screaming filled my throat and tore at my belly, at my heart.

'No,' I protested, but my tongue was dry and clumsy and the word stuck to the roof of my mouth. I licked desperately at my lips. 'No! Please!'

Mary's feet slapped at the stairs.

'No wake,' she panted. 'Mister Bla, can' wake. Eye close.'

'For pity's sake, girl,' Mrs Black snapped. 'Must I do everything myself?'

Pushing past Mary, she hustled down the stairs, my infant cradled in her arms. On the floor below I heard her thundering on the door of the apothecary's study, demanding to be let in.

My heart stretched out after her, tight and sick with fear and longing. As I lay in my tangle of filthy sheets, my broken body weeping blood, a ravenousness began to open up between my ribs, pressing outwards with such ferocious certainty that I was certain the bones must shatter. Pushing away the agony that shrieked through me when I moved, I tried to stand up.

'Come back!' I pleaded.

The sweat stood out upon my forehead. Bent over in a half-crouch, my arms clutched around my belly, I lurched towards the door. My legs were treacherous. The room tilted dangerously, spangled with glittering dust, and the sloped corners twisted and dipped.

'Please! I beg you, please, bring me back my child!'

At least I think that is what I said. I remember I felt the hot rush down my thighs, for I looked down then and thought the blood on the floor unnaturally red. In the centre of the puddle there was a thick slab like uncooked liver. It shone glossily against the rough boards. The silver dust in front of my eyes thickened to a blizzard. I could no longer see the door. I was quite cold. My hands floated up to my face, white and unfamiliar.

Then my legs failed me and I fell.

★ ★ ★

I remember little of the days that followed. I drifted in and out of wakefulness, lost in the bitter heat of fever and despair. It was only afterwards that I learned that the apothecary had disappeared. When I dredge my memory I believe I can hear doors slamming and voices raised in argument but the recollections are roughly sketched, unreliable.

In the two weeks before sitting-up, when I would at last be permitted to be bathed and to have my soiled bed linen changed, Mrs Black had Mary nurse me, bringing up poultices and herbal washes to clean and soothe my privities. She brought broths and cordials, as well as sweetmeats to tempt my appetite. I turned my face from her, towards the wall. In my stained and stinking bed, I clutched my misery around me like a blanket. I could not look out of the window, out towards the dome. Its haughtiness was intolerable to me now.

Instead, I kept my gaze fixed upon the flaking hole in the plaster, the crumble of dust and damp, the rotting strips of wood that stuck out from it as my womb clenched and cramped, folding itself back into its old shape. I hugged the pain in, letting it take me, although I could see no purpose in it. It would surely have been better for it to have been expelled along with the child. The first time Mrs Black came into the room and stood over me, she wore the black weeds of mourning. Her face was greyer than usual and dark shadows pressed down into the skin beneath her eyes. She walked carefully, her neck tall, and her face was sharp as folded paper.

I knew before she told me. The infant was dead. The words were hands around my throat, squeezing down. I shook my head, backwards and forwards, and breathed in shallow sips. Mrs Black's mouth was pressed so small there was barely room for the words to come out. No one was to blame, she said. There was nothing she or any other midwife could have done. The labour had been too protracted, the ordeal too great. She had done all she could, giving the infant a little softened butter and sugar to purge it and clear its breathing, even squirting a little warm wine up the nostrils, but to no avail. The child, fatally weakened by the travails of delivery, had survived only an hour or two.

I screamed then and wrenched myself up to grab at her arm. It was not true! She was wrong, I cried out, my fingers pressing into her flesh. She was wrong. I myself had seen the child alive, had heard it cry, felt the warmth of its mouth around my finger. It had looked well, strong. She was wrong. The child was not dead. It slept. She must go to it without delay, bring it to me so that I might suckle it. It would be hungry, in need of sustenance, in need of its mother. She was to bring it to me immediately.

The tip of Mrs Black's nose was white. She prised my fingers from her arm.

'No, girl,' she hissed, sinking to her knees beside me and gripping my wrist. Her face was so close to mine I could smell the gravy on her breath. 'Do not say such things. It is a common deception that the mind plays upon the mother, to think that all is well with her infant. Your child was too weak, its pulse too soft. It would never have lived. Be grateful instead that there was time to baptize it. It is with the Lord now. Surely there is comfort in that. I gave it the name of Grayson, after Mr Black.'

A boy. He was a boy. I shook my head, my breath coming unevenly. I wanted to sink my teeth into her hand, to see her face crumple in pain, to taste the crimson of her blood upon my tongue.

'Where is he?' I demanded, and my voice soared high and tight, fierce with desperation.

'Bring him to me now, do you hear me? I want my son!'

Mrs Black grimaced. Her lips were twisted and bloodless.

'Listen to me,' she hissed. 'You are not the first mother to have lost a child, nor shall you be the last. Infants die. Many die unsaved, before they can be accepted into the Kingdom of Heaven. You should thank God for His mercy. Your child has been taken from a world of suffering and sorrow to a place of inconceivable happiness. Cry if you must. It is a mother's fate to mourn the loss of a child. But it remains her duty to endure it.'

★　★　★

I did not cry, not then. All the tears, every drop of juice in my body, massed instead in my hardening breasts, bloating them with salty senseless milk until the straining skin threatened to split. My eyes were dry, hot and gritty. It hurt to keep them open but it hurt more to close them. When I closed them he was there. A child with eyes as dark and deep as a well, wrapped in his swaddling bands and sucking upon my finger as though he would pull the flesh from the bone. How I loathed that finger and its repugnant failure to nourish him, my own most precious child. No matter how much I studied it for signs that it had somehow changed, it remained no more than a finger, the oval nail ragged, the blistered burn at its tip hard now and flaking. No mark of my son was left upon it, not even the palest pink imprint of toothless gum on its underside. I crushed my hand between my thighs, the knuckles bent painfully inwards, so that I might be spared the sight of it. It did nothing to ease the pain.

As my breasts engorged with useless milk, I ground my knuckles into their bloated mass. My child had never set his forehead against their blue-veined swell, had never closed his mouth around the brown nipple that chafed, vigilant and futile, against the rough stuff of my nightgown. If I had only nursed him, allowed him to drink from me, who remained so resolutely, so brutally alive, my son would have lived. I knew it with bleak certainty. If I had not let him be taken from me, if I had somehow found the strength to drag myself downstairs, to close his dying mouth over my breast, he would have lived. But I had surrendered to the weakness of my own body, the heedless demands of my own flesh. Other mothers clasped their infants to their breast as lightning cleaved the very ground beneath their feet, curving themselves over, around, their ribs spread like umbrellas so that they might shield them from harm. Not I. Too craven to defy my pain, I had opened my arms and watched him fall.

Worse still, it was I who had caused it, who had made it happen. I had done everything in my power to kill my own child. It was not only the gladwin. Night after night I had lain in this very bed and wished for the creature to vanish, to unexist. I had wished it with all my heart, my thumbs squeezed in my palms, my brow furrowed with longing.

I had not thought anyone was listening.

NOTES FOR ANATOMIZING:

Follow <u>order of Mondino</u>, beginning with the abdominal cavity, thorax, head, brain & finally the extremities:

1. wax model to be made of specimen prior to dissection, representing <u>precise</u> damage to specimen's head & thorax
2. soft parts to be individually labelled with appropriate weights/measurement, each one set against their matching part in human infants of similar size & preserved by the injection of quicksilver — particular care to be exercised with brain, heart & lungs
3. skull & skeleton to be cleaned & assembled with hanging hook for display

<u>Critical dissimilarities</u> in canine & human anatomies:
— skull narrower & flatter in canines than humans — see comparative illustration in Vesalius Bk II showing human skull resting upon that of dog
— lower jaw of canines comprises <u>two</u> bones; humans <u>one</u>
— certain foramina described by Galen occur only in the canine skull
— do not stop now you do well think clearly look closer it will be there if you only look closer

— tongue considerably longer in quadrapeds than humans YES
— & in dogs, rectus abdominis extends considerably farther toward the neck
— Eustachio's *Opuscula Anatomica* (1564): comparative figures of ear ossicles & tensor timpani in humans & canines
— analysis of structure/form of canine versus human kidney — Realdo Columbo?

GOD BE IN MY EYES, & IN MY LOOKING

17

I do not know how many days passed before Mrs Black returned. I turned away as she entered the room but not before I had seen that she carried something in her arms. Though my heart leaped I closed my eyes, drawing my knees up to my milk-hard breasts. I would not be tricked into something as treacherous as hope.

'God in His mercy has sent us a child,' Mrs Black said briskly, holding the bundle out towards me. 'Its mother is unable to care for it. It is sickly and shall not live long but by nursing it you may prolong its life a little and do yourself a service besides. It is unwholesome to permit milk to collect in the breast. It will grow sour and impede your recovery.'

Hope died. Vultures both, loss and grief swooped and settled. I clamped my jaw, pressing my face hard against the pillow. Mrs Black sat beside me and pushed the child into my arms.

'Take it,' she instructed.

I shook my head again, more desperately, squeezing my eyes shut.

'No,' I insisted, twisting my face away. 'No. I — I can't.'

'Oh, but you can,' Mrs Black said, and her tone was almost cheerful. 'And you shall. If you are to remain here you must earn your keep. An ailing servant is a considerable expense. If you cannot help us to meet that expense, we must put you out into the street. Today. It is hard to imagine how you would manage alone and without lodging so soon after your confinement. Mary!'

Mary peered through the door, her mouth open. Her gaze slid uneasily around the room.

'Mary, you will remain here with Mrs Campling until she has fed the infant. Then you will return it to me. Is that understood?'

Mary lolled her head forward in a reluctant nod as Mrs Black deposited the child in her arms, touching its cheek very lightly with the back of her finger. Mary held it awkwardly, away from her body, as though it were hot from the oven.

'Call for me if there is any difficulty. As for you, Mrs Campling, it is high time you banished this morbid disease. This infant has reason enough for melancholy spirits without you infecting it with your own distemper. It would go badly for you if you were found to have turned your own milk.'

When Mrs Black's footsteps had faded, Mary darted over to me and, balancing the bundle in her lap, placed a cautious hand upon my hair. Her skirts brushed my cheek, filling my nostrils with their cooking smells. My throat clenched so painfully that I could not swallow.

'Lize sad,' she said sorrowfully. 'Poor Lize.'

'Go away.'

'Poor Dan'l,' she said. 'Dan'l sad so.'

I whimpered. If only she would stop, take the creature away. I could not breathe.

'Poor lil' bab',' crooned Mary. 'Bad hur', see? Bad bad hur'.'

With her tongue pressed between her gapped teeth, she began very carefully to unwrap the parcel on her lap. When it mewled my breasts tingled, oozing milk, and a single tear slipped down the slope of my cheek.

'Look, Lize,' Mary said softly. 'Poor lil' bab'.'

Miserably I opened my eyes.

'Oh, my — no!'

When I pushed it away the infant scrunched its face unhappily but it did not cry. Its head was covered with a thinly woven cap of hair and the skin on its cheeks was scaly and raw-looking. The ribs stood out on its chest like the cross-pieces of a half-finished boat. It was neither large nor small, fair nor dark. Its face was neither angelic nor brutish. It was merely an infant, indistinguishable from one hundred other infants. That was, until you saw that it had no hands. What it possessed by way of arms protruded from its trunk in two stumps that extended not quite to the elbow. Each stump bore an approximation of a thumb and a single flailing finger, blunt and stubby as the pollarded branches of a lime tree.

Carefully, Mary reached out a chewed finger to touch one stump. Then she lowered her face and kissed the shiny twist of skin that sealed it. For a moment the child was silent. Then it began to wail, a thin high shriek like wind in a chimney.

'Hung'y,' said Mary, stroking its head. She looked at me, her forehead creased with anxiety, and her eyes slid across each other until she seemed to be studying the tip of her own nose.

212

With her other hand she reached out to touch my hair, tucking loose strands behind my ear. 'Poor Lize.'

I said nothing. I wanted to shriek, to vomit, to throw the freakish thing across the room, but I could not move. My tongue was a wedge of wood in my mouth.

'Milk,' Mary urged. 'Wan' milk.'

Violently I shook my head, pushing the child away with the flat of my hands.

'No,' I whispered.

'Yes. Or bab' die. An' Lize go. Don' wan' Lize go.'

'No,' I whispered again. I rocked back and forth, my arms wrapped around my breasts. 'Please, Mary, no. Take it away. I — just take it away.'

'Can,' Mary whispered back. 'Mar' here. Mar' help.'

Very gently she pulled back the blanket, loosening my arms. Frozen with misery, the tears spilling on to the thin cotton of my nightgown, I let her do it. I clenched my eyes closed as she unbuttoned my chemise and pulled it from my shoulder, exposing my swollen breast. When the child whimpered, the brown disc of my nipple clenched obligingly, a drop of milk budding at its tip. My shoulders shook at the betrayal.

Mary bent down beside me and kissed me awkwardly on the ear. Then she pressed the child against my belly, her hand behind its head, guiding its mouth towards my breast. I felt the whisper of its tiny lips upon my skin, tasting, searching. Then, abruptly, ferociously, the

213

creature seized my nipple between its jaws and clamped down hard. The shock of pain and intimacy thrust a blade between my ribs, so that I cried out. Cramps tore at my womb. I wanted to scream and scream until the house shook with the pain that consumed me. I wanted to rip it from my flesh, to hurl the creature across the room. I could not endure its warmth, the pulse at the crown of its head, its urgent sucking mouth. I wanted to stifle it, to smash it, to stamp the life from it. I raised my hand. Mary caught it in hers. She squeezed my fingers hard.

'Is good,' she murmured. 'Lize good.'

The door opened. In that instant I saw plainly the grotesque tableau that we made, the desolate jilt, the idiot maid, the monstrous child, and the anguish tore through me like poison, shrivelling what was still soft inside me. I was lost. I placed my hand over the infant's nose and mouth and pressed.

'I'm right obliged to you, miss. For your kindness.'

The voice was rough, unfamiliar. Mary tugged away my hand, clamping it in hers. The child began to howl. A young woman stood in the doorway, ragged and dirty, with a torn apron and a scrap of a cap that barely covered her hair. Her lips were scabbed with sores. As she bobbed a clumsy curtsy from the doorway, something clinked in her apron pocket.

'May the Lord bless you all,' she rushed. 'Yes, indeed.'

Gathering up her skirts, she hastened into the room. She touched the screaming infant briefly

214

upon the shoulder with one blackened finger and hurried out again, her hand clutched tightly around her pocket. The stairs clattered, the front door slammed. Gently Mary lifted the child and latched it to the other breast. This time, when its mouth closed around the nipple, I felt nothing at all.

My son, despise not the chastening of the
LORD; neither be weary of his correction: For
whom the LORD loveth he correcteth; even as
a father the son in whom he delighteth. Happy
is the man that findeth wisdom, & the man
that getteth understanding. For the merchandise of it is better than the merchandise of
silver, & the gain thereof than fine gold.

There is no such thing as a failed example,
only new information & fresh insight

Thomas Sydenham

ALL WICKEDNESS IS
BUT LITTLE TO THE
WICKEDNESS
OF A WOMAN

18

I nursed the armless infant for close to a month before it died.

Although I never ceased to dread the first fierce tug of its mouth upon my breast, the treacherous surge of milk which sent a shock through my belly, there was all the same a sombreness in the child's round black eyes that eased my hostility towards it. It never smiled. Nor did it grow distressed when I wept, pushing it from my lap. Instead, it gazed at me without blinking, as though it knew already all the inexpressible horrors of the world. Its acceptance of the inevitability of anguish was a kind of sympathy. It knew it would not live long. And so I let it suckle, wrapping my misery about us both like a shawl.

The sultry weather did not break. A breathless glittering stillness shimmered like shallow water across the city. Mrs Black burned perfume in the main rooms of the house and scattered lavender along the skirtings, but nothing could keep the stench out. Beneath its slate roof the garret stewed, releasing a foul odour of rats and drying mould. The lice rampaged through clothes and bedding. Mary lay on her back, her mouth open and her arms outstretched, her hair dark with sweat. The heat came off her like a warming bottle.

After several weeks, at the end of my lying-in,

Mrs Black had me rise. Short-tempered and sour herself in the heat, my low spirits infuriated her. She claimed I was sick from contrariness and insisted upon all kinds of violent purges to restore me to myself. If she discovered me seated, she would have me climb up and down the stairs to open the bowel and encourage my blood to circulate. She cupped me, drawing out the air until I thought the glasses would explode against my flesh, and scarifying the skin of my back with a sharp blade in a series of inch-long cuts like those made upon a loin of pork for roasting. I never cried out. Punishment or cure, the pain was the only part of me I was sure of.

It was after one such bleeding, as I pulled myself shakily up the stairs towards the garret, that I saw the ragged woman again. Seized by an attack of giddiness, I had paused, leaning against the wall, to catch my breath. She did not see me for she never looked up. Instead, she backed out of the apothecary's study, her head lowered, her hand once more closed around her pocket. The ribbons of her cap were lank and stringy, as if she had chewed them. I thought of the infant then. It had been fretful that morning, unwilling to latch on. Mad with impatience, I had slapped it. It had stared at me then, its black eyes round and expressionless, but it had not cried. I had watched as a scarlet print bloomed upon its back and the stab of grief had been so sharp and sudden I had gasped out loud.

'Thank you, good sirs,' she cringed. 'Bless you both. May the Heavens smile upon you for your kindness.'

The door to the study closed with a click. Immediately the woman dug into her pocket. I saw several coins glint upon her palm as she raised them to her lips and kissed them. She jumped when Mrs Black called out from the hallway. Swiftly she raised her skirt and, pushing the money into a cloth bag she had hidden beneath it, she scuttled downstairs.

Before I might move the study door opened once more. A gentleman I had never seen before stood on the landing, as glossy and sleek as a fine horse. His fashionable wig was plump and freshly powdered and lolled indolently against the richly decorated stuff of his coat. Under one arm he carried a velvety-edged hat from which a magnificent feather bloomed. His stockings were as white as a thief's.

The visitor extended a meaty hand and gave my master's hand a perfunctory shake before turning to leave. I caught a glimpse of snowy-white neckcloth secured with a pearl pin and, above it, the most commonplace face I had ever seen, as round and red and as marked with pocks as a strawberry. A butcher's face, perhaps, or a knife-grinder's, roughened by work and coarse suggestions and creased, at this moment, with ill temper.

'It is hardly your place, sir, to tell me to whom I may or may not extend my generosity,' the butcher said tightly.

'On the contrary,' my master muttered. 'I consider it my duty to defend your purse against every last hard-luck story in the parish.'

'What then of yours? You would not deem

your case among that number?'

The mark on my master's cheek darkened.

'If you had even half so much wit as effrontery, sir,' he hissed, 'I might consider you a worthy patron. As it is — '

The butcher was silent for a moment, his mouth working.

'For God's sake, man,' he said at last. 'Let us not quarrel. But we must have results, do you not understand that? I have no intention of appearing a fool.'

'With respect, sir, there may be little I can do in that particular. Only a fool could imagine that the meaning of God's mysteries may be plucked from a tree like an apple!' Mr Black banged the door jamb with his fist. 'I am a man of science, sir, not one of your plaguey mechanical monkeys. You cannot turn a key in my back and have me dance for the amusement of your damned associates.'

'Is that so? But you would make a monkey of me, all the same? Good day to you, sir. I shall see myself out.'

The butcher's footsteps echoed in the stairwell. The master remained where he was, his breathing forced and loud, his fist still clenched against the door jamb. Dizzy with standing, I tried to creep away. A board creaked. The master looked up. In the windowless gloom his dark cheek was an absence, his eyes gleaming above half a face. I pressed myself into the wall, wrapping the shadows about me.

'Do not think you shall not be punished,' he hissed. 'Look at you, all impudence, careless of the injury you inflict. But, let me assure you, a handsome face is no more recompense for a treacherous soul than a cloth laid over a cesspit. You are still quite rotten. I can smell the stink on you from here.'

His half-face loomed towards me, his hands clenched. I smelled his burnt breath. Ducking beneath his raised arm, I fled.

* * *

A little before dark that afternoon, the infant died. When they told me I wept like a child. Mary lay next to me, her tears mingling with mine, her arms around my neck. I clung to her as an infant monkey clings to its mother, my fingers wound in her hair. They say that, by nourishing a child with the milk of her breasts, a wet-nurse passes on the fundamentals of her nature to the infant she suckles. My mother had often advised those of her patients wealthy enough to have one that care should be taken to avoid a nurse of a crude or violent temperament. What then of a nurse mired in sin?

There was no coffin for the child when its body was fetched away. It was wrapped in waxed paper, like a dead fish. If it had had a name I never knew it. Now, whenever I think of it, for all that it was assuredly a girl, I think of it as Daniel.

Hewlitt & Bain, Solicitors at Law, Newcastle

Dear Sir,

We acknowledge receipt of your letter, dated July 11th 1719, & have, as you asked, made your request of our client.

However, we regret to inform you that he is prepared to countenance no alteration to the contract currently in place. While he appreciates the difficulties presented to you by such an arrangement, he would wish to stress that his own situation is equally problematic, given the delicate negotiations surrounding the impending marriage of his son.

Since the announcement of said marriage, a number of threats to my client's reputation & property have already been received from the mother of the ward, Eliza Tally. While these are hardly lawful, my client would prefer that they be dealt with privately & with discretion & he asks that you may oblige him with your continued tact & good judgement in this matter. He has therefore required us to extend the terms of the existing agreement between yourselves for a further twenty-four months, with an option to prolong the term further as necessary. Given the absolute necessity of preventing any attempt at return to the village of her birth, we would require in addition that you intercept any correspondence written by, or on behalf of, the mother & return it to our office, so that we may deal with it in the most appropriate manner.

My client recognizes that these requirements run counter to your personal wishes &, in acknowledgement of his gratitude for your cooperation, has instructed me to inform you that a single payment of thirty guineas will be dispatched to you upon receipt by ourselves of the enclosed papers. We would therefore ask you to sign & return them to our offices at your earliest convenience.

I am, Sir, your humble Servant &c.

NICHOLAS HEWLITT

19

It was the hottest summer anyone could remember, soupy nights spilling into thick, breathless days. The city rotted in its skin. At Swan-street the windows swelled in their frames until they could no longer be opened and the shut-up house was stifling, its air solid with cesspits and the reek of rotting food. The smell of it sickened me. When the mistress locked us into the garret at night the scrape of the key turning in the lock screeched against my spine. The master remained in his room, seldom venturing out, but the malignity of him seeped into the breathless half-light, making shapes of every shadow. The darkness clung to me as I walked up and down the stairs, insinuating itself like tobacco smoke into my hair, my clothes, and down into the impossible void I buried in the still-slack skin of my belly. Each closed room sucked at me like a physician's cup, draining me of blood. I lashed out at Mary at the least provocation, inflamed by a rage that frightened us both. As for Mrs Black, I could no longer stand to look at her. The sight of her sewed-up darn of a mouth was sufficient to flood me with an antipathy so strong that it clamped my jaw and clenched my hands into teeth-white fists.

I had to get out. When I pressed the grocer's boy, who was hardly a boy at all but a loquacious man of considerable years and very few teeth, he shrugged.

'There's several households 'tween here and Lombard-street asked me if I knows of anyone,' he assured me. 'There's footmen aplenty but it seems there's a shortage of your kind, like, the maid-of-all-work not too proud to do the rough work. It's Change-alley, see. A hundred new schemes every day and more comin'. They say there's a better chance of winning a fortune at Change-alley than there is at the Guildhall.'

'Change-alley?'

'Stocks market. Look round yer. The Lottery's one thing. But now they's found out the secret of how to turn paper into money a maid with a good character can make five, six pound a year.'

Before he left the grocer's boy gave me the names of two families and promised to put in a word for me with both on his next delivery. All day long the soles of my feet itched. Several times as I stood at the sink, a pile of muddy potatoes before me, I dropped my knife and ran up into the lane, certain I had seen his lopsided gait in the tangle of feet that passed the window. Each time I returned to the kitchen disappointed, the dim room seemed darker and more stifling than before. When Mrs Black came to the kitchen a little before supper to rebuke me for my extravagance with water, I could contain myself no longer. I knew myself imprudent, even foolish, but the promise of liberty intoxicated me. I wished, I informed her, to tender my notice. I thought a period of two weeks sufficient for Mrs Black to find a replacement. Mrs Black considered me for several moments, her white lips pressed together, before she replied.

'It is quite out of the question,' she said, her voice clipped.

I gasped, a wild laugh of a cough that caught in my throat.

'Excuse me but I don't think — '

'I have said it is out of the question. That is the end of it.'

She turned to leave. I wanted to seize her by her vile white ears, to shake her until her eyes rolled from the white casket of her skull.

'You may think you can stop me but you cannot!' I cried. 'Yours is not the only household in London.'

Very slowly Mrs Black turned back. Her white nostrils stretched tight.

'Listen to me, girl, and hold your tongue. I have no more wish to keep you than you do to stay. But stay you shall. Blame your mother, if you wish, for it is her insistence that keeps you here. The deal is struck and there can be no reversing it. We must endure each other for as long as is required.'

'I don't believe you,' I said defiantly, clasping my hands to keep them steady. 'My mother would not wish me held prisoner.'

'You waste my time with such foolishness. You are not free to leave and that is the end of it. Should you be imprudent enough to attempt such a thing, be warned: we shall find you out. There is nowhere in this city you might hide from those who require you here. Besides, what employer would offer you a position when appraised by a well-wisher of your partiality to thievery and whoring? I fear, Mrs Campling, that, though neither of us wish it, you shall remain here. And in the meantime, and so that something may be made of you, it is agreed that I shall withhold your pay until that time is complete. It is to be hoped that such a measure may prove effective in subduing your insolence.'

'You cannot do that! That money is mine, by law!'

'I find the law seldom troubles itself with people of your sort.' She leaned close to me, her eyes cold. 'Know this: what you wish for is not of the least consequence. You are here because others will it. And you shall remain here until they will it no longer. There is no more to be said on the matter.'

When she was gone I leaned back against the wall, unclenching my hands and holding them out before me as though they belonged to somebody else. The nail beds gleamed yellow-white in the gloom.

Until they will it no longer.

They. But who were they, these others? My mother? *It is her insistence that keeps you here.* I pressed my fingers as hard as I could against my forehead, leaning into the powerful ache in my temples. What manner of a deal had my mother struck to keep me a prisoner here, against my will? And with whom? She had already sold me once and proven that she would do anything for money. But not this, surely? She had taken money from the Campling boy's father, it was true, but had she not believed it to be for my

227

own good? Perhaps she thought that, by keeping me here, she guaranteed my safety. She might think that a girl without reputation would not find another position and, cast out on to the street, might easily starve. She could not know that London's appetite for servants had grown voracious. Nor could she have the slightest notion of the nature of this place. She could not know the malevolence that quivered and turned in the air of the house, as dust turns in a beam of sunlight. If only she knew she would not want me held here, against my will. Surely she could not want that. She was my mother.

Upstairs the front door slammed. I swallowed a blade of dread so sharp that it seemed to pierce my gullet. I would never escape. I would grow old here, forced to submit, meekly and without protest, to the tyranny of murderers, until the shadows extinguished my spirits and shrivelled my hair to dust. All my life, made to swallow the bitter bile of hatred that rose in my throat until it rotted me from the inside out.

I could not do it.

★   ★   ★

That afternoon the air in the kitchen was liquid with heat and the floor sweated a fatty skin that tugged at the soles of my feet. Mary slumped in the bentwood chair, scratching at herself incessantly. I felt like I was drowning. Seizing the buckets, I shouted at her to rouse herself.

'We are going for water.'

Mary shook her head, her fat fingertips tearing

228

at the crevices of her armpits.

'No pipe.'

She was right, of course. During the hot weather the turn-cock had as good as disappeared, and what water there was came out at a dribble for less time than it took for the bells to sound out two quarter hours.

'We aren't going to the stand-pipe. We're going to the river.'

Mary gaped at me. In all the time I had been at Swan-street I had never ventured as far as the river, though it was hardly four streets away. Truth to tell, I was afraid of it. It was said that unwary children were stolen from the wharfs and taken to foreign lands as slaves. Certainly the violent and blasphemous abuse of the watermen, known to city dwellers as water-language, was notorious. Edgar had even declared the stream cursed, claiming that no one who had ever fallen into its fiendish depths had ever been seen again. Though I knew better than to believe him, the river oozed black and oily through the cracks in my imagination, its sinuous churn shifting to expose a brief gleam of fleshless bones and teeth before it rolled them up and hastened them away to the sea.

'They say it's clean enough,' I snapped. 'Now, let's go.'

I pushed Mary in front of me as we hurried up the kitchen steps towards the lane. The urge to get out drove all other considerations from my head. In my haste I almost fell over a hog nosing lazily in amongst a heap of rotting rubbish. I kicked out at it and it grunted irritably and ambled away. The lanes were narrow and dark with dust and shadow, the torn strip of white sky between the houses slung about with the rusting laundry of shop signs. The air barely stirred. As the slope steepened there was a powerful sea-stink of mud and rotting fish.

There was a press of warehouses and then, beyond them, a shifting shimmer of light and movement. I pushed forward, towards the quayside, until I stood at the edge of a narrow jetty, its grey planks curved and cracked by the sun. And yet even then I could barely see the river beneath its burden of skiffs, wherries, sailing barges and water taxis of every size and description, hacking at the hidden stream with a barrage of oars. It was a riotous mass of green and red and tarnished gilt. Barges were garlanded with swags and flowers. The noise rose up from it as relentlessly as the stench, the air crammed with scurrilities as putrid as the slicks of mud and black weed that greased the struts of every quay.

Along the length of the shore, for as far as I could see, passengers yelled and signalled conveyances to attend them at scores of stairs, landing stages and pontoons. Not twenty yards from where I stood, a swarm of men as black as ants unloaded a coal barge so heavily weighed down by its cargo that the scrolled lettering upon its flank was half-buried in the brown murk of the river water. A villainous-looking child, so black with dirt it might have been its own shadow, darted between the coalmen's legs, pouncing upon dropped lumps which it wrapped

230

in the tails of its ragged shirt.

I let the noise fill me, surrendering to its authority. Then someone behind me called and pointed. I turned, following their finger, to look downstream in the direction of the bridge. I blinked, hardly able to make sense of what I saw. For there, straddling the river as though it were no more than a muddy puddle, was not a simple crossing but a full and shameless street of houses, handsome elegant dwellings several storeys high, their windows throwing back the fire of the sun in a glitter of light, the columns which supported them braced like mighty thighs against the brown roar of the tide.

London Bridge is broken down, broken down, broken down. London Bridge is broken down, my fair lady. Bricks and mortar will not stay . . .
The children in the alley sometimes chanted the song, tossing stones into the mud, so close, sometimes, that I feared for the window. Now I thought of my long-dead forebears who had for many centuries believed that the only way to placate an angry river, and to safeguard the bridge set across it in defiance of its will, was to offer up to it a child as a sacrifice. I had a sudden unwelcome memory of a tiny mouth, a bead of flesh at the bow of its upper lip, and my nipple stiffened, sending a jolt through my breast. Another year. My stomach flipped. Tightening my fingers around the handles of my pails, I turned away.

It was only then that I noticed Mary was gone. Hastily I jostled a path through the throng, calling out her name, scanning the crowd for her distinctive face. There were too many people. I could make out only a chaos of cloth, wigs and hats and bundles shifting and changing shape, forming nothing. As I stretched on to my tiptoes a man in a rusty coat thrust a handbill into my face. It was covered in close writing with some kind of woodcut at the bottom, smudgy with ink.

'Sign of the Fountain by Shoe-lane till Sat'dy,' he hissed. 'Make yer eyes pop, it will. Y'ain't niver seen nothin' like the Hedgehog Boy. Bristles hard as horn.'

'Did you see a girl come past here, an idiot girl, brown stomacher — ?'

'Only sixpence,' he added encouragingly. 'Be chargin' a shillin' for this anyplace else.'

He waved the handbill in front of my face. I glimpsed a smudged picture of a boy covered all over in spines before the man slid the handbill into my pail.

'For the love of God!' I snapped, and I banged my pails hard against his shins. He yelped like a dog as I pushed past him. The crowd was thicker now, more sluggish, as folk stopped to look about them or to exchange pleasantries. Their indolence infuriated me. My pails caught on legs, on barrows. I could barely move my arms.

And then I saw her. She stood amongst a cluster of people before a low stage decked out with banners and gay strings of bunting upon which a monkey and a clown gallivanted. While the clown was a regular Jack Pudding, sweating profusely in his heavy costume with its donkey's ears and sawing away at his fiddle, the monkey swaggered in a red velvet cloak and a hat with an

232

elaborate plume, a clay pipe held aloft in one tiny hand. The joke was that, each time the clown contrived to draw something resembling a tune from the instrument, the monkey would leap up and settle itself upon the strings, leaning back on the bridge like a gentleman in a coffee-house. Holding its pipe to its lips, it would blow out mouthfuls of smoke with great contentment. Mary gazed at it enchanted, her hands pressed over her mouth like a lid to keep the laughter in. I pushed my way through.

'How dare you bolt like that?' I rebuked her. 'Do you want to be stolen?'

Mary nodded happily, intent upon the stage. A thread of spittle spooled from her mouth. I scowled at her. In her own idiot way she would always be free.

'Monk'!' she exclaimed, nudging me in the ribs. 'See, Lize? Monk'!'

On the stage the monkey leaped on to the clown's head, snatching the bow from his hand so that it might beat him about his ass's ears. The clown tried to swipe at the creature with his fiddle, but the monkey was too quick for him and the clown succeeded only in delivering a sharp blow to his own forehead. Mary's eyes bulged with held-in delight as the crowd roared their approval.

'Mary!' I protested angrily, tugging at her sleeve, but she only nodded impatiently and strained towards the stage where the clown was somersaulting in frantic circles, his arms over his head as he tried to escape the monkey's hailstorm of blows. It did him no good.

Dropping the bow, the monkey darted over a rope to seize the clown by the ears, tying them neatly together so that his arms were imprisoned. The crowd shrieked with laughter and Mary shivered, every inch of her stretched tight with pleasure. As she squeaked and craned for a better view, she slipped her arm through mine, and I felt my anger cool to a sort of exasperated tenderness. At least she did not want to go home.

Reluctantly I allowed my attention to be drawn to the stage where the clown ran in circles, his arms still trapped above his head, begging the audience to come to his rescue in rhyming couplets of increasing coarseness. The audience cheered and stamped but it served the clown no purpose. The monkey, matching Mr Punch in his violent use of any weapon that might come to hand, trounced him roundly at every turn and finally chased him clean off the back of the stage. There was a cry, a crash, and then silence. The little creature straightened its cloak, smoothed its whiskers and set its fiddlestick behind its ear. Then, sweeping off its plumed hat, it effected a deep bow. Mary squealed and clapped, her hands slapping together like fish. With my fingers in my mouth I whistled.

As the audience applauded an extravagantly dressed gentleman ascended the platform. Beneath a cape secured at the throat by a chain of large golden links he wore a lace collar and breeches decorated with shiny buttons and a mass of silken tassels. His head was crowned with a wide, soft-brimmed hat and from his jewelled and buckled belt there hung a long sword, its hilt the head of an exotic bird. With all the authority of an Admiral upon the prow of his ship, he strode to the front of the platform and gazed down upon his audience, his hands wide. Behind him the monkey clambered up to his tightrope and proceeded to peg out a series of papers, most of them crusted with seals.

'Lords, ladies and gentlemen,' the gentleman sang out from beneath his curled moustache. 'I, Aengus O'Reilly, favoured physician to the Grand Duke of Tuscany, declare myself your true and faithful servant.'

There was a hum of chatter from the audience. Several observers, mostly fish fags recalling their duties at the nearby market, began to drift away.

'Beautiful ladies,' O'Reilly called out, 'take heed of my Elixir Vitae! In no more than three doses this unparalleled preparation restores in full the lost bloom of girlhood and stirs the womb again to fruitfulness. Not to mention fastening loose teeth to a miracle. Why, I have a certification here from the Tsarina of Muscovy herself to testify to its consummate efficacy.'

The quack flung his arm behind him to gesture at one of the papers that the monkey had put up. The fishwives muttered and scoffed but they paused all the same, their eyes narrow beneath their battered hats.

'As for you gentlemen, pray do not think this reason to abandon me. I have here also a sovereign remedy of extraordinary virtue, ground from no less than sixty ingredients and so powerful that it can in a single draught undo the damage of the Devil's own vice. If any here have anchored in strange harbour and fear themselves corrupted, let them come to me. And ladies, listen well, for it cherishes up the drooping spirits of a married man and does quicken them again just as a rose that receives the summer's dew.'

At this the mountebank winked hugely and a rumbling of laughter and muttering broke out over the crowd. The mountebank pressed home his advantage.

'Ladies and gentlemen,' he gasped, and the tears seemed almost to stand in his eyes, 'contained in these two phials are medicines of such force and vigour that taken together they might revive the very Dead. Were that not a mystery set aside for God. Their true value is two guineas but I seek profit in the next life, not this one. For you, a shilling each. May Heaven and all its angels smile upon you.'

The audience pressed up against the rickety stage, watching as the first customers fumbled for coins. Mary tugged at my hand.

'Home,' she mumbled, and she ran an anxious finger over her palm. It sparkled with sweat, the red welt across it fat as a lip. I shook my head. Not yet.

'Water,' I said firmly.

As we turned around Mary gave forth a yelp. A man stood before us, a startled smile upon his face. It was a moment before I recognized him as the butcher-faced visitor to Swan-street, Mr

Jewkes. To my astonishment, he seized Mary's hand.

'Mary!' he exclaimed. Seeds of sweat stood out upon his strawberry face. 'There you are, Mary. Off for water, are you? Buckets'll be fearful heavy in this weather, I don't wonder.' He patted her hand awkwardly, his eyes upon the ground. 'It's been some weeks, I know. Forgive me. It is only that — well, with things as they are — '

Snatching up her hand, he placed a kiss upon the tips of her fingers before thrusting his own deep into the pockets of his coat. Mary blinked at him, her mouth loose as, with the same rough haste, he took up her hand once more and pressed something into the palm, folding her fingers over it.

'A little something,' he muttered with a shrug. His ears burned crimson. 'Goodbye, my dear. I shall come again when I can. Till then be a good girl and obey your mistress.'

He had hardly rounded the corner before I had seized upon her hand in my turn and opened her fingers. Inside there was a shiny half-crown.

'What in the name of the Devil is that for?' I cried, snatching the coin from her hand and biting upon it to see if it were real. Mary did not protest. Instead, she bent slowly over and took the smeared handbill from my pail, gaping at the picture upon it. I ripped the paper from her hand, throwing it to the ground. My lips tasted of money.

'Why, Mary?' I demanded, thrusting the coin in her face. 'Why the money? Bewitched by the

237

sheer loveliness of your face, is he?'

The cruel words were out of my mouth before I could stop them. There was something so infuriating about Mary's slowness, her half-witted incuriosity. It made you want to hurt her, to slap her cheek or take her soft wrist in your hands and twist the skin between them until she cried out. Mary said nothing. Instead, she squatted down to pick up the discarded bill, smoothing it out and staring at it. I wanted to shake her.

'Well?' I shouted.

'Like Mar',' she said simply. 'Kiss Mar'. Kind.'

'You stupid little bawd!' I screamed, seizing her by the shoulders. 'You let him touch you?'

Mary blinked at me in astonishment and slid the bill into her apron pocket.

'Kind,' she repeated, more hesitantly this time. 'Kiss Mar'.'

'You let him kiss you for money? You addle-headed trull, what else do you let him do? This is half a crown, for pity's sake! A man expects more than a few kisses for half a crown. So what does he do to you, Mary? Just what do you let him do?'

Mary shook her head, backing away from me.

'He like Mar',' she muttered again. 'Kind.'

'Are you so soft in the head that you think that a kindness? Is that what he tells you when he hoists your skirt, when he thrusts himself between your legs? That he is being kind? Mary, what the — are you such a mooncalf that you would let him make a whore of you and not even know it?'

238

Mary raised her head. The set of her jaw was mutinous, her pink eyes bright with tears and refusal.

'Kind,' she whispered, and then, seizing up her buckets, she fled up the alley towards home.

'You stupid little — ' I called after her. 'Well, don't come crying to me when you find yourself Frenchified half to death with a hole where your nose should be!'

She was gone. My heart pounded, my skin liquid in the heat. I could not rid my head of the image of the butcher as he ripped at Mary's petticoats, at his own breeches. I stamped after her.

At the end of the lane I saw the top of her cap as she ran down the kitchen steps. The house looked flat and ordinary from here, a house with a door and windows like any other, no different from its neighbours. A high note rang against the side of my pail, then another. Then a sharp sting like a wasp upon my elbow. I looked up. Across the lane two boys lurked at the entrance to a shadowed alley, their fists full of pebbles. When they saw me they cackled and darted away. I bent down and lifted the pails. They were light and, apart from two tiny stones, quite empty.

I had forgotten all about the water.

Yet another conversation with the boorish Jewkes in which I am certain he had not the faintest notion of what it was I said. I could swear he has never even heard of Descartes, let alone grasped the fundamentals of his opinions. How such a dullard has contrived to become so very rich is both a mystery & a gross injustice

All the same the frustrations of our exchange have left me in a pensive mood & it occurs to me even as I write that, while the Cartesian assertion that neither brain nor soul are required to manage the 'machine' or animate body cannot possibly be true of Christians, the same is not necessarily true of <u>savages & idiots</u>

Surely, since imagination & memory are organs with specific functions equivalent to heart & liver, an idiot whose body conforms to the involuntary facilities of breathing, heart beat, digestion &c. must also be subject to the involuntary functions of imagination & memory

What is more, without the intercession of the rational mind (explaining away the causes of fear, passion &c) or the godly soul (providing protection from the excesses of imagination) how significantly are the effects of imagination increased?

Oh God, oh my dear & merciful God.

In the idiot may be found <u>the most formidable imagination of all</u>

20

That night I dreamed of my mother. It was an uneasy dream, filled with objects I knew to be ordinary but which I was unable to identify. It was not the cottage I dreamed of but some other place, a place which, just as the other aspects of the dream, was at once familiar and quite foreign. In this place I reached out to my mother, trying to touch her, to strike her or embrace her or perhaps both, but however much I extended my hands, she was always beyond my reach. She wore upon her belt an iron key the size of a man's hand which she played with, stroking it tenderly like a cat, and, when she turned to smile at me, she had no face. When I woke, a spiteful headache smeared across the underside of my skull, I remembered that part, though the other particulars of the dream eluded me. I told myself it was her due punishment, that I could no longer remember what she looked like.

Until they will it no longer.

All that day, I toiled up and down the dark stairs, my shoulders screaming with the weight of water and of coal. In the relentless heat the house was more oppressive than ever and, in each room I entered, the sashes of every window set bars against the white sky. I banged the mop against the floor until my palms blistered, defying Mrs Black to punish me for making too

241

much of a disturbance. Mary was with the apothecary again, the third time in a week. I had a sudden memory of Mr Jewkes, his greedy butcher's face leering at her, the sticky coin forced into her hand. Could it be that — ? I pushed the thought away but it lingered, insinuating itself beneath my scalp between those relentless six words until I was obliged to kick over the fire irons with a startling clatter.

We took our dinner in silence. Mary ate with a dogged determination, stuffing wads of bread into her mouth which she chewed in circular, open-mouthed motions, like a cow. Again I saw the goatish Mr Jewkes, one hand clamped upon her shoulder, the other tugging at the buttons of his fly. Mary blinked when I slammed my fist upon the table and pressed another mass of bread into her mouth. So my mother had struck a deal. It mattered not at all whether she had intended it for her own advantage or mine. What mattered was that she unstrike it.

Pushing away my plate, I rose from the table, my legs suddenly restless. I would send my mother a letter. In that letter I would inform her that, although I understood that she had sought to safeguard my position through the terms of her arrangement, I wanted no part of it. On the contrary, I now wished to take up employment elsewhere, with immediate effect. I trusted that she would therefore relinquish any further claims upon my future at Swan-street and return any outstanding monies owing to the requisite parties. In return I would pledge her a regular stipend from my own pay, a pension for my freedom. As much as I begrudged such an assurance, I was sage enough to know an appeal to her good nature would hardly be encouragement enough.

★ ★ ★

Mrs Black's stringent government of household provisions extended even to the master's paper and ink powder, which she kept in the tea cabinet and gave out only in careful rations. It was fortunate for me that Edgar was a poor copyist and a worse shot. I had to wait only a matter of days before I was able to retrieve a balled-up piece of paper from the kitchen range, its edges only a little charred. After supper that night, as Mary dozed in the bentwood chair, I took the discarded paper from my pocket and smoothed it out on the table, folding Edgar's attempted calligraphy and slicing it away with the boning knife. A stub of pencil was kept in the drawer of the kitchen dresser so that Mrs Black might make notes of provisions required or jot a new recipe in the book she kept on the shelf over the mantel. I took it out and licked it, my bottom lip caught between my teeth.

I had had little opportunity to practise my letters. Slowly and with considerable effort I pressed my hand against the page. The rushlight burned down until it was no more than a greasy smear in the cup, more smoke than light, and still I pored over the paper. I was so intent upon my business that I did not hear Edgar until he slammed the door, filling the kitchen with the stale port and tobacco stink of taverns. Hurriedly I tried to smuggle the paper into my apron pocket but Edgar was too quick for me. Seizing my arm, he twisted it behind my back, extracting the paper from between my fingers. The noise roused Mary, who startled up from her chair, her hands flapping like a frightened hen.

'Well, well,' he slurred. 'How interesting. A rustic attempting the rudiments of penmanship? With whom can she possibly be corresponding?'

I made a grab for the paper but Edgar extended his arm upwards out of my reach and fluttered it above my head.

'Patience, you cunning little doxie, patience.'

Turning his shoulders away from me, he tilted the paper towards the light of the fire and studied it. Again I snatched for it but again he twisted out of reach. Mary whimpered.

'Give that back!' I cried.

Edgar did not reply. Instead he considered the paper a little longer. Then he turned to face me, the page extended with a flourish between his fingers.

'Well, well,' he said again as I seized the paper and thrust it furiously into my pocket. He smirked. Taking hold of a chair with the careful precision of intoxication, he sat, patting the seat of mine in invitation. I glowered.

'Please yourself,' he shrugged, regarding me. Then, to my confusion, he began to laugh, his hand over his mouth like a girl.

'What?' I demanded, crossing my arms. 'What is it you find so droll?'

Edgar opened his mouth. Then he closed it

again, shaking his head and clutching his soft belly with amusement. Beside me Mary reached out to squeeze my arm. I shook her off angrily.

'What?'

'It is — it is nothing. It is only that — well, you must confess it is amusing. The idea that your toothless crone of a mother of all people is responsible for your position here. It is — well, you must admit, it is something of an absurdity. I mean, where do you imagine she would get that kind of money?'

Edgar chuckled again. I hesitated.

'What the Devil do you know about it, anyway?' I asked sullenly.

'More than you, it would appear.'

I said nothing but only stared at the floor.

'I happen to know, for example, that our esteemed master receives a stipend to keep you here. A considerable amount, too. And that, unless she is recently married into the upper ranks of gentry, it most certainly does not come from your mother.'

'You expect me to believe that the master told you this himself? It is no more than hearsay, idle gossip.'

'Doubtless there is all manner of that kind of talk about you, sluttish little jade that you are. But in this case you are mistaken. An apprentice must keep a close eye on all aspects of his master's affairs, if he means to profit from the arrangement, and have at least as firm a grasp of the finances of his business as the master does himself. For as long as his patron requires you here, it would appear that you, dear Eliza, are

245

one of the master's few assets.'

'His patron?'

'I use the term loosely. Your patron perhaps. The gentleman who pays to keep you here. And pay he does, handsomely. Why so shocked? A girl in your unhappy predicament should be grateful that Mr Black is in no position to negotiate.'

I stared at Edgar. My mouth was dry.

'They cannot make me stay,' I protested. 'There are many households in London that require servants. I can leave whenever I choose.'

'Without a character? I hardly think so. And even if you found an employer fool enough to take you without recommendation, you think he would not find you? The apothecary is a dolt, it's true, but not so much of a dolt that he might readily surrender his golden goose. If you try to leave he will put advertisements in every newspaper and coffee-house in town until he finds you. And should your patron come to hear of your exploits — well!' He chuckled, pinching my cheek hard. 'Who knows what reward might be tendered then for your most unfortunate demise?'

★　★　★

The following day I was dispatched once more to Islington. It was the first time the mistress had sent me there since — well, certainly, it had been many weeks. Mrs Black sat stiffly on the shop's high three-legged stool, the leather-bound ledger of accounts open on the counter before her, listing her requirements as she copied the details of the week's business into the great brown book. Her nails clicked insistently against the worn wooden beads of the abacus.

There was a knock at the door, two men in velveteen coats, one pushing a handcart lined with straw. Mrs Black let them in, nodding towards the barometer that hung upon the wall opposite the hall mirror. As his companion lifted it from its nail, the smaller one appraised me with the cool efficiency of a coffin-maker.

'What the Devil are you staring at?' Mrs Black snapped harshly. It was a moment before I understood that the rebuke was directed at me.

Muttering, I ducked my head and slouched downstairs. Mary was with the apothecary again and the linnet hunched listlessly on its perch, its feathers dull and mothy. For some moments I stood motionless in the gloomy silence, staring into the earth-crumbed depths of my basket. Then, with a great effort of will, I snatched it up and flung open the door, taking the kitchen steps two at a time. For weeks now, pickled in the bricked-up stink of Swan-street, I had longed for such a task, longed to breathe in the vast bowl of the sky, to feel the jostle of the streets stretching my loose nerve-strings and quickening the flow of my blood. Now, as I toiled up the narrow lane, the heat pressed down on me, drawing the vigour from my body like a poultice. My legs dragged, heavy and disobliging. The house at Swan-street seemed to pull at me, sucking me back, its stale breath hot on my neck. Several times I stopped, twisting around abruptly to scan the crowd for

247

someone who might be following me. *Unfortunate demise. Unfortunate demise.* The words clicked across my skull, precise as an abacus.

The wooded glades of Islington were lush and airless, their silence too conducive to reflection. I gathered the required plants as quickly as I could and I hastened back to the city. The sky was a hot white glare, as though the sun had infused every part of it, and the sweat greased my bodice and slicked my forehead, stinging my eyes. At Butcher-hall-lane the stink of the shambles was so powerful that the tumbling in my belly threatened to overwhelm me and I was obliged to stop and cover my mouth with my apron.

I was still nauseous when I returned to Swan-street. The drapes were drawn and the house wore the blind blank look of Fate itself. I could not endure to go back there, not yet. Instead I turned, slipping down Artichoak-lane towards the river. There the sparkle of salt upon the air might pass for a breeze. I pushed my way through the press of warehouse-men loading barges with barrels of preserved fish. Beneath the white sky the river had a densely metalled glint, as though the water were not liquid but a solid thoroughfare of mud, churned by countless striving oars.

Beyond the wharf the mountebank had returned. A crowd of people, most of them women come directly from their work at the fish market, strained to watch the monkey that, having trounced its ass-eared opponent, rolled about on its back, its hands clutched over its mouth, convulsed by merriment. Then, leaping to its feet, it snatched up three phials of green glass and began frantically to juggle them, tossing them high into the air. The crowd roared and stamped as the mountebank solemnly ascended to the stage.

'Beloved women,' he cried, 'who are the admirablest creatures that ever God created under the canopy of Heaven, to the preservation of whose beauty, health, vigour and strength I have dedicated my studies, nay, truly, my life itself!'

The monkey bowed its head and solemnly placed all three bottles in the mountebank's hand before slipping from the stage. The crowd of women nudged one another and grunted and pressed a little closer to the quack whose voice carried easily on the windless air. Already several of them had their hands upon their purses.

Miserably I turned away.

I am resolved. There is no other way forward. When I think of how He came to me, how He stood before me, the Light pouring from His divine countenance, & required me, in that voice at once so mellifluous & so dreadful, to do His will the tears once more spring to my eyes. I am His instrument

Oh sweet God, no. It is back, the dark figure that lurks in the corner of the room, eyeing me with its cold crocodile eyes, choking me with its sulphurous breath. It sees my fear & it laughs, a vile laugh containing all the evil sounds of the universe. I lower my head to my work but the creature insinuates itself beneath my skin, torments me with its cancerous embrace, its abominable eyes besieging me in one thousand thousand repetitions that leer at me from outside & within. They twist in my belly writhing ripping my stomach torments me. More tincture. The opium shall open my eyes to the shadows & drive back the horrors to their loathsome brimstone lairs

Work. The simple precision of thesis and proof.

These alone shall keep me steady, protect me from the evils of doubt & the purposeless ravings of the outside world. Listen not to the voices. It is they who corrupt you, not *the work which must be done, which must always be done, whatever the cost, to the greater glory of the Lord*

Thy kingdom come, Thy will be done on Earth as it is in Heaven

21

And so the days went on, marked out by the grinding repetition of household work. The stifling summer eased its garrotte, though the cooler air did not penetrate far into the house. I fell into a low distemper, my stomach disturbed, my bowels loose and stringy. Mrs Black glared at my chamber pot and warned me that any attempt to shirk my responsibilities would be punished. Each time the door to the house or the shop stood open I imagined lifting my skirts and running, running, until I was nothing but a speck on the smudged Surrey hills, ant legs still running, never turning around. But when I turned around I was still there, pale but definite in the speckled glass of the hall, my eyes smudged around with coal dust and fatigue.

I missed Mary. The sticky hiss of her breathing had always irked me but it seemed I had grown used to it. Without the ballast of her bulk beside me the room had an insubstantial feeling about it and the cries and shouts of passers-by sounded closer, more shrill. Long after they had ceased, the room quivered with the echo of them.

Mary had begged not to be moved to the kitchen but Mr Black had insisted, claiming himself driven close to distraction by her relentless snoring. The first night, I watched as she pushed the table across the flags and rolled out her palliasse. She was crying, but silently, her back turned towards me. I felt the twist of vexation that her misery always roused in me and, beneath it, something else, something more desolate. She pulled a mess of rugs from the dresser shelf. The trailing hem of a rug knocked a pewter plate from the dresser, so that it clattered noisily upon the floor.

'Why must you always be so clumsy?' I hissed angrily. 'If the old sow hears you she'll beat us both.'

Mary said nothing. Instead, she wiped her nose on the back of her sleeve and crouched to pick up the plate. I wanted to kick her.

'Get a hold of yourself,' I added sharply. 'I have slept here myself, remember? It's not so bad.'

Abruptly a spasm of memory clutched my belly. Turning away from the dark window, I stared hard at the dresser, examining with uncharacteristic attention the tea service on the top shelf. One of the cups was chipped at the lip and the raw edge of the china had a yellow crust, like a cut gone bad.

Whimpering, Mary crept over to me and buried her wet face in my skirt. I pulled away, tugging the fabric roughly from her hands so that she fell forwards, catching her forehead upon the corner of the dresser. The wound gaped white, shocked as a mouth, before the blood leaped up into it, flooding it with crimson.

'For the love of God!'

Snatching a rag from the line above the fire, I

thrust it at her. Her face was grey, the blood that cascaded over her brow startlingly red. Awkwardly, she turned her head, moving her arm in front of her face as if to conceal the wound.

'Mary, please!' I admonished her, seizing her head. 'Would you bleed to death?'

Mary looked up at me as I pressed the rag to her brow.

'Mar' wan' stay wi' Lize,' she said, her pink eyes pleading.

I said nothing. The wound was wide but not deep and the bleeding seemed to be slowing a little, although Mary's face was fearfully pale. I closed her fingers round the rag but she let it fall away. Blood seeped into the faint arc of her eyebrow, white stitches of hair against the scarlet.

'Mary!'

''Fraid,' she whispered.

'Don't be. It's not so deep. But you must staunch the bleeding. Come now, help me, at least, I can't do it by myself,' I snapped, snatching up her hand more harshly than I intended.

'Lize — Lize, I — please — so 'fraid — '

Her voice split. Squeezing her eyes shut, Mary rocked herself back and forth. The tears gathered beneath her eyelids and issued down her cheeks, sending pinkish tracks through the smeared blood and pasting strands of sticky hair to her face. Something broke open inside me. Without stopping to think, I dropped down beside her and took her in my arms. She clung to me like a monkey, her hands gripping the stuff of my dress.

'Oh, Mary,' I murmured. 'I'm sorry. I was — there's no need to be afraid.'

The kitchen door slammed.

'How very charming. The idiot and the whore.' The viciousness in Edgar's voice was only slightly softened by the slur of liquor. 'A pietà worthy of Michelangelo. Of course, it would be more authentic if the mooncalf were indeed dead. All over, that is, rather than from the neck up.'

'Go fuck with yourself,' I hissed, tightening my arms around her.

'Ah, I would but, thanks to the close attentions of a spirited little creature upon London-bridge, the fucking is already done,' Edgar sniggered. He collapsed into the bentwood chair and fumbled off his shoes. Then, stepping with exaggerated care in his stockinged feet, a finger against his lips, he helped himself to a bottle of the master's best wine from the top shelf of the pantry and tiptoed upstairs.

For a moment the kitchen was still. In the fire a charred lump of wood shifted a little, the ash sighing as it dropped. Mary was quiet in my lap now, her breathing gluey but even. Licking a corner of my apron, I wiped the streaked blood from her face, tucking her hair behind her ears. In sleep Mary's pink lips pressed together, closing the gap in her upper lip so that her mouth looked almost ordinary. It was not only her mouth. Sleep and candlelight smoothed the skewed mismatch of her features, neatening her face so that, rather than discerning its deficiencies, you noticed instead the pale creaminess of her skin, the sweet curve of her chin. Above the black gash upon her forehead, her hair glowed red-gold.

Tucking the blankets more tightly around her, I kissed her very gently upon her damp cheek and blew out the candle.

★ ★ ★

Now that the rains had come, the stand-pipe was open again. Several times each week Mary and I were required to fetch water and each time she insisted upon circling by the river to see if the mountebank was there.

'Monk',' she said, and she rattled her empty buckets longingly. 'Lil' monk'.'

I obliged her, less to please her than because I felt too weary to protest. While she watched the monkey's antics, I watched her. Her hands flapped at her sides and her tongue thrust from her loose mouth, frantic with pleasure. When she laughed, her head rolled giddily on the stem of her neck. Mr Jewkes had not been to the house for weeks. I hoped the vile lecher was sick or injured or both. We never spoke of him. Indeed, she hardly spoke at all. Perhaps she feared the unpredictability of my humour, for it was true that I was often snappish and sometimes cruel. There was a native wisdom in Mary for all her idiocy.

As the mountebank took to the stage, the monkey passed him, flinging itself into the audience. Mary pushed forward into the crowd, trying to get closer and trampling the foot of a sharp-faced knife-grinder.

'Watch yerself, you plaguey rattle-head,' he cursed, raising his right fist to reveal a sleeve quite eaten away by his wheel.

'If there's a rattle-head round here, I'm looking right at him,' I spat back.

'Is that right?' hissed the knife-grinder, and he pushed me hard so that I stumbled backwards.

'You all right, miss?'

I blinked. The mountebank's clown stood beside me, his ass-eared hood slack upon his shoulders. He was taller than he looked on stage. My head came only to his shoulder.

'You wouldn't be wanting any trouble now, would you?' he said flatly to the knife-grinder, who muttered under his breath and, spitting into the dust at my feet, stalked away.

'You didn't need to do that,' I said to the clown. 'I can take care of myself.'

He shrugged, his toe scuffing the whorl of sputum into the dirt.

'Fighting ain't good for trade,' he said.

'And bastards like that aren't good for anything.'

His mouth twitched.

'Enjoy the show,' he said and, whistling, he ducked into the crowd.

I had to push through the throng to find Mary. She stood at the very front, bent almost double over the rough stage. On the boards before her, almost sitting upon her hands, was the monkey, its whiskery face held up towards hers.

'Come now,' I hissed, tugging at her arm.

Mary twisted obstinately as the mountebank

257

turned, throwing out a ring-heavy hand towards me.

'Now, see here a girl with the complexion and humour particular to green-sickness. Miss, you are well advised to come here today. In but three doses the noble Syrop shall cure your poor skin colour, your listlessness, your want of appetite and digestion, and in every way necessary restore you to yourself.'

'Mary,' I hissed again. 'Or do you want a beating?'

Reluctantly Mary bent to pick up her buckets. Even as we walked downriver towards the stand-pipe I could hear the mountebank's voice carrying over the clamour.

'Proof enough that it is a matchless fool who takes an idiot as an adviser!'

'Pay no heed to him,' I muttered to Mary. 'It is those women who are the fools, parting with their shillings in droves for quack medicines that are no more than water and dye, when the proper cures to their ills grow wild a mile from here.'

★   ★   ★

And so the idea began to grow. The city was crowded with fools who might part with their money upon the least provocation. What then was to prevent another Elixir from luring the pennies from their pockets, an Elixir of my own devising that mixed together all the most efficacious roots and herbs known to medicine? My mother had made little from her endeavours

258

but my mother had proved herself a poor businesswoman in all matters but the trading of her only daughter. Persuasively labelled and prettily bottled, my Elixir might be taken up by any number of taverns and coffee-houses. One day it might become as famous as Stoughton's Grand Cordial or Anderson's Scots Pills. For did I not know as much of herbarizing as any other?

As my arms ached with the effort of scrubbing the linens or hauling the coal or even the foul and headachy task of painting the bedsteads with mercury against the lice, my mind turned over the teachings of my childhood. Foxglove for dropsy. Laurel and white hellebore to destroy the tooth worm before it grew strong in the jaw. Cowslip flower and madder root to restore the skin to youth. I was not entirely displeasing to look at, when I was well. A shrewd woman might use the impediment of her sex to her advantage. Now when we went for water it was I who insisted upon visiting the mountebank's pitch, I who listened attentively as he declaimed the wonders of his nostrums. And although I found myself daily altering the recipe, it was with considerable impatience that I waited for Mrs Black to dispatch me once again to the abundant fields and woods of Islington.

Edgar was there when she summoned me a week later. I turned my face from his. For all his flabby self-importance, his eyes were discomfortingly sharp.

'We must have marsh sow-thistle and Jack-by-the-Hedge in particular,' Mrs Black instructed as she spread a green-flecked paste upon a strip of leather. 'And mugwort. I require quantities of the herb rather than the flowers. Wrap it in a wet rag to keep it fresh. It must not become dried out. And dove's-foot. I have had about all I can endure of your foul expulsions.'

'Yes, madam.'

'Do not turn away from me like that, girl,' Mrs Black snapped, frowning at the plaister. I lowered my eyes, my countenance studiedly blank. 'You are also to collect a parcel from the bookseller Mr Honfleur. The master is not well enough to venture out today.' She cleared her throat sharply. 'You will find the shop in St Paul's Churchyard, close by the sign of the Hand and Scribe at the western end. Do you read?'

There was something in the way her hand protected the letter she drew from her pocket that made me think it might be important. I shook my head.

'As I thought. Very well, give this to Mr Honfleur. Tell him I do not expect a reply. Mary, why are you loitering there? The floors shall not scrub themselves.'

Mary startled, hastily thrusting a much-thumbed handbill into her apron pocket. She was too slow. Mrs Black snatched it from her hand.

'Where did you get this? Have you been in the master's room? You know perfectly well that is quite forbidden. Well, have you?'

She fingered the birch at her belt and Mary backed away, shaking her head.

'It is not the master's,' I said quickly. 'It's mine. A man gave it to me. At the stand-pipe.'

Mrs Black peered at me and then at it, narrowing her eyes.

'Nothing but cheap trickery,' she said at last, crushing the paper into a ball. 'The spines are surely fixed upon that child with glue.'

Lifting the plaister with both hands, she left the room.

Edgar belched as Mary rubbed her face gratefully against mine, leaving a smear of spit across my cheek. I wiped it on my sleeve and tried not to think of Mr Jewkes and his butcher's eye for flesh.

DOCTOR JAMES TILBURG

Now living at the Rising Sun in St-Giles in the fields, over against Drury-lane end, where you shall see, at night, three Lanthorns with candles burning in them upon the Balcony

FIRST, he cures the French Pox, with all its dependents

SECONDLY, he takes away all pains in the shoulders, arms and bones, therefore all ye that are troubled, come to him before you are spoiled by others

THIRDLY, if any have anchored in a strange harbour, fearing to have received damage, let them come to him

LASTLY, he helps them that have lost their Nature, and cherishes up the subdued spirits of a marry'ed man, by what occasion soever they have lost it, and does quicken them again as a Rose that hath receiv'd the Summer's dew

22

I did not open the mistress's letter to the bookseller until I had gathered all I had come for. Though I was still unable to settle emphatically upon a single remedy, I had secreted beneath the wrapped parcels of shop herbs several I thought might serve me well, including sweet balm and mint which my mother considered peerless in quickening the faculties of Nature and encouraging a cheerful heart. What untold hundreds of people must there be cloaked in the grimy folds of London, I thought, who yearned for a cheerful heart?

My head was full of Tally's Quickening Syrop as I unfolded the letter and studied it. The script was cramped, hard to decipher, and hardly merited the effort of it, being only to do with matters of accounts and payment. Disappointed, I folded it up again carefully, fitting the knotted twine over it like a bridle. Even Edgar would have struggled to profit from a letter of that kind.

★ ★ ★

The churchyard was crowded with booksellers, each with tables of books spilling out in front of their premises and a doorway in which the shopkeepers leaned as though petrified, a pair of finger-smudged spectacles set low upon their noses. So motionless was their posture, their

263

heads settled low between their rounded shoulders and their arms wrapped around their plump chests, that they resembled sleeping pigeons upon the roost.

Mr Honfleur's shop, when I found it, was a quite different-looking place. For a start, the books on the table outside were not bundled together higgledy-piggledy and tied up with lengths of twine. There were no stacks of loose papers or dog-eared periodicals, all jumbled together with packets of sugar and tea. Instead, they were arranged in neat rows, the spines all facing outwards so that they might be easily inspected, and above them a broad awning of canvas had been stretched to prevent the sun from fading their bindings. A lanky boy of perhaps seven years sat upon a three-legged stool beside the table, his back stiff but his arms and legs wrapped around themselves in a series of complicated knots. As I approached, out of breath, he untangled himself and stood, peering at me with a severe expression. His brown hair was long in the front and fell over his eyes.

'I would show you in myself,' he said. 'But I cannot leave my post. You might think that, here, in the very shadow of the House of the Lord, you would be safe from the perils of thievery. But you would be mistaken.'

The evening sun did not penetrate the shop, for thin calico drapes had been drawn across the windows, but the dim light had a pearly sheen, a quiet contemplativeness that was quite different to the sealed-up dark of Swan-street. I stood in the doorway, afraid to enter. I had never seen so many books in all my life. Not an inch of wall was visible. Even the slice of space above the window contained two narrow shelves, both crammed with volumes. As for the shop itself, it was a maze of bookshelves, all of them higher than my head and with barely enough room for a grown man to pass between them. Where there was a crack of space between the books there were piled neat sheaves of writing paper, quills, ledgers, letter cases, sealing wax, wafers, slates, pencils, ink powder, even on one shelf a box of spectacles. It was impossible to imagine that a proprietor might be accommodated in such a place unless he too was bound in leather and his name tooled upon his spine in letters of gold. As I stared about me, my mouth open, a mote of book dust caught in my throat and I coughed.

'Yes?'

The woman who stood before me wore a simple dress of plain dark stuff. Her face bore not the faintest trace of paint, not even a reddening of her pale lips, and her hair was hidden beneath a white cap that put me in mind of a nun's wimple. Even her features were neat and plain, answering impeccably to the requirements of a face without attempting the slightest embellishment. The only decoration she wore was a brooch at her bosom. It was in the shape of a flower, with shiny petals of a deep blood red. A green enamelled stem curled from its underside and upon one of the red petals there rested a single tiny pearl like a bead of dew. I stared at it entranced, the letter in my outstretched hand forgotten.

'If you are possessed of a tongue, I would be obliged if you might use it,' the woman said dryly. 'I have many other matters to attend to.'

'Forgive me,' I stammered. 'I am sent by Mr Black. To collect his books.'

'Ah, the inestimable Mr Black. The apothecary who seeks to be the next Mr Harvey. *But happy Thou, ta'en from this frantic age, Where ignorance and hypocrisy does rage! A fitter time for Heaven no soul e'er chose — the place now only free from those.* But then it is reasonable, is it not, to assume your master is not a great admirer of the likes of Cowley, however wise their epitaphs?'

I shifted unhappily as she sighed, her fingers at her throat. If she thought I understood her she was mistaken.

'I — I have this too,' I managed, proffering the letter.

'Indeed. Doubtless my father will be greatly interested in the contents.' She considered me. 'Wait here. I shall fetch him down, in case there is to be an answer.'

'The mistress said — '

She was already gone. The dying sun lit the calico windows like candle shades. The shop smelled of dust and beeswax and a warm brewery aroma that was, I think now, the moulder of old paper but which I took to be the smell of learning. I had not known that such a place could exist. I thrust my raw, red hands into the pocket of my apron, suddenly ashamed of them, and wished the discomfiting woman would come back. Without her as

266

chaperone, I felt illicit as a thief.

Before me, a sweep of books fanned the low table, the linings of their worn covers poking through like tongues. One stood open upon a stand of dark wood, a dark blue ribbon hung between its pages. It looked old. The ribbon was frayed, a pulled thread wrinkling the silk along one side, and the paper was thin and delicate, almost transparent, edged in a tarnished gold and covered all over in thick black words. So many words! They swarmed at you so that you could not see where one ended and the next began. Not daring to step closer, I craned my neck towards it, screwing up my eyes. Perhaps if I concentrated all of my efforts on just one tiny part —

'You are fond of Marlowe?'

I startled upwards, my face burning.

'I beg your pardon, sir, I — ' I stammered, my eyes on the floor. The bookseller's shoes were plain and narrow, his ankles trim as a girl's.

'Please, look all you wish. Books are like people. They do not bear loneliness well. Those that remain unnourished by another's touch wither and die. Here, hold it, read a little. So long as your hands are tolerably clean, that volume shall be grateful for your favour.'

The bookseller spoke with an unfamiliar accent that buzzed upon his lips and set certain words to spinning at the back of his throat. His tone was gentle but there was more than a little of the daughter's dryness in it. I watched his long fingers unfold my mistress's letter. As he read it his lips twisted a little. Surreptitiously I wiped

267

my hands upon my apron.

'Hmm,' he murmured. 'So that is why he sends you and does not come himself.'

'My master is confined to bed, sir.'

'If the man allowed himself more air and a great deal less self-satisfaction he would enjoy considerably better health.' A faint smile upon his lips, the bookseller refolded the letter and pushed it between the covers of the large black ledger on the counter. 'He might even find men like myself more inclined to extend him the terms he asks for.'

Lifting a wrapped pile of books on to his counter, he proceeded to cut the string. From the pile he took two of the largest volumes and set them to one side. Then he pushed the smaller stack and their mess of paper and string towards his daughter, who sighed and set down her book.

'You shall take only these. Your master will understand me, I think.'

'Very good, sir.'

He considered me thoughtfully until I squirmed beneath his gaze.

'A fine face. But not a native of London, I think?' he mused, tapping a finger against his lips as his grim-faced daughter handed me the wrapped books.

'No, sir.'

'A foreigner, then, like myself. It is better so. This great city blinds its citizens, with the dust of all its rush and bustle and its desperate grubbing about in the dirt in the hope of a little profit. We foreigners are more fortunate. We see things more clearly, I think, standing a little way off.

Alors. Bon soir, mademoiselle.'

The bookseller bowed and, stepping around me, held open the door. I hesitated, then, inclining my head, I walked through it with a rustling flourish of my skirts. It was the first time in my life anyone had opened a door for me.

her eyes in the darkness the gleam of the rag
about her mouth but she does not cry out not
any more it is not her screams that haunt me
but her breathing the sticky choke of her
breathing the way her hands clench the knuckles bright as bone sharp as bone rotten as

Steady now. Dear blessed laudanum. Perfume
in my veins. Breathe. Better. Slowly now. The
pen jumps upon the paper like a cricket. Pulse
easing. Better.

notes
- no knowledge/understanding of act of copula-
  tion nor process of conception
- physically mature: developed breasts & pubic
  hair
- sexual organs normal, although labia unusually large & pronounced
- menstruation regular
- passivity: imagination driven by passion;
  anger fear grief where are they where are
  they idiot insensate vacant dumb
- nerve-strings slack heart slack muscles slack
  blood slack
- imagination dormant dead mind dead
- plough her punish her rent her in two slap
  strike twist bite burn
- force her to fear to flinch to cower to weep
- to feel

SEPTEMBER	OCTOBER	NOVEMBER
1	1 †	1 [M due]
2	2	2 † no M
3	3	3
4	4 M [conf.]	4
5	5 M	5 †
6 †	6 M	6 †
7 †	7 M	7
8	8 M?	8
9 M [?]	9 †	9
10 M [confirmed]	10	10 M? [spotting]
11 M	11 †	11 clear
12 M	12	12 clear
13	13 ††]	13 †
14	14	14
15 †	15 †	15
16 †	16	16 †
17 ?	17 X	17
18 †	18 †?	18
19	19	19
20 X	20 ††	20
21 ††	21	21
22	22	22 †
23	23 †	23
24	24	24
25 †	25 X	25 vomiting
26 †	26 †	26
27 X [?]	27 †	27 vomiting
28 †	28	28 fatigue/vom.
29	29	29 fatigue/vom.
30	30	30 please God
	31 †	

23

If proof were required of the efficacy of Tally's
Quickening Syrop it might have been found in
the improvement to my spirits in the weeks that
followed. In the kitchen I mixed a distilled water
of the two herbs, which I sweetened with sugar I
chipped from the sugar loaf, making sure to
carve it where my pilferings might not be
noticed. The dozen bottles I bought cheaply
from a slippery-eyed druggist who occupied a
small grimy crevice of a shop in an alley behind
Newgate-street and brought back to the house
wrapped in a rag. They clinked together quietly
beneath the master's bundle of books, like coins.

Once I had corked and sealed them, I hid all
the bottles of Syrop but one in the garret, tucked
into the hole in the corner of the ceiling. At night
I liked to reach up into the crumbling plaster
and stroke their smooth skins. The remaining
bottle I concealed in the bottom of my basket,
beneath a scrap of sacking. Each time I was
dispatched upon an errand, to the bookseller or
in search of herbs, I made sure to visit at least
one tavern or coffee-house so that I might
attempt to convince them of the wondrous
properties of this extraordinary medicine.

And although I did not enjoy the manner of
immediate success I had wished for, I refused to
be discouraged by the repeated rounds of
discourtesy and rebuttal, by the small anxious

voice in my head that woke me before dawn with its peevish doubts, its ceaseless fretful worrying and prodding. I moved the bottle from the basket to new hiding places, fearful of discovery, and at night I slept with it concealed beneath my pillow. When I woke, I took it in my hand and told myself to be patient, to hold steady. The Syrop was my only chance. Did I not grow more fluent, more assured and more mendacious with every petition? Surely, then, it would not be long before Tally's Quickening Syrop was as favoured a cure as Dr James's Powders themselves.

★ ★ ★

As autumn shrivelled into winter, it was Mary's turn to sicken. Her condition alarmed me. When I suggested we sneak once more to the mountebank's show, she shook her head listlessly. Even my Syrop, which I fed her hurriedly and in secret, failed to restore her. Unless I roused her and dressed her and pushed her up the stairs, she only huddled in the kitchen, staring into the fire. Mrs Black had taken to leaving the key of the kitchen door in the lock when she turned it at night, and most mornings I came downstairs to find the door still locked and Mary asleep upon her palliasse. She slept deeply. When I shook her shoulder she jolted upright as though a strike of lightning had passed through her, her eyes wide with shock. Sometimes she screamed. When I placed my hand over her mouth to quiet her, she bit me. Then, as abruptly as it had come, the convulsion would pass. Her body would go slack and her eyes would close and she would fall back on to her pillow, hauling the blanket over her head. Some mornings it took all my strength to haul her upright.

Mrs Black brewed her a tea of her own devising. The foul-smelling tisane had to be sweetened before Mary would drink it and even then she sometimes dropped the cup, her hand slipping away from it as though their fibres had been cut. It effected no improvement. Her distemper proved so unyielding that after several weeks I went myself to Mrs Black and begged that something more be done. Mrs Black eyed me beadily and informed me that the master was doing all that was necessary. Mary suffered sluggish blood thickened by a poor digestion for which he had prescribed purgatives and regular clysters which he administered himself.

The purgatives made Mary vomit until she retched nothing but a thin yellow bile but the clysters were worse. On those days Mary emerged from the apothecary's room glassy-eyed and trembling, her hands pressed between her thighs. When I tried to embrace her she was stiff as a corpse.

She did not improve. I watched her anxiously, certain that the apothecary had mistaken her disease. But although she limped a little and complained of pain in her lower belly, Mary showed none of the usual symptoms of failing health. She had no fever, no coughing, no sores nor blisters. Thanks to the master's clysters her evacuations were plentiful and of good colour.

Even the frequent vomits resulted in no loss of appetite. On the contrary, she ate constantly, rapaciously, devouring mouthful after mouthful of barely chewed food as though the demands of her stomach would never be satisfied. Even when she was finally finished, she sneaked as much as she could manage into the pocket of her apron. When we rolled her bed away in the mornings there were greasy fragments of cheese and buttered pastry caught amongst the blankets. She grew fatter. Her cheeks puffed and her belly, which had always been round as a child's, nudged out the skirts of her loose dresses. When she held my hand her fingers were damp and spongy between mine, her knuckles a line of dimples in the doughy flesh.

But it was plain that she was far from well. She might have been one of the waxworks in Mrs Salmon's museum, down to the yellow skin and glassy eyes. She stumbled through the days like a cow plodding to and from the milking shed, her head low between her shoulders. She chewed at her lips and her fingernails until they bled. Her duties went undone. She had taken to pulling out her hair so that the bald patch on her scalp, which had once been no bigger than a child's palm, now extended over almost to her ear. Amber hairs clung like cobwebs between her plump fingers.

In the evenings when our duties were finally finished I took to dressing her hair. The rhythmic strokes of the brush were soothing to both of us and, with Mary seated at my feet, I was saved the burden of her eyes upon my face. We did not talk much. I spent hours with curling papers and rags to create heartbreakers, the two small curls at the nape of the neck that were supposed to set men's pulses racing, and confidantes, smaller curls near the ears. For all its fineness Mary's hair held the ringlets well.

There was a glass in the kitchen, a cheap scrap of one with only the most cursory of frames, which Mrs Black had put there so that I might ensure that my appearance was presentable before I went up to the shop. For some reason that had always irked me, the glass agitated Mary. Even when I took her over to examine my handiwork, she would look only when the reflection contained us both.

'Mar'?' she would say then and, despite the uncertainty in her voice, her mouth curved up slightly at the corners. Not a smile exactly, though it looked as though it might permit itself to be coaxed into one. 'Is Mar'?'

'Look at you!' I encouraged. 'See here, how it curls over your shoulder. Don't you look handsome?'

Mary gazed and gazed, smiling and not smiling like an angel in a chapbook. She never dared lay a hand on her own head. Instead she would reach out and touch her reflection in the glass with no more than the tip of one finger, as if the picture were wet and might smudge. Frowning with concentration, she would follow the elaborate crest of her scalp, the looping whorls of hair that framed her face. Then abruptly she would turn away, laying the glass face down upon the table and crouching in front of the fire with her forehead resting upon her knees. She was quiet but I never doubted that she liked it, in her own way. She never asked me to stop.

Then, one evening, quite without warning, she snatched up the glass with both hands and slammed it down hard upon the kitchen table. Mercifully it did not break. Seven years is a very long time. Quickly I put the glass on the high dresser shelf where she could not reach it. It was a moment before I realized that she was tearing violently at her hair, ripping at its fixings so that pins skittered across the floor.

'Mary, stop!' I cried out, anxious, but angry too at the ruin of my careful artistry. 'For God's sake, you'll hurt yourself — '

I tried to pull her hands away from her head but she was too strong for me. She glared at me stonily, a hank of hair tumbled over her face, her mouth making silent shapes. Then, pushing roughly past me, she fled from the kitchen. I shouted after her then that she could shave her head bald for all I cared about it, for I would never trouble to dress her hair again.

She must have hidden in the coal hole for when at last she came back her dress was filthy. When she took my hands in hers and rubbed them against her cheek, I saw that her chewed nails were rimmed with black. I imagined her, squatting in its chill blackness, the whites of her eyes swivelling, and the thought of it vexed me unbearably. Mary was terrified of the coal cellar.

She did not let me comfort her. I tried kisses, I tried threats, often both at once, but nothing worked. She recoiled from my touch. It was as though the warm soft parts of her had been cut away and all that was left between the slabs of cold flesh that shaped her was an empty, hungry hole. She ate and ate, pressing down handfuls of bread into the sack of her belly, but the hole could not be filled. When she looked at me I could see the black depths of it in her glassy, desolate eyes.

To Grayson Black,
Apothecary at the sign of the Unicorn, Swan-
street

Black, sir,

I do not think that it will surprise you greatly
to receive this letter. In recent months I have
made no secret of my dissatisfaction with both
the nature of your work & the manner in which
you choose to conduct it. On the several occasions that I have attempted to discuss my
misgivings with you I have gained the distinct
impression that you regarded my intercessions
as no more than a tiresome interruption to the
business of your day.

These difficulties would be of little consequence to me if I was assured that you were
intent upon producing the paper which, when
we met two years ago, you promised would
make both of our names. I suffer no illusions
about the extent of my usefulness to you. I was
always content to provide the funds & leave the
intricacies of science to you. However, your
secrecy, your obdurate refusal to discuss your
progress with me, always an impediment to our
partnership, has of late become insufferable. I
have no idea whether you have subjects for
study &, if not, how else you mean to seek out
your proofs. I understand from the girl that you
rarely go out. You tell me nothing at all.

Once I might have excused such silence as
little more than your habitual ill manners. No
longer. Time and considerable expenditure has,

at last, made me wise. You are silent, sir, for the simplest of reasons, because there is nothing to tell. I can no longer deceive myself that a successful outcome to your work is certain, or even likely. I enclose a little money in conclusion of our arrangements.

I shall of course continue to support the girl, as I have always done. I remain much troubled by the matter of her persistent ill health & would wish nothing in the world to impede her swiftest recovery. I trust that you are gentleman enough not to permit the hostility between us to affect your conduct towards her, who is quite without blame.

I remain, sir, &c

MAURICE JEWKES
2nd day of February 1720

24

Her voice when she told me that the master wished to see me was barely audible. I set down the coal bucket with an awkward crash and turned away, crossing my arms tightly across my chest.

'Me?' My agitation made me harsh. 'I don't think so. What would he want with me?'

Mary shrugged dully, her toe scuffing the edge of the ash pile.

'Don't do that!' I snapped. 'Don't I have enough to do around here without you making me do everything twice?'

Mary's expression did not change but her fingers tangled in her hair, twisting and tugging.

'Why must you do that?' I cried. 'Damn it, Mary, do we all not suffer enough?'

* * *

I clenched my fist when I knocked, striking my knuckles painfully hard against the wood. When he instructed me to enter I had to force myself to turn the handle, to step across the threshold. I felt dizzy and wild. The thought of his damaged face thrust towards mine, his importunate questions, gorged with his wheedling grasping inquisitiveness, scraped the skin from my spine. Taking a deep breath, I set my jaw. It was a matter of enduring. I would not look at him. I would stare at the wall and I would seal myself up against him, answer him in monosyllables, endure until he grew weary of my obduracy and the blank, resistant wall of my dreamless nights. If that bastard thought he could rip anything more from me he was grievously mistaken.

It was months since I had last entered his room. The shades were pulled, so that the room was filled with a dim light like liquid dust that smelled sickeningly of over-breathed air and aniseed. The master himself sat hunched over the table, a blanket around his shoulders. I could not see his face, for his wig hung in loose flaps on either side of his face, but his posture and smell were those of an old man. His bony hands were clasped on a pile of papers set before him. Blue veins ran like ink blots beneath the yellowed skin.

'Sir.'

'Sit, girl, sit.'

I sat, turning my chair so that it faced the wall.

'I wish to speak to you of Mary.' His voice was metal on stone. 'You cannot have failed to observe that she ails.'

Mr Black broke off, shaken by a fit of coughing. It was some minutes before he was able to resume, his voice thinner now but harsher too, tight as a fiddlestring.

'Mrs Black says she is attached to you. What then is the nature of that attachment?'

I thought of Mary's fingers pulling out her hair, her hand in mine in the dark, and I stared harder at the wall.

'She is a half-wit, sir,' I said tightly. 'She

depends upon me as a child might, because she cannot manage alone.'

'And like a child, without the wit or reason of their elders, an idiot is given to foolish and powerful passions. You see her daily. Doubtless you understand her better than she understands herself. You may help me help her. Come now, what arouses her appetites, what causes her to laugh, to weep, to jump out of her skin?'

The question took me so much by surprise that I glanced sideways. His hands were clenched so hard that the knuckles shone white.

'I — I have never thought about it.'

'Then do so now. Let us start with a simple one. What gives the girl pleasure?'

I paused. I thought of Mary laughing, her tongue loose as she clapped her hands together in clumsy delight, and my spine softened a little.

'The usual things,' I muttered. 'The things a child likes.'

'Which are?'

I shrugged. Surely so innocuous a question could do no harm.

'Honey. Sweetmeats. Chocolate. She loves chocolate.'

'Of course. What else?'

'Baked wardens.'

'Nothing but food? Surely she is not so much of a savage.'

I hesitated.

'She likes it when I make shadow puppets. With my hand.'

'They do not frighten her?'

I shook my head.

'I do not make frightening shapes, sir.'

'So what do you make?'

'Rabbits, birds, you know. The usual things.'

'Mary is fond of animals?'

'Yes, sir.'

'Any in particular?'

'Any she can find, so long as it is small and soft. The yellow cat. The linnet. Even mice, when she finds them.'

The apothecary scribbled and looked up.

'She has a favourite?'

'Of those? The cat, perhaps. But it is the monkey she truly loves. The one that belongs to the mountebank's clown on — '

Immediately I tensed, clamping my lips closed. I knew quite well that the very mention of mountebanks sent the master into a rage. But he said nothing, only jotted something upon his paper and poured more cordial into his glass. After he had drunk, he held the glass for a long time in both hands, considering it. I waited, biting my lip.

'Mary has been with us for many years,' he said at last. 'Her mother succumbed to a fever when she was but an infant.'

He paused again. Then, swallowing, he continued. Not long after, Mary's father had taken a second wife, a young woman, who had agreed to wed upon one condition. She would have nothing to do with the half-wit. The girl must be removed elsewhere.

The master's voice cracked and, coughing, he took another long draught from his glass. His hands trembled as he set it down. Before Mary had come to Swan-street she had never spoken a word. Indeed, she had proved so slow to understanding that they had assumed her deaf. When distressed she had not cried but had beaten her head rhythmically against a wall. Mr Black was the first person to assume her capable of human sensibility. Her progress under his tuition had defied all probability.

'Not that there is any recognition of her exceptional recovery,' he said bitterly, draining his glass. 'Idiots, apparently, are worth nothing. How can they look at Mary and say that she is worth nothing? They are blind fools, the lot of them, blind bloody fools!'

He slammed his hand against the table, wrenching his chair around so that I could not see his face. It was a moment before I realized he was weeping.

'Damn those bastards,' he rasped. 'Damn them all!'

There was a long silence. Carefully he cleared his throat. Then he turned back to face me. His eyes were huge and black and he extended his hand towards me, the fingers plucking at the air. I stared at the wall, my teeth hard against my lower lip, my hands clasped tight in my lap.

'Do not defy me,' he said in a strangled voice. 'If she were to die now, if she — oh God, it would finish me, I swear it. Finish me. I could not endure it. Shall you have that on your conscience? Shall you?'

Despite myself, I turned. I had thought myself the only person who cared for Mary at all. The master closed his hand around the phial of tincture and my heart squeezed as though he gripped it instead. The neck of the bottle struck the glass so that it chimed.

'Help me,' he whispered, raising the glass to his lips. 'Help me to make her well.'

The silence lasted a long time. Then, very slowly, forcing my throat open with a considerable effort, I began to speak. At first the words came unwillingly, painfully, in ones and twos that hooked in my throat. My chest ached. I was obliged to draw saliva into my mouth so that I might describe, stumblingly, how she loved to eat potatoes hot from the ashes of the kitchen fire, grabbing at them so rashly that she burned her fingers and had to cool them upon the glass of the kitchen window. I paused then, remembering the way she had blinked at me, her eyes round with surprise and outrage and a child's impatient greed, and tears sprang unbidden into my eyes.

'Go on.'

I hesitated. The ache in my chest had moved downwards to my gut and for a moment I hugged it silently, holding it in. Then, very quietly, I told him of the way Mary would jump up and down and clap her hands together in a frenzy of delight whenever the organ-grinder struck up at the end of Swan-street and how she would sometimes grow so excited that she would urinate upon the floor. I told him of how she ran her finger around the base of his chocolate cup when it was returned to the kitchen for washing and how, as she sucked the dregs of chocolate from it, her eyes would close in dreamy pleasure. I told him how she loved to knead the bread

286

dough, moving her elbows with such ferocious energy that the flour billowed around her like smoke from a soap-boiler's chimney. I told him how, to amuse her, I sometimes shaped the leftover scraps of dough into mice or butterflies. Once I made a spider, with eight fat legs, which I set upon her plate. It made her shriek. Mary was terrified of spiders. She would not kill them, though. She would have made a lousy butcher's girl. The sight of any dead creature made her weep. I told him of how she liked to burrow into our bed like a badger and how I would often wake to find her toes against my cheek and, beneath the blankets, her heavy head upon my shins and her fingers tangled in the hem of my nightgown.

Behind me the apothecary coughed. I stopped abruptly. Caught up in my recollections, I had grown almost fluent. Immediately cold worms of compunction set to squirming in my belly.

'If you wish her well, sir,' I hurried, 'I think that if she were only allowed to return to the garret — she fears the dark, you see, and the kitchen — '

The master's quill, which had scratched tirelessly at the page, fell from his hand. He moaned, laying his head upon the table.

'Sir?'

'Why can you not leave me alone? I only wish to sleep. Just to sleep.'

'Are you ill, sir?'

I scraped back my chair. Mr Black's eyelids fluttered, his hands clenching and unclenching

287

as if he meant to catch something. White scum chalked his mouth.

'Where is the boy?' he murmured. 'He is a comfort, the boy, always a — oh, how my hand aches, it is an agony to me. Write for me, madam, as you used to. I always liked the neatness of your hand.'

'Mrs Black is not here, sir.' I stammered. 'It is only I, Eliza.'

Suddenly Mr Black snatched his head back up from the table. Clutching the arms of his chair, he cast around the room, as though he was searching for something, for someone. I stumbled stiff-legged towards the door.

'Mrs Black! I shall fetch the mistress, sir, and she shall come directly — '

'You may not show yourselves, you are sly, so sly, but I can see you. Don't think I cannot see you!'

Snatching up his inkwell, he hurled it past my head. It struck the panelling with a dull thud, sending an arc of dark ink up across the wall. I fumbled behind me for the door handle as he reeled around, his head swaying like a snake's. His eyes were holes in his skull, black and red at the same time. Tearing open the door, I fell down the stairs, screaming for my mistress, for Edgar, for anyone.

The shop door opened and Edgar peered out, a small bottle in one hand.

'Cease in your hysterics, damn you,' he hissed. 'We have a customer.'

'But the master,' I sobbed. 'That bastard, he — I think he means to kill me.'

Edgar snorted and rolled his eyes.

' . . . my clumsiness.' Mrs Black backed into the hall, a box in her hand. 'Permit me to fetch you another dose.' She closed the door and her shopkeeper's smile shrivelled on her lips. 'What the Devil is going on here?'

'It is the master,' Edgar drawled. 'He has another of his tiresome fits.'

'Then go to him, Edgar,' she ordered. 'Directly, I implore you! Mr Jewkes is expected here shortly. Mr Black must be ready for him.'

'He asks for you, madam,' I whispered.

'Does he indeed?' she retorted, snatching a jar from the shelf. The pills rattled against the lip, scattering across the table. 'Do you think food appears on the table by magic? Who will manage the business if I do not?'

She fumbled two pills into the box, leaving the remainder where they lay, and stalked back into the shop. I leaned unsteadily against the jamb of the door. I could not comprehend how I had failed to see it before.

Mrs Black was more afraid of her husband than I was.

To Mrs Grayson Black at the sign of the Unicorn at Swan-street

Dear Madam,

I received your letter by this morning's post & accept your gracious apologies for your husband's unfortunate letter.

In response I would seek to assure you that I bear no lasting grudge & have no desire to cast a shadow over what has been a long & mutually advantageous association with your husband's family. I know that during the long years of their acquaintance my late father regarded Daubeney Black as a friend as much as a customer. Like you, I would consider it most regrettable if hot words on either side were to bring an unhappy end to that fine tradition.

Nevertheless I regret that it remains impossible to extend to you the terms of credit you wish for, despite the considerably more courteous terms employed on this occasion. A woman of your business sensibilities cannot fail to appreciate that I must manage my business as I am certain you seek to manage your husband's, judiciously & with prudence. Such scruples are become quite rare in these reckless times — people of our kind are, I fear, a dying breed. Therefore as a gesture of good will, & given the urgency of your patient's requirement, I shall have my boy deliver with this letter some 100 grains of opium. In the same spirit, I would ask that I may depend upon your husband to settle his account with us _in full_ before the end of the month.

I remain, madam, your humble & respectful servant &c.

ISAAC THORNE
Thorne & Son, East India House,
Leadenhall-street

18th day of February 1720

25

Through the darkest days of winter Mary did not improve. Neither did Mr Black, though he continued on occasion to receive visitors. Snow fell, a grimy grey veil, and the lanes froze in toothed ridges. But although the master's indisposition required him to keep a fire in his room at all times, we were no longer permitted to light one in the parlour and, after supper, Mrs Black had me pick the remaining coals off the grate in the kitchen so that they might not be wasted.

Her thrift extended to every aspect of the household and she punished the slightest of squanderings. There was no more Indies tea. I was no longer permitted vinegar to clean the windows, nor soap for the heavier linen. The sugar loaf was locked in the dresser, the level of the salt box examined closely. In the evenings when my other duties were complete, I made rushlights, as I had done as a girl, from reeds and bacon fat. I was required to rise a half-hour earlier than before so that Mrs Black might get to the market ahead of the rest and secure the cheapest cuts of meat. They had to be boiled for hours before they were soft enough to swallow. But, although the apothecary hardly slept and Mrs Black's face grew thin and pinched, there was no abatement in his demand for books. Though such errands robbed me of any time to rest, I thanked God for such mercies. I clung to my visits to the bookseller as a sluggard clings to sleep, refusing the wearisome grind of his daily life. I willed that vile rogue to read faster, more widely, to recall volumes long forgotten or to find out a crucial new pamphlet that he could not manage without.

It was not only the shop itself that drew me. My thoughts as I hurried along Cheap-side, my thin cloak clutched against the wind, were all of money, of liberty. Out of the dark house, my Elixir in my basket, I might imagine myself free.

★　★　★

Even when the thaw came the mercury barely rose. A spiteful wind shivered over the skins of the puddles as I hurried along Cheap-side and the sky was a purple bruise, threatening more rain. Beneath my shawl my neck dragged at my aching shoulders. Mrs Black had roused me at four so that I might clean and polish all the jars and bottles in the shop which she thought grimy and an affront to customers. I was already awake. The master had been shouting again, screaming at someone to stay away from him, to get their filthy hands off him. The first time I had lain paralysed with fear, certain an intruder had broken in. Now I had grown so accustomed to the nightly hollerings that, had Mrs Black not thundered upon my door, I might have turned over and gone back to sleep. I could hear the master's screams as I stumbled down the night-choked stairs.

293

The early start had fatigued me. My hair was lank with dust and fragments of dried herb, my hands raw. In recent weeks I had ventured further afield, seeking out establishments that I might persuade to take the Elixir. But still my efforts yielded little. It seemed that there were one hundred such nostrums jostling with one another for space upon their shelves every day, with every physician in the land promoting a powder or a pill named for them. A dark little chop-house with greasy windows took three bottles for sixpence and told me to come back in a month. Everywhere else I had been turned away.

This morning I had ventured further than ever, seeking out a druggist who traded close by the Temple. He had hardly allowed me to open my mouth before bidding me leave him in peace. Smarting with disappointment, I walked doggedly, my hood pulled high and my head lowered against the miserable wind, so that when the monkey leaped on to my shoulder I feared myself assailed by a thief and struck out with my basket. I pushed away my hood, basket still raised, as, with a frightened chirrup, it leaped away.

'So you are still hot for a fight, I see.'

The mountebank's clown no longer wore his ass-ears but a suit of clothes in a hairy brown cloth of the kind favoured by country tradesmen. The monkey cowered on his shoulder, clutching his ear for support.

'I — he frightened me,' I muttered.

'And you him, so justice is done. I fear the

poor creature's bored half to death. It is time we got him some honest work.'

I sighed and was silent.

'You are walking this way?' He pointed west towards the Strand. 'I'd appreciate the company.'

I shook my head.

'Well, perhaps I'll run into you again. I've taken lodgings with the laundress in Little-whalebone-court, off of Drury-lane. Do you know her? Face like a mangle.'

My mouth twitched, despite itself.

'There, I knew you could do it. Take it from one who knows, you can forget your fancy Elixirs and all that foreign rubbish. Fight less, laugh more. The only secret of a long and healthy life.' He held out his palm. 'That'll be a shilling, thank you kindly.'

I turned so abruptly then that I almost overturned the buckets of the milk-seller behind me. By the time I reached the Churchyard it was late, and darkness had begun to fall. All around me windows flickered and swelled with light. I hurried through the throng, the first chips of hail stinging my face as I ducked through the low door and inhaled the now familiar smell of leather and old paper. I did not attempt to understand why it comforted me when it served as a persistent reminder of my own ignorance. It was enough to breathe it in and feel the way my shoulders eased and the clenched spaces between my ribs relented a little.

The bookseller's daughter glanced up as I entered. She held a small volume in her hand and, although she had half-closed it when she heard the jangle of the shop's bell, she had kept her finger between the pages to mark her place. When she saw it was me she sighed and returned immediately to her reading. She did not take her eyes from the page as she reached down with her other hand and drew a single cloth-bound volume from a shelf beneath the counter. In my turn I took a parcel of books from my basket. In recent weeks it had been agreed that the books my master no longer needed might be returned to Mr Honfleur for resale.

'Tell your master that the other book he wants must be sent from Holland,' she added sharply. 'If he wants it he must pay for it in full. And in advance. We shall not lend it, nor accept it for return.'

I nodded, glancing shyly past her towards the open door behind her. My feet ached and I longed to sit down. The daughter crossed her arms. The brooch on her chest glowered.

'My father is gone out.'

I shrugged, concealing my disappointment, and hurried through the formalities of the exchange, eager to be gone. Without the Huguenot to admonish them, the books grew haughty, disdainful. They pulled in their bindings as I passed the shelves, the leather curled with fastidious contempt. The daughter encouraged them. But when he was there they did not dare. For all his scholarship he was quite without airs. At first I wondered if he did not know that I was nothing but a maidservant for he was never curt nor condescending. He talked to me easily, familiarly, making no attempt to moderate his language. From the beginning he assumed I understood exactly what he said. It was not always so but I was resolved that he should never know it. When he spoke to me I had the same sense of solidity that I experienced when, by refusing to concede the wall, a gentleman was required to step around me in the street. I felt present, definite, as though by being there I changed things a little.

I found myself caught not only by what he said but by the manner in which he spoke, the way the words buzzed and gurgled in his throat. Although he had lived in England for more than thirty years, he had adopted nothing of the London way of speaking. He was, he told me, sipping at his little cups of thick black coffee, a *réfugié* from France who had smuggled his family to England in the terrible times after the Revocation of Nantes. I did not know what that was but I nodded all the same. His own father had been burned at Nerac, accused of having irreverently received the Host. His house had been demolished, his woods seized. The rest of his family had been fortunate. They had managed to escape to England. Honfleur had purchased an illegal passage on a coal barge while his daughter, whose name was Annette, and who had been no more than a babe in arms, had been smuggled with her nurse on to a ship bound for Dover, concealed in a fish barrel. It was a thrilling tale — I could have heard it daily and never tired of it.

There were often other Frenchmen crammed into the shop, most of them refugees too, who spoke a pepper-and-salt mixture of English and their own language. They talked mostly of men of their acquaintance and several in particular whom they never tired of discussing: Mr Wren, Mr Boyle, Mr Hooke, Mr Pope. It was some time before I understood that these men were known to them by reputation only, for the Frenchmen talked of them as fathers talk of their sons, their affection marbled with exasperation. Except for Mr Newton. They had nothing but respect for Mr Newton.

When the Frenchmen went home the Huguenot talked to Annette and to me too, when he remembered I was there. But unlike ordinary men, he did not tease us nor tell bawdy stories, though he laughed often. He talked instead of governments and laws, of the discoveries of science or the wonders of astronomy. Occasionally he would take up a volume and, raising a finger for silence, would read aloud from it in support of a point he wished to make. Often, too, he touched the books as he talked, his fingertips absently tracing the gold tooling of a binding or fanning the edges of the soft gold-dipped pages between his thumb and forefinger. Mostly, however, he sat in his shop much like a chandler sits among his soap and candles, steeped in their distinctive exhalations, at once an extension of the essence of his wares and aloof from them, as if they were already in his bones. He left the tending of them to his daughter, who was never without her nose in one. She even borrowed the words from them instead of using her own. Though I seldom understood them, it was not hard to tell when Annette was speaking other people's words, for her voice grew deeper and her fingers stretched into stars.

'*Come, let us go, while we are in our prime! We shall grow old apace*,' she would chide if her father dawdled.

Or, '*The glorious lamp of heaven, the sun, the higher he's a-getting, the sooner will his race be run, and nearer he's to setting.*'

'Take pity upon the inestimable Mr Herrick, I implore you.' Her father would say with a sigh then, his slow smile starting to pull up the corners of his mouth, and he would wink at me, so that I blushed. 'The man would turn in his grave to hear his verse pressed into such disreputable service.'

The bookseller did it himself, mind, stealing the words from books, only it was harder to tell when he did it. There was neither the swollen voice nor the reverent spaces around the words. Instead he spoke as he might observe the weather, easily and without the expectation of an audience. Maybe it was because I never saw him, as I so frequently saw his daughter, with his head bent over a book in study, but I fancied that, unlike Annette who scribbled notes in a journal as she read, the words entered the bookseller by stealth, suspended like dust in the bookshop air that he drew into his lungs. I could not see otherwise how he might have swallowed so many.

299

I could hardly believe my ears when, after I had been coming for a few weeks, he asked if he might seek my assistance.

'Excuse my presumption, but you read, do you not? I am wrong, perhaps, but there is something in the way you look at the books that suggests you understand their secrets a little.'

I blushed.

'I do not read well, sir. That is, I have learned my letters but these books — '

Mr Honfleur laughed.

'I do not mistake you for a scholar, my dear. You are far too young and pretty for that.'

Behind me Annette released a sharp breath. My blush deepened. I dreaded that he would ask me to read something and that I would not be able to manage a word. He would be kind, of course, but he would never speak to me again in the same manner. As though we might almost be equals. Mr Honfleur laughed again.

'Do not look so alarmed. I am embarked upon a new venture, books of stories particularly for children. There is quite a vogue for them, it would appear, and you are not so pickled in erudition that you would dismiss the lot of them as injurious to health.' He rolled his eyes at Annette and winked at me. 'I should like your opinion of them.'

I need not have feared. I was accustomed to a hornbook, a flat piece of board with a handle upon which was tacked a paper printed with the alphabet and the Lord's Prayer. But though the gold-tooled volumes the Huguenot brought me bore no greater a resemblance to such a primer than a hog bears to an Arab stallion, they were simple enough, with easily deciphered script. I pretended that I attended to them only on Mr Honfleur's account but in truth I loved to look at them, to peel the words from the page and set them in my head, one upon another until the story formed its own special shape. There was a small chair in one corner of the shop tucked beneath a high shelf where I might read without being under anybody's feet and I tried to arrange it so that I might manage a few minutes curled up there before I was required to head back to Swan-street. They forgot about me there. If I sat quietly enough the dusty air of the shop stilled and I had the curious sense of knowing what it felt like when I was not there.

One evening, as I set down the book I had looked at, Mr Honfleur came into the shop. He did not notice me. He stood behind his daughter, leaning down to place his arms around her neck. She did not close her book, nor did the stiffness in her spine relent, but she tilted her head just a little, so that the back of it rested against his chin.

'I am a very foolish, fond old man,' he murmured into her cap.

She smiled, her eyes on the page, and reached up a hand which she placed gently against his cheek.

'And I your Cordelia? To deal plainly, I fear you are not in your perfect mind.'

He laughed then, but softly, closing his eyes

and drawing her against his chest. I thought of
my mother then, the press of her fingers upon
my jaw when she rubbed her nose against
mine, the way her sharp chin rested upon my
shoulder when she slept, and the tug in my
chest pulled tight as a stitch.

Quickly, while there is sense in me. I have increased the dose again & again but I cannot silence these infernal nightmares. I wander through Hell itself with Death always on my heels, its eyes red with greed & lesser men's blood, but I can find no exit. There is no exit

I vow I shall not take it. But the pain, the agony takes me over until I can think only of the poppy. I would crawl upon my belly & lick up the dust from the floor with my tongue if I might be allowed one spoonful of that precious liquid. I am an animal, a miserable howling beast, as bereft of wit & reason as a maddened dog

Oh Lord God, what am I become? This flower is become my God, the altar before which I prostrate myself, the treacherous ease of the Devil. I close my eyes & he looms from the red velvet of my lids, the poppy in his black hand, his voice curling about me like smoke. Drink, he says, & I drink. Feel nothing, he says, & I smile & feel nothing. Sleep, he says, & I lay down my pen like a child. It is he who laughs then, when the words stop, he who claps his hands in delight. Now, he says, I am in you & of you. While your soul sleeps, I flow through your veins, blackening your blood, & set up my shrine in your unfeeling heart. Now you are mine

I cannot succumb. Life is suffering. Did our Lord Jesus Christ not endure agonies upon the Cross & call only for water to ease the dryness of his throat? The Creation shall not surrender its mysteries to an indifferent observer. Only in the pain may we find the Truth. Oh God, fortify my resolve & give me the courage to do Your will

AMEN

26

On the first day of March, when the cold peeled the plaster from the walls and it seemed that spring would never come, the city was seized by violent gales. The wind howled in the chimneys and clattered at the windows, causing the shop signs to swing and groan ominously on their brackets. In his room beneath the garret, the master howled back, so that my nights reeled with the clamour of it. In the streets men clutched at their hats and the horses whinnied fretfully, startled by fierce spirals of dust or gusting cabbage leaves. A woman died in Paternoster-row, struck upon the head by a dislodged tile. But, though fleshy clouds fattened and bruised beyond the distant hills, it did not rain.

It was restless, reckless weather.

'The master refuses to take his medicine,' Edgar announced on the third day of the storms. 'What a fool he is! Any apothecary worth the name knows that a man is one hundred times more likely to die of the lack of opium than the taking of it. Mrs Black shall be a widow within the week.'

It was no longer possible to dismiss Edgar's pronouncements as the lazy exaggerations of a braggart. I had never seen my mistress so discomposed. She did not eat. Nor do I think she slept. Instead, at night as the wind raged about the house, rattling handles and locks, she crouched over ledgers in the parlour, clicking at the beads of the wooden abacus. The glow from the smoky rushlight made silver wires of her hair and scooped dark hollows in her cheeks. At her elbow a pile of letters was secured against the draught from the window by a heavy slab of flint, its rough husk broken open to reveal an interior of smooth grey cut with white like a frozen puddle.

'Five pounds, no more,' Edgar urged her, his hand fluttering over her shoulder. 'How can the business prosper if we do not invest? There can be no dividend for those who do not own shares.'

'Five pounds? You may as well ask for five hundred.'

'Come now, surely the situation is hardly so calamitous.'

'Edgar, it is worse! He swore this work would be finished months ago. But if he should die now, his debts — how shall we live?'

The rising edge to my mistress's voice was interrupted by the shop bell and Mrs Dormer's high-pitched wheedle. But I hugged myself, smouldering with a grim excitement. At last the time had come. Had I not seen it with my own eyes? For that very morning the mistress had insisted upon my bringing fresh water to the master's room. I had not seen him in weeks and the lurch of disgust and exultation I had experienced still had the force to make my heart beat faster. I had not imagined a man could so resemble a corpse and still draw breath. His cheeks were yellow and sunken, the port stain on his cheek the used-up colour of dried blood. Beneath his nightgown his body was hardly more than an empty husk, its contents already plundered of anything wholesome or juicy. The moans seemed to seep from his skin like sweat, like the final cries of the animal spirits as they abandoned his body. There was hardly anything human about him. It was as if his layer of flesh had been no more than a disguise, allowing him to live among ordinary mortals undetected. Stripped of it, he was revealed as he truly was, stinking and malign.

The master was dying, steadily and with great suffering. Each morning that week I rose quickly, eagerly, certain that before nightfall there would be black drapes at the window and hushed voices on the stairs. I was certain that they could not keep me here, surely, if he did not live. His agreements, whatever their nature, would expire with him. I would be free. But his endurance defied reason. Each day he clung to life, just warm enough, the breath no more than a shiver in his mouth. At night he screamed, tortured by his dreams and the rattling of the windows in their frames. I had stuffed the parlour window with rags to prevent it breaking but I did not trouble with his. Our neighbours protested angrily at the disturbance and I suspected that many avoided the shop for fear of contamination, for there were few customers. Mrs Black's fingers flicked and flicked at the abacus, sending the beads spinning dizzily along the frame.

The house held its breath. Only Edgar seemed blithe, impervious to the heightened atmosphere, the feverish silences. For Edgar, spendthrift proponent of one hundred failed schemes, in debt to a score of creditors across the city, had a new plan.

'This house belongs to the master, did you know that?' he announced to me one day, his feet upon the kitchen table as he cleaned his nails with the cheese knife. 'Extraordinary, is it not? He has always allowed Mrs Black to think it rented, doubtless as an inducement to frugality, but blow me if when I was arranging his papers I did not turn up the deeds. It is his, outright.'

'What did she say, when you told her?'

'You foolish whelp. Tell her? Where would the profit be in that?'

He meant to marry her, and he wasted no time setting about it. All that week, as we waited for the master to fail, his attentiveness was grotesque. Edgar had no instinct for moderation, for the chessboard strategy of the long game, and no taste for it either. The appeal of subtlety, of quiet manipulation, evaded him. Besides, he was desperate. The mistress's slightest remark, even if it were no more than a tight observation that the rain was easing a little, was wont to elicit gasps of admiration. He hastened to open doors for her, to help her on with her cloak or to bring her a chair so that she might rest between customers. Almost every day he presented her with a little trifle, a plum tart or a pretty length of ribbon.

I dismissed his ambitions as the outlandish manoeuvrings of a lunatic. The mistress was distrustful by nature, alert to the faintest whiff of a swindle. I was confident that Edgar's

308

obsequiousness would, before long, provoke her ire. But it was clear that she too was hardly in her right mind. Although she repeatedly bid the prentice to hush, there was no severity in her reproaches. She had a way of saying his name, snapping the first syllable against the roof of her mouth and drawing out the second in something close to a sigh, that made the hairs upon my arms bristle. It was not unusual to walk into a room and see them together, Edgar's head bent over as he mixed or pounded something while Mrs Black's gaze fluttered against his face like a moth.

One morning at the end of that week, as the mistress sat with Mr Black and waited, Edgar pressed himself against me. I felt the stiff thrust of his yard on my thigh.

'Like that?' he whispered and poked a finger into my ribs. 'When I'm master here you may have as much of it as you like.'

The very next day, when I returned to the kitchen for water to bathe the master's sores, I discovered Edgar lolling in the bentwood chair, his feet on the chimneypiece above him.

'So you see,' he was saying to Mary, who squatted before the fireplace, 'once the master is gone, I shall be your master. So it would be prudent to oblige me, do you not agree? After all, what chance do you have of employment elsewhere?'

Leaning down, he placed a hand upon her shoulder. Mary hung her head but, although she shuddered, she did not shrug him off.

'Get your greasy hands off her!' I cried,

slamming the door. Edgar blinked and snatched his hand away, but when he saw it was me he let it drop once more.

'Good God!' he drawled, palpating Mary's flesh with his fat fingers. 'Your mistress is right, the scarcity of good servants these days is a scandal.'

And, even as I snorted in disgust, I saw our future. Edgar, our master. Edgar haggling with me, with us both, day after day like a fish fag at Billingsgate, bodies for board. It was all the currency we had.

TO THE CUCKOLDE APOTHECARY,

YOU HAVE BEEN MADE A FOOL OF
LONG ENOUGH.

I HAVE NO ARGUMENT WITH YOU. I
PITY YOUR DIS-EASE AND KNOW YOU
AS A GOOD AND HONEST MAN. BUT
CAN YOU NOT SEE THAT YOUR OWN
ABODE IS BECOME A CESSPIT OF
LEWDNESS AND DEBAUCHERY?

OPEN YOUR EYES TO THE FALSE FOR-
NICATING PRENTICE WHO TILLS YOUR
WHORE WIFE WITH THE PLOW OF HIS
PRICK & DELIVER TO THEM BOTH
THEIR MOST DESERVED PUNISHMENT.

A CONCERNED FRIEND & NEIGHBOUR

27

The master refused his tincture a full week. Then, on the eighth day, when it seemed impossible that he could contrive to cling to life for another day, he called for Mrs Black and declaiming her a monstrous whore, asked for laudanum. And, in the days that followed, Mr Black of Swan-street returned from the dead.

I can only guess at the manner of pact that bastard struck with the Devil but, if he surrendered what charred scraps remained of his soul, he regained, for the most part the vigour of his spirits. Had I not seen it with my own eyes I might not have believed it, so astonishing was his recovery. Although his body remained frail and perilously thin, the master exhibited a high-strung vigour that danced in his fingers and stretched his eyes wide open so that he appeared both unnaturally wakeful and quite astonished. Once he had swallowed his breakfast of opium, he rose from his bed to sit at his desk where, with few exceptions, he remained for the rest of the day, covering sheet after sheet of paper with his frenzied script. He took more of the medicine at dinner-time and often another draft at sunset, often as much as ten grains in a single day. Sometimes he found himself strong enough to venture downstairs or even to take a short stroll in the lane. When, in the afternoon, he found his vigour flagging, he had Edgar apply leeches in clusters behind his ears so that he might rub opium directly into the puncture marks. While the leeches fixed and swelled, he lay upon the settle with a cloth upon his forehead, soaked in a mixture of opium and rose water.

The Devil extracted his punishment all the same. The poppy-juice dried his mouth and bent his hands into hooks. If you stood outside his room you could hear the whimpers of pain and frustration as he tried to write. Frequently he was obliged to put down his quill and part his fingers, rubbing life back into their whitened tips. It closed his bowel too, causing the build-up of putrid matter which poisoned his blood. His rare stools were tiny black buttons, laced with blood.

His discomforts were something of a consolation. When my skin crawled with the thought of him and I longed to break something or someone, I took some solace from knowing that the Devil lurked in that villain's chamber pot, his brimstone breath hot against that monster's scabbed and blistered buttocks. But it was hardly enough. Whenever I thought of what I had told him about Mary I felt a spike of such pure loathing that I was sure I would vomit. It was not that I had lied or exaggerated. I had broken no promise, divulged no secret, said nothing that Mary would have denied or protested. But I had betrayed her all the same.

I intended to punish him for it.

*　*　*

313

He gave her a monkey. He told her it was to lift her spirits. It was a mothy little creature and clearly advanced in age but, though it had the mournful eyes and wizened complexion of a whiskery old man, it was possessed of a small boy's impish disposition. When she brought it down to the kitchen to show me, her words mangled with pleasure and her eyes stretched with disbelief at the extent of her good fortune. She could not put the creature down but kissed it over and over, cradling it in her arms, stroking its fur, her fingers seeking its infant grip. When at last the creature wriggled free and leaped across the room away from her embrace, her face crumpled. Gently I took her arm and pointed to the punchbowl upon the dresser where it peeked over the blue-edged rim, its eyes bright and mischievous. Mary blinked, her mouth working. Then she laughed out loud, without covering her mouth. Mary had not laughed for months.

The change in her was close to miraculous. She was still weak and easily distracted but her dull gaze quickened. Her cheeks grew less pale. She regained something of her old childish vigour. She no longer ate with the unthinking relentlessness of a starveling and she lost something of the puffiness around her face, although her belly still protruded in the manner of a hungry infant, the weak curve of her spine exaggerating the shape of it. When I bid her stand straight she only whispered in the monkey's ear and coiled its tail more tightly around her throat. At meals it sat on her lap and she fed it the tastiest morsels from her plate.

314

Across the table it eyed me suspiciously, curling against Mary as though it meant to protect her from me.

It was the master who insisted that Mary give the monkey a name of her own choosing. After much tongue-chewing deliberation she settled upon Jinks, which suited the ill-behaved whelp very well. Each afternoon she was required to bring Jinks to see the apothecary, who claimed himself as much a beneficiary as Mary of its restorative powers. Certainly they laughed together a great deal over its antics and indulged the creature dreadfully, petting it and feeding it sweetmeats by hand.

If that was not enough, the master even had Edgar bring up an old cradle from the coal cellar in which the wretched thing might sleep. The sight of it stretched the skin across the back of my neck.

'Not here!' I snapped as she set it before the fire, and, snatching up the poker, I stirred the coals fiercely, sending up a flurry of red sparks that stung my hands. 'The way you indulge that louse-ridden beast! Do you wish to burn down the house?'

As for Mary, she spent precious hours laundering and pressing the tiny linens that fitted inside the crib. At night she lay curled up beside it, singing softly as she rocked the beast back and forth. She even attempted to cajole the wretched creature into donning a little bonnet and a shift which she had uncovered from somewhere. Mercifully Jinks would suffer no such indignity and I was glad when she abandoned her efforts

315

and put the garments away in a drawer. I had laundered them myself, a long time ago.

Wrapped up with the monkey, Mary hardly remembered I was there. Briskly, I bade myself be thankful for it. All winter, as she had ailed, I had strained against the weight of her, her need of me an iron shackle that chained me to the house. Now she was recovered I need concern myself with her welfare no longer. The master was fond of her, was he not? And she had managed quite well alone, before I came. Besides, she was not possessed of the finer sensibilities of ordinary people. If only I might find a way to contrive it, I was once more free to go.

★ ★ ★

The master's appetite for opium grew more voracious. Mrs Black kept the resin locked in an iron cabinet with the other exotics but every morning she unlocked it and, her jaw rigid with concentration, silently measured out the apothecary's daily requirements so that Edgar might mix it up. *Ten grains of opium with eight of rhubarb pounded with a little camphor & taken in a tumbler of Canary wine, bloodwarm.* Edgar claimed that he repeated it in his sleep and even I, who was expressly forbidden to enter the laboratory, knew the recipe by heart.

It was late one evening as I took myself wearily to bed that I heard a whimpering noise coming from the laboratory. I peered through the hinge of the door. Several illicit candles burned as

Edgar spooned opium into the glass beaker beside him and stirred the mixture with a long-handled spoon. It was a long time since I had seen so much light and, moth-like, I found myself drawn to it. Edgar glanced about him but he did not see me. Wiping his nose roughly against his sleeve, he quickly added another spoonful of opium and another, until the liquid in the beaker was black and syrupy. When he poured it into a bottle it fell from the beaker in sluggish gobbets. Taking a paper package from his pocket, he tore it open and tipped its contents into the jar of opium grains, shaking it to blend them. Then he took the bottle and, pulling one of the master's old books from its place upon the high shelf, concealed the bottle behind it and pushed the book back into place. My face was pressed so close to the door that it swung a little, creaking on its hinges.

'Mrs Black?' he called uncertainly. 'Is that you?'

I darted away from the door, stumbling upstairs before I might be discovered. Edgar meant to be my master. I no longer doubted he would succeed.

* * *

That night I could not sleep. I stood in the window, peeling clumps of moss from the slates outside my window and hurling them as hard as I was able at the thick black hole that the dome stamped upon the night. But the moss was light and the night breeze fresh. The dome towered upwards, perfect and impervious. Mr Honfleur had told me that its builder had thought being an architect a poor profession. *I should have been a physician*, the old man had reputedly said. *At least I should have been rich.*

RESURGAM.

The strange word came unbidden into my head, a remnant of another of the bookseller's stories. When the architect of the Cathedral was first marking out the dimensions of his new dome upon the razed foundations of the old church, he had fixed upon the precise centre point and ordered a labourer to bring a flat stone to be laid there as a mark for the masons. The labourer quickly happened upon a broken gravestone of the appropriate dimensions and brought it to the spot that the architect had indicated. It was only when he laid it down in its allotted place that he saw that one word survived of its original inscription, carved in large capital letters at the centre of the slab. The labourer, unable to read, paid it no heed. But when the architect saw it he fell to his knees, thanking God for His blessing upon the mighty endeavour. For the single word carved upon the stone read simply *RESURGAM* or, in English, 'I shall rise again'.

Ten grains of opium with eight of rhubarb pounded with a little camphor & taken in a tumbler of Canary wine, bloodwarm. Not the two-bit balsam of a country cunning-woman but a miraculous remedy, capable of bringing a man back from the dead. The unsheathed sword of the murderer, pressed against his own neck. In

Edgar's hidden bottle there was dissolved enough opium for a dozen phials.

RESURGAM.

The boards of the stairs were chill against my bare feet but they made no sound. I was almost at the master's landing when I saw him, his marked face a darker patch of shadow. Holding my breath, I pressed myself back against the wall but he did not look up. Instead, he slipped silently into his room, closing the door with a click that echoed through the stairwell.

When my breathing was steadier I stole past his door, every part of me alert to the slightest noise. When I took the chamberstick from its nail on the wall, scraping the iron loop of its handle against the plaster, the hairs on my neck prickled like pins. But no one came. I would light it from what remained of the kitchen fire and take it directly to the laboratory. Although the kitchen door was kept locked at night, my mistress had for months left the key in the lock when she turned it so that I might rouse Mary and begin our duties while she was still at market. When I slipped through the door Mary turned over, expelling a noise half-way between a sigh and a snore. I stepped over her, squatting before the fire. Her face shone pale in the glow of the embers, the lump of her strangely swollen in the crimson light. Kicking at the fire, I held the wick of the candle to a red coal until it caught and held it up. The flame dipped and curtsied. Shivering, I looked over my shoulder. The door leading up to the lane stood ajar. Holding a hand around the candle to prevent it from going out, I hastened across the room to close it, glancing uneasily about me. Every customer to the shop had their own grim tale of thieves and vagabonds. I did not see the foot until I almost fell over it. I might have cried out, had I not recognized the shape of it. Instead, I seized the blanket and ripped it away. Mary moaned and turned, burying her face in the pillow. Crouched beside her, fully dressed, was Edgar. The stink of taverns rose from him like shit from a pigsty.

I kicked him. He groaned and blinked, his eyes swollen and unfocused, his nose crusted with dried slime.

'You poxy bastard! If you have laid so much as a finger on her — !'

'That thing? I'd rather *die*,' Edgar slurred. Then his face contorted and he began to bawl noisily, his face slack with wine and self-pity. 'Oh, sweet Jesus, Eliza, help me, I beg you. Don't let me die. I don't want to die.'

And so it was that he made his confession, clutching my skirts in desperate appeal as though I were the Madonna herself. Edgar had the French pox. He had discovered the first pustules a few days before and already was driven half to lunacy with the dread of it. He dared not consider the mercury cure. How would he explain away the loosened teeth, the black saliva, the endless spitting, the distinctive fetid smell? If Mrs Black were so much as to sniff the stink of it upon him, he was finished. The only other cure of which he was certain was to fuck a virgin, the younger the better, but where was he to find one? The madam at the bawdy house had set the price for one at ten guineas, a sum entirely beyond his means.

'After all my years of patronage how could she turn my misery to her own profit?' Edgar sobbed. 'Oh, Eliza. They say the pain is unendurable.'

He fell into a cataract of weeping. I said nothing but waited until his sobs subsided to hiccups and he rocked miserably, his arms around his knees. Then I made my own silent prayer, holding my thumbs for luck.

RESURGAM.

'My mother had her own treatment for the pox,' I said slowly. 'Without mercury. Often it worked.'

Edgar sniffed.

'I am reduced to the defective poundings of a country witch?' he snivelled.

'My mother was no witch. But if you think yourself too high-up for such — '

'No, no!' Edgar pleaded. 'Let us try it, I beg you. I beg you.'

'Of course, if I am to make it up for you I shall need your help. I would have to get into the laboratory.'

'Of course.'

'And it shall cost you. A shilling a bottle.'

'A shilling a bottle? But — ? Very well. Yes. Anything, anything, whatever you need.'

When at last I crept back to bed dawn was a ribbon of oyster silk threaded through the chimney pots. In the pale light the lead struts of the dome looked like fingers, pressing down on the still-dark skull of the cathedral.

'*RESURGAM*,' I whispered to myself, gripping the iron catch of the window so tightly that it impressed its curled pattern upon my palm. '*RESURGAM*.'

in search of paracelsus
the father of modern medicine

the irony of it does not evade me
for did paracelsus himself not say that 'what
makes a man ill also cures him'?
behind the books tucked out of sight a bottle of
tincture
my opium
mrs black tells me she locks the opium so that
she may prevent its misuse & yet here it is
from the smell & thickness of it a concentrate
50 or 60 grains per pint, perhaps more

intended as some manner of insurance for her?
now for me

i hold the precious bottle in my hand enough
to kill a man & i have to wonder:
does she mean to save me or to drown me

28

I scrabbled behind the row of aged volumes, sending up clouds of thick dust, but my fingers closed only on cobwebs. Agitatedly I pulled one tome down, then another, peering into the shelf. I had hardly any time. Mrs Black had gone for provisions and Mary and the mothy monkey were once more secreted in conference with the master, but I could hear Edgar as he clattered bottles restlessly in the shop. Hurriedly I groped again, reaching as deep as I could. But though I ran my hand along the very back of the shelf I found nothing.

The bottle of opium tincture was gone.

Hustling the books frantically back into position, I struggled to think calmly. The shop's supplies of opium were kept locked in an iron cabinet to which only Mrs Black held a key. Even if I contrived to pocket a little when I made up the master's tincture it would not be long before she grew suspicious.

There was an alternative. I might purchase it on my own account. Such a purchase would require guile and a large part of my mother's money but, as the days passed and the walls of Swan-street pressed inwards and downwards, snuffing out the first green flickers of spring, I knew it worth the difficulty and expense. What more fitting end than that the money from my sale be used to purchase my freedom? Tally's

Elixir. Powerful enough to bring a man back from the very brink of death. At night, straining out of the casement window, my thoughts were all of pestles and strainers, wine and herbs, bottles and seals of wax. When at last I slept I dreamed of holding in my hand a delicate phial the dark red of Annette Honfleur's brooch. But when I pulled the cork the liquid inside it dispersed in a coil of black smoke, leaving only the acrid, choking smell of burnt caramel.

★　★　★

It was a full three weeks before the apothecary required me once more to venture abroad to the bookseller. The waiting curdled my stomach. Though the weather grew warmer the house was damp and chill. Pale sunlight caught in the veils of dust on the windows and fell away. Malign and triumphant, the shadows crept across the floor unchecked, and the master grew stronger, sustained by opium and malevolence. And by Mary and the monkey, whom he summoned every morning after breakfast. I laboured through the work alone, scrubbing and pounding and beating with a ferocity that banished thought. The only subject worthy of consideration was how soon I might get out.

It was a little after dinner when I saw the packet of books on the hall table. My hands were black from polishing pewter but I tore open the front door without bothering even to untie my heavy canvas apron. My lungs and legs ached with the need to run. I flung myself down

Cheap-side, barging and pushing, gulping down the sharp spring air as though it were beer until I reached Newgate-street and the druggist from whom I had bought my first dozen bottles. He had made it plain by the slip of his eyes that he would do what he could to favour me with a bargain.

When I emerged a few minutes later with the pound of opium concealed beneath the folds of my apron, I had parted with six shillings and a promise to walk out to Hockley-in-the-Hole with the druggist the next Sunday. I had forgotten the promise before I had closed the door behind me but the opium bumped reassuringly against the books in the bottom of my basket. It was a tentatively warm afternoon and I tipped my head backwards as I hastened southwards, relishing the stroke of the sun on my face. When at last I reached the Huguenot's shop I paused on the threshold to remove my apron and stow it in my basket I could taste the metal tang of nerves on my tongue. I was sure that the Frenchman would have forgotten me.

'Well, look who is here!' Mr Honfleur cried delightedly as I tapped the door softly with my knuckles. 'What a pleasant surprise! We thought you surely dead — or, worse, married. Is that not so, Annette? You are not married, are you?'

I blushed and shook my head, my basket awkward against my thighs.

'*Coquette and coy at once her air, both studied, tho' both seem neglected; careless she is, with artful care, affecting to seem unaffected,*' Annette said under her breath, lowering her head once more over her book.

Her father frowned at her.

'Pay her no heed,' he whispered to me, loudly enough so that she might easily hear him. 'Still, it is hardly any wonder that my daughter is unwilling to embrace what is new. No man has yet written the words to express them for her.'

'And so you expose your folly,' Annette replied tartly. 'There is wisdom and prudence enough for your grandchildren's grandchildren in these volumes, were you to pay any heed to them.'

'And I know of no grandchildren ever begotten by the reading of books.'

Annette's mouth tightened.

'Besides,' Mr Honfleur continued more gently. 'Did not Mr Marvell himself remind us that *'tis time to leave the books in dust and oil the unused armour's rust*? He understood that there was a time for study and another for action, for enterprise.'

'You would take a man's paean to a moral war to defend your disgraceful bubbles? You should be ashamed of yourself, Father.'

'We must seek our counsel where we can. A poet may claim the hidden secrets of a man's heart, but only a fool would take a bard for a financial adviser.'

It was with a rush of pleasure that I realized, for all my absence, nothing whatsoever had changed. I smiled. Mr Honfleur studied me thoughtfully.

'Take Eliza, for example. Ignorant of Shakespeare as a babe-in-arms. But in Paris a sensible girl like her would have begged, borrowed or stolen the money to take a stake in the Mississippi Company, and by now she would doubtless have her own equipage and a handsome Comte of a husband, to boot.'

Annette grunted and said nothing.

'So many investors from all walks of life that at night the troops are called to clear the crowds from the Rue Quincampoix,' Honfleur marvelled. 'What kind of an alchemist is this man who has made paper more valuable than gold?'

'Why, if that is so, you should consider yourself most fortunate, Father,' mocked Annette. 'Your hoards of paper would shame Croesus himself.'

I tried to imagine Mr Honfleur in a suit of gold brocade, his fingers heavy with rings, stepping from a gilt-flashed barge to the fanfare of liveried musicians.

'It is nothing but a confidence trick,' insisted Annette. 'Heed the words of the wise Lucretius: *nil posse creari de nilo*. Nothing can be created out of nothing.'

Honfleur shrugged. 'Had Lucretius been fortunate enough to know the redoubtable Mr Law he might have come to a rather different conclusion. Doubtless he too would have begged the Englishman to favour him with the secret of his success, not to mention an allowance of shares.'

'*Look round the habitable world! How few know their own good; or knowing it, pursue,*' scorned Annette, in the special voice she used for the words she copied from books. 'Mr Law is a charlatan. He means only to line his own pockets at the expense of ordinary men.'

'On the contrary, *ma petite*, John Law is a visionary economist and the ordinary men, as you call them, have a good deal to be grateful for. Thanks to his reforms, France is rich and there is no longer any tax on wine, bread, oats, oil and one hundred other staples. Coal is half the price it was a year ago. So it is not just his stockholders but every Frenchman who profits. Every Frenchman in France, that is,' he added, and he cuffed me gently on the arm. 'Pity me, Eliza. For it is a poor time indeed to be *réfugié*.'

I blinked. I had been so occupied with my own thoughts I had forgotten where I was. Annette watched me over the edge of her book, her eyes narrow.

'Does your mistress not require you home?' she said sharply.

'Annette,' her father reproved her, 'she does no harm.'

'She does nothing at all,' Annette retorted. 'A fine life for a maidservant.'

'I — Miss Honfleur is right,' I stammered, seizing my basket. 'It is time I was going.'

Annette's mouth twisted. 'Would it be too great a trouble to take the book your master ordered?'

I flushed unhappily as, with nose wrinkled, she dropped a volume into my basket, string tied in a cross over its bindings.

'I have not wrapped it,' she declared. 'Paper is an additional expense, after all. Tell him he may have the rest when he settles his account. It is already six months overdue.'

329

Honfleur frowned at his daughter as I stumbled out of the shop and through the press of the Churchyard. A red sun rested briefly upon the low roofs and was gone. The clouds were rosy strips, their bellies polished to gleaming copper, and the evening was filled with the pale pink promise of spring.

★ ★ ★

The very next day I tipped away what remained of the Quickening Syrop. It had grown greenish and foul-smelling and I had to rinse the bottles repeatedly to rid them of the slimy residue. An agitated Edgar unlocked the laboratory door and reluctantly handed me the key. His eyes twitched as I closed the door and locked it behind me. I could hear the squeak of the boards in the hallway as hurriedly I made up the one bottle of the decoction of white love-lies-bleeding that was his weekly medicine, and a dozen bottles of Tally's Elixir. *Ten grains of opium with eight of rhubarb pounded with a little camphor & taken in a tumbler of Canary wine, bloodwarm.* As I bent over my mortar I repeated it under my breath, over and over until it had the metre of a prayer.

tumour
advanced
no mistake

lower part of belly, close to right hip
size of small apple, hard/tender to touch
black in colour
skin yellowed in centre with reddish-purple
outer area
network of black veins securing it to surrounding skin

second smaller lump in 2 parts, 2 inches above
small & purple, like small grapes
skin puckered all about

application of red lead plaisters to draw out
infection
juice of ground-ivy boiled with honey & verdi-
gris
cream of arsenic
<u>opium provides temporary relief from pain</u>

no other treatment known

29

For all the apothecary's apparent improvement no visitors came to Swan-street. Even the butcher-faced Mr Jewkes did not come back, although letters from him were sporadically delivered by his boy, a pockmarked lad in a showy livery of silver-blue who always asked for a sip of small beer and sat in the kitchen, the cup untouched in front of him, staring at Mary across the table as if she were a long word he was determined to decipher. Mary blushed then and covered her face with her apron, dusting her hair with flour. Otherwise we saw only the tradesmen and then only infrequently. As for the master, he remained closeted in his room, the door locked.

Tally's Elixir. The thought of it caused my toes to curl in my boots in anticipation. At the first chance I had I took it directly to a coffee-house on London-bridge famous for its purveyance of patent medicines. At Swan-street Mrs Black spat the name of the place from her mouth like a tainted oyster for she blamed it bitterly for many of her difficulties. In the lane I breathed deeply, filling my chest with the ripe, polluted stench of city air. Somehow it had become spring. The farmers' waggons were lush with green and the peeping of birdsong seasoned the raucous city like the glint of salt over the Thames, ticklish and new.

At the coffee-house I was required to wait so

long I knew I would be punished, but still I did not leave. When at last the proprietor received me I knew immediately from his expression that my wait had been purposeless.

'Now Dr James, he's a fine physician, that Dr Daffy too. Even Mr Ward I've the time of day for. But a chit of a maidservant, thinking she can mix up a soup of a nostrum in her kitchen and pass it off for physick? You must think me a perfect fool.'

Outside the coffee-house I wept, though I knew the tears wasted, even before they had ceased to fall. That night I stared out at the dark shape of the dome, my hand smarting and my heart grim as lead. It would require better planning, I saw that now. Proofs, warranties, testimonials. I had not the faintest idea of how I might obtain them.

I was still turning over the same questions in my mind when I returned two days later to the bookseller, and again several days after that. I was required to pass several coffee-houses on my way but on neither occasion did I take the Elixir with me. Although I pretended to myself that I had no choice, that there was not the time for it, I knew myself simply too weary for refusal.

On those mornings, as he had before, Mr Honfleur enquired after my master as he examined the books I returned to him for signs of wear or damage. I squirmed at the question, replying as briefly as propriety permitted. But the bookseller could not be so easily deflected. The second time he shook his head, flapping his hands as though clearing tobacco smoke.

'No, no, enough! When a man underwrites another's hopeless endeavour, with no prospect of reward in this world, he seeks more in recompense than dreary platitude,' he protested. 'He wishes to be amused. Now, try again, my dear.'

Annette frowned and declared her father nothing but a common gossipmonger, but the bookseller merely held out his hands to me, his face contorted in a parody of entreaty.

'I am certain life with your quack of a master brims with humorous incident. Come, sit by me and tell me all about it.'

My tongue was wooden in my mouth.

'Sir, I do not think — '

'For pity's sake, Father, leave the child alone,' Annette chided but, when I glanced at her in gratitude, she looked away. 'Can you not see that you discomfit her?'

'This one? Surely she is not such a milksop. On the contrary, I would wager from the look of her that she has sharp eyes and a sharper tongue. Am I right?'

I hesitated, torn between discomposure and my eagerness to oblige him. Behind me Annette grunted scornfully. I had not noticed it before but there was something of Mrs Black's sharpness about her features. I felt a prick of dislike.

'I fear you may be, sir,' I replied, and was rewarded with a smile of triumph.

'There, what did I tell you? Then I shall expect regular dispatches.'

* * *

After that the bookseller always demanded the latest news from the apothecary's house and was disappointed if I had no new morsels to impart. I did my best to satisfy him for I was quick to discover the consolations of indiscretion. In rendering the details of my life at Swan-street as comic tales, I stripped them of their menace. It helped me endure it.

For instance, I told him of the night when, on my way to bed, I had encountered the apothecary on the stairs, bareheaded and with nothing to cover his nakedness but a small blanket, and how he had raved that the Devil had stolen his nightgown. I said nothing of how he had leaned close to me and spat full in my face or of how fright had made icicles of my bones. There was no amusement in that. I simply rolled my eyes in long-suffering ruefulness at the master's weak head for liquor. The bookseller's laughter wove a kind of armour of lightness about me that, if I husbanded it carefully, might last for hours or even days.

I plundered both my memory and my imagination for stories that might amuse him. I told him of Edgar, of his hopelessness in the laboratory, and even, in a fit of audacity, of his plans to be my mistress's next husband, although I had the sagacity to make light of my master's illness, given what I guessed were the Frenchman's generous terms of credit. Instead, I elaborated upon Edgar's vanity and the implausibility of his ambitions. I told him of Mary and her monkey and how fat and alike they grew with every passing day. Mr Honfleur laughed until his sides ached. It made me feel safe, at least as long as I was in his shop. But it grew harder and harder to return to the smothered shadows of Swan-street. At night I lay awake, picking over the carcass of our conversation till it was stripped bare. Above me, the broken lathes poked like fingers from the hole in the ceiling and the hidden bottles of opium made a dark bulge in the damp plaster.

★　★　★

As spring strengthened, something changed within me. It was as though my skin contained two of me. At Swan-street I was tentative, pale, silent. At supper I watched Mary fooling with the monkey, and the bread grew mould in my mouth. It was as if the shadows of the house had finally taken up occupancy inside me. I grew as jumpy as Edgar, as grim and grey as Mrs Black, my skin stubbled with unrelenting gooseflesh.

But when I entered the Huguenot's shop I was transformed. I grew bolder, less prudent. One day, when urged for the latest intelligence, I batted my eyelids a little at the bookseller and then, in precisely the reverent tone Annette favoured for the regurgitation of books, I declared:

> 'Cock a doodle doo!
> My dame has lost her shoe;
> My master's lost his fiddling stick,
> And knows not what to do.'

I meant only to amuse him, but before I had even finished speaking I knew that my enthusiasm had overcome my reason. Annette was his daughter, after all. I stared at the counter, my mouth dry, and my armpits prickled with shame and apprehension.

'You are a sharp mimic,' he observed at last.

I swallowed, not daring to meet his eyes.

'So sharp indeed that I would prefer my daughter to remain innocent of your skill. I do not think you would wish to cause her distress, non?'

After that I fell into the habit of rehearsing my stories as I made my way to the Churchyard. Most bore only a passing resemblance to the truth, but I did not think Mr Honfleur the type of man to favour bare fact over an amusing tale. Annette might prefer her stories on mouldy paper in strenuously small letters, but her father's learning, it seemed, had not hardened him against mirth.

I did not see the handbarrow until I struck my shin against its strut and, with a cry that was as much surprise as pain, fell to the ground with such force that the contents of my basket tumbled out on to the road. The mackerel-seller, an ancient crone with a palsied face and puckered eye, spat curses at me as she rearranged the tarnished fish on their bed of straw. I swore back, groping for the master's book as a pair of soldiers in tattered uniforms stumbled past me, one almost setting his boot upon my hand. Sodden with gin, their eyes were as milky as newborn kittens'. They clutched at each other, their laughter fragile and desperate-sounding, before they reeled away again, their shoulders pressed together for support.

Leaning against the wall, I inspected the book anxiously for damage. Although the bindings looked unharmed, some of the pages were bent, revealing a pale gash in the smooth gold band of paper between the covers. Tugging loose the cross of string that secured it, I opened the covers so that I might smooth them flat.

There was only a little writing on the page, an unfamiliar curling script that looked like numbers. In place of words there was a large illustration, inked in colour so that it more resembled the chapbooks of my youth than a learned manuscript. But, while the chapbooks contained pictures of fairy palaces and dragons, the woodcut in this book showed a freak-boy of the kind you paid to see at fairs, only this one did not have the usual horned head or excessively hairy body. Instead it had stunted arms and legs, one hand having only two fingers and each leg reaching only as far as a knee might be. One of these half-legs ended in a foot, the other in a twisted stump that resembled the branch of a tree. On his head, he wore a jaunty green hat with a feather. It came down almost over his eyes.

I turned the page. There was a plain sheet of paper so fine you could see your fingers through it and then, behind it, another tinted woodcut, this time of a man with a second head growing out from his belly. The next showed a boy with the beak of a bird, the next a man and a horse, conjoined at the shoulders, a third an adult woman with the head and tail of a monkey. There had been talk of things like this, when I was a girl. Of women who indulged their desires with animals and even with fish. Once, at a fair, I had seen a grown woman of only fourteen inches tall. The mother had been seduced by a fairy or perhaps terrified by one, I could not remember which. Either might have as powerful an effect.

I licked my finger, tasting the thick smell of parchment upon my skin, and turned first one page and then another. Even such an amateur as I was could see that these pictures were drawn with considerable skill. As I moved the pages the eyes of the monsters seemed to follow me, as though they silently begged me to rescue them from their paper imprisonment. Something swelled in my chest, dark and knotted like a great clump of hair, but I could not stop looking. Faster and faster I tore through the pages until something stopped me, something that froze my fingers and set the blood singing dizzily in my ears.

A picture of a boy with the head of a dog.

I stared at the picture, and the clot of hair in my chest grew so thick that I could hardly breathe. The boy on the page was no more than an infant. The soft defencelessness of his pale naked body, the plump folded flesh of his wrists and ankles, his tender stub of a penis, contrasted violently with the head upon his shoulders. There was nothing charming about this head, nothing puppyish. It was the head of an adult dog, black as coal and with a murderous constriction to its eyes, which glared up at me with undisguised hostility. The artist had set the dog's jaws open in a snarl, exposing a curl of scarlet tongue between rows of pointed teeth, and it slavered a little, a loop of drool falling from its lips. I could almost hear the growl vibrating in its throat, the bellicose stink of its breath. The fur about its neck was matted and spiked. Its ears pricked forward, intent upon weakness and fear, as it strained from the child's round innocent shoulders.

I closed my eyes but it did not recede. The ghastly dread of lying there in the darkness of the kitchen. The explosion of terror as the monster burst through the open frame and roared until its lungs seemed sure to burst, its teeth a terrible bright white in the darkness, the saliva dripping from its jaws as it came closer, closer, closer . . .

★　★　★

'Well?'

Mr Honfleur extended his hand to take back the book, an anthology of Greek myths. I had stared at its plates for a long time but instead of the snake-haired Medusa or the maze-maddened Minotaur I had seen only the dog-child, its slavering jaws sharp against the white infant flesh of its chest, the ghastly black pelt of its matted neck.

'Did you think it as agreeable as those stories of Ancient Rome?'

'Rome — yes.' I blinked. ' I — I am sure it is a fine book.'

Honfleur frowned. 'Are you unwell? If so you

should go home. Fevers favour Frenchmen.'

'I am quite well, sir.'

'You are pale. Go home and get that quack of a master of yours to dose you with something suitably unscientific. Hurry now. And leave the door open when you go.'

I stared at my lap.

'I wondered, sir, if I might — if I might ask you a question?'

Honfleur gestured towards the door. I stood reluctantly.

'I never make promises I might be obliged to break,' he replied. 'Now, get along with you.'

In the door of the shop I paused. 'I only wished to ask — what exactly is the nature of my master's work?'

'If he has not told you, perhaps he does not wish you to know.'

I swallowed, biting my lip. 'With respect, sir,' I murmured, 'I think it likely there are things I have told you that he would not wish you to know.'

Mr Honfleur's mouth twitched. 'I was right, then, about the sharpness of your tongue,' he observed dryly. 'But though you are pert, you are not without wit.'

For a moment the shop was silent, dust turning on a treadle of sunlight between the shelves. Then Mr Honfleur sighed, snapping the covers of the Greek book together with a clap.

'Ah, it is hardly a secret. Your esteemed master writes a treatise. Has been writing it, indeed, for a number of years, although not a word of it has yet been published.'

'And his subject?' I whispered.

'The notion of maternal impression or something close. He declares himself always upon the verge of categorical proof of his singular theories but so far we have seen only his ability to beg, steal and borrow the ideas of other, wiser men than himself. Of which, I must confess, there is no shortage.'

'Maternal impression?' I stammered.

'The effects of strong emotions, fear, desire and such like, upon the physical form of a foetus. You have perhaps heard of the Dutch woman who saw a man broken upon the wheel and delivered a child whose bones were all broken in the exact same manner and could never be set? This and her ilk are the subject of his study.'

I stared at him dizzily. The roaring in my ears made it difficult to make out exactly what he said and I had a sharp pain in my side as though I had been running.

'Of course, as your master liked to remind me, the eminent gentlemen of the Royal Society have long been fascinated with monsters. It would be unreasonable of me, then, to draw a comparison between those who take a scientific interest in the subject and the rough hordes that ogle freaks for entertainment. You seem shocked. But what kind of living might a man make if he did business only with those of whom he approved? Your master's work may be profitless and injudicious but at least it is harmless. In the meantime I live in the false but glorious hope that, one day, he shall sell his ramblings to one of my rivals at an inflated price and I shall be properly paid!'

Galen on cancer:

excess of black bile which causes cancerous
tumours may be _stimulated in any man, if he
must endure a prolonged period of excessive
cruelty or low spirits_

tumour but the outward & visible sign
of his inner anguish

OF THE MALEVOLENCE
& _PERFIDIOUS DECEIT_
OF MY TORMENTORS

30

I took great gulps of London air as I stumbled back to Swan-street, filling my lungs with its comforting stinks. The pain in my side had eased a little but I trembled violently and several times I doubled over, certain I would vomit. *Maternal impression*. And then, like a chorus, in a harmony that danced and dipped around the principal melody, *my son*. Round and round they went, in their infernal a cappella, round and round, as insistent as the sawing fiddlers at the Covent-garden. *Maternal impression. My baby son. Maternal impression*. I squeezed my hands around my temples until my head ached. The clamour on Cheap-side sharpened itself on my spine. *Maternal impression. My son. My precious baby son*.

At Swan-street I crept to the garret and pulled the rugs over my head, but still the words poured like spiders from the cracks and fissures of my brain until my head swarmed with them. Black and indisputable as print, they declaimed their vicious chorus: *maternal impression, maternal impression. Eliza Tally, you blind fool, how could you not have seen, not have known?* And then softer, more gleefully: *you might have saved him, if you had only seen. If you had chosen to see*.

I turned over, burying my face in the mattress, but my skull was alive with them and they spun their venomous webs around me, holding me captive. *Maternal impression, you dumb trull,* they gloated. I could not escape them. They gripped me by the ears and peeled back my eyelids so that I might be forced to bear witness to their irrefutable truth.

The apothecary had brought me here to make a monster of my child. He had done all he could to pervert and distort him, to rip apart the godly parts of him and seed at their centre the brutish spirit of a beast so that from his innocent neck might thrust the vile neck and slavering jaws of a cur. The picture from the book pressed itself into the jelly of my eyeballs until I moaned out loud. Somehow, I did not know how, my child had thwarted him. I imagined him then, curled like a new fern in my belly, his fingers plugged into his ears as the taut strings of my nerves played their terrible music around him. He had held tight to his human form and he had prevailed. When I had held him in my arms, there had been not the faintest trace of the brute about him.

Despite it all, he had been perfect. Despite the apothecary's worst endeavours. Despite my own.

My stalwart, unyielding, perfect son.

The supper bell rang, three brisk tolls. I did not move. I stared instead at the ceiling and wondered distantly how long I might remain here before someone was sent to find me. It would not be long. In the meantime, if I was not present in the kitchen Mrs Black might punish Mary for it. She had done so before. I thought of Mary's sweet enduring face and heavily I dragged myself to standing. I could not bear to be the cause of more pain, more misery. My face felt swollen and stiff, my eyes puffy and my hair and ears wet with tears. I had not even known I had been weeping.

Mary.

The thought caught in my throat. Her loose mouth, her divided lip, her child's sensibilities, were they too the results of his vile chemistry? Had the apothecary not managed things as he had, would Mary have been perfect?

* * *

Leaning heavily on the banister, I made my way falteringly downstairs. As I passed the master's study the door opened a crack and the apothecary thrust out his head. His face was withered and pale, the purple stain upon his cheek scummed with grey, his eyes dark holes into his skull.

'You may pursue me all you will,' he whispered stickily. 'I shall never succumb to you or your cancerous embraces. Never.'

His voice caught in his throat and he convulsed in a choked coughing.

'You bastard,' I whispered. 'You vile, vile — '

'Never!' he rasped, and he slammed the door shut. The dark landing trembled with the force of it.

' — bastard,' I managed and my ribs screamed with the effort of not weeping.

'Did you not hear the bell?'

Mrs Black stood outside her chamber on the lower landing, her hands upon her hips. Her mouth was pinched into a knot.

'Answer me, girl! Did the master summon you?' she demanded. 'No? Then what exactly do you think you are doing?'

'I . . . ' I protested, hardly audibly. 'Nothing.'

'Nothing. You idle good-for-nothing puss, your consistency might be a credit to you, if you were ever to direct it towards your work. Now, get yourself to the kitchen immediately before I whip you there myself.'

Mary looked up as I entered the kitchen and her face puckered a little, spilling her tongue on to her bottom lip. When she handed me the bread for the master's supper she frowned.

'Quick, quick,' she urged. I took the bread woodenly, dropping some upon the floor. Mary clucked her tongue and pushed me towards the fire where a pot bubbled. I stared at it, my arms slack at my sides. I longed to scream, to weep, to hold Mary in my arms, to beg forgiveness for what I had done or not done, to her and to my beautiful flawless son, and at the same time I had no notion of how to be or what to do, no idea of what came next. The not-knowing lodged like a fishbone in my throat.

My legs trembled and I sank into the chair, my hands tight around its arms, my gaze lost somewhere in the dark hollow at the heart of the flames. Casting a nervous glance over my shoulder, Mary squeezed my wrist and laid her cheek briefly against my shoulder. The bone jabbed so that I could not swallow.

That evening Mary managed the chores alone. It grew late. I knew I should go upstairs but I could not find the will to rouse myself from the chair. At last, when the lights in the houses opposite were all extinguished, Mary rolled out her palliasse upon the floor and, taking me by the arm, urged me into it. She was agitated but insistent, hustling me beneath the covers. I did not resist her. When Mrs Black knocked upon the door, reminding Mary to douse all the lights before retiring, she did not see me, curled behind the kitchen table. As was her habit, she left the door a little ajar and the long thin shadow of her wriggled like an eel in the narrow stripe of light from her candle as she mounted the rough wood of the stairs. Then it was gone. Mary padded across the floor, snuffing out the last low light on the windowsill, and scrambled into bed beside me. I had forgotten how dark the kitchen was at night. I had a sudden longing to be somewhere else, anywhere else, and I struggled to sit up, my arms invisible in the thick darkness.

Very gently a hand reached out and coaxed me back towards the pillow. Mary murmured gently as she folded herself against my back, her arm heavy around my ribs, her lips against my shoulder. Reaching behind me, I took her hand and clasped it between my own. It was damp and slightly springy, like fresh bread dough.

Time crumples into unfamiliar shapes in the darkness, bunching and stretching so that you lose yourself in the dips and creases of it. When I next heard the night-lanthorn he was calling three of the clock. The fire was almost out and it had grown cold, the stone floor exhaling its chill

348

breath beneath the thin mattress. Mary had shifted round a little, so that she lay with her back to me, my right arm caught beneath her. When I eased it from beneath her it was numb, and I flexed my fingers, feeling the prickle of life returning to their tips. An answering prickle nudged in my chest. I sighed. Mary sighed back, turning round once more and snuggling up against my back. Squeezing my eyes shut, I pressed myself against her comforting warmth.

When I felt the first kick, I thought she had just twitched in her sleep. She had always suffered from poor digestion. I pulled my knees up to my chest, waiting for the familiar rumble of her fart. Then it came again, a distinct nudge against my spine. I opened my eyes. The kitchen flared with the light of a passing linkboy before returning to darkness, leaving his shrill shout lingering like smoke on the night air. Turning over, I placed the flat of my hand upon Mary's stomach.

Even in the pitch darkness there was no mistaking it. Around her hips and across the surface of her belly the flesh was soft and pliable as it had always been but beneath it there was a curved bowl of muscle, pulled taut. As I rested my hand upon its slope I felt again the pressure against my hand, a hard square shape there for a moment and then gone. I pressed down harder with the palm of my hand. There was a shifting, a larger rounder mass briefly pushing against my fingers, a ripple of moving parts. Mary sighed and mumbled in her sleep as she humped herself over on to her back. The firelight made a dome of her stomach, its lantern the soft pastille of her protruding belly button. In the red glow her skin had an alabaster fineness, the chapped areas around her mouth like the chipped edges of a china cup.

Of course I knew. For months I had seen it and not seen it. I had told myself it was not possible that an idiot might conceive a child. True, Mary had suffered from her monthlies, disconcerted and alarmed each month by the shock of blood, but in every other way she was barely more than an infant. I had observed her swelling and told myself only that she grew fat. In the cradle beside the bed the monkey muttered in its sleep.

Sweet God above, the monkey. My hand trembled as it traced the arch of Mary's belly. The creature was still now beneath its canopy. Perhaps like my son it would be perfect, the strength of its virtue protecting it from the beastly impressions that would force themselves upon its waxy flesh. But even as I longed to believe it I knew it could not be true. Mary herself was formed of unresistant clay, her passions fierce and free of the restraints of wit or discretion. She loved that monkey with all her heart. How then could it not be so, that it might be a child and not an ape-foetus that crouched in the liquid darkness of her child womb, its wildness tethered only by the choke of the birth-string?

Mary stirred and lifted her head. The crumpled rugs had left a dark red crease upon her cheek. She blinked at me in sleepy bemusement, clumsily smoothing away the tear that ran down my face.

'Poor Lize,' she murmured, hardly awake. 'Still sad.'

The grief twisted my heart.

'Oh, Mary, sweet, sweet Mary.'

I reached out and touched her creased cheek. Mary stroked my hand briefly and then, closing her eyes, she curled up once more.

'Sleep,' she yawned, and she held up the rugs so that I might cuddle down beside her. I lay down, my face towards hers, our noses almost touching. Her lashless eyelids were translucent, etched with lilac. She breathed deeply, already almost asleep.

'Oh, Mary,' I whispered. 'Forgive me. I can't bear that you have endured this all alone.'

I squeezed her hand tightly under the covers. She murmured something and pulled away. I knew that I should let her alone but I could not stop myself.

'Mary, you know, do you not, that — you know that you — that you shall — ?' I broke off. Then, brusquely, I shook her shoulder. 'Mary, this thing, this thing that is happening to you, that is growing inside you, in your belly, do you know what it is?'

Mary rolled over away from me, making a shield of her shoulders.

'Sleep,' she insisted.

'I can't sleep. Not until you've told me everything. Oh, Mary, who has done this to you? Is it that Mr Jewkes, is that who? That monster, I swear I could — '

Mary twisted around, her eyes suddenly wide awake and round with fear.

'No. No. Hush. No talk. Never. Secret. Big secret. Mus'n' say.'

'Who told you that, that dog Jewkes? Or our murderer of a master? Who, Mary?'

'Mus'n' say,' she said again, but her voice quavered and the chewed tips of her fingers pressed into my cheeks. 'Prom's' to Heav'n. Be punish'. Mus'n' say.'

Her eyes pleaded with me, bright with fear. I took her into my arms, wrapping my arms about her so tightly that the creature in her belly squirmed. I hugged her closer, swallowing my shudder.

'Oh, Mary, my dearest love, what is it they have done to you, to us both?'

There was a stirring amongst the knotted shadow of rugs beside her. The monkey pressed itself against Mary's side, tugging at her undress before skittering on to her shoulder and wrapping itself in her hair. It peeked out at me, its dark eyes bright, its ginger whiskers glinting. In the dying firelight, it was hard to see where one ended and the other began.

★ ★ ★

I stroked her hair until she slept again, her fingers plaited into the monkey's tail. I could neither bear to look at it nor bring myself to part them. From what I could tell, Mary was five months gone, possibly even six. Whatever the grim vitiations to be wreaked upon the child,

352

they were likely already complete. And though I longed to rip the beast from her embrace, I could not deny her the consolation of it. Her situation was already bleak enough. All the same, I looked down upon the creature, nestled against her cheek, and I wished it dead. And the child inside her too. Wiped clean from memory, so that, somehow, in some way I could not quite imagine, we might be able to begin anew.

I did not sleep again. I stared at the kitchen ceiling and I thought of the dome and the way it alchemized with the darkness to stamp a thick black hole upon the sky. Daily in its shadow its people were falling sick, starving, grieving, facing ruin and miserable death, but it never looked down. Instead, it kept its gaze upon the horizon, impervious as God Himself to the agonies of the petty lives that surrounded it. Mr Honfleur had once told me that it was the opinion of Mr Wren, the Cathedral's architect, that every building should aim at eternity.

I stood quickly, pulling the blanket up over Mary's sleeping shoulders. She sighed in her sleep, sucking on her tongue. My head ached with unanswered questions. I knew only that we could not remain at Swan-street. Whatever the cost, we had to escape it. It might be too late for the doomed child, its waxy bones already distorted into the grotesque form conceived for it by our monster of a master. It was not yet too late for her.

It was still night when I slipped out of bed. I lit a rushlight from the embers of the fire and hurriedly dressed myself in its smoky light. We

353

could leave before anyone might know we were gone. I had a little money to keep us from destitution, the remains of my mother's guineas. I would find employment for us both with someone kindly who might neglect to observe the swelling of Mary's belly. It could hardly be so very noticeable if I had failed to see it. I would —

I stopped, my bodice only half-laced, and my hands fell to my sides, heavy and palsied.

I would ruin us both. The ravaged beggars on Cheap-side plucked at my skirts as the fire that had lit my belly flickered and went out. There was no one I could go to for help. With neither commendation nor character I would never find work and without it I had barely enough money to keep us alive. Where would we lodge, what would we eat, how long before the filthy kennels of the city opened to swallow us whole? My entire fortune comprised a few shillings and several bottles of Elixir that no one wanted to buy. Mary had nothing but a swollen belly and an idiot's features. I was hardly more fortunate, a woman without relatives or reputation. What hope did either of us have of sympathy?

My knees buckled. I squatted on the side of the mattress, staring at nothing. I could feel the tiny movements of my ribs as I breathed in and out. Beside me Mary snored, one arm thrown out beside me upon the covers. Upstairs Grayson Black paced his room, making his endless figures of eight.

Grayson Black. Murderer, rapist, maker of monsters.

Master.

* * *

It was past dawn when the door banged open, setting what was left of the pewter clattering in the dresser. As I startled up blearily, Edgar flung himself down on the mattress, tugging at my arm.

'The medicine, you have to make it stronger,' he begged me. 'The sores — oh God, they — '

Beside me Mary stirred, kicking the mess of rugs away from her legs. I gasped as the memory struck me open-handed, Edgar sprawled where I lay now, his face crusted with tears and snot.

The only other proven cure was to fuck a virgin, the younger the better.

Edgar fell backwards as I clawed at his face, kicking with all my strength at his shins, grinding my knuckles into the soft slope of his nose. His blood spurted against my fist. Had he done it alone? Or had he offered himself for hire to Mr Black, a duty performed for the advance of his master's great work? The discrepancies of dates and probabilities were a faint murmur, powerless against the blind frenzy of my fists. As sharply as I could I brought my knee up into the slack of his groin. Edgar groaned, doubling up. I struck out with my boots, kicking him hard in the back of his knees as I slammed my fist once more into the mashed disorder of his nose. Perhaps he had even secured himself a payment for the unappetizing task, two birds slain with a single stone. Had he congratulated himself for the perfect symmetry of his subterfuge, when he left Mary sprawled and weeping upon her mattress,

355

his vile sediment sticky on her thighs? He groaned again, an agonized clutching at breath, before collapsing against the leg of the table, heavy as a felled tree.

Mrs Black appeared in the doorway. Edgar hauled himself to stand, turning his head away so she could not see his bloodied nose.

'I want the two of you upstairs in five minutes. The master desires to see Mary later and there are one hundred duties to be done before she can be spared.'

The door slammed shut.

Edgar moaned and clutched at his face. Disgusted by us both, I threw a rag at him and snatched up a comb to tidy my hair. The teeth gouged my scalp, steadying me. Edgar suffered still. Was that not some small comfort? Edgar's condition was not yet obvious, with none of the crusted scabs and foul stinks of the advanced disease, but they would come and then it would be he whom others regarded with revulsion, he who found himself alone and abandoned. What hope would he have then of gathering into his lap the last crumbs of the Blacks' fortune? He would die a dreadful death, his body decaying from the inside, his petty ambitions as rotted as his flesh.

It was then that I saw my chance. Edgar gaped at me as I outlined my terms, his mouth working furiously beneath his swollen nose, but, although he was witless, he was endowed with sufficient of the worldly form of wisdom to recognize that he had no choice in the matter. My silence was perhaps of even greater necessity to him than my medicine. He appealed with pleas and threats in turn to my conscience, to my shame, to my instinct of self-preservation, but I only informed him coolly that, of the trinity, I possessed only one and that it left me with no choice. My terms were fixed. Five shillings a week for my silence and another for the medicine, take it or leave it.

'You are a contemptible little bloodsucker,' he hissed when he surrendered his first payment. 'You shall not get away with this.'

I curtsied, my face grim.

'Please come again, sir,' I said. 'We so appreciate your continued patronage.'

That evening I sewed the coins Edgar gave me into the hem of my dress. The way it dragged a little to one side when I walked was my first presentiment of freedom.

★   ★   ★

The gladwin pessaries had dried to ancient chrysalises beneath the cloths in the kitchen dresser. When I picked them up, they crumbled in my hand, flecking my palms with brown. I threw them on the fire and watched them take. They burned fiercely, privately, rolled in orange flame.

I made no more. It was much too late for gladwin. Any attempt to expel an infant so much grown would require powerful and dangerous intercession and would most likely take the mother off with it. I might have taken such a risk on my own behalf. I could not countenance it on Mary's. What scandalous loss of reputation might be suffered by one who had never been permitted the privilege of claiming one? Besides, the spectre of her writhing upon her palliasse, her cheeks clay-grey, fatty sweat greasing her hair as she screamed, the puddle of scarlet blood spreading its stain beneath her — the image of it was intolerable. It would be safer for her now to carry the creature to term, whatever the horrors that awaited us then. It was the monster the master wanted, not Mary. Every day, he had her come to him. The hours she spent with him unspooled in slack loops that caught around my neck and made it hard to breathe. I began the same duties over and over again, completing none. At night I stared up at the ceiling and I made lists in my head.

Lists of herbs that might bring down a child before its time: alkanet; anemone; barberry; brake; bryony; calamint; gladwin; hellebore; hyssop; sabine; wormseed.

Lists of the words I had mastered in my reading practice and must commit to memory: capital, constable, conscience, candour, cataract.

Lists of the perils of the maternal imagination taught to me in childhood: if an expectant mother urinated in a churchyard or crossed a water-filled ditch, her child would be a bed-wetter; if she peeped through a keyhole he would squint; if she helped to shroud a corpse he would be pale and sickly; if she spilled beer on her clothing he would turn out a drunkard; if she ate speckled bird eggs his skin would be thickly freckled.

Lists of the fates that faced a poor woman

without employment: thief, whore, beggar, corpse.

Lists of remedies for the curse of the mother's imagination: if a hare should cross your path, tear your dress; think upon gods and heroes; baptize the unborn child with holy water. Avert your eyes from cripples and felons hanging from the neck.

Lists of infusions against the French pox: mezereon spurge; sarsaparilla; soapwort; spikenard with dandelion, burdock and yellow dock; walnut.

Lists of the ways it was possible to kill a man: aconite; agaric and other toadstools, the flowers of the buttercup distilled in wine; the root of the daffodil, cooked in place of onions; dog's mercury; foxglove taken daily over the course of a month; juice extracted from the roots, leaves and berries of belladonna.

To Mr Grayson Black
Apothecary at the sign of the Unicorn in Swan-
street

Mr Black, sir,

I am of course glad to know that your health is
a little restored and hope that each day that
passes hastens your recovery.

I enclose for your attention once again the
outstanding account of monies owed by yourself. As you can see, the sum is grown
considerable. I was diverted by the contention
in your last letter that my best chance of payment lies not in withdrawing my services but in
permitting you the completion of your studies.
How neat is your reasoning! In order to pay me
you must have me send you more books. I only
hope you are half as good a scientist as you are
a logician.

Still, harbouring no particular affection for
the grim processes of English law, I therefore
suggest the following. I shall continue to supply
you with the books you require. I shall however
increase the cost of each loan by 6d., which I
shall set against your outstanding debt. As
before I shall expect each one returned
unmarked and within three weeks of receipt. In
addition I shall accept for resale any books you
have already purchased from me, if they are in
sufficiently good condition, and credit any
monies accrued thus to your account. As for
the balance I shall take no action if the full
amounts is settled six months from today.

I believe my terms to be generous. If you wish to oblige me further, you should continue to send that charming maid of yours with your books. You are fortunate that her pretty face provides me something of a consolation.

I am, sir, your obedient — not to mention commendably patient — servant,

ETIENNE HONFLEUR
Bookseller at St Paul's Churchyard, London

2nd day of June 1720

31

This time I took two bottles of the Elixir with me. Two weeks passed before I was sent to the bookseller's again. It was a white, weatherless day, the bandage of the sky wrapped tight around the sun, and the door to Mr Honfleur's shop was propped open with a heavy iron weight. Just inside an artist's easel had been set up and upon it were pinned a number of handbills, some covered thickly with words, others illustrated with woodcuts. The largest showed a man seated at a table, quill held aloft, as an angel descended from a cloud above his head, an open book in her hand and a banner covered all over in tiny words streaming from her mouth. I squeezed past it into the shop. In the bottom of my basket the rag-wrapped bottles of opium sounded softly together.

'Ah, the prodigal is returned!' Mr Honfleur declared. 'And what do you think of our latest business venture?'

'You would be well advised to study the hearts of the men who trade so frenziedly at your beloved Exchange,' Annette protested, as though I was not there. 'I defy you to find anything but venality and greed and the determination to profit at the expense of his associates.'

'If you don't mind, I am in something of a hurry today,' I murmured, taking the books from my basket. Beneath my skirts my legs twitched impatiently. If I was quick. I might have time to visit two coffee-houses and not be missed.

'But all profit is at the expense of another,' the bookseller declared, unwrapping the master's books and idly studying the bindings. 'There is meat upon our table because our enterprise answers more readily to its customers' demands and at a better price than that of Mr Roe's next door. This is all you have brought?'

'Yes, sir,' I nodded, willing him to make haste. 'And if I could — '

'And because you turn away from books,' Annette interrupted. 'Which may teach a man how to live, in favour of selling patent medicines and life insurance, which prey upon his basest fear of death!'

'Medicines?' I burst out, before I might stop myself.

'What nonsense, Annette! If a man chooses to purchase a packet of pills or a policy along with his Plato, it does not devalue the currency of print. Why might a man not leave our shop richer in both happiness and health?'

'While you, sir, grow richer in coin? How very convenient.'

'Do not pretend naïveté, Annette. This is commerce, not coercion. A man may profit only by satisfying the needs of his customers.'

'*Vain wisdom all, and false philosophy*,' pronounced Annette, pressing her lips together.

'It is declarations of that kind, daughter . . . ' Mr Honfleur threw his hands above his head and rolled his eyes at me. 'Truly, she

363

is impossible. Come, we shall pay her no more mind. She can busy herself with your master's order. As for you, sit here, beside me, and tell me what news you bring from the apothecary's house.'

But I could not sit. I stared at the bookseller, excitement rising in my chest.

'Mr Honfleur, do you truly sell patent medicines? I had — '

'*Mon Dieu!*' Mr Honfleur cried. 'No more! You women — I am quite tired of the subject. If you wish to stay we will talk only of agreeable things. Annette! Here. I wish this seen to immediately.'

I flushed. From behind her book Annette considered me coolly, the faintest trace of a smile upon her lips. I ached to stamp down hard upon her smug little foot. Instead, summoning all the false gaiety I could muster, I launched into a wild tale of the monkey's latest antics. But even as my tongue tumbled over the words, my head resounded to a single rhythm. Medicines. Here. Here of all places. I gazed at him as he laughed and my blood pounded until the pulse in my neck throbbed with it.

'If it is monkeys you are fond of,' he chuckled, 'I shall have to have you accompany me to Exchange-alley one day. The place is more awash with simians than the forests of the tropics themselves.'

I managed a smile. My cheeks were flushed and I could feel the sweat trickling between my breasts.

'And now I have an appointment. Good day,

my dear. We will not wait so long to see you again, I hope.'

Saluting us, he straightened his wig and was gone. I paused as Annette slowly lowered her book and sighed, reaching with limbs slow as treacle for the apothecary's books. Then, snatching up my basket, I ran from the shop, casting about me until I made out the sway of his back, pushing through the throng towards Paternoster-row.

'Mr Honfleur, sir, please stop,' I shouted after him. He turned, frowning a little, and I seized his sleeve. 'Excuse me, sir, but stop a moment, I beg you. I — '

'You forget yourself, child,' Mr Honfleur protested not unkindly, detaching my fingers from his arm.

'Forgive me, sir,' I pleaded. 'It's — it's only that — there is — I mean I have — well, you were speaking — with Annette — she talked of — you sell patent medicine, do you not? And, well, there is — that is, I have prepared — I call it Tally's Elixir. I have it here, in my basket. The preparation is close to a miracle and may relieve the most agonizing suffering. Look at Mr Black. He has been so unwell and yet — and I — well, since you said . . . '

Mr Honfleur studied me. Then very slowly he began to smile.

'You wish to sell me a remedy you have stolen from your master?'

Although his lips still smiled, his brow creased with incredulity. Immediately I understood the terrible extent of my misjudgement. The bookseller found me amusing, perhaps even charming. He was not so antique nor I so very plain. But my master was a customer and a fellow merchant. Beside the mutual obligations of London's respectable burghers, the frail amity of master and servant was no more than a loose thread, quickly brushed away, as quickly forgotten. It was the iron girders of shared citizenship, of common interest, that held the structure of the metropolis aloft.

'It isn't like that,' I whispered, staring at my boots, and my treachery quivered in the space between us.

'Well then, I think I must see what it is you have to sell, do you not agree? Bring it to me tomorrow and I shall consider it.' Gently he placed a hand beneath my chin and raised my face till our eyes met. His mouth twitched. 'Why so disconsolate? It is a fine idea. Together we may contrive to recoup a little of what your master owes me. Besides, how may I resist the chance to drive my dearest daughter perfectly to distraction?'

He was still laughing as he disappeared into the crowd.

* * *

The very next day I took my two bottles of the Elixir to Mr Honfleur's shop. The bookseller took one of the phials and, uncorking it, sniffed at its contents. I watched him, my throat tight with hope.

'So this is Black's preparation,' he murmured.

366

'I hope, for his sake then, that it relieves that most disabling of human afflictions, false vanity.'

Carefully I outlined my pitch as I had rehearsed, making my claims soberly and without excessive embellishment. When I was finished Mr Honfleur did not speak but lifted the bottle once more to his nose and inhaled. I waited, my hands in fists in my lap.

'You have copied the apothecary's recipe exactly? You are sure?'

'I have only added some herbs, sir, for a better flavour.'

Mr Honfleur placed the cork carefully back into the bottle.

'Very well,' he said at last. 'I shall consider it.'

'Oh!' I gasped. 'Oh, Mr Honfleur, sir, thank you. Thank you! You shall not regret it, I promise.'

The bookseller laughed and held up a hand to silence me.

'I shall need to satisfy myself as to its efficacy. For all my daughter's misgivings I am not entirely without scruple. Send me a dozen more bottles and I shall give you my opinion as soon as I am able.'

'But how — ?' I hesitated.

'How? You are the Woman of business, my dear. You work it out.'

I hesitated.

'I — I am sorry, sir,' I blurted out. 'But the Elixir is dear and I have a pressing need for money. If I am to make more. You are a gentleman, I know, and honourable, but . . . '

My voice trailed away. Mr Honfleur sat back

in his chair, his arms crossed over his chest, and considered me, his head on one side. I stared back, my chin jutting out, biting my cheeks so that I would not cry. I could not read his expression.

'*Ma petite*,' he said, shaking his head, and a smile began to ripen around his mouth. '*C'est possible que deux filles peuvent être si différentes?*'

'I — I don't understand.'

'No.' Mr Honfleur reached into his coat and plucked out a crown. 'Shall this be sufficient? Until we are agreed?'

I stared at the coin and the tears sprang into my eyes. 'How long — how long until you shall know? It is only that — I cannot wait long.'

Mr Honfleur regarded me thoughtfully. 'Perhaps this shall do for now?' He held out his handkerchief and smiled as I took it and wiped my eyes. 'As to the rest, I shall let you know as soon as I am able, I promise you that. You drive a hard bargain, *mademoiselle*.'

★ ★ ★

All the way back to Swan-street I kept my fingers curled, crossed over one another for luck. *He shall take it, he shall take it not.* As a child I had cheated when there were few enough petals to predict the way it would come out. I wished I could manage things so easily now.

I slipped across the hall. But as I reached the kitchen stairs the laboratory door opened and Edgar emerged. His face was flushed and his eyes glittered.

'Not so fast, my little sluttikin,' he hissed, grabbing my arm.

'Edgar, please,' I muttered, alarmed. 'Let go of me.'

Edgar's grip tightened.

'But I have some good news for you, my little Hackney whore. Although I fear perhaps it shall not delight you wholly. At least not so much as it does me.'

'Good news is always welcome.'

'I wonder if you shall think that for long. It transpires that those blisters you were treating with such — such *dedication* — were not the French pox, after all, but only a local infection, quite common and happily now cleared. Which means I am no longer at your mercy, either as cunning woman or confidante.'

The heat drained from beneath my skin.

'I am pleased for you,' I said shakily. 'It must come as quite a relief.'

'Oh, it does. It does. For it is not only the burden of illness that I have contrived to escape. It defies belief, I know, but there are those out there, those so wanting in the slightest shred of humanity, so untrammelled by conscience or compassion, that they would not hesitate to extort blood money from a dying man.'

I said nothing, but my skin tightened into gooseflesh.

'Shocking, is it not? I knew you would be sickened by such a thing.' Edgar reached out dreamily and pinched my cheek hard between his thumb and forefinger. 'Of course they shall return all they have taken. In full.'

'But what — what if they have it no longer? If it is spent?'

Edgar snorted.

'You think a moneylender considers that adequate explanation for his losses? If it is spent it must be found elsewhere. All of it. Not to mention the interest due upon the capital sum at a rate of two pence for each shilling taken.'

'Two pence? But that is — ?'

'To increase by a penny each month that the debt remains outstanding.'

The self-satisfaction upon Edgar's face was intolerable. I crossed my arms.

'I only hope that you can prove what you claim,' I declared. 'Otherwise I imagine you have little hope of recouping your losses.'

Edgar seized my wrist. 'Don't you even try — '

'Edgar, I do not know what it is you talk of. Perhaps we should take this matter to the mistress to decide.'

'There is no need of the mistress in this matter. For they shall pay. And, if they do not, I shall seek my revenge upon such leeches. They will pay a heavier price in the end for their treachery.' He thrust his face so close to mine that our noses grazed. His breath was sour and hot. 'They would be advised to think on it, you know. I shall endeavour to exceed their worst imaginings.'

the laughter of the neighbour woman it torments me she comes to me in
my dreams & she quivers her chins & licks her
lips to whisper in my
ear & the telling arouses her & greases her fat
white thighs

she fucks him here in my house my wife that
cunt bitch fucks the
apprentice i see it in her eyes in her scorn she
scorns me & brings the
stink of him in on her cunt she takes from me
all of what is mine by
law mine my business my money my house my
wife

is there no limit to the baseness of woman

then let them starve
& see if the poor-house is as fine a master as i

371

32

Edgar proved as good as his word.

If I walked into a room where he was he walked out. On more than one occasion I found him in my garret, rummaging through my box. And whenever he could he made a point of whispering with Mrs Black, sending me significant glances that made me both angry and afraid. Each time my mistress summoned me I was certain she knew of my extortions and meant to beat me or worse. The atmosphere was worsened by a feud of some kind between my mistress and her neighbour, Mrs Dormer. Frequently I saw the chandler's wife standing in the window of her first-floor chamber, her arms crossed over her bosom, glaring like a gaoler across the lane. She seemed to be waiting for something.

When, a week later, Mr Honfleur greeted me with the news that he would take the Elixir for three months, by way of a trial, I almost kissed him in my relief. He raised an eyebrow when I pressed him about how soon we might expect to see a return. What proceeds there were, he declared lightly, would be divided directly down the middle. I was to remain responsible for the Elixir's manufacture which, in order to avoid difficulties at Swan-street, would from henceforth be undertaken in what had been a tiny storeroom at the rear of the Huguenot's shop.

Mr Honfleur in his turn would take charge of the Elixir's promotion.

The preparation, he informed me, would be sold under the appellation of Dr Huppert's Febrifuge. Perhaps I was not aware that only last winter this miraculous nostrum had brought the King of France himself back from the brink of death. The grateful King had pressed ennoblement upon the doctor but the good man had refused, asking instead for the freedom to practise his religion without concealment and the permission to share his medicine with his family in the Protestant faith. Unable to refuse the man to whom he owed his life, the King had agreed.

'He is a fine and pious man, is he not?' Mr Honfleur declared happily. 'A man to set every Pope-hating heart in London a-pounding. I have been acquainted with him for only a matter of days and yet I myself am already exceedingly fond of the good *docteur*. It is a privilege indeed to act as his representative here in London!'

He pinned a notice to the easel extolling the virtues of the elixir in French, scattered with dashes that gave the words quizzical eyebrows. He meant to print labels for the bottles to match it, each with the doctor's signature and seal. Though I feigned enthusiasm, in truth, I could hardly control the impatience that twitched in my fingers. There was so little time. Such absurdly elaborate preparations only delayed the tincture's sales. The medicine was miraculous and that was the end of it. Surely we had only to

373

tell the customers that and we would sell it by the waggonload.

'Trust me,' the bookseller reproached me. 'The educated man does not purchase an item only because he requires it. He buys it because every possession he acquires holds up a mirror to his imaginings and reflects a superior image of himself.'

I sighed. Outside the bells of the Cathedral scrambled to sound out the hour. So little time. Honfleur frowned.

'But of course I am right,' he protested, as if I had contradicted him. 'A man purchases a trifle, a silk scarf from Persia, let us say. How much softer and more colourful then is the silk if he can be persuaded to imagine the cloth that he now holds in his hands was once entwined around the sweetly perfumed shoulders of a dusky princess? How much sweeter the sugar chipped from King George's own sugar loaf?'

I ached for money, strained towards it with an effort that pulled at my neck and made my ribs ache. But for the bookseller the pleasure was all in the scheming, and in irritating his daughter. He relished the thought of arguing with her on the subject and longed to provoke her to ire.

'The flood of money undammed by the South Sea Company laps daily further into the provinces,' he announced to her. 'All over England men have money to burn and they yearn for long and healthy lives in which to burn it. Surely it is my duty to offer them this Febrifuge. For only God may set the allowance of a man's life.'

But, to his perplexed vexation, she said nothing. She kept house as she always had, she saw that her father visited the barber and wore clothes of adequate cleanliness, she even assisted in the shop when required to, although she obstinately refused to take money for anything but books, but she did so without uttering a single word.

At first the bookseller considered her silence a great joke. He engaged in elaborate displays of dumb show and, when that failed to amuse her, he declared himself delighted with the unexpected peace of it. And though at first I had feared it as yet another reason for delay, I was soon to understand the advantage in it. For, to provoke her, the bookseller took the books from the front window and replaced them with an exhibition of the Febrifuge whose merits he made a point of rehearsing to every customer who came in. As I gazed at the display I prayed she would not relent.

She did not. Mr Honfleur grew impatient. He criticized her publicly, rebuking her for her idleness, her lack of filial piety, and, when that appeared not to affect her, made much of my attentiveness, my humility, the readiness with which my opinions converged with his own. I was, he declared provokingly, the model of a dutiful daughter. He found simple books for me and encouraged me to read to him, to memorize lines of poetry which he had me recite, all the while pressing her for her opinion on my progress. Her eyes were chips of ice but she said nothing.

In time he grew morose. The Frenchmen still came to talk at the shop but Mr Honfleur no longer led the discussions. Instead he wandered about the shop, picking up books and flicking at their pages in weary disgust.

'*Far more numerous was the herd of such who think too little and who talk too much,*' he spat, slamming a volume with such ferocity that I imagined the poems crushed between its pages like flies. 'Why the Devil must poets insist on such commonplaces?'

And then, one pale triumphant morning in May, Mr Honfleur greeted me with a bow and handed me my first purse of coins.

'We are not yet rich, I fear,' he said dryly, 'But, *alors*, it is begun.'

I blinked at the bookseller and I felt a rising in my chest like a great wave.

'Six shillings. Spend it wisely.'

'Six shillings?'

'Every fortune begins with shillings.' He raised his little cup of coffee. 'To Dr Huppert — and the future.'

I did not trust myself to speak. Instead I nodded and squeezed the bag of money in my hand, feeling the press of the coins hard against my palm.

'Why so glum?' He pulled a face. 'It is a cause for celebration, is it not?'

Shaking his head at me, he seized me by the waist, spinning me round in a clownish dance. I ducked my head and blushed and begged him to stop, but he only laughed and stamped his feet like a rustic at harvest-time. Then, without warning, he stopped, snatching his hands away from me so abruptly he almost pushed me away.

'My dear, to what do we owe the pleasure?'

I twisted around. Annette stood framed in the doorway, her outline stamped against the light.

'I hate to interrupt your celebrations,' she hissed. 'But — '

'She speaks!' Mr Honfleur threw his hands up. 'A miracle indeed.'

Annette's face tightened.

'I wished to inform you, Father, that I can no longer remain in this house while you make free with your whore.'

The bookseller exploded like a firecracker.

'How dare you speak to me so! You are not too old, daughter, that I may not take you across my lap for such insolence!'

Annette's contempt might have turned a tree to ash.

'It would be my husband's place to strike me, Father, if such action should be necessary.'

'Until you have such a husband, I — '

'Oh, did I not tell you? How foolish of me. Father, I am to be married.'

The words seemed to strike the breath from Honfleur's belly.

'Why so aghast, Father?' Annette enquired sweetly. 'He is a curate, a man who venerates God, not Mammon. It should comfort us all that, in these days of madness, such men survive. He shall make a very fine husband.'

Honfleur gaped at her, his mouth working like a fish.

'Do you not mean to extend us your blessing?

Not that I require it, of course. We shall be married directly.'

'But — ?'

'But what about you? Dear Father, have you not already secured the services of an obliging little whore of a maidservant? Surely the slut is dexterous enough to keep one hand in your breeches as she empties your chamber pot?'

Then, with a swish of her skirt, she was gone. As the door slammed behind her, Mr Honfleur sank against the table, his legs bowing beneath him.

'Sir, are you — ?'

He looked up, and his face was crumpled and purple as an infant's.

'Go!' he roared. 'Get out! Take these damned books and get out!' Snatching up the books, he hurled them at me. 'I said, go!'

I knelt and clumsily stacked the books into my basket.

'You should not suffer her to slander me so,' I whispered, but if he heard me he said nothing. Instead, he bowed over the table, his fingers pressed hard into the tight curls of his wig, and exhaled the strangled cry of a rabbit caught in a gin.

'We are still in business, are we not?' I asked in a tiny high voice. 'The Febrifuge — ?'

'Damn it, girl, did you not hear me? Get out!'

There was nothing else to be done. Picking up my basket, I walked stiffly away.

★　★　★

378

At Swan-street the kitchen was empty and supper not begun. There was no sign of Mary. Quickly I hid my bag of coins in the back of the dresser drawer. A painful lump lodged in my throat as I chopped vegetables, wielding the knife like an axe. It was some time before I heard Mary's heavy footfall, the chirruping voice she used to the monkey.

'Where the Devil have you been?' I rebuked her, my distress curdling to anger, and I hurled a handful of vegetables into the pot.

'Wi' master,' Mary said in a faraway voice, holding the monkey against her cheek. It wore an infant's lace bonnet tied tightly over its whiskery face and it tugged at the ribbons, shaking its head unhappily. 'Jinks baby.'

'For pity's sake, Mary, it's an animal, not a child!' I cried, snatching at the bonnet. 'Why can you not — ?'

Mary swayed backwards and forwards as though intoxicated, cradling the monkey against her breast.

'Mar' nurse Jinks,' she murmured. 'Like Lize.'

I frowned. 'Milk. Like Lize.' For a moment I did not understand her. Then the shock burst like a bag of soot in my chest, black and deadening.

'Mary, no! You did not do it, did you? Tell me you did not let him do it.'

Mary cradled the monkey against her chest.

'Like Lize,' she said again more softly, and a single tear fell upon the monkey's bonneted head and quivered there. I swallowed, but the stone in my throat was not so easily dislodged.

'We are going to get away from here,' I whispered, and the pain in my throat choked me. 'We shall go where you shall be safe, where he will never find you. Just a few more weeks and it shall be over, I promise. All over. We shall be free.'

'Is that so?'

Mrs Black stood in the open doorway, the white blade of her nose slicing the shadows.

'This is how you would repay our kindnesses?' she enquired coldly. 'With theft and cozenage?'

'And whose kindness swells Mary's belly?' I spat back. 'Whom may we thank for that generous bequest?'

In the silence that followed the fire hissed with dismay.

'We are not felons,' I said shakily. 'You cannot keep us here against our will.'

'It would seem that you oblige me to do precisely that. Mary, come here.'

She snapped her fingers. Her head bowed, Mary rose leadenly and went to stand beside her in the doorway. Without looking at me, Mrs Black walked across the kitchen and locked the door to the outside steps, putting the key in her sleeve. Then, gripping my wrist, she turned my hand palm upwards and struck it six times as hard as she could with the birch at her belt. The pain was distinct but disconnected from suffering, like a memory of pain, and I made no sound. Only Mary whimpered, covering her face with her hands. When she was finished, Mrs Black stalked back to the door and, taking Mary by the arm, pulled her out of the room. The door

380

slammed. I heard the scrape of the key in the lock, then nothing. I did not rattle the door nor demand to be let out. I only stood there, immobile, as the fire sighed and the throb of my sore hand marked time, as regular and purposeless as the ticking of a gaoler's clock.

★ ★ ★

At dawn Mrs Black unlocked the door. She looked as weary as I, her face white and pinched.

'You shall not see Mary again,' she said and the act of speaking seemed to cost her prodigiously. 'She is to be kept apart from you and from anyone else who might seek to undo the master's work, under my close and constant supervision. Any attempt to see or speak with the idiot girl shall be severely punished. You shall not ruin us, do you hear me? I should see you dead before I let you ruin us.'

At the door she paused, her hand at her throat.

'From today, you shall perform her duties as well as your own. I can only hope that the burden of work shall teach you something of humility.'

An hour later I crouched in the hall, scrubbing the floor. My hand moved the brush mechanically over the boards, backwards and forwards, backwards and forwards. The scraping of bristle against wood muffled the voice in my head. *List them*, it urged, *come now, Eliza, list them —*

'To the kitchen! Now!'

Mrs Black stood over me, her boot against my

ribs. Slowly I put down my brush and stood. Gripping my arm, she dragged me to the top of the kitchen stairs.

'Lize.'

'Silence!'

I twisted around. Mary shuffled a little out of the shadows, her hands twisted into knots at her mouth. Her clothes were filthy, her face wan and streaked with soot. Smeary black shadows circled her eyes and her cheeks were rucked with twists of dried and blackened snot. Her distended belly poked against her soiled skirts like a deformity. She blinked, squinting up at me as if the dim light hurt her eyes.

'Mary, my dear one,' I pleaded, 'everything shall be all right, I promise.'

Very slowly Mary raised her head. Her eyes were pink, raw with misery. As I held out my hand to her Mrs Black wrenched at my arm, twisting it painfully in its socket.

'Lize.'

The anguish crumpled Mary's face and she squeezed her eyes tight, rocking backwards and forwards on her heels, her hands wringing and twisting together.

'Oh God, Mary — '

Mrs Black struck me so hard across the cheek that I bit my tongue. I choked, tasting blood.

'For every time you say her name she'll have another night in the coal hole. Is that what you wish for her? Now, get down those stairs before I throw you down!'

'Lize.'

I half-fell down the stairs. My cheek smarted

and my tongue swelled in my mouth. I thought of Mary crouched in the darkness, her arms hugging her shins, her forehead pressed hard against her knees, rocking back and forth to the shrill, tuneless sound she made when she was distressed, and my throat ached so sharply that I could hardly breathe.

Mary feared the coal hole more than any other place on earth.

I, Grayson Moses BLACK, Apothecary & Scholar of Swan-street in the Parish of Saint Martin-in-the-Fields in the County of Middlesex, being weak in body but of sound and disposing mind and memory, do make and ordain this my last Will & Testament in manner following so that all difficulties and controversies about the same may be prevented after my decease. That is to say,

Item: I commit my soul unto the hands of Almighty God, my Creator & Redeemer, and my body to Christian burial

Item: I give and bequeath to the Royal Society the full extent of my writings & other papers so that they may be preserved for the nation in the manner due to them

Item: I revoke the bequest sworn to in my previous testament to grant unto my wife Margaret BLACK the remains of my Estate & the full guardianship over any such direct dependants as shall exist at the time of my decease or afterwards. Margaret BLACK is an adulterer and a whore & it is my Will that she shall know the agonies of poverty & destitution due to the harlot who cuckolds her husband under his very roof.

Item: I declare as null and void the apprenticeship of Edgar Horatio PETTIGREW, who has, through his vile conduct while under my tutelage, so cruelly betrayed my trust that neither shall any part of the three hundred pounds of his indenture be considered due to him from the remains of my Estate nor shall he have consideration within his lifetime for admission

to the Worshipful Company of Apothecaries.
Item: May it be noted that, instead, I give and
bequeath all the rest and residue of the moneys
owing to me from any person or persons
whomsoever and of all my money in the public
stocks or funds and of all my other goods,
chattels, and personal estate whatsoever that I
shall be possessed of, interested in, or anyways
entitled to at the time of my decease, together
with the full & lawful guardianship of the sum
of my dependants & any offspring thereof, unto
my brother, John BLACK of Newcastle, to
have benefit thereof during his natural life on
condition of the construction of an appropriate
and public monument to the name of BLACK
and all that has been achieved in that name for
the greater glory of God.
In witness whereof I have hereunto set my
hand and Seal this eighteenth day of July in the
year of our Lord one thousand seven hundred
and twenty, Grayson BLACK

    in the presence of two witnesses as under-
signed Silas PEEL Sampson MATHER

33

I did not see Mary again. Mrs Black made sure of that. I prepared Mary's meals in the kitchen and Mrs Black took them up to her on a tray. On the second day I placed a tiny feather from the linnet's breast beneath her soup bowl. When the tray came back it was gone. After that I hid something beneath the plate every time. It was never much, only a curl of my hair or a scrap cut from the hem of my dress or even the paring of a fingernail. I prayed that she was safe and that she understood.

There were no errands. I kept Mr Honfleur's handkerchief tucked in the pocket in my skirt, a knot tied in it to hold in the luck, and I took it out when I was alone to give me courage. And still the days passed and the time of Mary's confinement grew ever closer. The handkerchief grew limp and grey from handling. I tried not to think of the anger with which the Huguenot had ordered me from the shop. Instead I brooded upon the ways in which I might once again secure his favour. I prayed that he did not remember my remonstrations, that we might pretend the whole episode forgotten. Desperation, after all, is no ally of dignity.

The wait was unendurable. Mrs Black did not speak to me, folding her lips closed whenever I encountered her. When she took Mary for her regular interview with the apothecary she locked

386

me into the kitchen so that I might not attempt to intercept her. She kept the front door to the house locked. Even the shop door was kept bolted and only opened when a customer rang the bell. I was as much a prisoner as Mary.

And then, after nine days, there was a book on the hall table. I touched it with one finger, barely able to believe in its solidity. When Mrs Black unlocked the door for me, she withdrew the key from her belt like a knife. She said nothing but the air around her smelled scorched, like the air after a strike of lightning. In the lane I ran, simply to feel the stretching in my legs. All along Cheap-side I pushed and jostled, giddy with desperate liberty. It was only outside the shop that I hesitated, suddenly afraid to enter. When at last I forced myself to step across the threshold, the Huguenot looked up and smiled. Although he looked tired and not altogether clean, there was nothing in his manner to suggest we had parted on ill terms. Rather, he greeted me as he always did, rubbing his hand over his unshaven chin.

'You have books for me?'

I nodded, staring at my feet. I thought of the sight we must have made, dancing together in the crowded shop. I did not know what to say.

'Annette is to be married,' the bookseller said at last.

He wished it forgotten. Everything was going to be all right.

'She is?' I said, relief pinking my skin. 'But that is fine news.'

'Is it?' he asked. 'It came as something of a

shock to me.' He sat heavily in his chair, tipping it back on to its hind legs. 'I had become accustomed to her.'

'She is already gone?'

'She tells me she will lodge with her aunt till he has enough set aside. I have offered to assist them but naturally she will not hear of it. My coin is clipped with chicanery, you see.'

'Surely not — '

'It is hardly unusual, of course,' Honfleur continued bitterly. 'Every daughter should use the institution of marriage to advance themselves in society. The only difference is that Annette wishes not to become the lady of the manor but the *principessa* of high principle. It makes no difference in the end. Either way, they consider themselves justified in despising you.'

I shifted unhappily.

'She is a respectful daughter,' I protested. 'Surely she will soften.'

The bookseller let forth a snort of mirthless laughter.

'How little you know her,' he said.

We were both silent then. The clock ticked upon the wall.

'*Tell us, pray, what devil this melancholy is, which can transform men into monsters,*' Honfleur sighed to himself. Pressing the pads of his thumb and forefinger into his eyes, he pinched his nose hard. Then he raised his head. 'So. You thrive, I hope? It has been some days since your last visit, if I am not mistaken.'

'Yes. I — I was hoping for news of the Febrifuge. You see, I have an urgent need — that is, I wondered how it went. How profits are.'

Honfleur shrugged.

'I do not recall. Still, the market rises daily, despite Paris. There they use banknotes to wipe their arses. But we pay no heed to them. In London every last man is turned stock-jobber. Most of their womenfolk too, for that matter.'

'Except Annette,' I said, attempting a joke.

Honfleur's mouth twisted. 'Except Annette. And her censorious sophist of a husband.'

'Then our partnership flourishes?' I asked, despite myself. 'There shall be more profits?'

Honfleur did not answer. Instead, a smile began to twist his mouth.

'Why, of course!' he declared, slapping a palm to his forehead as his chair thudded forward. 'Of course! I cannot believe I did not think of it before!'

'I beg your pardon?'

He held his hands out, palms up.

'We shall be married!' he announced. 'I shall take you as my wife. Such an arrangement would suit us both. We shall be married and live like kings on the proceeds of the Febrifuge!'

'Married?' I repeated dumbly.

'Married,' Honfleur said, and a mist of impatience rose up from him. 'I have the right word in English, do I not?'

'Your English is impeccable,' I stammered.

'Then we are agreed,' he said. 'We shall marry. The sooner the better.'

I stared at him as he leaped to his feet, my face slack and stupid.

'But — '

389

'But? Eliza, I wonder if you appreciate your good fortune. I should have thought 'Yes' a better answer.'

The lightness of his tone did not quite balance the reproof. Still I could not answer. My heart raced, my mouth opening and closing in soundless disbelief. Mr Honfleur wished to marry me. It was the answer, the answer to everything. I would be free, Mary too. She would come to the bookseller's as my maid. We would leave Swan-street for ever and we would never have to go back. We would live here together. We would be safe. I could hardly imagine it, the sheer unimaginable good fortune of it. The tears filled my eyes as I looked up at the bookseller, holding out both my hands to him in mute gratitude.

'Look at this — you are shaking, my dear.'

I nodded helplessly and the tears spilled over and fell unchecked down my cheeks.

'Why, you are overcome. Then I shall ask you again. Shall you be my wife?'

I opened my mouth but my tongue was palsied and my lips trembled so violently I could not speak.

'Still no answer? Be careful, the market for marriage is come like the market for stocks — there is a grave shortage of profitable opportunity for those women without fortunes to trade.' There was a peevish edge to his teasing. 'Tomorrow I might wake a more prudent man.'

Hastily, I pressed my hand to my mouth, forcing a little sense into my foolish lips.

'Forgive me, sir,' I whispered, and I bowed my

head. 'My answer is yes. Yes, yes, of course I shall marry you. I can think of no greater honour.'

'I should hope so.' He shook his head humorously, extending his hand towards me. 'Look at you. How very simple you are, for all your boldness and bluster.'

Taking my face between his hands, he kissed me very softly upon the mouth and wiped my tears away with his thumb, licking their salt from his skin. The taste of them stirred something within him, so that his mouth grew hot and greedy. Pulling me towards him, he pressed my body against his, kissing me hard upon the mouth. I clung to the stuff of his coat and parted my lips. When he thrust his tongue deep between them he tasted not unpleasantly of bitter coffee and pipe tobacco. His hands closed around my breasts as he kissed me more insistently, his tongue quickening and his breath coming in hard gasps. I forced my own mouth to move, responding to the bookseller's own parries. I wished to please him and it was not so difficult. Gratitude has much in common with affection.

The bookseller groaned, a long gluttonous grunt, and ran his wet mouth down my neck before burying his face between my breasts. His chin was gritty with stubble. I thought of my mother and her ambitions for her only daughter and I suddenly felt very old.

'Be mindful of my virtue,' I murmured, caressing his face gently with my fingertips. 'We must wait till we are wed.'

Honfleur looked up at me. He looked quite unlike his usual judicious self. His eyes were bright and feverish, his lips a deep crimson, their edges smeared against the surrounding skin like wet ink. Two circles of scarlet flared upon his cheeks. With powder and patches he might have passed for a courtesan, an ancient and wanton courtesan. His hands circled my upper arms and he pulled me to him once more, his hand reaching beneath my skirts. I pulled away, this time more firmly.

'Mr Honfleur, come now, I beg you. I must go home.'

The bookseller shook his head and sighed, rubbing his hands along his thighs.

'*Mon Dieu*, very well.' His lips pouted into a smile. 'But I will countenance no delay. We shall beat Annette and her whiffler to the altar, you may be sure of that.'

I walked back to Swan-street in a dream, my heart darting and wheeling in my chest like a swallow. We were safe. Safe. Our future secured, mine and Mary's, by a deliverance of such miraculous fortuity that I should never have dared to have hoped for it. As I made my way along Cheap-side, the smile spread stupidly across my face and my feet danced. Mr Honfleur the bookseller, a man I admired, a man who had shown me kindness, wished to take me, Eliza Tally, a maidservant without wealth or reputation, as his wife. What angels gazed down from the Heavens upon the grimy reaches of my soul and set upon my sinning head the light of their celestial blessing? What acts of goodness had I performed, asleep or unknowing, that now repaid me so?

I knew myself undeserving of such extraordinary good fortune. But now that, by whatever accident of Fate or seraphim, it was indeed mine, I would endeavour to merit it. I would permit no fissures, no cracks into which ill luck might creep and breed, but I would steep myself in those qualities that would preserve my undeserved good fortune as vinegar preserves onions, humility and obedience and the bowed kind of gratitude that knows it can never repay the debt owed to it.

Mrs Eliza Honfleur.

Mrs Eliza Honfleur and Mary.

We were saved.

formal invitations to hand-picked members of
royal society to attend delivery
    Halley
    Sloane
    Tabor
    Cowper
archbishop of london?
wright? But he asks only for money & more
money that exchange of his has a maw like a
great whale
fine wine & roasted meats & pies & pudding

Conversion of parlour to exhibition hall
skeleton of monkey to be displayed alongside
that of human infant idiot in cage to underline
simian association?
or formal lady's gown in order to emphasize
transformation by impression?
everywhere apparatus of science finest micro-
scopes & orreries those bastards shall not
dare to deem me less of a scholar than they

10 shilling entrance charge — note well Mr
Wren how much more my creation is worth
than that popish grotesquery of yours out
there

fecundation of the other whore girl debts must
be settled if they insist upon keeping her here
they must surely permit me to make use of her
worthless harlot
begin again & again while there is still time

394

subsequent proofs categoric proofs proofs for
all eternity

bring the whores to me & i shall make monsters of them all

OF THEM ALL

34

As the days passed, and still the master had no books for me, my exhilaration faded. I grew distracted and then anxious. What if Annette had persuaded her father to change his mind? What if he had regretted his proposal? Or forgotten it altogether? There had been no witnesses, nothing to make the offer binding. What if, when I entered the shop, he acted as though nothing at all had happened? What would I do then?

When on the sixth day I came upstairs to find in the hall a small package of books tied with string, I rushed through my tasks, banging brushes and coughing dust, so that I might spend careful minutes before the scrap of glass in the kitchen, combing my hair and pinching my cheeks to give them a pink glow. A little bacon fat gave my lips a glossy fullness. I pinned on a clean cap, using a damp finger to set a pair of curls upon my temples, and laced my bodice as tight as I could bear, arranging my breasts so that they curved generously above the muslin trim. Outside the house I looked up to the window where Mary was imprisoned, hoping to catch a glimpse of her, but as usual the drapes were pulled and the panes were milky-blank with borrowed sky.

'Hold your thumbs, Mary,' I whispered. 'Hold your thumbs for luck.'

Then, lifting my skirts, I ran so that I might be

at the shop before she forgot the instruction and let the wish spill carelessly out on to the floor.

'Good day, sir,' I called breathlessly as I pushed open the door, my pulse knocking in my throat. 'I hope I do not come at an inconvenient time.'

'My dear, come in, come in. Your mistress keeps you too close.' He smiled, half-raising himself from his chair and fumbling in his coat pocket with a forefinger. 'Look, I have something for you.'

He handed me a small roll of oyster-coloured silk and watched as I unwrapped it with clumsy fingers.

A ring.

'If you tremble so you shall drop it,' the Huguenot chided lightly. 'And it was not cheap. Here, let me.'

He slid the ring on to my finger. It was a tight fit but the bookseller twisted it like a screw, forcing it over the knuckle.

'There,' he announced. 'It looks fine.'

I gazed at my hand. The ring bit into my flesh, rigid and irrefutable.

'I can hardly believe it,' I murmured.

'How young you look when you blush.'

'We are truly contracted?'

'Unless you prove yourself in debt or quite insufferable, I believe we are.' Honfleur smiled, tapping my nose with his finger. 'I would urge you to make me a loving and careful wife. I have borne enough shrewishness for several lifetimes.'

I smiled, swallowing the lump in my throat,

and stood on tiptoe so that I might kiss him upon the cheek.

'Oh, I shall, I shall,' I assured him, and I knew that I had never before spoken with such sincerity. 'Thank you, sir. You shall not regret this. I mean to make you as contented a husband as there ever was in history.'

'Then we should set about satisfying that wish with all haste. I want nothing with the business of banns. Why declare one's business to all the world in a public place when the *curé* will do it snug and without to-do at Threadneedle-street? We shall have a couple of guests to serve as witnesses, eat a hearty dinner and consider ourselves well satisfied.'

My heart lurched. I thought of the Campling boy, of the ceremony at the cottage.

'But, sir, it must be done properly, must it not — ?'

'Dear God!' Honfleur frowned. 'I did not have you for one of these foolish girls who craves luxury and extravagance. You shall have a new dress for the occasion but you must not put on airs. Your humility has always become you.'

'On the contrary, I desire no luxury,' I insisted. 'It is just that I — I wish it properly lawful, sir. That is all. I should not want it underhand.'

'Underhand? Dear Eliza, do you mistake me for a Fleet man, all secrets and lies? I am a Frenchman, remember. It shall be done correctly, I assure you.'

I had vexed him. Quickly I took his hand and pressed it to my lips.

'Then I shall be quite satisfied, sir. It is

marriage I desire, sir, not ceremony.'

Mollified, the bookseller studied me thoughtfully.

'I myself have always been a great admirer of the gentler virtues: modesty, courtesy, patience. Powerful enthusiasms are treacherous. When they cool, as all enthusiasms must, they curdle into bile and bitterness. My countrymen would do better to learn from your Earl of Dorset: *'love is a calmer, gentler joy'*. Do you know the poem? Dorinda's Cupid he declares *'a blackguard boy that runs his link full in your face'*. A fine metaphor, *non*? The wise man has no desire to char his eyebrows.'

'I am quite sure you are right, sir,' I agreed, nodding vigorously.

'Do you mock me?' Honfleur grimaced. 'Truly, Eliza, you are in a most trying temper.'

I shook my head in distress. I did not know how I had contrived to provoke him when I was so intent upon the opposite.

'Forgive me, sir, if I displease you. It is only that I — I am overcome. Your kindness exceeds all expectation.'

Again I took his hand and kissed it. Mr Honfleur patted my cheek absently, his attention on the street outside. Then suddenly he stiffened. Turning to me, he seized me by the arms and pulled me towards him.

'Then favour me with a kiss,' he declared and, covering my mouth with his, he forced his tongue between my lips. There was a cold drip on the tip of his nose. The shop bell jangled. He kissed me again, more slowly, before raising his head, his hands clamped about my forearms.

'Annette, dear daughter,' he cooed. 'What a pleasant surprise. To what do we owe the pleasure of your company?'

Annette said nothing. The flower brooch flashed at her bosom.

'I — I should go home,' I muttered, attempting to free myself.

'This shall be your home soon enough,' Honfleur purred, and his fingers tightened upon my arms. 'Annette, you will doubtless be delighted to learn that Eliza and I have agreed a date for our marriage, St Bartholomew's Day, five weeks hence.' He thrust out my hand, displaying the ring. 'We may depend upon you and your curate to act as witnesses, may we not?'

Annette drew herself up taller, gazing at her father down the length of her nose.

'St Bartholomew's Day, but of course, how perfect!' She clapped her hands, a disconcertingly coquettish gesture. 'What other place for a girl of her quality to be married than at the Fair? Doubtless you have arranged for a dwarf to preside over the ceremony? Or perhaps a pair of Siamese twins? A grotesque of some kind would describe the character of the occasion so admirably.'

'Is that so?' Honfleur replied icily. 'To my mind, there is little more grotesque than religious fervour. There is no more certain way to leach the joy from this life than an excess of pious enthusiasm.'

'And no more certain way of ensuring eternal damnation in the next than the patronage of

400

sixpenny whores. *Il connaît l'univers et ne se connaît pas.*'

'You listen to me, you little — !'

But Annette was gone. Dust turned in anxious spirals in the sunlight and above the door the bell shivered, breathless with shock.

'I'm sorry,' I murmured, rubbing my bruised flesh. 'It — '

'No, no, it is I who should apologize.' Mr Honfleur's voice was weary. 'Excuse my daughter's intolerable rudeness. The curate has done nothing to temper her ill nature. She is — '

He broke off, his shoulders hunched. Tentatively I placed a hand upon his arm. He regarded it as a scientist might regard an unfamiliar specimen on the glass of his microscope. Then he clapped his hands, affecting briskness. I took my hand away.

'Since you are here, you must read,' he said. 'After all, we must begin work in earnest if you are to make sufficient progress before the wedding. A bookseller's wife must not be discomfited by her ignorance. Herrick shall do well, I think. His fondness for simple language favours the inexpert pupil.'

He handed me a thick volume bound in leather. I opened it, though I knew that it grew late, for I dared not risk his displeasure.

'Where do you wish me to begin?'

The bookseller said nothing but only sighed, leaning upon his elbows and pressing his fingertips into the sockets of his eyes.

'Shall I begin with the first poem, sir?' I attempted again.

'*I dare not ask a kiss,*' he murmured into the twin shells of his palms. '*I dare not beg a smile, lest having that, or this, I might grow proud the while.*'

'Perhaps you might direct me to the verse?'

'*No, no, the utmost share of my desire shall be only to kiss that air that lately kissèd thee.*'

The words hung in the air, turning slowly in the dust as I leafed through the book, hoping to find the poem. Honfleur sighed again. Then, slowly, he took his hands from his face and blinked at me, as though his eyes were not accustomed to the light. I smiled tentatively at him, unsure of what he wished me to do next. He did not smile back. Instead, he plucked the book of poems from my hand and tossed it on to the table.

'I have no appetite for the old fool. Let us talk of other matters.'

I hesitated.

'Come,' he said, somewhat roughly. 'It would appear you are shortly to be my wife. Surely there are things you would wish to ask me?'

He leaned forward, as though steeling himself against an onslaught of enquiry. It was plain that silence would only contrive to vex him further.

'Of course,' I said cautiously. 'How goes the Febrifuge?'

'No, no! I seek an affectionate wife, if you please, not a stock-jobber!'

I bit my lip. 'Forgive me. Then, if it pleases you, sir, I should like to know your name.'

'My name?'

'Your given name, sir. I know you only as Mr Honfleur.'

The Huguenot frowned.

'I hope you do not hold with the new fashion for addressing a husband by his first name. I am an old man, I know, and so likely out of step with the world, but it does not sit comfortably with me.'

I sighed, beset suddenly with weariness.

'No, sir. I should like to do as you wish in all particulars.'

'But you are curious, of course,' he conceded. 'I was baptized with the name Étienne. In English you say Stephen. It was a family name. All the same, I do not think of it as mine. My mother disliked it and always called me by my second name. It is that name that truly belongs to me.'

'And what is that name?'

'Daniel,' the bookseller said. 'I think of myself always as Daniel.'

* * *

I did not take the ring off until I reached the top of Swan-street. It comforted me to look down upon it and know myself neither ridiculous nor mad. Five short weeks and I would be his wife. Twisting his ring upon my finger, I forced away my uncertainties. It was not only the ring I had but also his daughter, reluctant witness to his declared intent. Did the law not regard such a promise as binding? It would not be a simple matter for the Huguenot to break his word.

To steady myself I gave myself over to imagining life at the Huguenot's house. I lit a fire in the grate and placed myself where Annette liked to sit, behind the counter, arranging Mary in the chair I had always taken. She had a soft smile upon her lips and a chapbook in her hand, held before her so that I could see the curve of her brow and the twin peaks of her knees. As for what came between, I pushed it away. For now it was enough to imagine her quiet and content. It would take her time to trust another master but she would grow to love Mr Honfleur for he would be kind to her. He might teach her to read, if she wished it. She would learn without being herself the subject of study, the various parts of her puzzled over and broken down into manageable syllables. She would make Mr Honfleur coffee just as he liked it and he would sip from his little cups, peering at her through the spectacles he balanced upon the end of his nose, and he would smile at her for he would see beyond the shape of her, which bore witness only to the disfiguring tyrannies of science, to her spirit, which lit her from within. When I thought of him then I felt a tender gratitude towards the bookseller that was not so very different to love.

I was required to lick my finger before I could slide the ring from it and my knuckle throbbed red as I concealed it in the hem of my sleeve. When I bent my arm the circle of it pressed against the crook of my elbow. Five weeks. Reflexively I looked up at Mary's window before crossing the kennel. The face that gazed back at me was unmistakable, white and gaunt, the damaged cheek lost to shadow, lips peeling away from brown teeth in a grimace that was neither smile nor snarl as it raised two clawed fists and squeezed them together as though intent upon strangling the air between them. Then it was gone. All that remained was a cloudy patch upon the glass that faded as I watched. Slowly, the drapes began to move across the window.

'Mary!' I cried, as though I might throw myself through the narrowing gap. 'Mary, can you hear me?'

Behind me Mrs Dormer, the chandler's wife, opened her front door, her chins shivering like a pork jelly upon their dish of lace.

'Is all well?' she enquired. 'I was just asking your girl here if all was well. I should not wish to think all is not well, Mrs Black.'

Mrs Black stood in the doorway of the shop. Her expression was grim.

'All would be quite well,' she said tightly. 'If one could only get servants of the proper quality.'

Mrs Dormer sighed, and her hands kneaded each other avidly.

'Although I understand you are more than content with Mr Black's apprentice. They say that you would be lost without him, is that not right, Mrs Black?'

'A dutiful wife does not permit her husband's business to suffer neglect, Mrs Dormer, while she amuses herself. Now if you will excuse me?'

Seizing me by the nape of my neck, she pushed me into the shop.

'How much trouble must you make before you

are satisfied?' she hissed, snatching up her birch. Twisting, I tore myself free, knocking from the table a basin that fell to the floor and broke in two. Scarlet liquid spread across the wooden floor.

'What does he do to her?' I screamed. 'That bastard — that bastard is killing her!'

'If you refer to my husband, he bleeds her, you stupid little drab,' Mrs Black said grimly. 'He bleeds her as physicians across the country bleed their patients; for their health. Our neighbours would doubtless be aghast at the scandal. Now, get downstairs before I whip you there, so help me.'

She pushed me so hard that I stumbled, striking my elbow against the counter. I clasped it against my belly, feeling the ring in my sleeve.

'Mary,' I whispered, bracing myself. It was worth the beating to ask it out loud. 'Is she — is she well?'

Mrs Black looked at me strangely, her pale lips working.

'She — she endures. It shall be a relief to us all when she is safely delivered.' Then she stiffened, clearing her throat. 'For pity's sake, girl, why do you gape so? Anyone would think idiocy contagious.'

She sent me to the laboratory to assist Edgar with its cleaning. The scrubbed wooden table was littered with dirty jars and beakers. I began slowly to gather them up, stacking them on a tray. In one corner Edgar hunched over a flame, watching a blackened glass tube in a metal frame.

'Where the Devil is my money?' he hissed without looking up. 'You test my patience exceedingly with your postponements.'

I opened my eyes wide.

'What money, Edgar? You know quite well I have none and never have had.'

'You could get it if you wished to. You could borrow it from your friend, the bookseller. From what I hear the old man is a perfect fool for you.'

'Then you hear wrong.'

Edgar turned slowly, his eyes narrow.

'Or do I?'

My neck reddened. Frowning, I tossed my head, clattering bottles and phials.

'So it is true? You dirty little strumpet! I had heard whispers, of course, but thought them nothing but rumour. So the bookseller fucks you, the lewd old goat!'

'Spare me your filth. The bookseller is an honourable man. Unlike some.'

'Which means what? That he intends to make an honest woman of you first?'

I was silent, my hands petrified before me.

Edgar stared, and a smile spread slowly across his face.

'Well, well,' he drawled. 'This *is* interesting. I presume, then, that the honourable Mr Honfleur knows that you are already married? And that there are some years still to pass before your husband might lawfully be declared lost?'

'You know quite well that that is not true!' I protested. 'That my marriage was — that it meant nothing. In the eyes of the law. You know that.'

'Oh, I'm sorry. So the child you bore, the child Mrs Black delivered in this very house, that child was a bastard? Mr Honfleur knows of the child, I take it?'

'It was not like that. You are twisting things — '

'I do not believe that in our past dealings you have concerned yourself unduly with the precise particulars of fact. You should be grateful that, in return, I mean to stick more closely to the truth as I see it. I am certain that your future husband would find the story most engrossing.'

'Edgar — ' I swallowed. 'I shall repay what I owe you. I swear it. As soon as I am married you shall get it all.'

'Ah, if only it were that simple.'

I gaped at him. 'But — what then? What is it you want from me?'

'Interest on my oh-so-generous loan. Ten pence for every penny.'

'Ten pence? But that is extortion!'

'Then you shall be familiar with its conventions. Ten pence for every penny. Or I shall tell the Huguenot the truth about his sweet little blowzabella.'

'But, Edgar, how many times have I told you? I have no money.'

'The Huguenot has money.'

'Which I may make use of only once we are safely married.'

Edgar frowned, his mouth working.

'Edgar, listen to me. If you go to Mr Honfleur now you shall have your revenge, it is true. But you shall also take away any chance I might have for setting things right. For you, for Mary . . . ' I faltered. 'Please, Edgar. I shall repay you. But I can only do it if you permit my marriage. It is all the hope there is. For any of us.'

There was a sudden sharp crack, like a gun shot, as, over the flame, Edgar's tube exploded in a glitter of broken glass.

'That bastard,' Edgar whispered, and he buried his face in his hands. 'When is that poxy bastard going to *die*?'

35

Upstairs, locked in her curtained solitude, Mary grew daily closer to the time of her delivery. And inside her, in its own liquid confinement, the tiny monstrous creation stretched and strengthened, thickening her blood with clots of its black primate hair, its simian skull pressing ever harder against the mouth of her womb. In perhaps two months it would be delivered. But in five weeks I would be married. Hold tight, I whispered when I passed her door, hold tight. I shall not fail you.

I was not fool enough to consider Edgar reliable. But when a week passed and still he did not go to the Huguenot, I permitted myself to breathe a little more easily. And though the days passed with painful slowness, little by little the wedding plans advanced. A mantua was chosen and brought to the shop so that it might be adjusted to fit me. It had a skirt of scarlet silk with a cream-coloured underskirt, the pale gold bodice tied across the stays with scarlet ribbons. When Mr Honfleur confessed that he had paid £1 8s for it, I gasped out loud. Such frugality became me, the bookseller commented approvingly, but there was something regretful in the way he smoothed the skirt down as I took the dress and hung it in the press.

'It is a silly game where nobody wins,' he murmured as I drew the curtain across it. 'Though a sensible man pays little regard to the views of Mr Thomas Fuller. It was he who claimed that *learning hath gained most by those books which the printers have lost*. He would have done better to recognize that catchpenny drollery makes a fool of us all.'

He paused, caught by his own thoughts. Then he smiled, patting my hand.

'Come, let us not be discouraged by such a dotard. Your books await you. A little Webster, perhaps, to sharpen our wits. *And of all axioms this shall win the prize, 'Tis better to be fortunate than wise.* And so forth. You will find much in it with which to concur, I fancy. Now, what is it you have memorized for me?'

I straightened up, my hand smoothing the skin of my throat.

'*'Tis just like a summer bird-cage in a garden: the birds that are without despair to get in, and the birds that are within despair and are in a consumption for fear they shall never get out.*'

'How quickly she learns.'

Annette stood in the doorway, her face grave, her hands clasped loosely before her. Her voice was almost gentle but her composure had a taut quality that set the sunlit shop dust to spinning more frantically upon its axis. She studied us both for a moment, seated side by side, the book on the table before us. When she opened her mouth, I thought she would say something more. But she only touched the tip of her tongue to her lips. Then, with a tiny nod, she turned and left, closing the door quietly behind her. Honfleur let out a breath and his fingers flexed.

Lightly I placed my hand on his.

411

'Shall I fetch you some coffee?' I asked.

'*There is nothing of so infinite vexation as man's thoughts*,' the bookseller murmured to himself. Then he sighed, forcing his mouth into a smile. 'Dear Eliza. But we have work to do. We shall make a scholar of you yet.'

★ ★ ★

As soon as I turned the corner into Swan-street and saw the front door standing open, I knew that something was seriously amiss. I ran down the lane, my basket bumping against my thighs, and in through the open door. The screams came in keening waves, so vivid with grief and loss that it pierced the chest to hear them. They cut through the walls of the narrow house, burying themselves like knives in the crumbling plaster until the splinters bristled in the floorboards and the glass in the sashes issued a low rattling moan. The agony in them was a kind of madness.

It had happened at last. Mr Black was dead.

The hall was deserted, occupied only by dust and shadows that pressed back against the walls, as though to accommodate the magnitude of anguish contained in the ghastly cries. There was none of the usual business of death, the gossips with their covered heads and expressions of assiduous piety. The doors to the laboratory and the shop stood open. Both were empty. Closing the front door behind me, I tiptoed up the stairs. I saw no one. The door to Mr Black's chamber stood open. It seemed to tremble upon its hinges as the wailing traced its desperate arcs up and down, up and down, shrill and savage as the cries of a seagull.

Trembling myself and with my face averted, I pushed it wider and, fearfully, stole a glance inside. The angle offered only the end of the bed, where a white foot protruded from beneath the weight of bedclothes. The toenails were ridged and yellow and curled over the end of his toes. The skin too was yellowish, with a chill waxy sheen. I shivered as another scream began to swell. Steeling myself to enter, I snatched another look and what I saw stopped my heart in my chest. The foot moved. It twitched quite distinctly against the bedclothes, so that the blanket fell away from it a little. By now I was truly frightened. I had known the master capable of unutterable wickedness. I had not thought it possible that he might triumph over Death itself.

I backed away from the door. I longed only to flee, to run from this house and never return. The air tasted poisonous upon my tongue and the shadows reached out to me like beggars, plucking at my skirts, sucking the spirits from me and drawing me into their dust and darkness. My hand closed around the stair-rail and I gripped it tightly so that I would not fall. For a moment the house was still, as though the scream itself drew in all the breath in the house, before another wild howl rattled through my bones.

And then, quite suddenly, I knew. It was not Mrs Black who screamed. It was Mary. All of her suffering, all of the raw and miserable incomprehension of her unformed soul, was contained in the anguish of those ghastly cries. I flung myself at the door so precipitately that I almost fell.

My master was not dead. On the contrary, his face, habitually grey and pinched, was lit by a strange pink glow. His hands shifted and jumped upon the paper he propped upon his lap as though unable to contain their vigour, and his lips moved in agitated wordless spasms. Mary lay half across his legs, her head in his lap, her body racked by sobs. In her arms she clutched a blood-soaked bundle which she pressed against her distended belly, rocking backwards and forwards as she was overtaken by yet another maddened howl of grief. The blood smeared the front of her bodice in thick rusty streaks and stained the fine hairs along her forearms. Her face was swollen, shapeless with grief.

In a moment I was beside her, taking her in my arms, holding her close. The smell of blood flooded my nostrils, hot and metallic and undercut with the reek of shit, the stink of a shambles on a summer afternoon. I stroked her head, crooning to her under my breath. She rocked back and forth against me, her nose buried in the bundle in her arms.

'Mary, Mary, I am here now. Sweet Mary, Eliza is here.'

'Get out,' the master said, and his voice was sticky and thin. 'Why do you come here? This is none of your concern.'

He laid a yellowed hand upon Mary's head. She did not resist him.

'Don't you touch her!' I cried, wrenching her away from him. 'What the — oh, Mary, Mary, my sweet girl, what has he done to you? What has he done?'

Tugging her by the arm, I tried to pull her to her feet but she fought me, twisting and biting at my hands like a savage.

'If it is your intention to aggravate the girl's distress, you do very well,' the master observed, and his face jumped as, with a shaking hand, he made a mark upon the page before him. 'You do very well indeed.'

'You — you are a monster!'

The master opened his mouth to speak but suddenly he was convulsed with a spasm of such ferocity that his whole body jerked and his black-hole eyes contracted in bewildered astonishment.

'Mary, dear Mary, please, come,' I whispered desperately in her ear. 'Let us leave now, while we can.'

But Mary only buried her face in the bloodstained bundle and howled like an animal. I held her, wrapping myself about her as though my flesh might protect her from her anguish, murmuring reassurances and urging her to collect herself, to trust me, to try to stand, but she only surrendered more completely to her anguish, her cries drowning out my words.

The colour quite drained from his face, the master fumbled upon the table beside him until his fingers closed around a cup which he endeavoured to bring to his lips. Some of the liquid ran down his chin as his hand and the cup dropped away, the cup falling with a dull thud upon the floor. The skin on his face loosened and eased as he took a series of shuddering breaths. When once more he raised his head his eyes burned with black fire. He licked his chalky lips.

'Come,' he murmured to Mary and, with an effort that strained the ropes of muscle in his neck, he eased the bundle from her arms. Mary did not fight him but only moaned, her eyes squeezed shut, her fists clamped around two handfuls of her own hair which she tore at as though she would rip it from her head. He murmured soothingly to her as he unwrapped the bloody bundle.

'See, Mary, see well,' he murmured. 'The creature is dead. It is not sleeping nor can it ever be restored to life, however warmly you embrace it. It will do you no good to pretend otherwise. Come, look. I wish you to see this for yourself.'

Uncovering the tiny corpse, he held it aloft. I gasped, the acid threat of vomit at the back of my throat. It was a dreadful sight. The monkey's head had been almost completely severed from its body. Worse almost than that, its arms had been hacked off just above the elbow joint, leaving only two stumps, black with congealed blood. Its narrow chest was a glistening plough of blood, flesh and splintered bone. Behind the pale curve of its left ear I could see the tiny nails that tipped its fingers. The monkey had been cradled in its own arms.

Mary's screams snagged and slowed as, with great gentleness, she extended one finger to caress the creature's blood-clotted cheek.

'It is altogether a most unpleasant incident,' my master observed and, taking an uncorked bottle from the crowded side table, he took a long draught. He sighed, leaning back against his bolsters. 'Mrs Black was a fool to leave the window unlatched. London swarms with thieves. Besides this, they took what remained of the pewter.'

'Thieves? You expect me to — what have you done?' My voice rose uncontrollably. 'This — you know the grief shall kill her!'

'I sincerely hope you are mistaken. But certainly her passions are as violent as any I have ever observed,' the apothecary agreed and, steadying his writing hand with the other, he picked up his quill and directed it towards the inkpot. 'See how she can barely breathe. She is quite undone.'

'You — you conscienceless dog!' I shrieked. 'How much more must you have her suffer before you are satisfied? Oh, Mary, come, I beg you. You cannot stay here.'

But Mary would not move. She clung to the bundle and to the bedclothes, writhing away from me, her elbows thrust out before her. The apothecary patted her hand, his eyes blinking at a point somewhere beyond her head. Then, leaning his head back upon the couch, he closed his eyes.

'See how your derangement distresses the creature,' he observed serenely. 'Her passions are inflamed beyond the bounds of human endurance.'

I stared at him. Mary huddled on the floor,

weeping silently into her hands.

'You dare stand here and blame me for her grief? A man who would corrupt the very essentials of Nature without the slightest conscience, who would destroy blameless lives, and for what? Money? Renown? Sweet God, you are the agent of the Devil himself!'

I swallowed, scrubbing roughly at my nose with my fist. Beside me Mary lifted the butchered monkey into her arms and tenderly pressed her cheek against its face.

'Why must women always prove themselves so lacking in the higher qualities of reason and intellect?' Mr Black remarked. There was no anger in his voice. Rather, it had a dreamy, sing-song quality. 'It is truly observed that a woman is but a child of larger growth. It is little wonder such damage is done to so many.'

'The damage is done by you, you bastard! By you!'

The apothecary did not reply, but only lifted his quill and once more placed the point upon his paper. I strained to see what he wrote but there was no sense to it, nothing but wild swoops and circles and black-edged holes where the pen had pierced the surface of the paper. When he raised his head it swayed slightly from side to side, as though his neck was insufficiently strong to support it.

'Madam, I am tired and wish to rest. I shall say only as I have said on many previous occasions that, but for us, this child would have suffered the fate of all those unfortunates who serve society no useful purpose. Now she may repay us and make her own small mark upon the understanding of Man. You would deny her this comfort, a child to whom Providence has proved so unkind?'

'A comfort? That she be forced to part her legs for whatever stinking cockstand you choose to thrust between them?'

'Madam, please, such lewdness does not become you. The advance of human learning will not falter before an onslaught of foul words or empty accusations. The hunger for earthly knowledge is a provision given to Man by God Himself. It is only through the precise and detailed understanding of its myriad complexities that we may see His creation clearly, in all its great glory. Long after we men of science are brought to dust, our discoveries will shine like beacons in the world, beacons illuminating the rough and rugged path towards enlightenment.' His hands reached upwards and his voice strained after them, taut with awe and shortness of breath. 'As I now trace the course set before me by my forebears and press forward into the darkness that they could not penetrate, so too the scholars of the future will place their feet carefully in the footprints I shall leave behind me, advancing further and further towards the horizon of perfect understanding, their bright-burning flares of wisdom held aloft until the darkness of ignorance and superstition is quite expunged and we stand shoulder to shoulder with God, made whole by His truth.'

His voice was faint and rasping but each word shivered with certainty.

'And if the child is unmarked?' I cried. 'What method of killing is it you favour? Stifling or burning, or crushing his tiny skull? It is clear from the monkey what kind of butcher you are. Is that how you killed my child, by carving him up like a chicken?'

Grief encircled my throat like hands. Mary whimpered at my feet but I paid her no heed. With an effort the apothecary raised his head, blinking and frowning as if perplexed to see me there. The purple mark on his cheek glowered.

'How the Devil did you get in here? Mrs Black! Where did that bitch go? How may a gentleman work with all these disturbances? Mrs Black!'

'You murdered my son.'

'For the love of God!' he rasped. 'When you came here, you wished me to rid you of a bastard child. To perform an illegal act, an act against God, so that you might be spared the consequences of your immorality. And you have been duly spared, though you hardly deserve such good fortune. No harm has come to you. You have been well looked after. The child is no more. Most importantly, your reputation has suffered no stain, although, given your insolent and reckless nature, I can hardly believe such a situation shall continue so for long. I struggle to understand your lack of gratitude. Mrs Black! Where are you?'

I stared at him. I wanted to plunge my fingernails into his face, to pull open the seams of his frown and score raw red lines in its pale implacability. I wanted him to shriek, to writhe,

420

to bleed. I wanted his pain to last for ever.

'You murdered my child,' I whispered. 'And now you kill Mary too. You destroy everything I have loved.'

'On the contrary, I saved you from ruin and provided for you a second, and quite unmerited, prospect for a better life. As for Mary, through my work she has found a purpose and, in all likelihood, a fortune too. I trust that, unlike you, she shall display the good sense to be thankful.'

Mr Black broke off, his voice lost in a spasm of coughing. His fingers groped once more for the bottle beside him but this time they did not find it. With a swift chop of my hand I knocked it over, sending a gush of liquid across the table. The apothecary howled, the coughs convulsing his thin frame as he struggled to raise himself from the bed. His hands clawed desperately at the sodden papers as I snatched the bundle from Mary's arms and ran with it from the room. With a wild cry she flung herself after me.

It was only afterwards that I thought of the candles. A trio of them had stood in a stick upon his table, bubbles of wax oozing down their lengths like spittle. I might have set light to his coat if I'd only had the wit to. I imagined the flames devouring him, seizing upon his cuffs, his stock, his wig, engulfing the narrow chaise until their orange tongues glowed bright as petals in the empty darkness of his eyes.

There was peculiarly little comfort in it.

To Maurice Jewkes Esq. at his house at
Jermyn-street in the parish of St-James's

Dear Mr Jewkes,

My husband acknowledges receipt of your
letter, the discourtesies of which he is prepared
to overlook, & has asked me to reply to you,
both to ease your anxieties & to remind you
once again of the terms of our indenture. Your
objections, sir, have no place in law.

As I have already informed you, the monkey
purchased for the girl had begun to stimulate
swift and startling improvements in her persistent ill health & we harboured strong hopes for
a rapid recovery. The sudden demise of the
creature is therefore greatly to be regretted.
However Mr Black counsels strongly against
purchase of a replacement as this will serve
only to provoke the girl's habitually feeble
memory and thereby deepen her malaise. He
has instead prescribed bed rest and regular
bleedings, supplemented with a nourishing diet
and a restorative tonic of his own devising. As
agreed, the bills for her treatment will be dispatched to you monthly.

In order to speed the patient's recovery you
will appreciate that every effort will be taken to
ensure that she suffer no undue excitement or
agitation. Mr Black would therefore have you
desist from an attempt to visit her here at
Swan-street until such time as we detect a
manifest restoration of her health. Neither shall
your boy be permitted entry. We shall of

course continue to send word of her, as required by the terms of our agreement, and hope that we shall soon be able to inform you of considerable improvements in her condition.

Mr Black has me acknowledge receipt of the monies as agreed and remains &c

MARGARET BLACK

2nd day of July 1720

36

I did not stop running until we had crossed the sluggish brown stream of the New Canal. No one would find us in the tangle of lanes that criss-crossed the undergrowth of the wharves. The water of the canal was lumpy with dung and dead cats. On the western side, in the scale-silvered turmoil of fishwives and eel-sellers that bellowed their wares around the foot of the bridge, I turned and held the bloodstained bundle out to Mary. She snatched it from me and began to weep, her head bowed over the blanket. The swell of her distended belly was rusty with drying blood and there were red-brown smears across her face and arms and around the chewed stumps of her nails. Her hair escaped her blood-streaked cap in whippy tails. Only in London could we have come so far unhindered.

It had begun to rain, a powdery drizzle comprised as much of soot as water.

'Mary, forgive me. There was no other — forgive me.'

Mary did not answer but only held the dead monkey closer.

'I shall take you to a safe place. Somewhere far away from him, where we can be together.'

I pushed Mary ahead of me. Beyond the makeshift market the lanes were noisome and narrow and the stench of the river so thick that it left a greasy tallow-skin upon your tongue. Curses and rough laughter spilled from tavern doorways, propped open with rocks or slabs of splintered wood. From blind walls and ash-heaps dogs and ragged children materialized like dark phantoms to swarm about our legs. On house after rotting house, pinned to warped door jambs or propped up behind cracked and grimy panes of glass, were faded signs depicting a man's hand joined with a woman's and the words MAR- RIAGES PERFORM'D WITHIN. Behind one I glimpsed a parson in a soiled surplice, his eyes empty and red-rimmed in his pale yellow face.

We skirted the high walls of the Temple and emerged on to the traffic-choked jostle of what I guessed was Fleet-street. I paused, holding Mary before me, so that I might judge where it was we were. Immediately a chairman bawled at us to clear the path before he walked right over the pair of us.

'Addle-headed numbskull,' he jeered as I pulled her out of his way. Mary gaped. Then, as though her knees gave way, she slid down the brick wall to squat upon the rain-spotted ground, her knees clamping the bloody bundle against her chest.

'Come on,' I urged her gently. 'I have a friend who will help us.'

'Home,' muttered Mary, and she bowed her head over the blanket. 'Home.'

'What? You would go back to that bastard, after all he has done?'

'Mast' make med'cine,' Mary said very quietly. 'Mast' make Jinks better.'

425

'Oh, sweet Mary.' A knot tightened in my chest. 'If only it were possible.'

'Mar' take care. Make better.' She gazed up at me longingly. 'Soon better.'

'Mary, don't. It's too late. There is nothing anyone can do for him now.'

Mary shook her head. 'No. Mar' help. Mar' mama for Jinks. Mama.'

'Yes.' I swallowed hard and, trying to smile, I reached out and took her hand. 'You were a fine mother to him. No one could have loved him better. I am so sorry.'

Mary stared at our hands, at our fingers plaited together.

'Mama. Make better.'

'No.' My mouth tasted of ash. 'No. Mary, please, listen to me. Jinks is dead.'

Mary turned over the package of our hands, twisting our wrists together. Then, slowly, she looked up.

'Dead,' she echoed.

I nodded, not trusting myself to speak and squeezed her fingers.

'Jinks dead,' she said again.

'Yes.'

'In Par'dise.'

I thought of Jinks's furtive attempts on the sugar loaf, the curl of his mothy tail as he scaled the dresser with a penny or a stolen teaspoon.

'Imagine Jinks with wings,' I murmured. 'There'll be no catching him now.'

'Wings.'

Mary leaned against me, her hand still woven in mine, and placed her head upon my shoulder.

426

'White feathered wings,' I said. 'Like a dove. And sugar for dinner every day.'

'Yes. Ever' day.'

'Feather beds too. From the angel wings. And — '

Her sudden yelp of pain startled us both.

'Clear out the bloody way, can't you? This is a thoroughfare, you smuts, not a bloody pleasure garden!'

The porter thrust his face so close to mine I could smell the Geneva water on his breath. His skin was porridgy with pockmarks, his handcart piled high with wooden tea chests. A row of iron nails bled rust into the raw wood. I pressed myself against the wall so that he might pass. He thrust the barrow angrily ahead of him as though it were a cudgel, muttering under his breath.

'Bloody doxies, clutterin' up the streets like they owned 'em — ' He hawked noisily, dispatching a bubbled pellet of saliva into the mud.

'In Paradise the spit is made of sugar water,' I murmured to Mary. 'And the mud is the thickest, sweetest chocolate you could ever imagine.'

Mary's hand twitched in mine.

'And the porters — the porters push little monkeys around all day, wherever they wish to go, when their wings grow too tired to carry them.'

'In Par'dise?'

'In Paradise. It sounds fine, doesn't it?'

★　★　★

We left the dead monkey in an orange box upon the steps of a small church near the river. The doors were locked and the stained brickwork exhaled an air of weary disuse but Mary stood quietly, her head bowed, as I murmured a few words about committing the monkey's soul to God. She made no difficulty about leaving then but only tore a fragment from the blanket that wrapped the mutilated creature which she held to her lips as we walked. Her quiet endurance was more painful to observe than all of her extravagant grief. I held her hand tightly, as we walked northwards towards the Churchyard. It was perilous to go directly to the bookshop, for I thought it one of the first places they would seek us, but I could think of no other possibility. Mary grew tired; before long she would be hungry. We had no money for board or lodgings. It occurred to me that I might manage the interview with Mr Honfleur better alone but I dared not leave Mary anywhere in case she was not there when I returned.

And so we made our way together, with me glancing over my shoulder every few steps to check we were not followed. At the pump close by Fleet prison we stopped so that I might wash from Mary's face and clothes the worst of the blood. The rain had stopped. The late sun spilled into the blue summer evening, reddening the roofs and polishing the bellies of the lingering clouds to gleaming copper. Somewhere, carelessly, birds sang.

The door to the bookshop was closed when we

reached it, the shade pulled down, but a light burned within. Swallowing my trepidation, I raised my hand to knock. Beside me Mary sidled up to the bow window and pressed her face and hands hard against the thick panes. Frowning and snapping my fingers at her to summon her back to my side, I knocked.

'Mr Honfleur? Are you there? I am sorry to trouble you so late but — well, it is I, Eliza. If you are there, please open up!'

I heard the sound of footsteps inside the shop. Again I hissed at Mary but she paid me no heed. There was no time to concern myself with it now. Taking a deep breath, I composed my face into a smile. I heard a cough before the shade snapped up and Mr Honfleur peered out. His chin was faintly stubbled with grey and crumbs gathered in the corners of his mouth. A wire-rimmed pair of spectacles rested upon his forehead. They winked in the light as he fumbled to open the door.

'Eliza?' he said, frowning sleepily at me. 'What brings you here so late? I have been closed a full hour at least.'

'Mr Honfleur, I'm sorry but I had to come.'

'Did you indeed?' He looked suspiciously at Mary. 'And whom, may I ask, do you bring with you? I would prefer it if she did not lick my windows. It does nothing to improve their efficiency.'

'No. Of course. Come here, Mary. This is Mary. She works — that is, she was maid to the apothecary. With me.'

Mary turned to face him. I watched his face

change as he took in her face and then the great curve of her belly.

'For God's sake, have you taken leave of your senses? You bring a pregnant whatever it is she is — there is no husband, I assume? You bring her here, at night, to a respectable establishment? *Mon Dieu*, what were you thinking of?'

'I beg your pardon, sir. I did not know where else I might go. Mr Black, he tries — he means to make a monster of it. Of the child. To put into his book. He — I fear it is already done. Inside her. Growing inside her. The thought of it — oh, Mr Honfleur, sir, please, I beg you, if you have but the slightest affection for me, take pity on her.'

'Not yet wed and already you would come here with your — this creature — and haggle with me like a fishwife? Eliza, I have misjudged you calamitously.'

I bowed my head. 'I have not come to haggle, sir, but to throw myself on your mercy. You are a good man, a just man. I know you shall direct me as to what is best to be done.'

'I shall indeed. You shall take that girl back to her master, where she belongs. The apothecary may be a philanderer as well as a fool but what he elects to do or not to do in the privacy of his own house is a matter of concern only to his wife and to God.'

'But what if he succeeds, if he has made a monkey of it?' I whispered. 'What then? I — I have seen the pictures. It cannot be imagined.'

'A monkey.'

'She was ill and the master said he gave it to

her to restore her spirits but — oh, God — she loved it like a child. And he urged her on, wants her only to — oh, sir, he did such terrible things, monstrous things, why, I have never told you but when I — and then he killed it. He killed it. So that the grief might — might force itself upon the child. Look at her, sir. She is quite undone.'

Honfleur regarded Mary as she breathed upon the glass and drew patterns with a wet fingertip. Sighing, he crossed his arms.

'So your master seeks to create his own monster?' he mused. 'It is a fascinating idea but I hardly think the old dog capable of such ingenuity. The man is a dullard, hardly capable of rendering the ideas of others in intelligible prose.'

'You are wrong, sir! I mean — there have been others.'

Even as I clamped my mouth shut, the chasm opened before me leaving me dizzy with the terrible proximity of it.

'Others?'

'I — I think so.'

'But you have never seen them?'

Miserably I shook my head.

'But you saw him kill this — this monkey?'

'No, sir,' I whispered. 'He claimed it for thieves.'

'So the sum of your proof is that he gave your idiot friend here a monkey as a plaything and that the poor creature died?'

I stared at the floor.

'And you consider *her* imagination unhealthily inflamed? You have built quite an edifice of presumption from an act of kindness, would you not agree?'

Still I said nothing. Mr Honfleur sighed.

'Take the girl home,' he commanded. 'If the child she carries is indeed your master's, then let him disentangle himself from the fix as well as he is able. I am weary of obliging the cantankerous old bastard. His wife shall doubtless take the news ill. As for me, I shall, I fear, take some small pleasure in witnessing his mortification.'

'But — please, might she not stay here, if only for a few days? With Annette gone, you surely require a servant and she works hard — '

'Enough!'

Mr Honfleur uncrossed his arms. His face was grim.

'For all your youth and inexperience you are, I am sure, sufficiently artful to know what a fragile creature is fortuity. It is unwise for a woman whose dowry resides all in her amiability to prove perversely troublesome, Eliza. Now, go home.'

It must have been my fear for Mary that made me reckless. I ploughed on.

'Mr Honfleur, sir, I do not mean to vex you, I swear it, but if I might only ask for a little money, against my share of the profit from the Febrifuge — '

'Eliza!' Anger slammed the word shut. 'Hold your tongue! I have given you my decision. Now cease in your insolence this moment or, God help me, I shall silence you myself!'

I hung my head. There was nothing else to be done.

'I — forgive me, sir,' I whispered, curtseying before him. 'I — I have vexed you abominably. I never wished to — I — please, forgive me. I beg you. I beg you.'

'Eliza,' he said sadly, 'why do you seek to try me?'

I swallowed. 'Forgive me, sir,' I whispered.

'There shall be no more of these — these fantasies, you hear? As for that poor creature, you shall return her to Swan-street directly. I desire no further quarrel with your master.'

Honfleur pressed his fingers into his eyes. Then he sighed.

'Then the matter is complete. Doubtless your master shall punish you as he sees fit. Endure it without complaint for my sake, for it shall make a wiser woman of you. It is your good fortune that it is not in my nature to harbour resentments. In my turn, I trust that you have learned a valuable lesson. From henceforth I shall hope to see a great deal less impetuousness in you and considerably more discretion. Now, since you are here, you may take a book to your master and leave me to my supper before it is grown quite cold. I shall expect you tomorrow at a more reputable time.'

He smiled a little then, shaking his head in reproof, and ducked into the shop to fetch the book. When he held it out to me, I took his hand and pressed my lips against his fingers. The Huguenot did not press his advantage, although he squeezed my waist a little.

'Oh, I almost forgot. Your master's apprentice came to see me yesterday. Weak-looking fellow, is

433

he not? But then your master was never much of a judge of a man's character. I fear he has wasted his time with that one.'

'What — what was it he wanted?'

'He did not say. Only that he wished to make my acquaintance. Since I have rarely seen a man less interested in books, I can only hope he has been charged with the clearing up of your master's accounts. So. Off you go. Tomorrow then,' he said, and his tone was almost gay.

'Tomorrow,' I echoed.

When I led Mary away across the dusky Churchyard, her hand tight in mine, he had the delicacy to look away.

To Jewkes at Jermyn-street

Listen to me, you bastard, you bring her back here do you understand me you have no claim upon her you signed her over, you & that ruthless wife of yours you could not be rid of her quick enough then, remember? Well, do you remember?

she is my property mine alone you hear in the eyes of the law & in the sight of god her & all that is in her all of it I have it signed & witnessed damn you you vile & plaguy thief bring her back or like a common thief I shall see you hung i swear it be glad tis only theft I threaten when the king himself discovers your treachery you may be sure it shall be treason

i should have known you would betray me you pox-ridden parvenu it is all profit & loss with your kind no number of south sea millions could make gentlemen of any of you fine porcelain could never be fashioned from such vulgar clay

bring her back she is all I have left what use do you have for her except to spite me she has only ever been a source of shame to your family shame & mortification shall you now betray everything I have laboured for given my life for i shall not let you destroy my legacy i shall see you dead first dead, do you hear me BRING HER BACK SHE IS MINE

GB

37

Mr Honfleur assisted us in one way, though he would have been dismayed to know it. Before it could grow warm in my hand I sold the book he gave me for my master to a merchant in a courtyard at the dingy end of Paternoster-row whose grimy window resembled nothing so much as the press of a slovenly man, its curtain drawn back to reveal a discarded jumble of worn coats and cracked shoes and wigs with the locks all askew. In amongst the chipped shaving cups and threadbare neckcloths, I could make out a handful of dog-eared volumes, but I chose it mainly because it seemed the kind of establishment that would be quite invisible to a man of the Huguenot's education and sensibilities. At the end of the narrow yard the low windows of a tavern spilled light and rough laughter into the deepening gloom. The raucous swagger in it put me in mind of Edgar. But I could not think of Edgar, not yet. One matter at a time, I told myself, or else I would go mad.

I sat Mary upon a doorstep in a shadowed corner as far from the tavern as I could contrive it and, kissing her, bade her not to move from her position upon any account but only to watch the shop. I would be back for her as soon as my business was complete. Dumb with fatigue, her shoulders slumped in piteous submission, she obeyed me. When, upon reaching the door, I turned to look at her, she was already almost asleep, her pale cheek propped against the crumbling brick. The proprietor, a man wearing a greasy velvet cap and the distrustful expression of a habitual swindler, glanced at the book's several plates with careful indifference and offered me a shilling for it. When I declared it was worth ten times that much, he only shrugged and declared his customers not greatly interested in book-learning. All the same, I observed how he kept his hands locked together beneath his chin and his index fingers against his lips, as though uneasy that, unconstrained, they might betray him, and, though it was almost night and I was in no position to negotiate, I demanded two and held his gaze without blinking. The proprietor was the first to look away. With a half-hearted exhibition of indignation, and much satisfied muttering about thieves and charlatans, he paid almost what I asked.

★ ★ ★

It was the taller of the two men I saw first, for he stood directly before Mary, his gait unsteady and both hands occupied in a drunken tussle with the front of his britches. His coarse laughter was a boast that rose vertiginously even as I ran across the yard, catching him off guard and sending him staggering into the wall.

'Poxy — whore!' he slurred, sliding unsteadily to a squat, and I saw, between his fingers, his slack member from which issued, down his leg, a steady stream of piss. In the doorway behind him his associate issued a screaming bark of amusement. He held Mary's head in his lap and her jaw open, as an animal's jaw might be kept open, by exerting the pressure of his fingertips at its hinge, but Mary did not struggle. She did not even look afraid. Instead, though her eyes were opened, I almost thought she slept, so blank and sealed was her gaze. Only her tongue moved, its rigid tip circling her lips like the hand of a clock.

Pulling back my fist, I struck the seated man full in the face. He stared at me in perfect astonishment before expelling a kind of breathless whimper and falling backwards so that he struck his head with a dull thud against the door. Seizing Mary's hand, I dragged her upwards. The other man lunged at me as I passed but gin dulled his instincts and weakened his grip and he only sprawled upon the ground, expelling his slurred curses into the summer dust.

★ ★ ★

We passed that first night in a chop-house near the Strand that advertised itself by means of signs in the grimy windows as both cheap and late to close, and then, at the recommendation of a fellow diner when we were at last required to leave there, in a coffee-house that opened before dawn to serve the river trade. As we staggered through the grey early morning, our limbs strange with weariness, I glanced about me, fearful every minute of seeing Edgar or Mrs Black coming towards us through the crowds. A girl of Mary's description might be easily identified, but at least here no one troubled to notice us. The wharves and landing-stages swarmed with people, stumbling beneath their bales and barrels like scuttling crustaceans. Chains and ropes clanked and shrieked as casks and crates and huge coarse sacks were sucked from the jetties into the dark narrow spaces between the warehouses. Porters shouted and swore. Amongst the frenzy of activity the stores and mills seemed to press closer to the water, reaching out towards the scramble of boats as though they would swallow them whole.

At the coffee-house I bought bread and a cup each of small ale, though Mary looked longingly at the bacon, and we ate and drank in silence, watching the hurried comings and goings of the other occupants, heads bowed beneath the low ceiling. It was a busy enough place, and its regulars too set in their habits for our presence to elicit more than brief twitches of curiosity, but all the same I sought out a small table at the back, away from the fire, where we might attract little attention or animosity. In the doorway a pair of ragged chimney-sweeps, refused entry, waited as the girl brought them their breakfast, wrapped in grease-pearled paper. They twirled their brushes as they shambled away, rousing a burst of protests from the mob outside.

I think we slept a little, propped together as the wall exhaled its chill breath into our backs. Certainly when we emerged day had taken hold and the dawn wharves had hardened into something more commonplace. I wrapped Mary's face in her shawl, so that her features might be obscured, and hunched my shoulders as we hurried north, staying away from the main thoroughfares.

We had spent as parsimoniously as I could contrive it and already I had parted with almost a shilling. Along with the money in my dress our savings might last us four or five days, a week if we were careful and did not care for hunger or a place to sit or to sleep. I thought of the man in the alley the night before, taking aim while his friend held Mary's mouth open in readiness, and I squeezed Mary's arm so that she turned and blinked at me.

'Home,' she murmured, but it was no longer a question and the word caught in the folds of her shawl, heavy and without hope.

★ ★ ★

It was the only other place I could think of to go.

Little-whalebone-court was a sliced-off corner of Drury-lane, tucked between a tavern with the sign of the Crossed Keys and a sag-roofed stables. I could hear the horses whinnying and thrashing in their stalls as we passed through the slit of an entranceway, navigating the mahogany-stained puddles and scattered hillocks of straw-bristled manure. Beyond the stable the courtyard opened to the sky but you would never have known it. The yard was criss-crossed with ropes and ropes of wet laundry, rising up in layers like the drapery of an elaborate tent so that, for all the harsh brightness of the day, the light in the courtyard had a vaporous quality, as

440

though we stood inside a cloud. Beside me, the crumbling brick wall echoed with the sharp hollow blows of horses' hooves striking wood, sending the taut-stretched sheets and cloths into a dance of shivers and jerks. Dark petals of water lay strewn across the dusty ground.

Pushing a sheet aside, I ducked beneath the line. The linen sweated the sour stink of lye.

'Hung'y,' Mary muttered mulishly.

'Mary, you cannot be!' Anxiety had me speak more harshly than I intended. I sighed. 'Come, let me get what I am come for. Then we shall find you something to eat. Although if we are to make do at all you shall have to learn to manage on less. You have the appetite of an elephant.'

I pushed aside another sheet, holding it up so that Mary might pass beneath it. There were beads of water caught in her coppery hair. I smoothed them out with my hand as she bent under my arm. The damp hair was darker and clung in sparse tendrils to the shape of her head, exposing the pale wax of her scalp.

'All is going to be well,' I murmured and, hiding my hands in my armpits, I crossed all of my fingers.

The laundry occupied a narrow steam-filled room at the rear corner of the courtyard. Piles of dirty sheets and cloths drifted like city snow against the long wall, while all about the room were baskets and barrels of cambrics and muslins and Holland shirts and other small linens, both dry and damp. Two girls of perhaps six or seven years old stirred at coppers of linen with long wooden poles, their bare feet straining upwards from their three-legged stools so that they might keep from scalding their elbows on the hot metal. Another girl, a little older, rubbed with soap at a ruffled collar thrown over a low table. The wooden tub beside her, which reached to her waist at least, overflowed with soiled linens. Behind her a fourth girl, smaller and slighter than the others but with a feverish flush to her cheeks, pumped at a handle that passed wet pieces of cloth between two great wooden rollers, squeezing the water in a steady stream on to the puddled brick floor.

The laundress was a glint-eyed woman with a high forehead and a choleric complexion coarsened by steam and lye. She was young, though, and vain enough to dispense with an apron so that her neat waist might be displayed to advantage. Her perse petticoat was streaked with spattered stripes the colour of thrushes' eggs. When I asked if the mountebank's clown still lodged there she wiped her nose on the back of her raw red hand and sucked at the gaps between her teeth as though they were sugarplums.

'You mean Petey Smart?' She looked me up and down disparagingly, as if I were a stained neckcloth. ''E ain't 'ere.'

'Will — will he be back?'

'What am I, 'is blinkin' keeper? Gawd almighty. As if I don't 'ave my fill of witless little doxies wastin' my time already.' She clapped sharply at the girls. 'What you gawpin' at? Heads down, unless you want to miss yer dinners.'

'Dinners,' echoed Mary longingly as she

442

stalked away. 'Wan' dinners.'

The girl at the table tittered and ducked her head at her friends, damp strings of hair catching in her mouth.

'Thirst,' Mary muttered, tugging at my arm.

'I know, I know. Just one moment, while I — ' I pressed my knuckles against my forehead, kneading my temples, but no thoughts came.

'Thirst,' she pleaded, and her face crumpled. 'Thirst, Lize.'

'Here.'

I looked up. One of the laundry girls stood shyly before us, holding out a dipper of water. Before I could thank her she had slipped away. I waited while Mary drank. Then I took the dipper back into the laundry. The steam clung to my hair as I thanked the girl for her kindness.

'Petey Smart, does he still lodge here? I — I'm trying to find him.'

The girl nodded, but jerked her head towards the door.

'Go, can't you?' she muttered. 'Or she'll have us, just like she said. Since the last girl upped and went she don't let up on us what's left, not even for a minute. There's more work than twice of us can do.'

When I presented the two of us for hire, the laundress laughed derisively. She had only a position for one, she sneered, and she would take neither an idiot nor a strumpet neither, for she disliked the quick-witted impudence of the street girl just as much as she abhorred the slowness of the simple-minded.

I bore her insults without flinching. Instead, I

443

suggested that we might share the position between us, each one offsetting the excesses and insufficiencies of the other. Two girls, paid the same as one, would work harder, I reasoned, being seldom fatigued. The laundress snorted but, as she watched Mary turn the handle of the mangle, her eyes were dark with calculation and her tongue worked busily between her teeth. She could not deny that we were strong and the work simple, mostly a matter of turning the handle and making up the lye.

It was fortunate for us that the laundrywoman was of that breed of woman who cannot refuse a bargain, however much its terms offend her. I was to bring the idiot to the wash-house at dawn to ensure her punctual arrival; tardiness would not be tolerated. I would then work from the two o'clock bells until the end of the day. The idiot would be required to make herself scarce at those times; the laundress would not have her fooling around and distracting us from our work. I looked at Mary then and the thought of her fooling around leaked a warm patch of wistfulness against my chest.

The laundress saw my face and frowned. Plain meals would be provided, though, as two halves of a single worker, she would provide only one between us. There would be meat once a week and small beer to drink. There was no room for us to lodge at the laundry but we might find accommodation in a rooming-house known to the laundress in the lanes east of the Tower, close by the wharf they called Cole-harbour. It was a considerable walk away but the rent was cheap and the landlord incurious. I hesitated. Lodgings at the Tower would require us to pass close by Swan-street every day. We could not risk it.

'Please, madam,' I begged her. 'Let us sleep here. We want for very little.'

'Fink you can 'aggle wiv me, do yer? Go on then. Go on and 'aggle yerself right out of a position an' all.'

I was silent. The laundress narrowed her eyes, crossing her arms over her chest. The pay would just about cover the cost of our lodgings with a bit over for necessaries. I hesitated only for a moment. Then I accepted. Spitting on her hand, the laundress had me shake it to seal the agreement.

Nothing was said of Mary's condition, though it was impossible she had failed to notice it. Still, keen perception was a gift of little value to a washerwoman of no particular scruple who had secured herself a pair of good workers at negligible expense.

Hewlitt & Bain, Solicitors at Law, Newcastle

Dear Sir,

We are obliged by our client to communicate to you the extent of his displeasure at your extraordinary letter.

It is unclear from the raft of reckless accusations contained within that injudicious document whether you meant to issue an apology or to seek one. However, from a legal standpoint the terms of the contract could hardly be clearer. Upon acceptance of our client's exceptionally generous terms, you undertook to guarantee that the girl might be retained in secure lodgings & on no account be permitted to return to the parish of her birth. That you have in all likelihood failed in that undertaking is a matter for serious & immediate concern.

Our client has therefore required that it be made clear to you that it is <u>your full & lawful responsibility</u> to locate the girl at the first opportunity & effect her secure restoration at your establishment. Should you fail to do so he shall not hesitate to seek reparation for any losses sustained due to the dereliction of the lawful duties detailed in the contract signed by both parties, by whatever means deemed necessary.

I am, Sir, yours &c.

NICHOLAS HEWLITT

38

We made sure to walk to Cole-harbour the long way, by way of Bedlam and the stinking market at Smithfield. Even so, I kept my head bowed as we hastened along, my skin prickling with the fear of discovery. When a harassed clerk pushed past me at London-wall, I was so convinced that he was Edgar that I cried out. It was only when we were past the Tower and lost in the maze of tiny alleys behind Radcliffe-highway that I considered us tolerably safe. It was impossible to imagine anyone even approximately respectable in a place like that.

The house itself was a ramshackle structure built of yellow brick, slimy to the touch. Towards noon, as the sun grew stronger, it exhaled a powerful smell of stale fish. Several of its windows were boarded up. The room we were offered was damp and dark, a narrow slice of the second storey that looked out directly on to the coal-stained wall of its taller neighbour, with only enough room between the two of them to accommodate the span of my hand and the mudflat reek of the river. It was furnished only with a straw-filled mattress and an ancient tea chest with a plank for a lid. Canvas was pinned across the window where once there had been glass. I took comfort in its gloominess. Matters might be managed here in a manner that could not be stomached in sunlight.

Once we had given the landlord what he asked to secure the room, we had no money left for food but we slept heavily, too bone-weary to be disturbed by the infestations of the palliasse. The next day, as agreed, I walked Mary to Little-whalebone-court some minutes after five in the morning. The houses were shuttered, breathless with sleep. As we passed the Tower we heard the fretful roar of the lions confined behind its thick stone walls.

I meant to walk a little, so that I might compose myself before going to the bookseller's. I knew what it was that I had to do. I would bow my head in shame and remorse, and with a few tears and the humble admission that I did not deserve his clemency, I would beg his forgiveness. When he reprimanded me, as he most certainly would, I would hang my head and accept it all.

Mrs Eliza Honfleur. Three weeks and two days.

Somehow, though, the hours skittered away. I walked west towards Westminster where everything was unfamiliar, scratching the bites on my arms and neck and watching the traffic. Around me on water and on land, boats and men and horses and waggons moved vigorously, purposefully, in no doubt of where it was they were going. When I grew tired I sat on a wharf, my legs drifting like weed from the damp wood, until a bargeman barked at me for blocking his mooring. I thought of Edgar pressing his fat hand into the Huguenot's long-fingered one, the smile pressing into his puffy cheeks and lighting up his sucked-bone eyes, and I hugged my knees against my chest and pressed the tips of my fingers into my eyes. Close by a group of ragged children played in the dust, their faces sunk with hunger. When I gave them half of the slice of bread I had bought for my breakfast, they fell upon it like rats.

When I returned to the laundry at two o'clock, the washerwoman hustled me into the laundry room, nodding at Mary's back, bent over the copper in the boiling room.

'She'll do,' she conceded. 'She's slow but she'll do.'

'And today she will do no more. You shan't have both of us, not for the price of only one.'

The laundress frowned. Then, snapping her fingers, she instructed Mary to give me her oiled apron. Mary blinked with fatigue as she fumbled with the strings. Her hair hung in dark tails about her face and her hands were red and chapped from the lye. I took one in mine.

'Poor Mary. When there is time I shall make up something to soothe the skin.'

'Came?'

'Me? Of course I came. Wait for me where I can watch you. I shall be done before long.'

'Came,' Mary repeated, and her eyes filled with tears.

'Oh, Mary. You shall not have to do this much longer, I promise you. I promise you.'

★   ★   ★

449

The work at the laundry was back-breaking and numbingly repetitive. It cracked and blistered our hands, shrivelling the skin to fish scales, and cramped our shoulders until we could barely lift our arms. The meals were plain, but there was enough bread and I tried to sneak sufficient scraps into my apron to give Mary something of a supper when at last I was finished. We hardly talked but I watched the way our feet struck the twilit roads in an unspoken rhythm and it consoled me. At night, on the lice-ridden mattress, her sticky breath stitched itself through my dreams. Sometimes she cried out in her sleep and the creature in her belly writhed and jumped but it did not come. I turned my back on it then, and closed my eyes. I did not talk to her about the child, or about the terrors of confinement or what we would do when the creature came. I had never attended any birth, except one, and had only the vaguest notion of how such a terrible miracle was managed. What did I know, whose only rehearsal for the delivering of an infant was a wrenching, drowning, blood-slippery scream of pain? There was no purpose in frightening her, in frightening myself. There was time enough for that, when things were more settled.

One matter at a time.

On the morning of the third day, I forced myself to go to the bookseller's. As I walked I rehearsed my apologies: I wanted to come before but my mistress had not permitted it. I had not dared to show my face, so ashamed was I of my disgraceful conduct. For three days I had wept inconsolably, terrified that, through my own

450

thoughtlessness, I had put in jeopardy a marriage that meant more to me than life itself. And with each pace I grew more certain that when I got there I would find Mrs Black behind the counter, her hands crossed like blades over her lap.

I could feel the sting of the birch on my palms as I rattled the handle. The door did not open. When I looked closer I saw that the window shade was pulled and a sign propped behind it declaring the shop temporarily closed. I gazed at my distorted reflection in the thick panes of the window and saw the rawness of my skin, the draggled dullness of my hair, the crumpled disorder of my cap robbed of starch by the ceaseless steam. My skirts were dusty and stained with dirty water, my hands red and itchy. There was nothing about me of a bookseller's wife, nothing at all. I did not look up at the Cathedral as I pushed my way out of the Churchyard, the lye stink of me hot in my nostrils, but fled to Drury-lane where the hunched press of houses had a dirty and defeated look, and dirty and defeated people hunched as they hurried along the dusty alleys, unjudged and unnoticed.

* * *

It was a windless day and the curtains of linen hung sullenly from their lines. I called out to Mary, who turned the handle of the mangle in laborious circles, her face shiny with sweat. When she saw me she straightened up and, kneading at

451

her sore shoulders, came out into the courtyard, blinking her welcome. Then, abruptly, she looked up, covering her mouth with one hand and pointing above my head. I turned. Behind me the sheets cracked and billowed, marked with faint shadow like spilled ash as, along the lines, the clown's monkey darted and swung. It was wrapped in its usual red velvet cloak but, instead of a hat, it wore around its head a lace handkerchief which it clasped beneath its chin with one hand. Then a hand sprang up and snatched the creature down.

'Bad boy,' the clown chided. 'Give me that.'

The monkey clucked at him, tweaking his nose. Mary laughed, a spluttering snort behind her fingers. Both clown and monkey turned.

'Hello,' I said shyly.

The clown's brow creased. Then he smiled. As for the monkey, it dropped the lace handkerchief upon its master's head and, leaping to Mary's shoulder, wrapped her coppery hair around his fingers and crooned in her ear. The clown clicked his tongue, calling for it to come, but it paid him no heed. Instead, very gently, the monkey rubbed its whiskery cheek against Mary's pale one. Mary squeezed her eyes shut, her fists opening and closing at her sides.

'Jinks,' she breathed.

'His name is Jabba,' the clown told her, looking sideways at me. 'He likes you. I have never seen him so affectionate with a stranger. What is your name?'

She did not answer.

'This is Mary,' I told him.

'Your sister?'

'No. Although I would think myself fortunate if she were. She is my friend.'

The clown looked at Mary and smiled, holding out an apple. The monkey bounced eagerly, his hand extended, but still it did not go to its master.

'He does not wish to be parted from you, Mary. Shall you help me feed him?'

He skinned the apple expertly, a curl of peel spiralling from his knife, and held the peel out to the monkey who, tearing it in two, offered one half to Mary.

'And you,' said the clown, slicing the apple flesh into pieces. 'I do not know your name either.'

'I am Eliza.'

'Eliza. And what brings you to Little-whalebone-court, Eliza?'

I shrugged, smiling slightly. The clown smiled back. He had a kind face. 'Fate,' I said quietly. 'And penury.'

★ ★ ★

When at last my work was done, Mary and I walked together in silence down towards the river. The summer night was purple-dark but on Bishopsgate-street we saw a pedlar selling birds in the light of an oil-lamp. They were a wretched lot, their feathers dull and patchy, but Mary crept towards them, pushing her fingers through the bars of the cage and chirruping softly. The birds shifted on their

453

perches, sending up a miserable creaking. The pedlar frowned. Idiots were bad for business.

'Buy,' Mary begged, and she pointed to a bird which cowered at the back of the cage, its abject demeanour quite at odds with the violent scarlet of its feathers.

'How can we?' I scorned. 'We have barely enough money to eat.'

Mary wriggled her finger. The bird buried its face in its wing.

'Buy,' she said again, more urgently.

'Why, Mary, it is nothing but an ordinary pigeon coloured red and half dead at that. Whatever could you want with it?'

Mary's hand tightened around the bars of the cage and her shoulders shook. I touched her gently on the arm, coaxing her away. When at last she relinquished the cage, the palm was striped pink.

'Hurt,' she wept, and she rocked, pounding her fists against her chest. 'Hurt, Lize.'

I held her tightly then, my cheek against her sticky one, and the desire for vengeance flushed my cheeks.

'I know,' I murmured. 'I know.'

'Yer buyin' or not?' grumbled the pedlar.

Gently I took Mary's hand and pulled her away from the birdcage.

'Come, let us go home. And how about sausage for supper?' I said recklessly.

'Saus'? For me?'

'Yes, for you. Oh, Mary, I will set things right, I swear it.'

Above me, beyond the shadowed jut of a roof,

something flashed in the early-evening sun. I did not have to look up to know it for the golden cross of the Cathedral. I had not seen it for weeks but it was always there, presiding over the metropolis with its ever-vigilant eye. There was no happening, however secretive or insignificant, to which it failed to bear witness. It saw everything, heard everything. Just as its creamy stone absorbed the city's foul air, assimilating its greasy soot into its bones, so too did that vast gilded cavern of an interior sop up all the fiendish vitality of the city, each foul thought or evil deed tarnishing a length of altar rail or flaking away at the angels that crowned its elegant colonnades.

Buildings should aim for eternity.

It would not bring the Cathedral down, the stench and corruption of a million lives ill-lived. On the contrary, it seemed to me that the Cathedral gained its strength from the squalor around it, each day sending its roots deeper into the tainted London soil while, above it, like a great lung, the dome filled magnificently with each and every foul-smelling exhalation, from the strident obscenities of the watermen and the shrieks of the robbed to the curses of murderers, the murmured whispers of confession, the rustles of bills and paper money. Sustained by the rich and abundant nourishment of London's sins, the Cathedral would surely outlive eternity itself.

I looked up at the cross without blinking, until the dazzle of it burned a hole in my skull. When at last I closed my eyes it branded the darkness, two fiery unflinching bars of red.

'Now come,' I said briskly, taking Mary by the hand. 'I am ravenous.'

she is gone quite gone no trace of her left

it is over

a single tide shall wipe my footprints from the
sand
no mark no shadow
no one to remember
the tide comes i can see the foam of it upon
the horizon
then nothing

it is in the striving that we find salvation not in
the success
    the grand task of life is preparing for death a
life well lived in the service of the lord
    he does not judge us by our worldly tri-
umphs but by our fitness for heaven

oh god how may it be borne

39

The next day I went again to the Churchyard. Outside the west front of the Cathedral I paused to smooth the chopped ends of my hair into my cap and, taking the ring from the hem of my sleeve, forced it back over the knuckle of my finger. It shone unnaturally yellow in the flat grey light. Before the western entrance a group of prosperous-looking gentlemen conversed in an unfamiliar guttural tongue, their complacent expressions at odds with the harshness of their language. Above them, St Paul gazed down from his pediment, holding aloft the sword that would be the instrument of his own execution, the dome swelling self-importantly behind him.

On the other side of the Churchyard a woman in a dark mantua stopped, turning to look in my direction. Her profile was sharp, the pinch of her waist narrow as a girl's. For a moment I stood frozen, unable to move. Placing her basket upon the ground, the woman lifted her hands, tipping her head backwards so that she might adjust her hat. Not Mrs Black but a young woman, perhaps twenty years old.

My stomach twisted, my bladder seized with an urgent need to piss. My knees trembled as I squatted in the shadow of a buttress, the books balanced in my lap. The urine mapped a brisk path through the mud, splattering warm droplets against my calves. Smoothing down my skirts, I pinched my cheeks to lend them a little colour and, adopting an expression I hoped both modest and blithe, I strolled through the Churchyard and pushed open the door to Mr Honfleur's shop.

As soon as I saw him I knew that something was terribly wrong. I smiled with stiff cheeks, my heart pressed up against my ribs.

'I am glad to see you,' I gabbled. 'I want to beg your pardon for what happened. I was wrong to ask you, to bring her here — I would have come before but Mrs Black is grown most suspicious. She suspects us, I think, though I do not know how. But then I should not be surprised if she were possessed of some dark power of prophesy. She has a great deal of the witch about her, don't you think?'

The words withered upon my tongue, desiccated by Mr Honfleur's grim face. I swallowed, bowing my head.

'I — I have come to beseech your forgiveness,' I said quietly.

'So I see.'

The shop looked dusty and unkempt, piles of books stacked higgledy-piggledy upon the floor. The table bore traces of several meals, dirty cups and dishes stacked together with old crusts of bread and yellowing bacon rind, the wood grained with sticky marks.

'Mrs Black visited me yesterday,' he said.

I said nothing, but clutched at the table, suddenly dizzy.

'She was considerably distressed,' he went on in the same flat voice. 'She wished to know if I

459

had seen you. When I said I had not she informed me that you had been missing since Thursday last. That you had stolen from them irreplaceable property of prodigious value and vanished. That you were nothing but a common criminal and that they meant to see you hanged.'

'If it is the book — '

'She made no mention of any book.'

I said nothing but stared at the table, tracing with one finger the pale circle of a cup-mark. The gold ring flashed.

'I fail to understand what it is you intend, Eliza. Perhaps you would be kind enough to enlighten me.' He crossed his arms. 'No? Very well, then, let me tell you something instead. You shall return the apothecary's property to him today. Today, *vous comprenez?* This nonsense must end. Then we shall decide how best to deal with you.'

'But — '

'My terms are plain. If you fail to observe them our contract is broken. Is that what you wish for?'

Still I did not speak. I could think of nothing to say.

'Come, Eliza, surely you can do better than that. You have acted unlawfully and against my express command. You are fortunate I do not throw you out this instant. The very least you can do is to fall to your knees and plead mercy.'

'Forgive me,' I whispered, not looking at him.

'Mrs Black made it clear to me that it is the idiot they want. Only the idiot. Should you return her unharmed the matter shall end there.

460

They shall take no further action. I trust you concede the generosity of such an offer.'

'Yes, sir.'

'You are fortunate too that I consider it time that my business arrangement with the apothecary be terminated and that another condition of the girl's return is the payment in full of their outstanding account. As it is, I blame that man for most of this madness. It would appear that, not content with taking leave of his own senses with the idiot girl, he has taken those of all his household with him. The sooner you are removed from Swan-street the better.' His lips curved. 'A wiser man would doubtless turn you out and congratulate himself upon a narrow escape. I trust that you appreciate the extent of my generosity. My affection for you renders me foolish.'

I managed a nod.

'Good. Now, if you would be so kind, I will have that ring.' He gestured at my finger. 'You shall have it back when I receive assurance that the idiot girl has been returned to her rightful place.'

I swallowed.

'Please, Mr Honfleur. I beg you, have pity on her. On us both.'

'What did you say?'

His voice was low, the blade of his anger still half-sheathed as he leaned over the table towards me. I raised my head and looked at him. My eyes felt hot. This was my chance. Surely, so long as I took care to describe everything exactly, the Frenchman could not help but feel sympathy. He

461

was a good man, a just man. More than that, he was an educated man, steeped in the wisdom and compassion of the greatest writers of all civilization. He knew the obligations placed upon humankind by the requisites of morality, of humanity, of the simple absolutes of love. He of all men would understand why it was that I could never leave her. It was simply a matter of explaining it properly.

I took a deep breath, my hands clasped tightly before me, aware that of all the words I had ever uttered in my life, these were the only ones that truly mattered.

The bookseller's face tightened ominously. 'Well?'

'Nothing, sir,' I muttered. 'I said nothing.'

To John Black at the sign of the Scroll &
Feather, Newcastle

Dear John,

I fear that this is hardly the letter you hoped
for. Your brother is dying. He has battled ferociously with his illness for many months but it
would seem that, in recent days, he has lost the
will to continue his fight & he weakens with
every passing day. It is therefore my duty to
request of you that you make the journey to
London with all haste. It would give him great
comfort to bid you a final farewell.

Your letters have made no attempt to conceal the extent of your rage & bitterness
towards your brother. A man is fortunate if, at
the close of his life, he may seek the forgiveness
of those he has wronged. But though there are
others against whom he has sinned most grievously, your brother has not done so with you.
It is not towards Grayson that you should
direct your invective but towards myself. So
that he might be spared the burden of your
financial difficulties, given the extremities of
our own, I have burned your letters before he
might see them. Blame me. All his life my husband could deny you nothing.

I do not regret my decisions for myself. It is
some time since Grayson's health permitted the
judicious consideration of matters pertaining to
money & business. However, aware as I am of
his particular fondness for you, I cannot allow
for him to pass from this world in the shadow

of your undeserved censure. My conscience is burden enough already.

I can send no money for your journey but I would ask you to come to London all the same, for your brother's sake. If this is impossible a loving letter would suffice.

I am, &c.

MARGARET BLACK

40

One matter at a time.

After that I kept Mary close, hurrying her through the streets before sun-up or after dark, when we might not be seen. I told myself that Mrs Black would never find us, either at Cole-harbour or at the laundry, hidden in its secret courtyard, but I was careful all the same. I had Mary remain in the room when I went for food, my shawl over my head despite the summer heat. In the afternoons she stayed where I could see her, playing with Petey's monkey while he went in search of work. Her belly had grown suddenly enormous, its bulk pulling her off balance. I watched her as I worked and I knew it would not be much longer.

I did not go to the Churchyard again. When I thought of my marriage and the graze of the bookseller's ring over my knuckle, it was without regret but rather with a kind of incurious bewilderment. My recollections had the elusive, half-remembered flavour of a dream, the Huguenot's face at once close to mine and at the same time blurring and becoming, with the ease and logic of dreams, the face of Edgar or of the dead monkey.

One matter at a time.

★ ★ ★

It was five days before the festival of St Bartholomew, a little before three in the morning, when Mary was seized with violent contractions. It was a warm night, the shadows rendered harsh by the glare of a round white moon, and, in bed beside me, Mary gave off more heat than a bread oven. For hours I had drifted in and out of sleep, my dreams restless with a woman I knew to be Annette, though she had the face of Mrs Dormer, dressed in a mantua with a skirt of scarlet silk and a pale gold bodice tied with scarlet ribbons. As soon as I heard Mary cry out I knew that it was time. Reaching beneath the mattress, I fastened my hare's-foot around her neck. She sat bolt upright, her arms clutched around her belly.

Holding tightly to her hand, encouraging her to breathe, I struggled to keep my face steady. The preparations had all been made. We would manage perfectly well. The laundress, for all that she remained resolutely blind to Mary's condition, had, little by little, allowed us to accumulate a small collection of scraps and rags that she had no use for. These we had boiled and dried and wrapped in a piece of muslin so that they might remain clean. We were fortunate too that the clown, lonely without the mountebank O'Reilly, had become a regular visitor to Cole-harbour, bringing food for supper and sometimes even wine too, the dregs of which I saved so that I might have something to give Mary after her delivery. Without his kindness we would have been more frequently hungry. Beside the door I set at the ready a pail of water from

466

the river. The bucket's muddy exhalations flavoured the air, insinuating themselves into the lye smell of our hair.

When the first pains began it was terrible to witness her distress. She clutched at me, certain she was dying. As her labour progressed and the contractions came harder and more closely together, she clawed at her belly, as an animal caught in a trap may bite at its own leg, as though she might tear the source of her agony directly from her body.

I could do little but wipe the perspiration from her brow and urge her to greater endurance, all the time praying that the birth be straightforward. I dared not call a midwife. She would require the identity of the father, so that the child might not become a burden on the parish. The more officious of the breed might even demand that the father be summoned and brought to the room during labour to confess his misconduct. As for the child itself —

No, I could have no witnesses. I thought of Cain, of Herod, of the Pharaohs of Egypt, all twisting in Hell like chickens on a spit, and I was grateful for the wall that stood outside the window of our room at Cole-harbour, obscuring any glimpse of the dome. Sometimes I felt God's hot breath upon my neck, thicker and saltier still than the smell of the river, but though it made me shiver, I did not doubt what I must do. A monster-child would make a monster of its mother, a brace of curiosities to be chained up and carved open and cackled over by boy-men disguised as scholars, their fingers greased with

467

duck fat so that they might thrust them in more easily. Mooncalf mother and monkey boy. Fairground freaks, the pair of them, to be stared at for a sixpence. For a shilling you might jab at them with a stick and marvel as they moaned, weeping tears so lifelike they were almost human.

It happened in a great rush of slither and blood. The crown of the infant's head was dark, streaked with hair. I dared not look at it. Instead I gripped Mary's hand, urging her to push. She screamed and writhed and begged God and all his angels to let her die and then, with a tearing moan, she set her teeth together and drove the child out. I had only to place my hands beneath its arms and pull and it was free. Its tiny body hung like a root from the bulb of its great head, the birth-string pulsating, blue and fatty. Without looking at the infant, I took up my knife and cut through it. It was resistant, muscular, like scrag end of lamb. The child opened its mouth and its eyes as wide as it was able, convulsed with outrage. Then it screamed.

Mary whimpered, pressing her hands over her ears. I murmured comfortingly to her as I washed the child. Morning was already advanced and the sun struck the smeared windows, filling the room with greasy light. Setting the child on the floor upon the clean muslin square, I knelt and forced myself to examine it with detachment.

The creature had no eyelashes or brows or any of the human arrangement of hair. Instead its entire body was covered in a fine pelt, not black as I had feared, but pale and downy, like the fluff of a dandelion clock. Its face was creased, its features squashed close together, and its limbs were unnaturally long, the knuckles of its hands curved in the way of larger apes who use them for walking. Its testicles, which I could hardly bear to look upon, were grotesquely enlarged and a dark red-purple.

And so it was. There could be no denying it.

The apothecary had made his monster.

Quickly I wrapped the thing up. In my arms, the monkey child fussed, its searching mouth open and quivering, nudging my breast. I swallowed my agitation, holding it away from me and tugging at the cloth until its face was obscured. The bundle was so light it might have been only an armful of laundry.

On the pallet Mary sighed and closed her eyes. Anxiety stabbed my numbness.

'No, Mary, no. You must not sleep,' I cried. 'I have some wine I have kept by. It will restore your strength a little.'

Setting the bundle on the floor, I rummaged in the wooden tea chest for the bottle. Behind me the bundle began to wail.

'For pity's sake, hush!' I muttered. 'Do you want us discovered? Here, drink.'

I knelt beside her, holding the bottle to her lips, but Mary turned her head away, clamping her lips. Her hands pressed over her ears, she rocked back and forth, her own moans drowning out those of the bundle.

'Make stop,' she wept, over and over. 'Make stop.'

On the floor the creature screamed steadily, its feet kicking against the tight swaddling, its knees pushing the stuff into corners. I crouched beside it, my hand on its chest, as though I might press the screams back into its lungs. It did not quiet. Beyond me, in my basket, I could see my shawl. It would take nothing to place it over the bundle and press down, press down, until at last —

My hand shook. I felt the creature move beneath me and the sudden strength of its jaws as it took the tip of my finger into its mouth. Immediately it fell silent. I closed my eyes, a blade of memory sharp between my ribs. Hardly considering what it was I was doing, I snatched up the bundle and dragged Mary upwards by the arm until she was half-sitting. Mary fought me but the efforts of labour had exhausted her. She had no strength left. Forcing her knees flat, I thrust the infant into her arms.

Mary gave a strangulated cry, twisting away from me.

'No!' she gasped, and her face was grey and scooped out with an adult anguish that made no sense of her childish features. Afterwards, I thought it was likely the pain in her womb that twisted her so. But then, at that moment, I looked at her and I saw myself. Then I knew that it was loss and longing that hollowed out her face and which would soon spread into the heart of her, eating away at the soft parts. I knew that she would carry with her always the sense of something absent, something amputated, without which she would never be complete.

Pulling back the blanket, I pushed the

creature's head towards her breast. It nosed at the skin for a moment, blindly searching, before it seized upon the nipple, clamping it hard in its mouth. Mary flinched and closed her eyes. Her face was slammed shut, her jaw set and twisted away from her body, refusing complicity. But she did not push the child away. Perhaps it did not occur to her that such a thing would be possible. Several times that day I put the creature to her breast. When I grew tired of holding it I fashioned a kind of sling in which the creature might be cradled. Mary never once looked inside the sling.

For four days we remained concealed in my room, the three of us. I slipped out for food when it grew dark. I tried not to think of how little money we had left. It was easier than I might have expected not to dwell unduly upon the gravity of our predicament. The powdery twilight of my nightly incursions bleached the colours from things, softened their sharp edges. Even in daylight, there was an insubstantial quality to the world beyond the covered window, its muffled clamour no more urgent than the gurglings of our own stomachs. Concealed in this place, we might stop the hands of time. Without time there could be no consequences.

The creature fed well and slept much of the time, as did Mary. As they dozed I prowled about the darkened room, my limbs fraught and effervescent in the half-light. I could hardly bear to look at the creature but at the same time I could scarcely tear my eyes away from it, interrogating every one of its movements for betrayals of its simian nature. When it slept it made tiny muttering noises with its tongue that raised the hair upon my neck. As for the moment when its fist first closed around a hank of Mary's hair and clung to it, I felt a spasm of such disgust that it made me dizzy. But I could not kill it. With every day that passed I knew more certainly that I could not kill it.

* * *

I was watching them both sleep when the knock came. As soon as I heard it I knew that I had expected it. I had known that they would find us. Sooner or later they were bound to find us. Now that they were here I realized that I had not the first notion of what to do. Frantically, my heart hammering, I snatched up the child and cast about for a place to hide it.

'Mary, Eliza, are you there?'

Not Edgar. Petey.

My head swam dizzily as I struggled to straighten my thoughts. Then, lifting the plank lid from the tea chest, I carefully set the child inside and covered it with my grey shawl. I could only hope that I could get rid of Petey before it woke and began to cry. The plank I set back at an angle so that it might have air to breathe.

'Why, good day,' I said, opening the door a crack. 'We had not expected a visitor.'

Jabba sat upon the clown's shoulder, intent upon grooming his hair. Shivering, I looked away.

'The laundress said you had not come to

work. So I presumed — the child. It's come?'

'Yes, it came,' I said hurriedly. 'But it — it died. It was too early, I think.'

'I see,' Petey said gravely. His kind eyes regarded me. I jutted my chin.

'Mary does well enough, though she sleeps now. She has a slight fever today.'

'Then perhaps when she is better I can bring Jabba to see her? She is so fond of him, he might cheer her a little.'

I shrugged awkwardly as the monkey bounced and chattered on the clown's shoulder. Then, without warning, he leaped to the ground and, streaking through the narrow opening, disappeared inside the room. I started.

'Come back, come back here, you little — '

'He has little respect for the opinions of others, that one,' the clown said dryly. 'Here, let me fetch him out.'

I hesitated. Then, biting my lip, I pushed open the door.

'But quickly. I don't want Mary woken.'

With its curtained window the room was dim, its grey light like liquid dust. Petey moved tentatively, chirruping in the monkey's own whistling inflection.

'Come, Jabba, Jabba. Come, Jabba, Jabba.'

Swiftly I crossed the room so that I stood in front of the chest. Mary slept on, her fist nestled into her cheek. Suddenly the monkey started out from behind me and streaked across the room. He trailed something behind him, soft and grey in the soft, grey light.

'Jabba, come now, give that to me,' Petey

473

reproved him gently.

Behind me in the box, the creature began to scream.

* * *

It was Petey who insisted on taking the sailcloth down from the window so that what little light there was might be allowed in. While I had Mary nurse, he went for food and brought soup and bacon which, despite her fever, Mary ate ravenously, splashing the sling with spots of grease. I could not eat. I sipped only at water, trying to calm my stomach as I watched Petey take the creature gently from its sling and into his lap. He stroked its simian head with one finger. I closed my eyes, burying my face in my cup. The water tasted stale, brackish with the sealed smell of sleep.

'I had thought you might . . . ' Petey murmured. 'But you have done well. The child thrives.'

I said nothing.

'I had thought she must surely bear another one. Like her. But this one seems quite ordinary.'

I choked.

'How can you — ?' I spluttered. 'Look at it. Look at it!'

Petey blinked. 'But — '

'Are you quite blind or have you simply spent too long leering at the freaks at the Bartholomew Fair? Can you not see that the — the thing — that it is — '

'He is come a little before his natural time but

474

he has suffered little for it. He is a bonny little bugger.'

I stared at him.

'Bonny? It is covered all over in hair. And the — the — '

'The balls?' The clown guffawed at my clumsy gesturing. 'Grand, ain't they? God's way of making sure even the dullards can tell the difference.'

'I suppose you are an authority on infants?'

'Aye. Well, me ma was a wet-nurse so I seen 'em all and some right sickly little scraps of flesh, I can tell you. Not this one. He's blooming.'

'But — you are certain? Nothing is amiss?'

'Don't look like it.'

'It's not — he does not strike you as — ' I took a breath and forced my unwilling lips to form the words. 'As resembling a monkey?'

The clown chuckled.

'All the scraggy ones look like monkeys, specially if they come before their proper time, which is what likely happened with this one. The fat ones, they resemble boiled puddings. There's only the two kinds.'

'So — ?'

'So he'll fill out. And grow up to be a worry to his mother, same as any other infant.'

I gazed at the child. It scrunched its face, twitching its nose.

'But I thought — '

'What?'

'You are certain? That there is nothing at all wrong with it?'

'With him,' Petey corrected me. 'Yes, course I am. Quite certain.'

Slowly I reached out a hand to stroke the child's face. My face felt starched, resistant to the crease of it, but I could feel the smile on it continuing to widen, forcing the flesh to give. In my cage of my ribs, my heart twisted like a landed fish.

'What do you mean to do next?' Petey asked later. 'The father, he can be found?'

I pressed my lips together. 'Oh, he can be found. But I do not mean to let him anywhere near us.'

The clown frowned.

'But how will you manage? You must have him pay his dues.'

I stared across the room. Beyond the window the damp wall bloomed with coal-stain flowers. I had given no consideration to the future, of what came next. For the first time in days I thought of Mr Honfleur and I was startled to see how very far away he was, his features tiny and blurred, his voice hardly audible. There was a river of ceaseless time and circumstance rushing through the gully beyond the window. In this room we might be safe, for now, but we were marooned all the same, stranded as the city swirled and rushed around us. It would always be the same, the secrecy, the fear, the swift furtive forays for food, the way my belly twisted every time I glimpsed a woman's sharp profile or heard voices in the stairwell. We might have escaped Swan-street but, without the funds to flee the city for ever, that bastard still held us prisoner. He always would, until he ceased to search for us. Until he knew himself defeated.

A sudden hot rush of saliva leaped from beneath my tongue.

'Petey!' I exclaimed. 'Do you know how to write?'

TO MISTER BLACK THE APOTHECARIE
OF SWAN-STREET

MAIRIE IS WITH ME OF HER OWEN
CHOOSING CONSIDER THIS LETTER AS
HER NOTIS PROPLY GIVEN

SHE IS BEGUN IN HER LABOR

IF YOU WISHE TO SEE HER AND THE
CHILDE IT WILL COSTE YOU 10
POWNDS IN GOLD COIN NO BANK BILL
I SHALL COM ALONE TOMOROW HAVE
THE FULL SUM READY

IF YOU FAIL TO PAY OR IF YOU DO ME
ANY NATUR OF HARM YOU SHALL
NEVER SEE MAIRIE OR THE CHILD
AGAYNE

I MENE IT BE IN NO DOWTE

ELIZA

41

It was plain, from the first, that Petey was uneasy about the arrangements. He considered the sedative unsafe, the scheme for the creature's retrieval risky and ill-considered, the likelihood of mishap considerably too great. He was, frankly, loath to oblige me. When, unsure how else to persuade him, I offered him money, the expression on his face convinced me that I had blundered irretrievably.

It was his affection for Mary that decided him, in the end. Petey might have struggled to claim for himself an immaculate reputation for honesty and candour in all of his business dealings but, at bottom, the clown was a decent and kind-hearted man, more honourable than most so-called gentlemen. Once he understood how grievously Mary had been misused, he could not stand aside.

And so it was, two nights later, a little after the bells had struck one o'clock, that we made our way west towards Swan-street. Mary's fever had finally abated a little and she slept, a light gasping sleep that made it hard to leave her. It was a dark night, the waning moon blotted by cloud, and Petey carried a small torch of the kind carried by linkboys. At the top of the lane we parted, as agreed. He took up a position in a doorway, his light aloft. As for me, I gathered up my skirts and ran to my master's house. I did not have to pretend to gasp for breath as I thundered with all my strength upon the front door.

'Mr Black, Mr Black! It is I, Eliza, come with urgent news. Wake up!'

I kept banging at the door until I heard the clatter of shoes on the stairs. The door opened a crack and a face peered sleepily out.

'Edgar, in God's name, let me in!' I shouted. 'I must see your master.'

A door slammed upstairs.

'What the Devil — ?'

'She is here?' Mr Black's voice cut across his wife's. 'That venomous little bitch is here?'

Grimacing at me uncomprehendingly, Edgar opened the door. I shook my head.

'I shall not come in. We shall speak down here or not at all. I have asked the lantern-man to wait.' I gestured towards Petey's torch. 'For my own safety.'

The apothecary had grown so weak that Edgar was obliged to put down his candle and carry him down the final flight of stairs, his arms crossed before him to make a seat. He had barely to strain to lift him. Mrs Black followed behind them, her white undress drifting down the stairs like ash. I could see the pale yellow gleam of her clenched knuckles upon the banister rail.

Edgar settled the apothecary in an upright chair upon the threshold. His cadaverous face was grey as he leaned forward, his roped hands gripping the arms.

'Where is she, you cunt-bitch?'

'Such civility. Very well, if you do not wish to speak to me — '

480

'Come back here, you stinking trollop. How dare you?'

'How dare I?' I replied smoothly. 'Mr Black, if you wish to see Mary again, it would behove you to address me with a little more courtesy.'

'She is mine,' he muttered, his breath painfully short. 'You have taken what is mine. You are a whore and a thief.'

'She is gone into labour,' I said conversationally.

Mr Black stared up at me, the dark centres of his eyes spreading like ink blots. Behind him Mrs Black gave a little gasp.

'She — '

'The child should come by morning.'

'Morning,' he breathed.

'It shall be yours. Upon payment of my terms.'

'It is blackmail!'

'Blackmail? No, sir. There are accounts to be settled. The laws of the parish make it clear that all such expenses should be paid by the child's blood father.'

'You — '

'Of course if you refuse me I shall find a benefactor for the child elsewhere. You are surely not the only man in London with an interest in freaks.'

The apothecary's eyes stretched as he battled for breath and composure.

'No! I shall not be blackmailed . . . by a common slut . . . '

Again his words were lost in a paroxysm of coughing. He twisted, gasping, in his chair. The

481

knobs of his spine made shadows down the back of his nightgown.

'As you wish,' I conceded. 'Good night, Mr Black.'

Raising my hand, I gestured towards the clown's light. The torch dipped in response. I kept my steps slow and deliberate, praying that I had not misjudged him.

'No!' Mr Black called after me. 'No. Come back.'

I paused but did not turn.

'Come back,' he said again. This time the sigh of defeat was unmistakable.

The agreement was much as I had hoped it would be. Mr Black would give me two guineas immediately, by way of a bond. I would get the remainder when I brought back Mary and the child. The apothecary instructed his wife to unlock the safe box where the money was kept. She counted it out and handed it to me, dropping each coin into my palm as though it were poisoned.

'You foul leech, how can you come here to demand money while she labours? What if she should die while you are gone? Have you not the faintest trace of compassion?'

'Mrs Black!' the apothecary croaked sharply. 'You shall be silent.'

Mrs Black closed her mouth. As I looked up at her she fixed me upon the points of her eyes, grinding her disgust into my face. I had a strange, fleeting compulsion to confess the truth. Then I looked once more at the apothecary's straining face and I closed my heart.

'And a good night to you too, madam,' I murmured and, nodding at the apothecary, I hurried away.

★　★　★

I returned the following evening, a wrapped bundle in my arms. When I banged at the door Mrs Black opened it almost immediately. I pushed past her, clutching my bundle, and, before she could stop me, I ran up the stairs. I did not stop until I reached the apothecary's study. There I banged once on the door before flinging it open.

The apothecary was lying upon his couch. He could hardly lift his head as I entered the room but his eyes flickered and his hands fluttered in front of his face.

'It is come?' he breathed, the words catching roughly in his chest. 'And is it, is it — ?'

I knelt before him, holding out the bundle, my face twisted.

'Truly, you are the instrument of Satan,' I said quietly.

Mr Black's hands shook violently as he fumbled with the cloth.

'Closer.'

Behind me I heard the door open and the deliberate footsteps as Mrs Black crossed the room to stand beside me. She said nothing. Taking a step towards the apothecary, I pulled the cloth away from the creature's face. Mrs Black gasped, a tight choking quickly covered by one hand. As for the apothecary, the muscles in

483

his neck pulled tight, stretching the yellow skin taut over the elbow-points of his cheeks. For a moment one might have hoped him dead. Then something in his face worked loose and his mouth spread in a slack and awful smile.

'It — it is a monster,' I said.

'Yes,' he murmured and his eyes closed over in a kind of rapture. 'Yes. It is come at last.'

Unsteadily, he tried to tug away the rest of the cloth but he had not the strength for it and instead broke off into a fit of coughing that caused his arms to jerk at his sides. Quickly Mrs Black crossed to the other side of the couch and, leaning down, lifted a cup to his lips. He drank clumsily, his brow creased with the effort of it.

'Open it,' he rasped at me as Mrs Black wiped the dribbles of liquid from his chin. 'Let me see it.'

Edging forward, I placed the bundle on his lap. It was Mrs Black who, with trembling hands, unwrapped the cloth. Jabba lay upon his back, his hands tucked beneath his chin. The Febrifuge had worked. He slept soundly, making little snoring sounds in his throat, as the two of them gazed. The corners of the apothecary's mouth worked.

'Perfect. It is perfect.' He sighed, the breath rattling in his chest, and a tear ran slowly down his nose. 'Where is the idiot? She must be brought.'

'That is not possible,' I said. 'She is not yet well enough to be moved.'

'Of course she is. The afterbirth, the proofs — I require her here within the hour.'

'No. The exertion would surely kill her.'

The apothecary reached out and gripped my skirts, twisting them in his hand.

'Bring her, I tell you. Or I shall — '

'You shall what?' The apothecary was weak and I detached my skirts without difficulty. 'Do not threaten me.'

On the other side of the bed Mrs Black bristled.

'If you care for the girl at all,' she hissed, 'you shall bring her here where she may be properly cared for.'

'Cared for? Is that what you call it? To be stabbed at and scrutinized like a felon's cadaver? I should rather die first.'

'And Mary? You would wish her death also, in service of your own petty extortions?'

'No, madam. I wish only to save her the misery of ever setting eyes upon the pair of you again. You have the — the creature. Surely that is all the proof you require. And you have me, who may bear witness to the birth. Why is that not sufficient?'

'You?'

'I shall give an account to whatever audience you choose. Mr Black has always declared the gentlemen of the Royal Society superior stuck-ups, has he not? Then summon them, to bear witness to his triumph.'

Mrs Black's eyes narrowed. Her lips pressed together, she looked at me and then at her husband. He nodded, his head awkward upon its stalk of a neck.

'Call that bastard Jewkes,' he whispered. 'Have

him bring those doubters here. And fetch me up another draught. Thirty grains, do you hear me? I must be steady now and clear.'

Mrs Black hesitated. Then, with swift, light steps, she crossed the room. In the doorway she stopped and turned. Her face was half in shadow and impossible to read. Then she was gone.

'So,' I said, 'let the show begin.'

There was a pertness to my tone that I regretted the moment it was out of my mouth for, to my ear, it spoke far too plainly of my intent. It was fortunate for me that the hubris of prideful men swells about them like a rising sea and fills their ears with nothing but the roaring of the ovations that await them. I might have told the apothecary every detail of the plot then, I think, and he would have heard nothing. If he had observed the opening and closing of my lips doubtless he would have taken it for applause.

'Great is Truth,' Mr Black rasped triumphantly as two tears fell from his eyes and quivered expectantly upon the sleeping monkey's chest. 'And mighty above all things. Praise be to God.'

blacks law
grayson black fellow chairman newton sloane
black

the pen is steady
the opium curls like a vine around my feverish
mind green & fresh & juicy it smells
like summer
the beginning of it
how clear it is how perfectly sweet

opium & joy what perfect salve for agony what
unusual power
I am weeping & my tears taste salt & sweet so
sweet

it is done sublime joy
& i am at peace
thanks be to god

42

I was put to wait in the room Mary had occupied in her last weeks at Swan-street. As the key turned in the door behind me I crossed the room and looked out of the window to the other side of the street. The scraping caw of crows caused me to look up. The angle of the roofs obscured them but I could just make out a cluster of the black birds settling upon the chimney pots.

It seemed that no one had been in this room since Mary left it. The bed was a tangle of rugs and, on a low table beside it, a plate stubbled with crumbs bore the dried-out crusts of a half-eaten slice of bread. I lay upon the bed, burying my face in the pillow. It no longer smelled of Mary but only, faintly, of mildew. The table bore a single small drawer, without a handle. The front of it was warped so that it did not quite close. Idly, I inserted a finger and pulled it out. It was so light I thought it empty but when I glanced inside I saw instead a mess of tiny scraps of fabric, small feathers, clippings of yellow fur from the cat. I stared at them without touching them, and their inadequacy tightened something in my chest. The poor furtive remnants I had sent up on her trays so that she might know that I did not forget her. She had kept every one.

When Mrs Black unlocked the door I was lying on the bed, staring at the ceiling. I longed now to be finished with it, for the whole ghastly circus to be over. Without speaking I followed her to the apothecary's chamber and waited as she knocked crisply at the door.

'Mr Black? May I enter? We expect Mr Jewkes and his associates directly.'

When there was no answer she pushed the door open. The room was still and perfectly quiet, filled with gently turning spirals of dust, solid in the sunlight. In the centre of the room in a pool of melted light was a crib of dark wood with high carved sides. In its shadowed centre lay the monkey, wrapped tightly in its swaddling bands. It slept, its face twitching with dreams.

Beside it, folded over in the prostrate posture of an Eastern mystic, was the apothecary. His hands were spread out wide upon the floor, the bony fingers splayed and their tips pressed against the boards, and his shoulders shook in silent spasms. He wore neither hat nor wig. His stubbled head shone silver in the sunlight, while his worn black coat had the green gleam of beetle wings. He was surrounded by drifts of paper. A little beyond his reach a quill lay abandoned, a drop of black ink quivering upon its crushed nib. There were holes in the upturned soles of his boots.

Mrs Black pushed past me and into the room. 'Sir, are you taken ill?'

Very slowly the apothecary raised his head. His face was a startling ghostly white, the purple of his stained cheek muddied to a dark brownish-grey. Even his lips were white. Only his eyes were red, the lids swollen around the great dark holes of his pupils. The tears ran down his cheeks, falling on to his coat and clinging there for a brief shining moment before surrendering to the weave of the fabric. In one hand he held an empty bottle of smudged green glass.

'We — we are vindicated,' he rasped weakly. 'The name of Black shall . . .'

His voice failed him. As he held his arms upwards his expression was of exultation, of almost beatific ecstasy. In the crib the monkey chirruped softly to itself and was silent.

'Mr Black, the — the creature, it wakes,' Mrs Black said with uncommon gentleness. 'There, there, do not fret. Perhaps you should entrust it to me until you are strong enough to examine it. I shall ensure it is fed and cleaned. When you are ready to resume your examination, inform Edgar here and I shall have it brought up to you. You look a little recovered already.'

With a clatter Edgar put down his tray. The apothecary gazed up at him with his punched-out eyes. The smile still curved his lips but his mouth had collapsed somehow into his face, peeling the flesh away from his teeth. Raising his hand with great effort, he brought the bottle down hard upon the floor as though making a toast.

'Edgar,' Mrs Black instructed, 'the brandy if you will.'

Briskly, she extended her hand but Edgar did not move. His eyes were fixed upon his master. Mr Black gave a hollow rattling snort, lifting his head a little as though with great effort. His eyes bulged in their sockets, then rolled backwards, and his head fell forward with as much force as though it had been cut from his neck, his nose striking the floor with a pulpy thud. A spasm of vigour jumped through his limbs as a puppet's limbs jerk when the strings are pulled. Then he was still. The bottle quivered in his uncurled fingers and fell, rolling idly across the floor, coming to stop against the iron grate of the empty fireplace.

'Edgar,' Mrs Black said again, more sharply. 'Must I ask you again? The brandy, if you please.'

She did not look at her husband. Instead, she stooped to lift the monkey from its crib, clasping the bundle tightly to her chest. It stirred and, with a soft surprised gurgle, she took a step backwards, raising the creature's face to hers until their noses brushed. Her movement dislodged the apothecary's arm from the edge of his desk. It fell, the elbow twisted outwards at an unnatural angle, the fingers of the pale hand uncurling. Purple stains marked the yellow skin. Mrs Black did not turn. Instead, she cradled the monkey in her arms, swaying a little backwards and forwards, her eyes half-closed.

'Be still, my little one,' she crooned into the bundle. 'My misbegotten little savage one. Be still. I am here.'

Again the monkey stirred, its tiny fists balled against its cheeks. Mrs Black clasped it against her chest and rocked it backwards and forwards, crooning a lullaby under her breath. It whimpered, wriggling in her embrace. With great deliberation Mrs Black walked upon stiff, straight legs, across the room and away down the stairs. Edgar stared at me, his face creased with bewilderment. Then, with the air of a man walking to the gallows, he followed her.

I remained where I was, suspended in silence. It was over. Dust stirred itself in slow circles into the white glare of the window, thickening the air, and a pair of fat flies buzzed, drawing zigzags across the room. One settled upon the apothecary's coat, the other on his head, insinuating itself into the details of his ear.

From downstairs came the muffled sound of raised voices, then the thud of feet taking the stairs two at a time. The butcher-faced Jewkes pushed me aside.

'That bastard! Where is he, that damned bastard!'

He stopped, frozen, staring at the apothecary slumped upon the floor.

'He is dead,' I observed, and I brushed reflexively at my ear. 'Already dead.'

Mr Jewkes hardly looked at the dead man. Instead he wheeled around, seizing me by the shoulders.

'Then where is she? Where is my little girl?' He thrust me away from him, covering his face with his hands. 'Oh, Henrietta, my sweet child, what have I done, what in the name of the Devil have I done?'

He pressed his fingers against his brow. His hands were pale and freckled, gilded with pale hairs, and I had a sudden startling picture of one of them moving down Mary's neck and over her breasts, as the other fumbled with the front of his breeches.

'You shall burn in fiery Hell for all eternity,' I said, and my quiet, steady voice seemed to come from somewhere very far away. 'For it is not the child you have made a monster of but yourself. Now, if you will excuse me — '

Mr Jewkes caught me by the arm. His grip was gentle, almost apologetic.

'Where is she?' he whispered. 'Is she here?'

'You disgust me,' I said, and I swallowed back the tears that clenched my throat. 'You think I would bring her back here, to him, after all that has happened? You are as much a monster as he is.'

'So where is she? Please, tell me, I beg you.'

His voice was pleading, wretched. I wanted to rip the hair from his scalp, his eyes from their sockets, anything to make him feel something of her pain, the pain he had devised for her.

'Somewhere you and your scalpel-sharpening cronies shall never find her. Somewhere safe.'

Mr Jewkes dropped his hand.

'Thank God. Does she require a physician, money, anything? I — I should like to help her, if I can.'

'As you have helped her already? Trust me, you have done enough.'

Jewkes lifted his head. He held my gaze steadily, humbly, as if he had forgotten I was only a servant.

'I have betrayed her most grievously,' he said quietly. 'I shall regret it always.'

The abruptness of his confession caught me off guard.

'So you acknowledge it? That you — that you

are the father of Mary's child?'

The shadow of a frown passed over Mr Jewkes's face.

'You mistake me. I am her father.'

'Her father? But I — I don't understand.'

'No. No, I hardly understand it myself. But I am her father all the same.'

I stared at him stupidly.

'You are Mary's father?'

'Yes. May God forgive me, her father. And she is not Mary. She has never been Mary. Her name is Henrietta. Henrietta Sarah Jewkes. My second wife did not — she wished to be rid of her. And I let her. I let them take her away.'

I shook my head, but still it would not clear.

'You are her father?'

'I am. Though I may hardly be considered worthy of the name.' He sighed miserably, staring at his hands. 'How is she? Does she do well?'

I thought of all the curses I had heaped upon his head, the images that had tormented my imagination. I thought of Mary's white face, greasy with sweat, the low pained murmurs as she turned in her sleep. He was her father. I could hardly look at him.

'Well enough,' I whispered at last. 'Though her ordeal has been considerable.'

'Might you permit me to send my physician, just to see her? It — it would give me some comfort. To know her in good hands.'

Immediately I knew myself tricked.

'If you think all your manipulations shall have me tell you where she is, you are quite mistaken.

In all this time you have been nothing of a father to her. Why should I trust you now, when so much is at stake?'

Mr Jewkes swallowed and his shoulders slumped.

'I — I do not know,' he said very quietly. He stared at the floor. Then, fumbling in his coat, he drew out a fat leather purse. Without opening it he thrust it into my hands. 'Here. Gold keeps its own counsel and betrays no one. Take care of her.'

I weighed the purse in my hand. It was heavy. After the birth Mary had seemed to improve. But when I had helped her up from the pot, last evening, she had moaned, half-falling, and I had wiped away the gush of dark blood that rushed down her thigh. In the pot, I had found more blood and a glossy wine-red slab like pig's liver. It was then that the fever had returned.

'Go,' he urged softly. 'There is nothing more for you here. And, if you will, tell my daughter when she is well enough that I shall never forgive myself. That I have always loved her, though I served her so ill.'

From downstairs there came a scuffle of voices, the sound of a door slamming. Jewkes sighed and, rubbing his chin, stared impassively at the apothecary.

'Have my boy come up. The priest must be sent for and the undertaker. The sexton too, so that the bells may be rung and the cause of death properly reported. The weather is warm and we should not delay. As for that — that creature downstairs — '

He broke off as Edgar stumbled up the stairs. His wig was askew, his cheek scored with what looked like scratch marks.

'I require your assistance, sir. With the mistress. The master's death has dealt her a severe blow. She — well, she is most discomposed. Agitated.'

'Surely — '

'Please, sir,' Edgar urged unhappily. 'Perhaps if you saw for yourself — '

'For the love of God!' Jewkes growled but, feeling my gaze upon him, he bit his lip. 'Very well. Take me to her.'

Almost pushing the man before him, Edgar hustled him downstairs. Holding the heavy purse in my hands, I looked around the apothecary's room one last time. It smelled of ink powder and old wigs. The surprise about death, in the end, was the ordinariness of it. In the lilac light of evening the iron dome beyond the window was tinted with lavender. It looked gaudy, foolish, a stout matron coiffed and rouged like a girl.

Closing the door, I walked slowly down the stairs. The house was shadowed, the doors off the stairway all closed. Like a skeleton, I thought before I could stop myself, the stairs like the knobs of a spine down through its hollow centre, and I crossed my fingers to drive away the ill fortune. I had only to retrieve the monkey and I might walk away from this house for ever. In the hallway two slim cloth-bound volumes waited on the table, fastened together with string, and angry voices set the parlour door trembling against the jamb.

'You have no claim upon the child,' I heard Mrs Black howl with a violence that rattled the door upon its hinges. 'The child is ours, do you hear me? Ours.'

'Child?' Mr Jewkes's tone was quieter but no less savage for all that. 'You call that — that *thing* a child?'

'It is ours. Ours alone. You shall not profit from it, you hear me? You relinquished any blood claim when you gave her up to us. It makes no difference that he is dead. You understand me? You have no claim. No claim whatsoever. It is ours.'

'You think I would want anything to do with that monster? You think I am not already so crushed by the burden of shame and guilt that I wish now to profit from my misdeeds? That creature is an atrocity, an act against God. It revolts me that I have been complicit in its creation. I have betrayed my own conscience. Worse, much worse, I have betrayed my daughter. You may have made an abomination of her child but you shall never make one of her. I would die first.'

'You defy all reasonable civility, sir,' spat Mrs Black. 'Mr Black has always thought you the coarsest of men. Give me back the child this instant and get out or I shall have him throw you out. Have we not told you? You are not welcome here.'

Suddenly the door flew open and Mrs Black stood swaying in the doorway. Though I stood directly before her, she showed no signs of seeing me. Her eyes had a glassy, unfocused look.

'Edgar!' she cried shrilly. 'Edgar, are you there? Mr Jewkes threatens me.'

Mr Jewkes pushed past her into the hall. He held the monkey aloft, his hands tight around its narrow throat. Jabba wriggled frantically.

'If you think I shall permit this — this freak to live — !'

'No!' I cried. Startled, Jewkes turned and, before he could stop me, I seized the monkey from him. 'Please. The monkey has done no harm.'

'Thank you, Eliza,' Mrs Black said smoothly. 'Now, return the child to me if you will. It requires feeding and then my husband must see it.'

'Your husband is dead, madam!' Jewkes roared, and he tore roughly at my arm. 'Give me that — that beast. I shall not stand by and let it live.'

'No, sir,' I begged. 'Listen to me, I implore you. This is not Mary's child. I fear I have — do not hurt him, I beg you. He is nothing but a monkey.'

'I shall not — '

'A clown's monkey,' I said again. 'Of the kind one sees in the city daily. I borrowed him. So that I might — I borrowed him.'

'The girl is gone mad!' Mrs Black declared hectically. 'Do you hear her? She is quite mad. Where is Mr Black? Edgar, fetch my husband so that he may finally put an end to these absurdities!'

'He entertains the crowds as part of a mountebank's show, sir,' I said quietly to Mr

Jewkes. 'His name is Jabba.'

At the sound of his name the monkey wriggled a little in my arms and opened his eyes. He gazed blearily at me. I kissed the top of his head. Jewkes stared.

'I do not — '

'Mary has a son. He thrives.'

'A human — an ordinary infant?'

I nodded.

'The child is with her?'

'Yes, sir.'

'And this — ?'

'Is a trick, sir. A hoax.' I stared at my feet. 'Mr Black — well, I thought — '

I did not see Mrs Black until she was upon me, pushing me backwards with such force that my legs folded beneath me. The monkey gave a little shriek and, leaping out of reach, fled up the stairs.

'You lying little slut!' Mrs Black screamed, seizing me by the hair. 'You bitch! You filthy foul-mouthed harlot! Edgar! You are lying! I know you are lying! Where is the child? Where is it? Edgar!'

Jewkes seized the old woman's arms and dragged her from me as Edgar peered from the door of the laboratory, his face rucked with fear and dismay.

'Fetch me something to calm her nerves,' Jewkes ordered the apprentice as Mrs Black kicked out at me savagely, her teeth displayed like an animal's. 'Quickly, I implore you. As for you, Eliza, take the monkey and go. Its presence here will only inflame her further.'

Mrs Black twisted and writhed.

'Get the child,' she hissed at Edgar. 'It went upstairs. I must have the child.'

Edgar hesitated. Then he drew himself tall.

'Jewkes, what in God's name is happening here?' he managed, though his voice squeaked.

'Edgar, for pity's sake!' Mrs Black shrieked. 'We must have the child. The papers too. All the papers. Fetch them from his study. Edgar, I beg you. Think what will become of us. We cannot let this villain steal what is rightfully ours.'

'Believe me,' Jewkes said grimly, 'I want nothing from you.'

Edgar hesitated, his eyes flitting anxiously from Mrs Black to Jewkes and back again. Then slowly he stepped forward and took hold of his mistress's legs. Together he and Jewkes began to carry her into the dining room.

'Mr Black!' Mrs Black's cry was piteous now, the mewl of a kitten in a sack. 'Mr Black, why do you let them treat me so? Why will you not help me?'

The door closed. Like dark water, the shadows quivered and settled. Suddenly there was a scampering on the stairs. Swift as a rat, the monkey streaked across the floor and into the laboratory. I followed him, calling him, but he did not come. In the dim room I could not see him, though I heard a scuffling amongst the bottle-crowded shelves on the far wall.

'Goodbye, Eliza.'

I turned to see Mr Jewkes standing behind me in the doorway, his shoulders hunched and his hands thrust deep into his pockets.

'And thank you.'

I nodded. Suddenly a clamp fell with a great clatter to the floor, so that both of us started. The monkey sat upon the table, something in its hands. The napkin around its waist glowed white in the dusty light. Bowing, the monkey held its hands out towards us. They contained a small pill box. Prising open the lid, the beast took from the box a dark-coloured pastille of which he proceeded to make a thorough study. Mr Jewkes and I glanced at each other and something in his eyes loosed the cords around my chest a little. On the table the monkey held the pastille up to its mouth and pretended to take a bite, rubbing its little stomach with its free hand. The napkin around its waist slipped. Mr Jewkes's mouth twitched. The monkey frowned and tugged at it before picking up the pill box and, jumping up and down, pointing a finger helpfully at its lid.

'I only hope your physician, when you summon him, is not such a charlatan,' I murmured.

Mr Jewkes squeezed my arm, his lips clamped in a swallowed smile.

'Thank you,' he muttered. 'For everything. Take care of her for me.'

I hesitated. Then I looked up.

'Is your carriage outside?'

'Yes. Yes, it is.'

'Then let us take it. Mary will be wondering where we are.'

★　★　★

501

Mr Jewkes sent his boy for the doctor and, calling up his equipage, required his coachman to take us with all speed to Cole-wharf.

'You are sure, sir?' the coachman asked doubtfully. 'It is a wretched place and hardly safe, even in daylight.'

'I am perfectly certain. Now, hurry.'

Shrugging his shoulders, the coachman whipped up the horses and the coach lurched forward. I perched on the edge of the seat, feet braced against the rattle and jolt. But close by the Exchange the narrow streets became choked with traffic and we slowed almost to a standstill. Mr Jewkes lowered the window and called up to the coachman.

'It's the Alley,' the coachman called. 'Been pandemonium there since dawn.'

'Try the river.'

The coach tipped as it turned, its wheel passing so close to a chair that the chairman dropped the struts to shake his fist at the coachman.

'You poxy dog!' he shouted. 'May your filthy mother be cursed with the warts of a toad!'

'Ah, take pity on the poor rogue,' sneered his associate. 'By tomorrow the sinking of the South Seas'll have taken him and his master's fancy conveyance with it and he'll be in the gutter where he belongs!'

Beyond the Tower the equipage elicited considerable curiosity. When at last we reached the wharf and the footman had put down the steps, the coachman looked ill at ease.

'Shall I wait here, sir?' he asked.

502

Jewkes nodded. The coachman and footman exchanged a glance as he gestured me forward into the lodging-house, the monkey in my arms.

'Send Dr Kingdom up when he comes,' he instructed.

'Very good, sir.'

The room was quiet when I pushed open the door. Petey half-stood, his finger to his lips. On the palliasse Mary slept.

'How does she do?' I whispered.

'Not so well,' Petey replied, holding his arms out to the monkey. 'The fever is stronger and she cries out in her sleep.'

Quietly I crossed the room and kneeled down beside her. Her closed eyelids sketched a delicate tracery of blue and purple across their pale curves. Her tongue lolled a little from between her parted lips. I stroked her cheek, taking her hand in mine. Both were burning hot. Jewkes stood in the doorway, his arms crossed over his chest, as though restraining himself from entry.

'The doctor shall be here soon,' I whispered. 'He shall make you well again.'

Jewkes turned to Petey.

'What have you need of here? Wine, water, soft food? Tell me and I shall send my man for them.'

The two men conferred quietly.

'We shall be back directly,' Jewkes said to me. He looked at Mary and his face twisted. 'Directly.'

Mary and I were alone. Dipping a rag in the basin of water beside the bed, I wiped her face with it. Her eyelids fluttered.

'No cry, Lize,' she breathed, and her hand

fluttered in mine. 'No cry.'

Rubbing my nose hard with the back of my hand, I forced myself to smile.

'I am not crying,' I rebuked her softly. 'Why should I cry when you are almost well? Mr Jewkes means to take care of you, you know. You were right, he is a good man. We shall be safe now, quite safe.'

Mary murmured something inaudible and closed her eyes. Settling myself beside her on the palliasse, I took her in my arms. At some point, when it was almost dark, Mr Jewkes entered but he said nothing, only stood with his back against the wall, watching and listening. I did not stop in my singing, not until the door opened again to reveal a fat little man with a kindly face, considerably out of breath. Mr Jewkes turned and extended his hand.

'How goes it, Kingdom?'

'Excellent, excellent,' the physician said, bowing as best he could over his globe of a belly. 'Though I hardly would have expected to find you in a place of this kind. For a moment there I thought myself certain to be robbed and never seen again!'

'It is an insalubrious spot, I grant you. I thank you for coming.'

The physician nodded. 'We shall need light, of course. There are candles?'

'In my carriage. I shall have Watkin bring some up.'

'Very good, very good. And you are well, Jewkes? Not caught up in all this nasty business with the markets, I trust?'

'There shall be no difficulty with your bill, Doctor.'

'Goodness, man, what a cynic you are! A courteous enquiry, no more. And here is our patient. Good, good. Now, missy, excuse me if you will.'

Very reluctantly I loosened my embrace. A pained flicker passed over Mary's sleeping face as the physician felt for her pulse.

'You shall make her better, shan't you?' I said, unable to help myself.

'That is why I am here,' he replied, his hands working circles upon his belly as he surveyed her, pushing aside her skirts to peer more closely at the bloodstained sheet beneath her. At the door the coachman handed Jewkes a lit candelabra. Shadows jumped, startled, against the walls as he brought it to the bed and set it down close to Mary's head.

'Thank you, Jewkes,' the doctor said thoughtfully, tapping his teeth with a gold pencil. 'Perhaps the girl could stay, in case I should require anything. Otherwise if you would wait downstairs . . . ?'

Though there was nowhere downstairs to wait, Mr Jewkes murmured his consent, closing the door. The physician considered Mary for a few long minutes, his head on one side as he moved around the low bed, then asked me for the details of her confinement. I gave them shakily, hardly able to remember.

'Hmm,' he said at last. 'I shall require some tea. Let it steep a while.'

'Mary prefers it weak, sir.'

The physician frowned at me.

'Does she indeed? Now, make haste. I cannot think well on a parched throat.'

It was an agony to leave Mary, even for a few minutes. I pressed my lips to her hand, squeezing her fingers between mine.

'Be brave,' I whispered. 'I shall be back directly.'

The physician gestured impatiently. 'Tea.'

I waited in the lane as the footman went with exaggerated apprehension to purchase the physician's tea at a small tavern near the water. The shouts of the sailors carried over the low hiss of the advancing tide. When the footman returned, carrying a cup of ale, his face was stretched with affront.

'The physician may have this and consider himself fortunate,' he snapped. 'I shall not risk my life for tea.'

Hurriedly I carried it upstairs. The physician had pushed Mary's knees up and tented them with a cloth which covered his head and shoulders. As the cloth jerked, Mary gave a strangulated scream and her eyes flew open. Clattering down the ale, I crouched beside her and gripped her hand. I felt the twitch of her fingers as she squeezed me back. Beneath the cloth the physician pushed her knees wider. She gazed at me wildly, hardly seeing me. The sweat stood out on her forehead and darkened her hair. Her breath came in ragged strips. Her grip tightened.

The physician lowered the cloth. His right hand was dark with blood, a metal hook protruding from his palm like a terrible sixth finger. A smudge of red rouged his cheek.

'It would appear I am become a man-midwife,' he observed, taking up a clean cloth and wiping his face fastidiously. 'You have my tea?'

'Only porter, sir.'

Dr Kingdom sighed.

'How does she do?' I asked, afraid of the answer.

'We shall not know for some hours. She is very weak. The afterbirth is corrupted and obstinate but I trust we shall do better with the proper instruments. Please do not concern yourself unduly. Such a process is not uncommon and is usually successful. Permit her to rest for now. She must conserve her strength for what is to come. I must talk with Mr Jewkes downstairs.' He paused in the doorway, nodding at me kindly. 'Keep her warm and have her drink as much as she can. I shall return directly.'

When he was gone I lay down beside Mary as she dozed, her nose close to mine, her hands hot between my cool ones.

'How does the patient do?

I turned my head. Mr Jewkes stood in the doorway, his hand extended towards me. I did not know if he intended to offer support or to seek it.

'I — I should never have left her,' I whispered. 'Forgive me.'

'It is not you who should seek forgiveness but I,' he replied softly. 'You have never abandoned her, never closed your eyes to her plight as I did, as I have always done. You have protected her. You have showed her affection. I, her blood father, was never a father, but in you, who owed her nothing, she found a sister. I shall always be grateful to you for that.'

'I have never loved anyone as I love her,' I murmured, and it was only as I said it that I knew it to be true.

'Then she is fortunate indeed.' He paused, gazing at the bundle asleep in the tea chest. 'And this is the child?'

'Yes, sir. Your grandson.'

Jewkes squatted, pressing his fingers against his lips.

'He is a fine boy,' he said at last.

'Yes, sir. He is.'

We were silent for a moment, watching Mary sleep. Jewkes's fingers played absently with the end of the infant's blanket.

'Kingdom should be back soon,' he murmured. 'Then, when he considers her fit enough to be moved, I shall take her home. Mrs Jewkes shall simply have to endure it.'

I blinked at him. In its chest the infant began to cry. I had brought Jewkes here, had accepted his kindness, his help. I had never thought that he might claim her.

'She shall not miss the laundry,' I managed, though my mouth was dry.

There was a knock on the door and Petey looked in. Jabba the monkey rode on his shoulder, his fingers around the clown's ears.

'The physician is returned,' he said.

'Show him up. And have the footman bring

fresh candles. These ones burn low.'

'Yes, sir.'

Petey made to withdraw but the monkey, spying Mary upon the palliasse, leaped down from his perch and skittered across the room to curl upon her pillow. Mary stirred and opened her eyes.

'Jab Jab,' she said dreamily and she smiled, her face ivory-smooth in the guttering candlelight. 'Ev'rythin' fine now, Jab. Ev'rythin gon' be fine.'

Peel Mather, Solicitors at Law,
Poultry, London

For the attention of John Black Esquire at the
Sign of the Scroll & Feather, Newcastle

Dear Mr Black,

We regret to have to inform you of the death
two days since, that is, the 4th September of
this year of grace one thousand seven hundred
and twenty, of Mr Grayson Black of Swan-
street, London.

Since you, his brother, are the primary ben-
eficiary of Mr Grayson Black's last Will and
Testament, we would beg your attendance at
our Offices at the earliest convenience so that
the terms of said Will might be fully and expe-
ditiously executed. Given the circumstances of
the bequest, such funds as may be required for
such a journey may be advanced from the
amount due to you if necessary.

We hope you will accept our most heartfelt
condolences for this, your sad loss.

We remain, sir, your humble servants & c

SILAS PEEL

SAMPSON MATHER
                              6th day of September,
                        the year of our Lord 1720

43

Mary died.

Years have passed but still my hand trembles when I write those words and a stitch of loss tugs at my heart. Mary died. Not that day, nor for several of the days that followed, but a week later. The physician first bled her from the feet in an attempt to bring forth the corrupted afterbirth and afterwards, when that yielded nothing, endeavoured to remove it with a scalpel, but it was a more difficult process than he had predicted, demanding several hours of cutting and scraping. Mary had scarce been able to tolerate the pain of his endeavours, frequently falling into a faint from the agony. At last, he had sighed and requested Mr Jewkes's permission to cease in his surgery. There was a chance that Mary's womb would expel the remaining fragments of tissue of its own accord. If he persisted, however, he feared that she would not have the strength for it.

And yet, perhaps if we had pressed him to continue he might yet have saved her life. He was a fine doctor and a decent man and would have done what we asked, even at the cost to his reputation, had we insisted upon it. As it was, we conceded, grateful to spare Mary further pain. The puerperal fever took hold two days later and she succumbed to it quickly, without a struggle. The memory of it still plagues me. If I had only had more courage on her behalf she might be sitting with me now before the fire, the flames warming her cheeks and lighting sparks in her copper hair. It might be her hand, and not mine, that strokes the child's head as he sleeps, his dark eyelashes quivering against the ripe swell of his cheek. She might look up at me, with that sweet slack smile upon her face, and call my name. Lize. No one but Mary ever called me Lize.

I miss her. At first I think that I imagined that there would come a time when I would not miss her, when the skin of the passing years would close over the wound of her, but that time has never come. It is true that the raw grief has softened into a tender bruise that is tolerable if I do not press it too hard, but even now I still find myself talking to her as I always have. I never stopped talking to her, not even in those bleak months immediately after her death when my heart stopped and my limbs withered and there were no words in the world for the ripped-out anguish of it.

I was hardly alone in my desolation that autumn. The great edifice of the South Sea Company had at last collapsed, bringing down with it the swarms of investors who clung to its crumbling brickwork. The year of soaring prices and reckless abandon was brought to a shuddering end and the wreckage was every-where. All of London was convulsed with the groans of the afflicted. Exchange-alley, which had echoed with such noise and excitement to the call of the stock-jobbers, sprawled, winded, alongside the Bank of England, shocked and silent. Overnight vast fortunes were obliterated while men who had purchased shares against future profits and believed their fortunes assured reeled at the mountainous extent of their debt. Paper money was suddenly worthless. Houses were left half-built; orders for ships cancelled; newspapers filled with advertisements for pictures, china and glasses. Long-lane and Regent-fair were full of rich liveries to be sold and on every street corner there was to be found a stall hawking gold watches and jewellery for a fraction of their true value.

Thousands of families were ruined. Even the bookseller's favourite, the brilliant Mr Newton, had proved himself greedier than he was astute and was rumoured to have lost more than £20,000 of his own fortune in the collapse. The disaster drove many to madness and more to put an end to their misfortunes through the taking of their own lives. The metropolis lurched and staggered with scandal and distress as, one after another, gentlemen and merchants of previously good reputation cut their throats or hung themselves by the neck or drowned themselves in the muddy waters of the Thames, leaving behind wives and children and the ruins of their estates. There were rumours of a gentleman who threw himself from the Whispering Gallery of the Cathedral, smashing his head open like a pumpkin upon the marble floor beneath.

Mr Honfleur was one of those who fled. It was Edgar who brought me the news when he came to say goodbye. Like Mr Newton, the bookseller had extricated himself once from his commit-ments in Exchange-alley only to be tempted to return for a final gamble. According to Edgar, he had pledged to purchase shares on an instalment plan that meant that, even before the worst of the crash, he had owed significantly more than his stock was worth. It seemed that he had slipped away in the hope that, in the great blizzard of paperwork that had snowed down upon Exchange-alley in the previous months, his promise might somehow be lost or forgotten.

'It is to be hoped, for his sake, he is not gone back to France,' Edgar remarked, watching my expression. 'They say the plague is at Marseilles.'

'And Annette, is she gone also?' I asked, but Edgar only sighed.

'How careless you are, Eliza, to let yet another husband wriggle from your hook,' he said instead, and a flicker of his old spirit lit his face for a moment. 'You see, it is proof that we were indeed intended for each other.'

'Or perhaps we were neither of us meant for marriage at all.'

'But you have your Mr Jewkes, at least. A mistress may manage at least as well as a wife, if she is canny.' I only shook my head.

Edgar looked sallow and ill. His face had grown thin and, as if his head had shrunk beneath it, his wig tilted oddly, slipping over one eye. When I asked him what it was he meant to do next he shrugged.

'There is the possibility of a passage to Virginia,' he said. 'They say the Thirteen Colonies are a positive Arcadia. Unlimited land

514

and Negro slaves as far as the eye can see. Cheaper than a wife and much more obliging. You may imagine me upon my plantation, a piccaninny girl on each knee and at least one of your erstwhile husbands to raise a glass with. What more could a gentleman wish for?'

He said nothing of his debts nor of Mrs Black. His plans, like the plans of so many adventures in London, lay in ruins, snatched from his hands just at the moment he had thought them secure. He could surely never have imagined that Mrs Black, whose mind appeared shut as tight as a trap, could have permitted herself to have become so deranged by the death of her husband. He knew nothing before their precipitate arrival of the family of Mr Black's brother who arranged her removal to an unwilling cousin and as swiftly took control of the shop and all of its contents. Edgar had had time only to bundle up the apothecary's papers which he supposed might have some value and which he now lodged with me for safe-keeping. Naturally, being Edgar, he had also had sufficient wit to offer his hand in marriage to the brother's oldest daughter. Doubtless it had not escaped his attention that she was not only much younger than her aunt but also possessed of a considerably more ample bosom.

Naturally, she had refused him. Edgar appeared resigned to the failure of his efforts. Something of Edgar, it seemed, had been dispatched along with Mrs Black and it was a smaller, quieter creature who took his leave from me that dark afternoon. I knew that I would

515

never see him again. I felt a tinge of affection for the apprentice but no regret. When he stepped away from the threshold he would carry away with him the final traces of Swan-street and of what I had become there.

'Nursemaid and whore,' he murmured softly and quite without spite. 'A secure future indeed and better than most in London have managed.'

I said nothing, but hugged my arms around myself as I gazed down into the crib. The sleeping infant yawned, showing the soft pink of his mouth, and his nose twitched like a rabbit's.

'He will leave soon,' I said silently to Mary. 'And we shall be peaceful once more. The three of us, as we like it.'

'You are not too solitary, here alone?' Edgar asked.

'I am not alone,' I replied.

'And when he tires of you?'

I bent down and took the child into my arms. He was waking up now and his eyes peered blurrily at me from beneath their heavy lids. I kissed him very gently upon the button of his nose.

'A boy does not tire of his mother.'

'You know I did not mean — '

'Goodbye, Edgar. And may good fortune go with you.'

When Edgar had left I took the sleepy child upstairs to the room occupied by the wet-nurse. The boy would be weaned soon and then she too would leave. She was a pleasant Scottish woman with an even-tempered demeanour but I would be glad to be rid of her. She was obliging in her own way and almost tender with the child she called the poor orphan bairn but, for all that, it remained difficult living at close quarters with someone who had never known Mary. The cottage was a small one and her idle chatter seemed to fill the spaces where Mary might settle, forcing her out. When she nudged me, and winked, and muttered gleefully that we had surely fallen on our feet in such hard times to have found ourselves so spendthrift an employer, I found myself frowning and charging her to be silent. It did not feel right to speak of Mary's father that way where she might so easily hear it.

I talked to Mary as I set Edgar's cup in the sink. The winter would have to be endured. But when the spring came, I would begin once more to collect plants. The cottage was on the edge of a small hamlet that reached out hopeful fingers in the direction of the larger village of Hampstead. There were many herbs that grew here and many more that might be cultivated in the scrap of garden behind the house. I wanted no more to do with opium or its other foreign relatives but I had conceived of an idea to produce potions to enhance the beauty of women, complexion waters for the face and creams to augment the swell of the breast or the whiteness of a lady's hands. With my preparations a woman might triumph over the vagaries of nature and find herself always young and beautiful. Mary, who had grown more ironic in death, thought the idea perfect.

I did not mean to tell Mr Jewkes of my plans just yet. He had insisted that he would always

517

provide for me and the child and had had lawyers draw up the necessary papers so that his wife might find no way to overturn his intentions. The money would, he assured me, last for as long as I required it. Unlike most of London, Mr Jewkes had emerged from the financial disasters of the summer unscathed and had contrived to purchase an estate in Norfolk at a price that would have been thought laughable only weeks previously. As he himself observed, he was in a position to be generous.

Besides, he was exceptionally fond of the child. Whenever he could he visited us and dandled the little boy upon his knee, singing snatches of nonsense and contorting his butcher's face into humorous expressions to make the child chuckle. Our cottage, he said to me once, as he flung himself contentedly into the chair by the fire, was not unlike the one he had lived in as a boy, a place where he might loosen his collar and his proprieties a little. I had the impression that in the Norfolk house he was careful as a caller, anxious not to dirty the fine carpets or break the porcelain. From what he said of his wife, it was easy to imagine her wincing as he set his feet upon the silk-upholstered chaises or blew his nose upon the lace-embroidered napkins. He never complained of her but there was a softness that came over his features, an easiness in his sigh of pleasure when I brought him muffins hot from the oven upon a battered tin plate, that assured me he was happy with the arrangements he had made.

I had no need to concern myself with the

business of making money. But all the same I wished to. It occurred to me that when I had made a little I might send for my mother, if she were still alive. The idea pleased Mary considerably. I would continue with my studies, improving my reading and writing so that our son might know the joys of scholarship. That way, too, I told Mary, I might be able to set down our story, so that one day, when he was old enough to be told it, he might know how, despite the attempts to deprave him, he had held firm and come into the world in his own fine form, untouched by the perversions of a fiendish imagination, truly himself and truly loved, as completely as any boy in history or fable.

Now it is done. Mary's headstone is mossy and the humped blanket of earth that covers her is thick with the juicy bright grass of May. Henry and I visited the grave yesterday and left flowers, handfuls of bluebells that Henry had picked himself. Clods of earth clung to their startled roots. His hands are plump with dimples for knuckles, not yet the hands of a youth, but they are strong and know nothing of hesitancy. I watched the child as we made our way back to the cottage and marvelled at the eagerness that springs in his limbs, as if he can hardly wait for the next minute of his life to begin. I do not know yet how much of this account I shall share with him, or which of the papers that Edgar left in my care I should permit him to see. I am not yet ready for him to learn that there are people in this world who may not be trusted.

As we closed the wych-gate behind us, Henry

spied a cat lurking beneath a hawthorn hedge and, dropping to his knees, crawled in beside it and set about engaging it in serious discourse. As I waited for him to finish, a lady in a dress of fine blue silk came up the path. She carried a flat basket filled with white and yellow flowers and looked for all the world like one of those shiny shepherdess figurines whose porcelain hands and glazed features owe nothing to ordinary work. Her expression stiffened a little when I did not immediately step out of her way, but when she saw Henry's bottom protruding from beneath the hedge she permitted herself a small smile.

'How engaging,' she said graciously, inclining her head towards me. 'Chattering away like a veritable monkey.'

The cat uncurled itself from Henry's embrace and, stretching, disappeared into the dark reaches of the hedge. Henry wriggled backwards, his hair stiff with twigs. His bottom lip protruded as he frowned up at me, ready to blame me for the cat's precipitate removal. Smiling, I shook my head at him and held out my hand.

'Oh no, madam,' I said firmly as I pulled Henry to his feet. His hand was warm and slightly sticky. 'There is nothing of the monkey about this boy. Nothing at all.'

Acknowledgements

There is insufficient space here to acknowledge each one of the many historians and writers whose work has helped to illuminate my understanding of eighteenth-century London, but there are some without whom I most certainly would not have been able to begin this book.

Eighteenth-century London boasted social commentators of matchless wit and acuity and I have plundered the writings of Samuels Johnson and Pepys, Jonathan Swift, Joseph Addison and the German visitor and chronicler Zacharias Conrad van Uffenbach, who in 1710 famously had his man carve his initials into the stone of the lantern of St Paul's Cathedral. My favourite among all of these, however, remains the diary of an ordinary visitor to London in 1704, one Ned Ward, who chronicled his innumerable adventures in the capital with laugh-out-loud gusto in *The London Spy*.

As for modern-day analysts, I am particularly indebted to the late Roy Porter. *English Society in the 18th Century, London: A Social History* and *Enlightenment* were all invaluable resources in understanding the society and sentiments of the period. The more colloquial perspective of the ordinary man was admirably provided by Peter Earle's *A City Full of People: men and women of London 1650–1750*, and *The World*

521

of Defoe. *Manners and Customs of London in the Eighteenth Century* by J.P. Malcolm, and Maureen Waller's *1700: Scenes from London Life* were equally evocative, while *The Monster City* by Jack Lindsay provided wonderfully vivid pictures of the seamier sides of London life. *The Criers and Hawkers of London* by Sean Shesgreen provided the double treat of his perceptive commentary and the wonderful drawings by Marcellus Laroon that bring the street sellers of late-seventeenth-century London vividly to life. I am also obliged to Peter Ackroyd, whose *London: A Biography* proved, yet again, an inexhaustible source of anecdote and inspiration. A special mention should also go to the late Dennis Severs, whose painstaking restoration of a Huguenot silkweaver's house at 18 Folgate Street, Spitalfields in London allows the visitor an unparalleled insight into the living conditions of the time.

In my quest to understand the medical structures and sensibilities of the early Enlightenment I am in debt once more to the indefatigable Roy Porter, whose *Quacks: Fakers and Charlatans in English Medicine* proved endlessly useful. A number of the works he wrote in partnership with Dorothy Parker, particularly *Patients' Progress* and *In Sickness and in Health*, were equally critical to my understanding of contemporary medical theory, as was the collection of essays he edited, *Patients and Practitioners*. On the subject of maternal imagination, Jan Bondeson's *A Cabinet of Medical Curiosities* and Dennis Todd's *Imagining Monsters* provided excellent starting points, while I relied heavily for the detail upon the several tracts published by two doctors in the 1720s, whose views on the subject were radically opposed to each other: James Blondel and Daniel Turner. Ulisse Aldrovandi's extraordinary collections of drawings of 'monstrous' humans, *Monstrorum Historia*, first published in 1642, directly inspired the books used by the apothecary in the novel. I would also like to thank the staff of the library at the Royal Society who allowed me access to their remarkable archive of original documents and who, on discovering my particular interests, went out of their way to dig out for me far more and better material than I had originally requested.

Two lively and informative studies of the causes and effects of the South Sea Bubble also proved useful in researching this book: *The Moneymaker* by Janet Gleeson and Malcolm Balen's *A Very English Deceit*.

Finally, thanks must go to Mary Mount and her team at Viking, to Clare Alexander, to Sophie and Stephen Paine whose invitation to visit their restoration of the dome at St Paul's Cathedral provided the inspiration for this novel, and to Chris for his never-ending support and enthusiasm.

We do hope that you have enjoyed reading this large print book.

Did you know that all of our titles are available for purchase?

We publish a wide range of high quality large print books including:
Romances, Mysteries, Classics
General Fiction
Non Fiction and Westerns

Special interest titles available in large print are:
The Little Oxford Dictionary
Music Book
Song Book
Hymn Book
Service Book

Also available from us courtesy of Oxford University Press:
Young Readers' Dictionary
(large print edition)
Young Readers' Thesaurus
(large print edition)

For further information or a free brochure, please contact us at:
Ulverscroft Large Print Books Ltd.,
The Green, Bradgate Road, Anstey,
Leicester, LE7 7FU, England.
Tel: (00 44) **0116 236 4325**
Fax: (00 44) **0116 234 0205**

Other titles published by
The House of Ulverscroft:

TUG OF WAR

Barbara Cleverly

Summer, 1926. Working for Interpol, Joe Sandilands is despatched to Reims representing British interests in an unusual case. French war-widow Aline Houdart runs a champagne estate on the Marne, and is determined that Joe should support her claim that a shell-shocked soldier in the local sanatorium, without speech or memory, is her husband. But a strange conflict has arisen — the patient has also been claimed by three other families ... Aided by Inspector Bonnefoye, he investigates all the claimants. Amid a tangle of lies and manipulation Joe uncovers a murder committed during the war. And when he discovers who the soldier is, Joe and Bonnefoye face an even greater dilemma. They must work quickly, not only to solve a past crime, but to avert a fresh tragedy.

THIRTEEN MOONS

Charles Frazier

Will Cooper's search for identity and home begins at the age of twelve, when he is given a horse, a key and a map, and sent to the edge of the Cherokee Nation to run a trading post as a bound boy. Between a Cherokee chief named Bear and the mysterious and beautiful Claire Featherstone, Will finds the passionate connections and the complications of manhood that will forge his character and shape his life. As his fate becomes intertwined with the destiny of the Cherokee, Will travels to Washington City to fight against the Removal of the Indians from their land and to protect Bear's people, their culture, and way of life.

THE ISLAND

Victoria Hislop

Alexis Fielding longs to find out about her mother's past. But Sofia has never spoken of it. All she admits to is growing up in a small Cretan village before moving to London. When Alexis decides to visit Crete, however, Sofia gives her daughter a letter to take to an old friend . . . Arriving in Plaka, Alexis is astonished at its proximity to the deserted island of Spinalonga — Greece's former leper colony. Then she finds Fortini, and hears the tale of her great-grandmother Eleni and her daughters, and a family rent by tragedy, war and passion. She discovers how intimately she is connected with the island, and how secrecy holds them all in its powerful grip . . .

THE QUEEN OF SUBTLETIES

Suzannah Dunn

Lucy Cornwallis, King Henry VIII's confectioner, sculpts valuable sugar into 'subtleties', the centrepieces for royal celebrations. One day, she has an unusual visitor, someone curious to meet the creator of the famed sculptures: gorgeous Mark Smeaton, singer and musician. During a troubled year at court — the final year of Anne Boleyn's brief reign — Lucy and Mark become close. Anne Boleyn's rise has changed the history of England. Politically astute, intensely ambitious and uncompromising, she had easily caught King Henry's heart. But powerful forces are now gathering to make her pay for her prize — and Lucy Cornwallis is unwittingly in danger of giving them the means to do so . . .